Praise for Mari Hannah

'Involving, sophisticated, intelligent and suspenseful – everything a great crime thriller should be'        Lee Child

'A gripping, twisty police procedural – fans of the Kate Daniels series will love this one'        Shari Lapena

'Mari Hannah has a rare gift. She can write compelling, page-turning suspense with the very best, but she adds heart to every page. Kate Daniels is a character to cherish, and Mari is a writer at the very top of her game'        Steve Cavanagh

'With a cast of compelling characters and a chilling plot, *Without a Trace* sets off at a cracking pace from page one and never slows down'        Rachel Abbott

'Mari Hannah is in the uppermost echelon of British crime writers and *Without a Trace* demonstrates why. It's her best book yet – compelling, emotional and intricately plotted with a procedural authenticity few can match. A stunning novel'        M.W. Craven

'I loved it – both compelling and incredibly moving'        Elly Griffiths

'*Without A Trace* is a deft blend of emotional drama and crime procedural that kept me hooked to the very end. Mari Hannah has a talent for writing about the light and dark of life, and creates characters who feel so realistic they almost pop from the page'        Adam Hamdy

**Mari Hannah** is a multi-award-winning author, whose authentic voice is no happy accident. A former probation officer, she lives in rural Northumberland with her partner, an ex-murder detective. Mari turned to script-writing when her career was cut short following an assault on duty. Her debut, *The Murder Wall*, (adapted from a script she developed with the BBC) won her the Polari First Book Prize. Its follow-up, *Settled Blood*, picked up a Northern Writers' Award. Mari's body of work won her the CWA Dagger in the Library 2017, an incredible honour to receive so early in her career. In 2019, she was voted DIVA Wordsmith of the Year. In 2020, she won Capital Crime International Crime Writing Festival's Crime Book of the Year for *Without a Trace*. Her Kate Daniels series is in development with Stephen Fry's production company, Sprout Pictures.

Find out more by following Mari on Twitter @mariwriter or visiting her website www.marihannah.com

### Also by Mari Hannah

STONE & OLIVER SERIES
The Lost
The Insider
The Scandal

KATE DANIELS SERIES
The Murder Wall
Settled Blood
Deadly Deceit
Monument to Murder (*aka* Fatal Games)
Killing for Keeps
Gallows Drop
Without a Trace

RYAN & O'NEIL SERIES
The Silent Room
The Death Messenger

# HER LAST
# REQUEST

*A Kate Daniels novel*

# MARI HANNAH

ORION

An Orion paperback

First published in Great Britain in 2022
by Orion Fiction,
an imprint of The Orion Publishing Group Ltd,
Carmelite House, 50 Victoria Embankment
London EC4Y 0DZ

An Hachette UK company

1  3  5  7  9  10  8  6  4  2

A CIP catalogue record for this book
is available from the British Library.

ISBN (Mass Market Paperback) 978 1 4091 9245 9
ISBN (eBook) 978 1 4091 9246 6

Typeset by Input Data Services Ltd, Somerset

Printed and bound in Great Britain by Clays Ltd, Elcograf S.p.A.

MIX
Paper from
responsible sources
FSC® C104740

www.orionbooks.co.uk

*In loving memory of my mother*

# Prologue

We all want to escape sometimes, even you. The difference between us is that my life depends on it. No, wait! If you're reading this, that sentence should be framed in the past tense because by then it'll all be over. If that's what's happened, you've already found this note. My days were numbered from the moment I set eyes on HIM.

Does red mist cover this note?

Has he read it too, you're wondering. I wonder that also, though there'll be no bloody fingerprints for CSIs to lift. He's savvy. Meticulous in everything he does. I wonder about other things too – about YOU mostly. I feel you rather than see you, if that makes sense. I wonder who you are and what you look like. I wonder if you're one of the murder detectives I've seen on TV. I wonder if you feel guilty scrutinising my thoughts, my note. No need – it was written for you.

You did well to find it.

Or did HE get to it first? If that is the case, he'll have torched the van with me in it, though I choose to believe that this note will reach you, otherwise there's no point. I really hope it has. I don't want your pity, but I feel your heart race as you read on. Bizarrely, even though we've never met in person, I feel I know you. When I think of you, you're in silhouette, backlit by a bright light. Immobile. Moved by what you see. You didn't expect to hear from me . . .

Not like this.

I picture your eyes bearing down on me. As you turn your head away, I imagine your sadness. Your outrage.

I second-guess the many questions my death has raised in your subconscious. Mentally you're processing the scene, wondering what went on here, trying to figure it out. I've asked myself over and over how you sleep nights, why you put yourself through it. I've wondered how often you've yearned to walk away, as I have. You won't. I know you can't. Not now you've seen what's left of me.

Not easy, is it?

You're as trapped by circumstances as I am.

Darkness isn't new to either of us, is it? We've both hidden in the shadows, hearts pumping, watching, waiting for the red flag. HIS triggers were visible only to me, so be warned.

This single sheet of paper is enough for one day. Still, I feel a need to communicate with you, though I'm in no doubt that you'll find the key to what went on here.

There you go again, unable to tear your eyes away.

Are you searching for clues?

You won't find any . . . from HIM.

I guarantee it.

He warned me the end would be slow and painful, that it would eclipse my worst fears – and some. Is it everything HE said it would be? Messy, I imagine. I told myself I wouldn't plead for mercy. He'd get a kick out of that. I suspect I did it anyway. With every blow, I probably begged him to spare me.

As you can see, he didn't.

I feel as if you and I are now one, joined by an invisible and dangerous thread; life at one end, death at the other – a space familiar to both of us. Take a good long look, because if you go after him, he'll come for you too. I'm begging you to take care. Does that give you pause for thought? It should. Do you still want to get to know me? On the one hand, I doubt that. On the other, I know you won't be able to help yourself.

You'll discover that I'm not entirely innocent.

Which of us is?

Are you judging me? Are you? Can't say I blame you. I imagine it comes as second nature. The fact that you're blameless doesn't make me guilty. The fact that you're strong doesn't make me weak. Do you think I had any choice in the matter? Calling you earlier would have signed my death warrant, so I fought back in the only way I knew how.

Please don't criticise without investigating the facts – all of them.

Make no mistake, I dreamt of a better life. I dream of YOU often, intangible though you are. I tried my best. It wasn't enough. I prayed that I'd get lucky, that I'd manage somehow to slip away, for good this time. I did, often. He found me.

HE always does.

He'll find you too, so watch your back.

I have one last request: find Aaron.

# 1

As an experienced Senior Investigating Officer, Kate Daniels was unflappable, ready for any eventuality, but the contents of the note had kicked a hole in her heart from the inside, delivering a sharp pain to her chest. She was boiling up, gasping for air inside her mask, pulling at the neck of her forensic suit, feeling hot and clammy in the small, claustrophobic space. Who and where was Aaron?

She glanced briefly at the victim, then shut her eyes tightly. She'd seen the results of excessive violence many times, but this was off the scale. The message passed on from the control room in no way prepared her for what was to come.

It wasn't this.

Never this.

The shell of the caravan closed in around her. Dealing with shit like this was hard enough at the best of times. When it came off the back of a fourteen-hour shift, when Kate was wrung out and emotionally vulnerable, keeping it together was almost impossible. Her heart was pumping fast. Too fast. The rhythm wasn't right. Palpitations were not something she'd experienced before.

The ringing in her ears stopped, replaced by Detective Chief Superintendent Bright's voice, calm and reassuring. *Steady your breathing, Kate. That's it. In. Out. Gently does it. First impressions are vital. Assess the scene. It holds many clues. What's it telling you?*

It was telling her to rip the mask from her face and get the hell out. It was telling her that she didn't have to wait for her professional persona to kick in. It was telling her that if she didn't want to do this fucking job anymore, she was free to leave at any time, had it not been for the fact that the author of that note had nailed her to the floor.

She was right too: Kate couldn't help herself.

Her mentor was no longer sitting on her shoulder.

The words she was hearing were her own. She reminded herself to breathe, to take as much time as required. The victim was in no hurry and neither was she. She was ready to take a look . . .

*You got this.*

Forcing herself to concentrate, Kate looked down at the transparent evidence bag she was holding in her gloved hand. Instinctively, she knew that the single sheet of cream-coloured paper inside would temporarily become more important than the dead woman whose handwriting flowed seamlessly across the page . . .

Assuming she was the author.

Desperate to know if there were other notes secreted there, potential clues to a brutal killing, Kate summoned her colleague, Crime Scene Investigator Paul O'Brien, asking where he'd found it.

'Almost missed it . . .' His voice was muffled through his mask. 'It was taped to the underside of the shelf beneath the sink.'

'It's quality stationery with a watermark.'

'Yeah, possibly from the writing pad I lifted from the seat over there.'

He pointed to a perfect oblong shape, the only space on the seat not covered in blood. The profile of the flowery fabric against a red background would haunt Kate, a symbolic and indelible reminder of what had gone on here. How desperate must the victim have been for the attack to end?

For a long moment, Kate couldn't speak.

She cleared her throat, holding up the note. 'Keep your eyes peeled. There may be more of these.'

'There are none, guv. I swept the place twice.'

Despite his confident claim, that wasn't what the first paragraph of the note implied, Kate thought, but didn't say.

Knowing O'Brien to be thorough, with twenty-five years' experience, she didn't challenge him. Instead, she photographed both sides of the page, an ice cube slithering its way down her spine. Shivering involuntarily had nothing to do with her imagination, or the uncomfortable narrative running through her head, though there was that too. It was zero degrees in the van, even colder outside, the weather closing in, heavy snow expected across north Northumberland – and yet the victim wore no outdoor clothing.

Kate bent down to examine a gas fire, the only heating appliance in the room. 'Did you see this, Paul? The valve regulating flow is turned on and the temperature dial is on its highest setting.'

O'Brien nodded. 'It was like that when I arrived, guv. It must've run out . . .' He thumbed toward the door. 'I asked one of my lads to check the LPG cylinder outside. It's empty.'

She didn't answer.

Her eyes had drifted to the Canada Goose coat hanging on a self-adhesive peg beside the door – a thousand quid's worth or more. It looked new. In her head, Kate imagined the IP wearing it, entering the van, perhaps lighting the fire, allowing the place to warm up before taking off her outdoor gear, which would rule out her being pushed inside by someone lying in wait.

Her attention was on O'Brien. 'Did you check her coat yet?'

Another nod. 'I found a key that fits the door, a few quid and some loose change in the right-hand pocket.'

'Not enough to live on,' she said.

'No, but I recovered in excess of five grand in a pocket sewn into the hood. Whoever searched the place was in a hurry.' He blushed. That was her territory, not his. He was there to collect evidence that might identify the victim and perpetrator, not interpret the scene. 'There's blood on and in the drawer of the bedside table. We have photographs of everything. Don't hang your hopes on prints. It's no more than a smudge. Looks like gloves were worn. There's so much blood here, it would be almost impossible not to transfer some of it.'

Kate turned her head, avoiding eye contact.

Her pulse was racing, her mouth dry. She wasn't ready to study the victim, though the 'invisible thread' mentioned in the note was securely attached, set to become unbreakable. It was tugging at Kate's heart, pulling her in a direction she didn't want to go. She felt tethered by it, like a prisoner in rigid handcuffs, unable to break away.

Her internal dialogue was interrupted by O'Brien's voice. 'I'll bag the coat now you've seen it. Guv, I found no bag, purse or credit card.' He went on to explain what he did and didn't have. 'I'd show you, only I've been passing the exhibits out to my crew.'

Kate could see why. There was no surface completely free of blood where he could set them down for collection later.

Through the window, O'Brien's colleagues were working under arc lights, blue flashes lighting up the night sky. They had reached the scene before her, discovering tyre tracks, evidence that two vehicles had recently been parked outside; one next to the caravan where deep grooves suggested a regular parking spot, presumably the victim's car, the other further away. On arrival, the Crime Scene Manager had told her that they had both been driven away at speed, tearing up the grass.

An accomplice then . . .

Two vehicles.

Two drivers.

'I'm done with the note,' she said.

In reality, she was undone by the note.

She fought hard to keep her composure. 'It's top priority. Get it processed. I need a replica in my hand urgently. Give everything the full works. Whatever you need to do, do it. Check the writing pad for indentations in case she or anyone else has written other notes in or on it. We need categorical proof that it was written by the deceased and not her killer.'

O'Brien bagged and sealed the exhibit. Kate watched him make a note of when and where it was found, adding his name and lastly the date, Tuesday, 18 February 2020. He put his pen away, prompting her to ask if he'd found one that might've been used to write the note. He'd found two, a Sonnet ballpoint and an Elmo rollerball. Expensive. Only one with blue ink.

'It'll all be in my report.'

Kate studied him. He'd said "my report", not *the* report, personalising the comment. Owning it. Her mind flew to the victim's note, a phrase she'd used that jumped out at her. Was she overthinking this? She didn't think so. She'd double-check when she got to base and, if still of the same opinion, raise it with her team.

Her mobile rang, pulling her attention away.

Lifting it to her ear, she listened a moment, then hung up, her focus on O'Brien. 'How much longer will you be? Stanton is ten, fifteen minutes away.' As pathologists go, he was the best.

'Should be done by then.'

'Good. Hank's outside. As soon as we can move the body, I want the caravan uplifted. Left here, it's vulnerable to a break-in. Tell him to set it up for me. You can finish the job off-site, right?'

'That would be perfect. I'd rather examine it on our own premises, away from the prying eyes of the press, any inquisitive locals and the finder, in case he's in any way involved.'

'I don't envy you this one, Paul. The sooner I can get out of here the better.'

On the one hand, Kate didn't want the case. On the other, there was no way anyone else was having it. Her relationship with the woman on the floor began the minute the note was found.

As far as Kate was aware, she didn't know her.

*She did now.*

9

The victim represented every murdered female the DCI had ever come across. Crime scene images scrolled before her eyes, hideous injuries to every part of the female form: broken bones, smashed skulls, stab wounds numbering one to fifty. These women had endured months, if not years of unimaginable pain and suffering. Their screams kept her awake at night.

'Guv?'

She swung round, unaware of how long she'd been reliving those cases, some solved, some not. Then there were the women who'd seemingly vanished off the face of the earth and were never found, the most deplorable of all.

'I'm off,' O'Brien said.

'Thanks, Paul.'

When he'd gone, Kate took in every inch of the scene, trying to work out what else it might tell her. Everything in her eyeline was covered in a fine spray of blood. Small items of crockery, cutlery and food lay smashed on the mini-draining board and in the sink where it had been scooped out of the cupboards by whoever had searched the place. O'Brien had all he needed for now. The entire contents, including the caravan itself, would be forensically examined in due course.

There was no rush.

'Who were you hiding from?' Kate whispered. 'You don't belong here.'

She crouched down to examine the victim more closely, taking pictures even though the crime scene photographer had already taken plenty. The injuries to her hands were proof that she'd put up a fight, deep nicks where the knife had caught her, a broken fingernail. Kate hoped she'd managed to scratch her attacker, collecting DNA.

The woman was well-dressed, one shoe missing, a classy watch, a gold locket Kate was desperate to open, hoping to expose an image of Aaron. Was he a brother, work associate or key witness? she wondered. Or was he someone the victim was determined to protect, her kid perhaps? The pathologist would confirm if she'd ever given birth. If it turned out to be her offspring, Kate was on the clock, looking for a potential second victim.

# 2

Scenarios came and went as Kate concentrated on the body. *Find Aaron* was a plea – or as the deceased had put it, a request. Her last request. If O'Brien hadn't found the note, Kate would have been hoping that death had come quickly. She didn't need it to work out that the opposite was true. The evidence was staring her in the face. Whoever was responsible had beaten the victim first and enjoyed doing it.

The extent of her injuries would fill a very long list.

Kate wandered into the bedroom. No blood here beyond the smudge O'Brien had referred to. The bed was upended, the covers strewn across the floor, including a pair of warm Liberty pyjamas O'Brien would send off to the forensics lab. In the tiny, adjoining shower Kate found costly toiletries scattered on the floor tiles, tossed out from a small cupboard over the sink, but no cosmetics. If there had been a hairbrush and toothbrush, the CSIs had taken it.

Wondering how a woman of obvious wealth had ended up here, Kate moved into the main room, glad of overshoes and small tread plates that raised her blue plastic overshoes off the sticky floor surface. She stood a moment, immobile, trying not to look at the deep gash to the IP's neck. Closing her eyes gave brief respite from the scene facing her. It was impossible to think in a horror chamber.

A rush of cold air hit her as the door swung open.

'Oh Jesus!' The familiar voice of her second-in-command.

It was safe to turn around.

DS Hank Gormley was more than her 2ic. He was her long-standing professional partner. Steady. Reliable. Trustworthy. The only copper she could be totally open with. More brother than colleague. He was standing in the entrance looking down. They would normally view a crime scene together. With O'Brien moving around, there wasn't sufficient room for two detectives in the van. Kate had asked him to wait outside, but Hank being Hank, with the CSI gone, his natural curiosity had taken over.

He'd be wishing he'd stayed away.

When their eyes met, Kate could see how moved he was by another man's rage. His weren't the only eyes on Kate. In her peripheral vision, she was aware of the victim's head turned at an odd angle. She appeared to be staring up at Kate, the connection between the two women already established. Her clothing was intact, though her shirt was torn, two of the buttons gone, possibly when she was grabbed by her attacker.

'Stanton won't require a rape kit,' Kate said. 'The motivation is personal, not sexual. This is about control, pure and simple.'

Hank's eyes were on the ceiling.

Kate followed his gaze.

Looking up she saw a large bloodstain. Directly beneath it, beside his right foot, was a round spot of blood with tiny splashes radiating from a central point. The size, shape and distribution of blood at a scene was a job for others to analyse but, in a moment of deep sorrow, Kate was overcome with grief. She couldn't afford to allow images like this to affect her, but they did. This one had shaken her to the core.

Now she'd seen it, she couldn't unsee it.

At every crime scene, there was always one thing that stuck in her mind: a child's toy, an old man's pipe, a shoe, the eyes of the dead. Those were the images that drove her on to seek justice for victims. On this occasion, that perfectly formed starburst pattern would act as a permanent reminder, a flashback to haunt her, day and night.

Until she got her shit together, she had nothing to say.

Already Hank was suspicious. 'Is there anything helpful in that note O'Brien took out of here?' He rarely missed a trick.

'The ramblings of a terrified woman.' It was at times like this that Kate hated her job. She knew he felt the same. 'It's the only thing we have of evidential value. O'Brien found no ID. No invoices, photos, passport or payslips. No devices, computer, iPad or mobile phone. A person who lives like that is in hiding.'

'Or she didn't live like that and the killer removed them,' Hank said.

Kate was shaking her head: he hadn't read the note she hoped had more to give.

He spread his hands. 'You don't think so because . . . ?'

'Tell you later.'

'Your face says you should tell me now.' He grimaced. 'You *know* her?'

'No . . . she seems to know me though.'

'You're talking in code again—'

'The note was written for me, Hank. Or someone very like me.'

'What do you mean?'

'Not now. I want to process it first. Call Jo. She's entertaining tonight. I hate to spoil her fun, but put her on standby. The three of us will put our heads together later. We need a handle on the victim. Our priority is the finder. He's the site manager, right?'

A nod. 'His name is Jack Shepherd.'

# 3

Kate and Hank walked to Shepherd's place, behind one another, rather than side by side, keeping to the southern edge of the path as directed by the Crime Scene Manager. It was pitch black on the dirt-track road, clouds obliterating the moon. The further they got from the caravan, the more eerie it became, trees on either side blacking out the surrounding landscape.

Without a flashlight, it would have been impossible to see.

Shepherd's stone-built single-storey cottage was located on the south-west corner of what had obviously once been a smallholding. Kate had passed it on the way in, all police vehicles, including her Audi, having been left on the main road, ensuring no contamination of the route in. Keen to get to the crime scene, Kate had taken little notice of the place.

Now she did so.

It reminded her of her father's home where she grew up. The curtains of the cottage were closed, though lights were on inside, the flickering of a TV visible through the thin fabric. Ignoring the dwelling once more, she used her torch to scan the immediate area. When she'd arrived, she'd noticed the name **SHEPHERD'S GATE CARAVAN SITE** and a sign indicating the months of the year when caravans were available for rent. For the site – and Kate's unidentified victim – the season was definitely over.

'I'd like to take a look around before tackling Shepherd,' she said.

Hank stopped walking. 'Looking for . . . ?'

'We won't know till we find it, will we? Check the entrance.'

They split up.

Kate stood a moment, listening to the waves crashing to land beyond the perimeter of the smallholding. Taking a much-needed gulp of sea air, she set off to examine two separate outbuildings, one large structure, one small, both locked and bolted, awaiting the spring. One was a shower and toilet block, the other a modest wooden chalet with a single shuttered window, the sign on which had faded over time.

She could just make out *Breakfast Hut*.

This, presumably, was a money-making sideline for the owners, a perk for those who preferred to camp under canvas and not in a tin tube. The hut was less than fifty metres from the house and neither building had a rear entrance.

The spot where Kate was standing suddenly lit up, casting a long shadow on the ground in front of her. She swung round and was blinded by the beam of a torch. Shading her eyes with her hand didn't help.

She called out to Hank.

No answer.

The torch was lowered, illuminating a pair of legs and the muddy ground on which they stood. Kate wasn't easily spooked, but having seen the state of her victim, she was taking no chances. Switching off her torch, making herself less of a target, she took cover.

The beam of light shifted from one side to the other, scanning the ground.

She held her breath.

'Kate, where are you?'

'Fuck's sake!' She turned her torch on, lifting her arm, pointing it in his direction. He was standing at the side of a rotting five-bar gate. It stood open, as it had been when they arrived. She made her way across the soggy ground toward him. 'Why didn't you answer when I called out?'

'I didn't hear you. Sorry, didn't mean to startle you.'

He had. 'Find something?'

'Maybe.'

He indicated a light patch on the gate. Hoping for a clue, she bent down to study it, finding two large chunks of wood missing. Corresponding splinters were on the ground a few metres away. The damage was recent. Bumper height. She noticed three sets of tyre tracks, presumably Shepherd's and two more. It didn't require a genius to work out that the gate had been hit by a vehicle taking the bend too fast.

She didn't need to ask.

Hank was already on the blower to alert the Crime Scene Manager.

Call complete, Hank followed Kate towards the single-storey cottage, asking no questions as she knocked on the door. He knew that she'd been deeply disturbed by what she'd seen in the caravan which was, he suspected, why she'd been so jumpy outside. He felt guilty for that.

It was his job to protect, not scare her.

He was concerned that she'd withheld the contents of the note O'Brien had found. Unusual. Normally, they collaborated on everything, in real time. His thoughts on what might be holding her back were interrupted by the sound of a key turning in the lock.

An arc of light flooded an overgrown front garden as the door was pulled ajar.

Shepherd was short, a stocky man with bushy eyebrows and the weathered skin of someone who spent a lot of time outside; a former smallholder, according to first responders, diversifying in retirement to make a crust on land extending to forty-five acres.

'Mr Shepherd?'

'Yes.'

Kate held up ID. 'Detective Chief Inspector Daniels and DS Gormley. May we come inside?'

Shepherd stepped away from the door.

Hank noticed no alarm on the property as Kate entered the hallway but, as the front door closed behind them, he took in heavy-duty bolts on the door, top and bottom. Catching her attention, he flicked his head and eyes downward, indicating the stock of what looked like a twelve-gauge shotgun. The weapon was propped up against the wall beneath a coat rack, the magazine and barrel partially hidden under a long, waxed coat. The gun was not cocked and he wondered if it was loaded. On the wooden stool beside it was the coil of brown leather, a cartridge belt.

Two were missing.

# 4

The house was unbearably hot, even though the fire in the grate was dying in the cosy living room. Shepherd introduced the detectives to his wife, Peggy, a small woman with white hair tied in a bun. Using a remote, she turned off the national news. Behind her gold-rimmed specs, her eyelids were red, a telltale sign that she'd been crying.

'Is this going to take long, DCI Daniels?' She was looking at Hank. 'We were just off to bed.'

'Detective Sergeant,' he corrected her.

Assumptions on who was in charge were not new. It happened a lot, especially with the older generation. Though it irritated Kate, she made nothing of it. No apology was forthcoming, except from her.

'We're sorry to keep you up, Mrs Shepherd—'

'Not at all,' her husband said.

Peggy bristled. 'You're tired, Jack.'

'Stop fussing, woman. Go to bed. I'm fine.'

'Actually, I'd like to talk to both of you,' Kate said.

Peggy Shepherd remained seated, though she had more to say. 'Jack's not been well. We told the uniformed officer all we know—'

With no time to debate it, Kate cut her off. 'Mrs Shepherd, I'm aware that you've already been spoken to, but a very serious incident has occurred on your property. I need to hear what you have to say, in case the officer you spoke to earlier missed anything. I appreciate the time of night and won't keep you any longer than is absolutely necessary.'

Peggy caved, getting up to move a pile of freshly ironed washing from an armchair, inviting the detectives to sit. They did. Jack Shepherd bent down, picked up a log and threw it on the fire, then took a seat on the sofa beside his wife. He cleared his throat, repeating the events of that evening without being prompted. 'We'd been out for an early dinner with our son. We arrived home around nine to find the front gate swinging open. It was closed and on the latch when we left.'

'Did you notice it was damaged?' Kate asked.

'Didn't look. I checked the house, then went to make sure we hadn't lost anything. Last time it was an off-road quad bike, worth six grand. Rural areas are unprotected. No offence, but we rarely see your lot up here. Anyway, that's when I noticed Helen's light on. Her car was missing and the door was ajar. I knocked. She didn't answer. I looked in.' His lips formed into a thin hard line. He was struggling to keep his composure. 'What kind of animal would do such a thing?'

Peggy slid a hand in his and gave it a squeeze. Her gesture suggested they were normally close. He pulled away. Kate felt that something other than shock and a police presence was upsetting them both. The atmosphere between them was unbearably tense.

'What kind of vehicle did she have?' Hank asked.

'A Fiat. Dark blue. 16 Reg.' Shepherd's expression was apologetic. 'I don't know the full registration number. I think it began with YA.'

'That's a Yorkshire plate,' Kate said. 'Does that fit with her accent?'

'She didn't have one. It was cosmopolitan, posh compared to our usual clientele.'

No surprise there, Kate thought, given the expensive kit found in the van. 'How long has she been here?'

'Two months.'

'Do you recall her having any visitors during that time?'

'No, never.'

'Have you?' Hank asked.

'No, we never get anyone here. No central heating. They're always cold.'

Kate couldn't imagine that. She was perspiring. She studied Shepherd closely. 'Have you seen anyone hanging about recently, anyone you didn't like the look of? Strange cars, people you hadn't seen before?'

'No, I'm always on the lookout. As I said, we've been robbed before.'

Kate took a moment to think. 'We couldn't help noticing that the other caravans are empty. The campsite is closed, isn't it?'

'Technically.'

'Well, either it is or it isn't.' Kate's tone was harder than before. 'Are you telling us she just rocked up here on the off-chance, knocked on the door and you made an exception?'

'I have an advert in the phone book.'

'She called you?'

'Yeah, I said no at first. She offered me cash, six months upfront at twice the going rate—'

'The call . . . did it come in on the landline or mobile?'

'Landline.'

'Who's your provider?'

'BT.'

Kate made a mental note to raise an action on this when she returned to base. The victim's telephone number would take them a step further to finding her identity. 'You said Helen, Mr Shepherd. I need a surname.'

'I don't have one.'

She gave a sharp look. 'How can you take a booking without a name? Surely, that would void your insurance.'

His silence made her think that he had none off-season. Kate couldn't have cared less how he ran his business, unless this seemingly nice man was aiding and abetting a murderer. She didn't think it likely. It was time to push the witness.

'Helen wasn't her real name, was it?'

Shepherd hesitated. 'I don't know.'

'Would you like to hazard a guess? I don't care about your—'

'Look, I hire out vans. I don't spy on people—'

'You don't value confidentiality either, do you?'

He didn't answer.

Kate took a moment to compose her next question. 'Who have you told about your lucrative arrangement?'

'No one.' Shepherd looked down at his slippers, avoiding eye contact.

'Someone knew she was here, Mr Shepherd.'

# 5

Kate left her comment hanging, carefully watching the interaction between the smallholder and his wife. A worried exchange. The DCI formed the impression that they'd already had that conversation, argued over it even. It explained the tension she felt when she entered the house. The victim's heartfelt note arrived in her head. It would act as her driver from this point on, compelling her to ask the hard questions, the ones witnesses would rather not answer.

She wouldn't hold back.

Swallowing her anger, she focused on the smallholder. 'Every action has consequences, Mr Shepherd. If you tell one person, you may as well put it on social media or stand in Eldon Square with a megaphone. People can't help themselves. Gossip makes the world go around. The woman you knew as Helen was vulnerable, living alone in the back of beyond. Now she's dead. I need the full names and contact details of anyone you told.'

Shepherd hung his head in shame, then raised it again. 'I mentioned it to one or two down The Bull. It's on the main road south, you can't miss it. The place is on its last legs. Very few get in there.' He rattled off three names. Hank wrote them down. Shepherd claimed not to have telephone numbers for any of them. Allegedly, he didn't like using the phone.

'We'd also like your son's details,' Hank said.

'You think I'm lying?'

'No, sir. It's standard procedure.'

Shepherd was angry. 'To corroborate what I told you? That's how it works, isn't it?'

'Jack, calm down!' Peggy said. 'They're just doing their job.'

Ignoring his wife, Shepherd got up and walked towards

the fireplace. At the centre of the mantelpiece was an antique wooden letter rack stuffed with what looked unopened post. He took his son's business card from it, handing it to Kate, asking if she could wait till morning to establish that he was where he said he was.

He remained standing, his back to the fire.

'Please don't bother him. Our daughter-in-law is in hospital after giving birth.'

He'd made no secret of the fact that he wanted the detectives gone. Kate had more questions. Slipping the card into her coat pocket, she moved on. 'Can I ask how Helen paid you?'

'Cash,' Shepherd said bluntly. 'I suppose you want that too.'

Kate caught the unexpected tell immediately. He'd had plenty of time to bank the cash. If, as he claimed, he'd been robbed, why hang onto it? She might benefit from this. 'Yes,' she said. 'Don't worry, I'll return it.'

'That's good to know, Inspector. We've struggled the last couple of years.'

'I understand.' Just how hard up was he? He should've have kept his gob shut. He was incriminating himself every time he opened it. 'If you could show DS Gormley where it is, without touching it, I'd be grateful.'

With his back turned, Kate eyed the letter rack, wondered if she was looking at unpaid bills. Had someone offered him money to take his wife and make himself scarce?

More to the point, had he taken it?

Shepherd opened the sideboard drawer, indicating a brown envelope.

'Did it come in this?' Hank asked.

'Yes.'

Hank put on gloves, took the money out and dropped it into an evidence bag Kate handed to him. She was betting that the retired smallholder wouldn't declare the cash as income. Fortunately for him, she had more important things on her mind to worry over it.

'Did Helen choose the van or did you?' she asked as Shepherd sat down.

'Why do you need to know?'

'Just answer the question,' Hank said. 'The sooner we get this done, the sooner we'll be on our way.'

Shepherd looked at his wife. 'Peggy?'

'Helen did,' she said.

Kate thought for a long moment, wondering if Helen's choice was significant, a memory of a happier time in her life, a family holiday perhaps. Given her expensive tastes, the DCI didn't think it likely, but it was important to cover all the bases. The Shepherds wouldn't necessarily recognise Helen if she'd been there as child. Still, it was worth a punt.

'Had either of you seen Helen before?'

'Not that I recall,' Shepherd said.

Kate switched her attention to his wife. 'Mrs Shepherd?'

'No, I'd have remembered.'

'Did she ever mention that she was familiar with the area or had been here before?'

'No, she kept herself to herself.'

'When did you last see her?'

'She drove by yesterday,' Shepherd said.

'Coming or going?'

'Coming.'

'Any idea how long she'd been out?' Hank asked.

'No, sorry. I was out myself fixing the boundary fence.'

'Another break-in?' Hank asked.

'No, it's been down for months, way before Helen arrived. People park on the main road and cut across our land to the beach from there. There's no right of way, but it happens all the time. We don't mind so long as they keep to the path at the bottom of the pasture and don't discard their litter.'

Kate asked: 'Did Helen use the path to the beach?'

'Yes, a lot,' Peggy said.

That didn't surprise Kate. They were so close to the

shoreline, they could almost touch it. Helen would be spoiled for choice, the small fishing village of Craster to the south, the spectacular ruins of Dunstanburgh Castle to the north. Kate had heard the North Sea angrily crashing to shore, bringing bad weather inland as she'd stumbled along the dirt road from the crime scene.

'When you saw Helen drive in earlier, what time was it?' she asked.

'Around two as usual—'

'As usual?'

Peggy glanced at her husband, then at Kate. 'We'd noticed that she seemed to have a routine. She'd go out at the same time every day, around noon. She was like clockwork. We came to the conclusion that she was collecting pre-ordered groceries, except I never saw her take any shopping from her car. Maybe she was eating out, popping out for a newspaper. I'm not sure.'

Or perhaps meeting someone, Kate thought. If that person was Aaron, a two-hour window meant that he wasn't far away. 'And tonight? What did you notice about tonight, before you went out?'

Shepherd shrugged, as if he didn't understand the question.

'Nothing unusual,' Peggy said. 'No comings or goings, if that's what you mean. Helen never ventured out after dark, which I found a bit odd for a young woman. Understandable at our age. At hers, I was never in, were you?' The question was rhetorical. 'And another thing I found curious. There was never anything in her rubbish bin. I mentioned it once and she didn't answer. I guess she had her reasons for bagging it up and dumping it off-site. We didn't pry, Inspector . . .' Her voice broke. 'We wish we had.'

'Have either of you received any enquiries about her?'

Both denied it, vehemently.

'OK, nearly done. Have you rented out any other caravans during the closed season? While Helen has been here, I mean.'

'No, this is the first time ever and it'll be the last . . .'

Shepherd's bottom lip began to quiver. He bit down on it, his face pained with regret. 'I couldn't live with myself if it turns out that my actions led to her death . . .'

Kate felt sorry for him. 'No one is accusing you of anything, sir.'

'With respect, that's not how it feels.' He stalled, wiping his face with both hands. 'She was such a wee thing. She didn't engage much. On the occasions she did she was polite and lovely. When she first got in touch, she was upset. I could hear the desperation in her voice. It wasn't about the money. I gave her refuge because it was no skin off my nose . . . because I knew she was in trouble and because we've been there before. Our Zoe got in with the wrong crowd when she was a young 'un and paid the price.'

'Is that why you took the shotgun with you?' Hank asked. 'Because Helen might be in danger?'

A nod. 'I'd have used it too.'

Kate had no doubt he was telling the truth. 'Do you have a licence, Mr Shepherd?'

'Of course.'

'A secure cabinet?'

'I do.'

'Then maybe you should use it.'

A resigned nod. 'Are we in danger?'

Kate hoped not. 'I doubt that, but I'll leave an officer here overnight. Last question. Did either of you see Helen with a laptop, bag or mobile phone?'

'We never went into the van,' Shepherd said, 'though Peggy used to take her eggs once a week, the occasional loaf of bread if she was baking. Helen must've had a mobile. If she needed her LPG bottle exchanged, she rang us and left cash on the step to pay for it. She never came inside or asked to use the telephone. Our conversations were brief. She gave nothing away. I did tell her that if she was ever in any trouble, or needed our help, she could contact us, day or night.'

27

'And what was her response?'

'Same as always . . . noncommittal.'

Thanking them for their cooperation, Kate stood up. 'We'll let ourselves out. An officer will be here in the morning to take a full statement and a search team will require access to out-buildings. We'll take possession of the gate. I've already made arrangements to uplift the caravan.'

Shepherd was welling up.

'Don't bring it back,' he said.

# 6

Leaving Hank to liaise with the pathologist, Kate headed back to base alone, telling him to beg a lift with the Crime Scene Manager. His team were almost done: photographs, impressions and measurements complete. Once the van was uplifted, Kate had given instruction for them to cover the base on which it stood and examine it in the morning when they could see more clearly.

They would be packing up soon.

As she drove away from the coast, it began to snow. Delicate flakes rushed obliquely towards her headlights, whipping into blizzard conditions, altering her perception of space and time, reducing her ability to determine her position on the road. As it blew towards her in a repetitive blur, traffic slowed.

So much for reaching her destination anytime soon.

She turned on the radio. A presenter reported further heavy snow overnight in north-east England. By morning, the area surrounding her crime scene and the entrance to Shepherd's property would be covered in a thick white blanket. If that happened, she should kiss goodbye to a more thorough search in daylight.

'Damn it!' she said.

Switching channels, she found music. It kept her company for a few minutes, then she turned it off. It was making her emotional. In view of the inclement weather, it was madness to continue to Northern Area Command HQ, Middle Earth as it was known among the rank and file. She was straining to keep her eyes open. There would be no one there. What could she realistically achieve while her team slept?

She'd just decided to call it a day when the brutalised faces of men, women and children who'd haunted her dreams for the majority of her career transported her to that grim caravan. Tonight's victim was impatient. Whoever Helen was wouldn't wait to creep up on Kate in the middle of the night. She was in her head now, her battered body superimposed on the windscreen.

Her note had seen to that.

When Kate finally reached the Major Incident Room it was empty, the cleaners long gone, lights dimmed, computers asleep, a deathly hush. She needed this time alone. Using her warrant card, she logged on to search the PNC for recent missing persons. In the past couple of months there were plenty. None that fitted the description and approximate age of her victim. None called Helen, though that didn't surprise her.

Deeply troubled, she stared at her monitor.

It would appear that no one had been looking for her victim, except the one person she feared the most. Accessing the images on her phone, Kate found the note. Sending it to the printer, she heard a copy spew out. Collecting it, she sat down to reread the text. Part of a sentence jumped out at her: *I'm not entirely innocent*. Should she take the words literally? If Helen had form, a fingerprint match would ID her.

Kate could do with an early breakthrough.

In her office, she made herself a decaf. As the coffee dispensed from the Nespresso machine, she texted Hank: **Stand down. See you at 7.**

**On my way in already.**

**Get yourself home.**

**Is Jo with you?**

**I'll call her.**

It had slipped Kate's mind that she'd put her partner on standby. Jo understood the demands and changing priorities of an SIO. There was a time the job had come between them. That was no longer the case. They had come to an understanding, past mistakes consigned to history. Kate was still a workaholic, but the relationship worked.

Kate tapped on her number.

The mobile was answered on the fourth ring. 'Kate, hold on!'

The coffee smelled good. Kate took a sip. She could hear laughter, loud conversations, the heavy beat of Sia's 'Elastic Heart', one of Jo's favourites. The music faded as she walked away, presumably looking for somewhere private where they could talk. Kate imagined her thundering up the stairs, throwing herself down on their bed, worn out from hosting the party they had both planned. They had spent last night preparing much of the food. If only she could press a button and rewind.

'Hey!' Jo said. 'Is it time to get rid of rent-a-crowd?'

Kate smiled at the in-joke. They had wrapped up early more times than she cared to remember due to an unexpected call-out.

'Is it a bad one?' Jo asked.

'As bad as it gets. I'm going to need your input in the morning.'

'Hank said you need it now.'

Kate checked her watch: 00:44. 'No, it's late. You carry on. Might be an idea to lay off the cocktails though.'

'Yes, guv.' There was a short pause. 'Are you OK?'

Kate wasn't. Far from it. She sidestepped the question. 'I should go.'

'See you later,' Jo said. 'If I'm lucky.'

'An hour and I'm all yours.'

'Why don't I believe that?'

'I'll be two hours, tops.'

'See you in three then.'

Kate laughed. 'Don't wait up.'

'The way things are going, this lot will be joining us for breakfast.'

'Then I might bail.'

'Don't you dare.'

Kate wasn't joking.

She was desperate to drive home, climb into bed with Jo and fall asleep in her arms, but they would end up talking about tonight's gruesome find, spend hour after long hour analysing the victim's note and still be there at dawn. Disconnecting, Kate wondered if Jo would now crash, leaving their guests to fend for themselves or rejoin the party. Helen had no one. There was no chance of Kate making it home tonight.

# 7

Detective work was often a hard slog – that was a given – but it was always fascinating and exciting, every shift different from the one before and the one after. You could never describe it as mundane. Predictability didn't come into it. Where violence was concerned, trying to second-guess the cruelty of one human to another was an impossible task. And just when you thought you'd seen it all, along came a new low to change your mind.

The MIT arrived in dribs and drabs, Jo included, everyone delayed by traffic chaos, some unable to get in from outlying areas, leaving the team depleted. A foot of snow had fallen overnight. It was still coming down and the gritters were struggling. Kate was glad she hadn't gone home. Hank was less happy when he found out, telling her she looked like death.

Ignoring the comment, she handed him a copy of Helen's note. 'Read, digest and distribute to the team with the same instruction.' It was essential that everyone read and interpreted the note themselves, not hear it second-hand from her. 'Make sure Jo gets a copy first. You have fifteen minutes.'

He took the copies and left.

Kate spent that time in her office, briefing Bright, her guv'nor. He was an exacting boss but one she respected and admired, a man who liked to keep his finger on the pulse of the Murder Investigation Team. The first few hours of any enquiry were as frantic as they were crucial.

Once assembled, Kate called the MIT to order, asking everyone to pay attention. She had to find a way to motivate her team. To do that, it was important to set the right tone, leaving no ambiguity about the type of murder or offenders they were up against. 'I assume you've all seen the briefing sheet and read the note found at the scene?'

Heads were nodding, the odd 'Yes, guv' reaching her.

'Then let's get started. I want to make this absolutely clear: we're not dealing with someone losing their shit in the heat of the moment. There was more than one set of fresh tyre tracks at the crime scene but no vehicles. Best guess, we're looking for two offenders who arrived in the same car and took a chunk out of Shepherd's gate on the way out. They didn't have to search for Helen. Her car was a giveaway, the only one on site. They were in and out. Job done, they ransacked the place and left in a hurry, taking Helen's car with them.'

Kate paused.

Even though she'd yet to confirm ID, she'd adopted the name Helen, personalising her at the earliest opportunity, knowing that it would spur her colleagues into action. Describing the victim as the injured party, the unident, the deceased were all too abstract. She wanted them to get a sense of the person she was, not the bloody remains she'd become.

'At this point in time we have no surname,' she continued. 'But there was nothing random or opportunistic about this one. There was an element of torture before her throat was cut, so we're not looking for some arsehole who happened to be passing the caravan, looked in through the window and thought he'd have some fun. Neither is it a robbery gone wrong. Helen's expensive watch and jewellery weren't taken. The attack was brutal, deliberate, planned and well executed, like a military operation.'

'And to some extent preordained, by the sounds of it.' It was Jo who'd spoken.

For a split second, their eyes met, a non-verbal message of solidarity passing between them. There hadn't been a moment to talk before the briefing began. Jo's insights into the criminal minds of dangerous offenders were as fascinating as they were crucial in finding those who kill. Kate was dying to get her take on the note.

'Yes, that too,' she said. 'What triggered her abuser to go over the top and kill this time is less clear. If any of you come up with a theory in the course of the investigation, I want to hear it, no matter how far-fetched it may seem. We're going after these men, no holds barred.'

'Too right,' Hank said.

'Please, all of you, heed Helen's warning. The man we're hunting is ruthless. Take him seriously and stay alert or you could end up as his next target. We all know it can happen.'

She had no need to elaborate. A few years ago, a colleague had fallen in the line of duty. Detective Sergeant Paul Robson had been murdered by an Organised Crime Group while acting up in Kate's absence, a warning to the police to back off.

They didn't do it then.

They wouldn't now.

# 8

Detectives and civilians were rigid in their seats. Kate gave instructions that they were to operate double-crewed until further notice. The enquiry into Robbo's death concluded that he'd been working alone without telling anyone where he was going. Lessons had been learned, procedures tightened. Bright had issued a directive that no one was to step outside of accepted guidelines from that point on, no matter the circumstances.

Kate would take no chances with their security or anyone else's . . . except maybe her own. Where she saw injustice in the world, she tackled it head on, even if it meant going off-book in pursuit of the truth, often incurring the fury of her boss and mentor. She'd do everything in her power to apprehend Helen's killer.

She caught the eye of Lisa Carmichael, the detective who'd been promoted into a dead colleague's shoes. She'd coped well as a DS, though every time Robbo's name was mentioned, or even hinted at, her head went down.

They had been the best of friends.

Time to move on.

'Helen's note moved me to tears,' Kate said. 'If it hasn't done the same to you, you're in the wrong job. As you've all seen, the note is unsigned, making our job a damned sight harder. It may contain clues and it's up to us to discover what they are. The copies you have I want returned, so please hand them in when this briefing is over. We can't afford for them to fall into the wrong hands.'

Hank said. 'I've posted a photocopy of it in the boss's office for reference.'

Kate thanked him and scanned the room. 'Now, I want you

to think about your wives and daughters, then imagine what the victim was going through at the time of writing. Take that sentiment with you when you're out making enquiries.'

'Why didn't she name her killer and tell us who she is?' DC Neil Maxwell said.

'I suspect she was protecting Aaron, who may now be in grave danger,' Jo said. 'Probably is.'

'I agree,' Hank said. 'But it's more than that, Jo. If the killer had found the note and suspected there were more – as the boss does, given the wording of the note – he'd have tortured her to give them up, then legged it for sure.'

'He didn't find it,' DC Andy Brown said. 'We did.'

'You're missing the point,' Hank argued. 'When Helen penned that note, she couldn't be sure it would find its way into our possession. It was taped to the underside of a low-level cupboard, hidden so well that O'Brien nearly missed it.'

'He's right,' Kate said. 'It could conceivably have remained in situ for years or floated off on the breeze when the van was crushed as scrap. Remember, Helen had no way of knowing where her body would be found. She might have been abducted, dragged from the van and kept prisoner elsewhere.'

'Or disposed of by other means,' Maxwell added. 'Weighed down in the river, buried, dismembered—'

'Spare us the graphics,' Kate said sharply. 'What we're saying is, Helen's death might never have been linked to that caravan or the note discovered. Shepherd had already been paid in full. If she'd disappeared, he may not have come forward, though I'd like to think he would. Plus, Helen had no idea of *when* we'd launch the investigation into her murder. It could've happened the day she died, next week, next year, in twenty years if ever. Lastly, and more importantly, if she'd named her killer and we made an arrest on the basis of the note alone, three things would happen: he'd deny it, we'd have been forced to let him go *and* we'd have shown our hand – the worst possible scenario.'

'I agree,' Jo said. 'Her priority is Aaron, then her killer, in that order. Clearly she believes we're up to the challenge.'

'And our priority is her ID. When we have it, there'll be no press release. We can't help her now – I wish we could – but we'll give it our best shot to prevent another slaughter. No one in this room talks to the media, on or off the record. Aaron could be her kid or someone else close to her. I suspect the former. She was wearing a gold locket. I just got word that there's no inscription on it, but it contains a picture of a toddler. We need to trace him urgently.'

'Was there no clue to his whereabouts at the scene?' Detective Sergeant Harry Graham asked. As the receiver, the result of all enquiries would cross his desk. He was the linchpin of the office, a detective who could spot inconsistencies in documents like a cat could spot a mouse.

'None,' Kate said. 'And her carefully constructed note drops no hints. He could be in foster care or with a relative, so all of you bear that in mind. He could be an adult for all we know. You see now why I'm keen not to disclose her identity when we have it. I don't need to draw you a picture. We have plenty.'

Kate thumbed over her shoulder.

All eyes shifted past her, concentration etched on the faces of the MIT.

The crime scene images uploaded onto the digital murder wall looked like a grotesque art exhibition where the prominent colour scheme was red. 'Take a good look. This has to be one of the most distressing scenes I've ever had the misfortune to attend. Whatever you're thinking, triple it.'

# 9

Kate didn't know how long the note had been taped to the underside of the shelf in the caravan. For all she knew, it could have been left there by a previous tenant, though deep down she didn't believe that. Two women with identical problems hiding from an abusive partner in the same caravan was a stretch too far. She was as sure as she could be that Helen had written it. Forensic examination might assist in that regard.

She wasn't hopeful.

'Why didn't she come to us before?' Andy Brown's hand was up. 'We could've put her in a safe house.'

'Unrealistic,' Kate said angrily. 'Women in need come forward every day and what do we do about it? You know as well as anyone that informing on an abusive partner isn't given the priority it deserves. Women are dying as a result. Two a week at the last count. Another million and a half live in fear of a partner. Had she come forward, she'd have been kicked out sharpish with a target on her back.'

Andy didn't know where to look.

Suitably ticked off, his eyes found the floor.

Kate didn't labour the point. 'It's clear from Helen's note that she was terrified of the man who murdered her and had been for a very long time. We're not dealing with a domestic that went too far, as bad as that is. We know she went out every day. Maybe to meet someone, a new man in her life perhaps. Maybe *he's* Aaron. We have no proof that he's her kid. I suspect the killer convinced himself that she was his property and, if he couldn't have her, no one else would. Think Moat.'

The room went very still.

Raoul Moat, a local thug, had shot his girlfriend, killed her new lover and blinded a police officer in a fit of rage, sparking the biggest manhunt in Northumbria's history. His name would never be forgotten in the corridors of Middle Earth or any other area command across every force in the land.

Carmichael broke the silence. 'Yeah, well maybe our target will do us all a favour and take the easy way out too.' Cornered by the police, Moat had killed himself. 'Not such a big shot, was he?'

Others were agreeing with her.

Kate understood their pain. She preferred to remember Moat's victims, especially Traffic Officer: PC David Rathband. His life had changed irreversibly as a result of that shooting. He'd since committed suicide, unable to live half a life. Kate had read his book: *Tango 190*. Heartbreaking. The man was a hero in her eyes.

'OK, I see you all got the message,' she said. 'I want your focus on this investigation, not on one we'd all like to forget.'

A mumbled apology followed.

'I suspect we're looking for more than a jealous loser with a death wish,' Kate added. 'The frantic search of her van suggests that she had something incriminating on her attacker and was silenced to prevent her passing it on. We don't know what the perpetrator was looking for or whether he found it. Everything we know implies that he's loaded, a man with more to lose than Moat and the means to escape justice. I'm relying on you to ensure that doesn't happen. Hank, anything to add before we move on?'

'Only that the investigation may not be as bleak as it sounds. We've amassed a lot of intelligence in the first few hours. Despite the worst the weather can throw at us, a search is ongoing on Shepherd's land, the toilet block, the breakfast hut and other sheds or byres on or near the property. House-to-house is up and running. Officers have been deployed to the beach to locate anyone who might have met and spoken to Helen over the past couple of months.'

Kate took over. 'The Shepherds said she used to walk the

shoreline regularly. Forensic examination of exhibits are on fast track: the note; the five grand recovered from Helen's coat; the cash she paid her rent with; her pens and writing paper; her watch and gold locket; the damaged gate and, crucially, the caravan in which she was found. Results are likely to come in thick and fast, so warn your families. We have some very long days ahead of us.'

Kate imagined CSIs emptying the caravan, painstakingly stripping it to a shell for clues that might identify a murderer. For her, and the MIT, waiting for others to fulfil their tasks was the hardest part of the job. With the team up to speed, pathologist Tim Stanton reporting back at any moment, she pushed aside what she couldn't do, turning her attention to the list she'd made in the small hours, raised actions the MIT could reasonably be getting on with.

'Jo, Hank and I will analyse the note as soon as we're done here. Unless it's absolutely necessary, we'd like no interruptions. This hideous offence didn't happen in the middle of Northumberland Street.' Kate was referring to the main shopping thoroughfare in Newcastle city centre. 'Shepherd's place isn't in the middle of nowhere. It's on the periphery of a small community where everyone knows everyone else's business. It shouldn't be beyond our capability to identify strangers near the scene.'

'Shepherd and his missus are the last people we know of who saw Helen alive. They have a son, Simon. He allegedly gave them dinner while Helen had company. Their daughter, Zoe, was apparently wayward, mixing with undesirables in her youth. We need to know more about the entire Shepherd family. They may have more to tell us.'

Andy Brown raised a hand, keen to volunteer and make amends for his earlier gaffe. 'I'll take that on, if you like, guv.'

'No, I need you for other stuff.' Ignoring his obvious disappointment, Kate gave the job to DC Amy Heads, the most recent member of the MIT. She lived in north Northumberland

and was from a farming background, so perfectly suited to the task Kate was about to ask her to perform. 'Amy, I want you to get to know Jack and Peggy Shepherd. They were in shock last night and may not be aware of the significance of what they've seen or heard since Helen moved in. Find out who's visited the site: postman, binmen, delivery drivers. They all need interviewing. Second, gather as much general info as you can about extended family. Hank and I will check out their alibis later. I want eyes on Simon Shepherd myself.'

'Yes, guv.'

Kate switched her focus to Carmichael. 'Lisa, I want you to check on Shepherd's shotgun certificate. His firearm was locked and secure when Hank and I left. I'm hoping it'll stay that way. Having seen what I saw, he's understandably nervous, though I don't think he and his wife are at risk. Whoever killed Helen would've seen that there was no one home when they were on his property, so they'll have no need to tidy up.'

'Right, guv.'

'While you're at it, talk to BT. We need the call history of Shepherd's landline. Oh, and see if he has an advert for his business in Yell.com. We only have his word for how Helen came to be staying there.'

'Would a man who is allegedly skint spend money on advertisements off season?' Harry said.

'I think so,' Carmichael said. 'That's when most people book up.'

'Then bring me the proof,' Kate said. 'And check on any suspicious incidents local to the crime scene, any emergency calls: police, ambulance, fire service. Helen seems to know us, Lisa. Find out if there were any social events that local coppers may have attended in the area. The more eyes on this the better. Offload those actions if you need to and keep Harry informed if you do.'

Harry raised a thumb to Carmichael.

Brown was looking sidelined.

'Andy, I have a job for you too,' Kate said. 'Shepherd gave us the names of three customers who knew about his long-term visitor. They're on your briefing sheet. I want you at The Bull public house ASAP. Talk to the landlord, see if he knows where they live, what they're like, then pay them a visit.'

Brown glanced through the window where the snow was bleaching down – a grimace. 'Not sure my old motor will cope, guv. I'll see if Traffic can give me a lift in a four-by-four. I can't imagine they'll have anyone spare. They'll be up against it this morning.'

'Fine! Do what you have to. Just get me that intel.'

Maxwell had his hand up. 'Am I the only one who thinks Helen might've been on the game?'

'No,' Harry said. 'You're the only one who thinks every murdered woman probably asked for it.'

Maxwell scowled at him.

There was a deathly hush in the briefing room, two dozen pairs of eyes on Kate. Years ago, Maxwell had joined the squad with a bad reputation and an outdated attitude to women, including colleagues, hence his transfer to a female-led team, his last chance to retain his status as a detective. Kate had told him straight: make the change or ship out. He'd worked hard to gain her trust and won over the rest of the MIT. For reasons she couldn't fathom, Harry was the exception.

Maxwell raised his chin defiantly. 'Guv, I meant no offence, neither was I talking about street-corner trading. You said Helen's gear was high-end. *She* said she wasn't entirely innocent. A high-class escort was my interpretation . . . unless Harry has a better idea.'

'Yeah, keep digging,' Harry scoffed. 'Fucking dinosaur—'

Kate shot him down, telling him to cut it out. 'The last thing I need right now is you two mouthing off at one another. Express your opinions without being offensive or button it. Didn't I just encourage input?'

'Yes, guv.'

'Right. Well, Neil is as entitled as anyone to contribute.'

'Fair enough, so long as he doesn't assume that women come by good gear by selling their bodies or because men gave them the funds to buy it—'

Maxwell exploded. 'That's not what I was suggesting—'

'No, it's not,' Kate said. 'As theories go, it's as good as any, exactly what I'm after from all of you. Personally, I'm not convinced. Helen's note demonstrates her intellect. She's as likely to be a woman of independent means—'

'I'm on CCTV then,' Maxwell said.

A ripple of laughter went around the room.

Even Maxwell was grinning, his spat with Harry over . . . for now.

Kate could see he was faking it. 'You excel at CCTV, but you're not getting off that lightly. I want you to liaise with ANPR. They've already been briefed to look out for Helen's dark blue Fiat. Yankie, Alpha reg, a 16 plate . . . we think. I doubt they'll spot the killer's vehicle,' Kate continued. 'Only a fool would stay in convoy after what he did. Clever offenders will have split up the minute they hit the main road.'

Maxwell's mood lifted. 'Liaise on what, guv? Sounds like you've got it covered.'

'I instructed them to concentrate on last night. I want the parameters extended to include the last week. We can extend further, if need be, but let's keep it tight for now. Helen had a routine the Shepherds described as "like clockwork", leaving the property at midday, returning around two in the afternoon. Let's see if we can identify where she went and if she was being followed. Sweet-talk local shopkeepers and residents to hand over CCTV if they have it, interior and exterior. They don't need to know why. We'll hit them with that later and follow up with photographs as soon as we have ID. I want ANPR to concentrate on that two-hour window with a half hour either side.'

'There's only one problem with that,' Hank said. 'If Helen

took the backroads, we're screwed. Once we left the A1 en route to the crime scene I never saw one camera. I tend to check if you're flying, guv.' He rolled his eyes.

The team laughed again, a chance to let off steam.

Kate only had one speed.

# 10

Kate needed a moment alone with Jo before Hank joined them. More than that, she needed a hug. Rarely did that happen when they were on police premises. After their relationship was made public, Bright had given special dispensation for them to continue working together, so long as they kept everything on a professional footing. What the hell? The blinds were down. She put her arms around Jo. Her voice stuck in her throat, arriving as little more than a whisper.

'I'm sorry I didn't make it home.'

Jo gave her a squeeze, her hand moving to the nape of Kate's neck, barely noticeable, but a thrilling sensation all the same. Kate struggled to keep her composure as a slender finger stroked her bare skin. Feather-light. Exquisite.

She was a breath away from losing it.

Reacting to the tension, Jo pulled away. 'I realised it wasn't the snow that kept you as soon as I read the note. Are you OK? I can't begin to imagine how painful it must've been to receive it, especially in the middle of a crime scene with O'Brien looking on—'

'It's my job.'

'Oh, Kate. Don't pretend a message from the grave is no big deal or deny how it made you feel. Why didn't you say you were struggling? I'd have called a cab and come in—'

'Which is why I kept it to myself. And, for the record, I'm not struggling.'

'Telling yourself that doesn't make it true.'

It was a long time since Jo had blown into Kate's life. Apart from Hank, she was the only person in the world who'd seen her with her guard down, at her most vulnerable, trying to keep up appearances at work. Being around her made Kate want to weep when she needed to be strong. It simply wouldn't do

The shutters went up.

'Please don't take this the wrong way. I didn't want you in last night because I needed you here now, with a clear head and your expertise, not your sympathy.'

'Shutting me out, pretending you've got this, won't help. Talking it through with someone who adores you might.'

Jo's concern was self-evident. She looked at Kate, really looked at her, and still she didn't speak. Kate dropped her gaze, then raised her head, a long look between them, a delicate moment.

It was Kate who broke the deadlock. 'Please, don't look at me like that. Not here.'

'Then where? You're hardly home. We've been here before, remember? Kate, you may be able to fool them . . .' Jo pointed beyond the office door. 'But don't try it on me. I know you're not that person.'

'I am that person. I have to be. People are relying on me, Jo. One of them is dead and I have no intention of letting her down.'

'I'm not asking you to. I worry about you, that's all.'

'I know you do, just save it till we get home. That's all I'm asking.'

On edge, Kate looked out of the window, avoiding eye contact.

There was no let-up outside. Tiny drifts of snow were forming on the sill, even as she watched, obscuring her view through the glass. The sky was heavy, much like her mood. She took a moment out, on the verge of losing it. Kate wasn't angry with Jo. Far from it. She'd be the one picking up the pieces when Kate let her emotions go. All she wanted was to stop her from being nice.

Kate turned to face her, a guilty expression. 'I'm sorry. You don't deserve to suffer because I'm an emotional wreck. I won't lie. The note floored me, but I don't have the luxury of falling apart.'

'I know—'

'Then back the hell off and let me get on with it.'

Jo's smile didn't reach her eyes. She understood the note would do one of two things: drive Kate on to solve the case or drive her insane. She'd always been torn between her love for Jo and a job that demanded her full attention.

She had no off switch.

Kate reached for Jo's hand, then snatched it away as someone arrived at the door. There was always something to interrupt a private moment. This time Hank's knock was welcome, her get-out-of-jail card.

Walking behind her desk, she called out to him.

The door swung open. He was balancing three coffees, waiter style, on a tray, a curious expression on his face. 'You psychic now? How did you know it was me?'

'When is it ever anyone else?' Kate said.

He eyed them in turn. 'Do you want me to bugger off for five?'

'No, we're good . . .' Jo kept her gaze on him. 'Kate's keen to push on.'

'Before or after you punch each other's lights out?' Hank back-heeled the door. It slammed shut behind him. Aware that he was about to cross an invisible line, he danced around the subject. 'Harry's mood must be catching. His constant bickering is beginning to annoy me. What the hell is eating him?'

'Don't know. Don't care,' Kate said.

'I could see that when I walked in. I could've sworn you'd had words. Imagine that.'

'Only nice ones,' Jo lied. 'Though unless you want your head on a plate, I'd drop the sarcasm.'

As he put the coffees down, Kate glanced at Jo, mouthing the word 'sorry' while his back was turned. She noticed a packet of Garibaldis sticking out of his pocket, a stash of which he kept in his desk drawer in case they needed a sweetener for their guv'nor – they were Bright's favourites – and sometimes for minor emergencies, such as now. Jo had brought pastries in for the team. They were devoured before Kate had a chance to grab one. Hank knew she hadn't eaten and was compensating.

She had a lot to be grateful for.

They all sat down.

Hank opened the biscuits and passed them on.

Though grateful for his generosity, Kate had no appetite. With a million things on her mind, even more actions to delegate, she passed up on the treats. 'This is not going to be easy . . .' She held up the note. 'Handwriting analysis isn't an option without a comparison document, which we don't have, but I'd like to have a stab at interpreting what's written here. Jo, it goes without saying that you'll need more time to study it, we all do, but would you kick us off with your first impressions?'

Relaxing into her seat, Jo placed her annotated note on her knee. 'I can't confidently predict Helen's personality in the way that a handwriting expert can, but I'm guessing that's not what you're after.'

'We'll take anything we can get,' Hank said.

'Well, as you've reminded me many times, in less professional language, graphology is far from an exact science, but it has its uses.'

'Oh really?'

'It's used extensively in professional profiling and in determining marital compatibility—'

'Are you taking the piss?' Hank said

'Yeah, if only we'd known,' Kate added.

Jo laughed.

Humour was the only way to deal with the effect of work on a happy home life. Over the years, their relationship had had its moments and so had Hank's marriage to Julie. On both counts, that was behind them now. There had been times when it was touch and go whether either union would survive.

They had all gone to the brink and survived.

Kate counted herself lucky to have kept hold of Jo. She had that look in her eyes now that made Kate feel like *she* was the only one in the room and that anyone else was invisible. Before Jo, no one had ever looked at her that way. And now, as if she'd read Kate's mind, Jo tapped her note, regaining her attention.

'As you alluded to already, I think we can all agree that Helen is intelligent, articulate and well-educated,' she said. 'The grammar is good and there are no mistakes or crossings out. The words flow. The letters are consistent. Given her assumed state of mind at the time of writing, that's unique in my experience. The content is measured, very personal and yet there's no sign that she's agitated, which is baffling. If that had been the case we'd have seen it in her scrawl.'

Kate nodded.

So far, so good.

Jo was still talking . . . 'From the first paragraph to the last there's no doubt that she feared the worst and wasn't expecting to live long. Not only does she talk about her demise, she imagines it, describing it in graphic detail, as I'm guessing she has many times over. It's also clear, as discussed at the briefing, that she's suffered a prolonged cycle of abuse. Kate, when you get an ID, you could do worse than consulting domestic violence organisations to see if she ever sought refuge.'

Kate gave Hank a nod.

He made a note to chase it up.

'I can take care of that if it would help,' Jo said. 'I have a few contacts I can tap into.'

'Yes please,' Kate said.

'I can't see Helen doing that,' Hank said.

Kate looked at him. 'Why not?'

'You said yourself, everything she owns is flash, from her clothing to her shampoo.'

'Since when is that relevant?' Kate rolled her eyes. 'I've got news for you. Men from all walks of life shower women with gifts, then rape or beat the living shit out of them—'

'I'm aware,' he bit back. 'The difference is, she had the means to get the hell out of there to a hotel—'

Kate cut him off. 'Has it occurred to you that money might not have been her only consideration?'

He glanced at Jo, clueless. 'Am I missing something here?'

Jo said nothing, preferring not to get caught between Hank and her other half.

Kate sat forward, elbows resting on her desk, hands linked together. 'Helen may be operating under a false name, but I believe Aaron is real, in which case he'd need more protection than a room key, even a digital one in an upmarket hotel. She may not fit the profile of a woman who'd use a refuge, but she wasn't living in a shitty caravan by choice, was she? Her abuser tracked her down before – and now she's dead.'

# 11

Kate suspected that Helen recognised the danger she was in, had weighed up the odds and come to the conclusion that there was less risk of being found if she hid somewhere other than in a recognised place of safety. Kate moved on, keen to analyse the note chronologically, line by line, word by word. 'The note is timed but not dated,' she said. 'We know only that it was written late on a Friday evening. We don't know which Friday and presently have no way of finding out. Why ten forty-five? It seems like an odd time to sit down and pen a letter. Any ideas?'

'Maybe she couldn't sleep,' Jo suggested.

'She hadn't been to bed,' Kate said. 'She was dressed when Shepherd found her.'

'OK. A lot of people sit down to reflect in the evening, especially those prone to dark thoughts. Maybe something happened that prompted her to write, a call that spooked her, a programme on TV—'

'*Newsnight* probably,' Hank said. 'It's enough to drive anyone to reach for the remote.'

Kate ignored the jibe. 'Jo makes a good point. I'd be interested to know what has been, is being broadcast at that time on a Friday night, if any of it includes police, a televised appeal for witnesses to come forward, that kind of thing.'

'Was the TV on?' he asked.

'Not according to first responders. Doesn't mean she hadn't turned it off or viewed it on her mobile, assuming you can get a signal up there. It was intermittent last night. O'Brien said there was no Wi-Fi in the caravan. I'd like to check the local news feeds, radio and TV.' She met Hank's gaze across her desk. 'I didn't see a Sky dish, did you?'

He shrugged. 'I wasn't looking for one.'

'Well you should've been. When we're done, speak to O'Brien, then call Shepherd. Find out what reception he gets up there, what channels are available. That far north he may pick up Border TV as well as Tyne Tees. If we're lucky, we might find something that'll help us.'

'Maybe she received a call from *him*,' Jo suggested.

'I don't think so,' Kate said. 'She'd have legged it if he was onto her. And if she was too frightened to leave, the very least she'd have done is alert Shepherd. Besides, there was no break-in, no damage to the caravan door.'

'Maybe her boyfriend arrived begging forgiveness and she let him in before it all kicked off,' Hank suggested. 'As ridiculous as that sounds, it happens. The question is, would she write and hide that note, then open the door to a man she knew might kill her?'

'I don't think so,' Kate said. 'I suppose it would depend on her state of mind at the time. Unless she was expecting someone else . . .'

Hank looked at her. 'Based on what?'

'She was terrified and yet didn't lock the door. O'Brien found the key in her coat pocket, so she wasn't ambushed as she arrived home. Her coat was off and hung up. It doesn't make sense. Shepherd said she received no visitors. Mind you, he can't know that for sure. He said himself that people walk across his land to access the beach. There's no direct line of sight from his place to her van so he wouldn't have seen anyone approaching from the other direction.'

'Might there be a spare key with Shepherd?' Jo asked.

'He still has it,' Hank said. 'I checked.'

A beat of time passed when no one spoke.

Jo eyed the note. 'We might not be able to make sense of them, but I think Helen is leaving clues here.'

'I'm not seeing any signposts,' Hank said.

'Be patient, these things take time to percolate. It's like watching a movie or reading a book for the second time around. You see things you didn't notice on first viewing. Helen mentioned the red mist. That's a police term, isn't it? An anger reference?'

'It's common enough language,' Kate said. 'Jo, I've read the note multiple times and I'm struggling to make headway. One thing struck me as odd though. She wrote *this* note, not *my* note. There's no ownership. She repeats it twice in as many paragraphs. *This* note to me suggests there are more, which is what Hank was alluding to at the briefing.'

Hank apologised to Jo. 'Sorry, I was going to elaborate on it and forgot. Helen also used the phrase "enough for one day", which again hints at more to come.'

Jo was nodding.

Kate said: 'I don't know about you, but I get the distinct impression that Helen's note is less to do with helping us detect her murder. It's about us finding Aaron, preventing her abuser from doing so. She's choreographing the situation. Taking control—'

'Wouldn't it have been simpler just to name him?'

'Not if we can't prove a case against him.' Kate reinforced what she'd told everyone at the briefing, before moving on. 'What Helen gave us is heartbreaking, as close to a dying declaration as you'll ever get, but it's not enough and she knows it.'

'And there were no further notes in the van?' Jo asked.

Kate shook her head. 'They're dismantling it now.'

'Might she have hidden them elsewhere on Shepherd's land?'

Kate thumbed toward the window. 'If she did and this weather keeps up, I doubt we'll find them today. It's bad here. Up there it'll be a whiteout.'

Jo wasn't listening. 'Assuming you're right about multiple clues, Helen's way too clever to have left them all in one place.' She drained her coffee and got up to stretch her legs. Even at home, she couldn't sit still for long. She swung around to face the others. 'This is pure guesswork, but I think it more likely that she'd have found other ways of connecting with us, if that's what she's doing.'

'Based on what?' Hank asked.

'Well, she was clever enough not to use a refuge—'

'Yeah, for what good it did her—'

'Oi!' Kate raised her voice. 'Wind your neck in or sling your hook. We need to work together on this. I think Jo's hit on something here. Opening different channels of communication is what I'd have done in Helen's situation. If she is on any social media platform, Carmichael will find her. If she left cryptic messages elsewhere, we'll find them too. As soon as we have ID, I want every newspaper ad and social media post scrutinised.'

Hank apologised for his negativity.

'Don't be daft,' Jo said. 'That note got to all of us. I detected only one discrepancy . . .'

Kate leaned in. 'Which is?'

'Helen is suggesting that our target is forensically aware,' Jo said. 'Clever enough to outwit us—'

'He won't,' Hank cut Jo off. 'Not as long as I live and breathe.'

'Good,' Kate said. 'Now shut up and let her finish.'

Jo ignored their petty squabble. 'Unless I'm reading this wrong, there's a contradiction here. Helen is also confident that we'll catch him. Now that is odd—'

'It's a warning,' Kate said. 'She's giving us the heads-up that it won't be an easy collar. That's my interpretation anyway.'

Jo underlined some text on her copy of the note. Kate strained her neck to read upside down. She was about to ask for an explanation when Jo posed a question. 'Why does she refer to him torching the van when everything else is so precise? The murder went down exactly as she described. Is it a throwaway comment or a hint at something specific?'

'He's a killer,' Kate said. 'Not an arsonist.'

'Then why mention it?'

'Who's to say he's not both?' Hank said.

Kate looked at him. 'He didn't set fire to the van, did he? Not even to get rid of forensics and burn his victim to a crisp, making identification more difficult. Surely, if he'd been that way inclined, he'd have struck a match.'

'Maybe he has.'

'What's that supposed to mean?'

Hank didn't come up with an answer. Kate didn't push him on it. He was thinking, not avoiding the question, exactly what she wanted from him. She made a note to look at arsonists in the system. Jo wasn't listening to either detective. Her head was down, re-examining the note, devouring every word.

She spoke without looking up. 'There is a lot of subtext here. Helen said, quote, "even though we've never met in person," unquote. I can't work out if she means she's had no dealings with the police generally, or just you, Kate.'

'We've never met,' Kate said.

'You *think* you've never met.'

'No. If we had, she'd have called me. I don't know her.'

'How could you possibly know that? Her mother wouldn't recognise that face. And don't be so touchy. I'm posing questions. That's why you invited me in here, isn't it?'

Kate didn't answer.

'Apology accepted,' Jo said.

Hank shook his head. 'You two crease me up sometimes. If we're sharing theories, I have one for you to chew on. Kate, you're not going to like it.'

'Go on.'

'I agree with Jo, Helen's note is mystifying. I'm paraphrasing now, but she said her abuser's triggers were difficult to spot, visible only to her. I thought she was warning us that he'd appear normal and wouldn't stand out. There is another interpretation. Might invisible triggers be a euphemism for a concealed weapon?'

Kate considered this as valid, though if Hank was right and the offender was armed, it upped the threat level. 'Good work,

Hank. I didn't see that on first reading. Pass that on to the team. As Jo said, we need more time to analyse the note. The more eyes on it the better.'

Jo had something else to say.

Kate spotted her hesitation. 'What?'

'I know you don't want to hear this, but I think Helen wrote the note specifically with you in mind.'

'That's ridiculous—'

'Is it?' Jo wasn't convinced. 'She's nailed you, Kate. She knows you're outraged. When are you ever anything else? Joined by an invisible thread? Well, she got that right. She understands what drives you. If she hasn't seen you in person, I'd wager that she's seen you on TV—'

'That note could describe any SIO on the force.'

'You don't really believe that.'

'I do. Helen had no way of knowing who'd turn up at the crime scene. She's personalising the note, that's all. She wants Aaron found and she's prepared to stroke our ego to achieve that—'

'Oh please, she does it again and again. Right now, she has you wrapped around her little finger.'

Hank remained silent, intrigued by Jo's theory.

It was like watching a drama play out on stage, two Alpha females with opposing views doing battle. He couldn't get a word in edgeways and didn't try. Instead, he grabbed another biscuit, bit into it and waited for the intermission.

Jo wouldn't back off. 'Kate, I'm only verbalising what you've been thinking ever since you read that note. What's the first thing Bright does when you crack a high-profile case?' She didn't wait for an answer. 'He wheels out his golden girl in front of a camera. Helen knew her death would be brutal. She's talking about a sadist here. Why *wouldn't* she assume that the head of CID would put his most revered SIO on it, no matter who was on call-out or who turned up at the scene?'

'That's a bit of a stretch,' Kate argued.

'Is it? You may not realise it but when you're shoved in the limelight your passion shines through to anyone watching. The author of this note knows a bit about psychology, her own and other peoples. Notice how she writes "YOU" and "HIM" in block capitals. She's matchmaking, measuring up two opponents of equal stature.'

Hank raised a finger. 'Can I speak?'

Kate glared at him.

'You asked the team for theories,' he said. 'Jo's is as good as any. I also have one. You can stamp on it if you like. God knows I'm used to it but, if I'm right and you're wrong, we have a serious problem.' He held up the note. 'Anyone reading this text could be forgiven for thinking it was written by a woman. It's almost poetic . . .' He paused for a long moment. 'Or made to look that way.'

'You're not convinced she's the author?' Kate's eyes widened. 'Jesus, are you serious?'

'Who's to say it wasn't written by someone with a score to settle, hinting that he's a match for you, not the other way around? It could explain why the handwriting flows, couldn't it? Maybe *he's* the clever, articulate one. You stressed in the briefing the need to be careful. You made a point that we're looking for a player or two, as well as a potential second murder victim. What if the note was designed to lead us down that path? What if Aaron doesn't exist and that second victim is you?'

# 12

Carmichael arrived with Stanton's preliminary post-mortem report before Jo had time to digest Hank's theory. The implication that some tooled-up egotist from Kate's past might be playing mind games was a possibility that Jo didn't want to acknowledge. The thought scared her. Kate had put some twisted men and women behind bars during her career, some who'd rub her out in an instant if they got the chance.

What did that make Helen?

Collateral damage?

A ploy to pull Kate into an investigation fraught with danger?

The idea was unthinkable.

Jo had been watching Hank. He'd spent the majority of his career shadowing Kate. He took the job as her 2ic seriously, loved her almost as much as he loved his wife. Jo had never seen him so worried. Her attention shifted to Kate. She was in denial, on autopilot, asking Carmichael to precis the document in her hand.

'Guv, before I do, you should know we have ID. Helen's real name is Hannah Swift. Before being attacked, she'd been super fit with no sign of pre-mortal disease that might have contributed to her death.' She paused, a sad expression. 'There was evidence of old injuries: a broken bone in each forearm, a fracture to her left cheekbone, a massive scar down her back Stanton described as deep, as if the bastard inflicting it had tried to cut her in half diagonally. On this occasion, her injuries were consistent with a sustained beating.'

'Skip to the conclusions, Lisa.'

'Severed carotid artery was the cause. In short, she bled—'

'Time of death?'

'Yesterday, between five and seven p.m., give or take an hour or two either way. Hannah has one conviction for possession of Class A, more than could be explained away for personal use.' She handed Kate a printout that included a photograph of the deceased, and her antecedent history.

Kate stared at it for a long time, then looked up. 'How long did she get?'

'Strangely, a hefty fine, not a prison sentence.'

Kate examined the printout, checking the details of the conviction. 'For a kilo? That's a street value of around £50K.'

'I know, how lucky was—'

'There's nothing lucky about Hannah's life, Lisa.'

'No, guv. I didn't mean . . .'

'Relax, I know what you meant.'

Carmichael blushed.

'Anything else?' Kate asked.

'There was no evidence that she was a significant player, dealing or supplying. The officer in charge was Chalky White. He's tied up with a serious assault in the West End at the moment. He's on earlies, goes off at two.'

Kate checked her watch. 'You mean half an hour ago?'

'I told him it was urgent. He's coming straight here when he's done.'

While she waited, Kate held on to Carmichael, who'd just informed her that Hannah Swift had given birth. Kate didn't speak for a long while, then: 'Get Maxwell to email the registrar. We need two things: a copy of Hannah's birth certificate so we can trace her parents; a search for Aaron in the register, assuming he is the child she gave birth to and she hasn't given him an alias.'

Jo and Hank exchange a look: *Assuming he even exists.*

Kate ignored their scepticism.

'Given that she's begging you to find him,' Jo said, 'I think it unlikely she'd make it more difficult for you. Wouldn't she have said find my son?'

'Maybe.' Kate turned her focus on Carmichael. 'Issue Hannah's photograph to the house-to-house team. They already have a description of her vehicle. I want them canvassing local farms, doctors, garages and shops. If people saw her, stationary or on the move, I want to know about it. Oh, and see if she's on social media.'

'Already on it. I've also spoken to the child protection team and put a call in to the NSPCC. Hannah never made a complaint to us but maybe she used one of their hotlines to ask for advice.'

'Good thinking.'

Kate had given Carmichael a lot to do. She was up for it, quick and efficient, but she didn't want to overload her. An awful thought came out of nowhere that Kate hadn't considered while analysing the note with Hank and Jo. Did 'find Aaron' mean the killer had the boy?

Unthinkable.

Unwilling to indulge that thought, Kate turned her attention to the case file, homing in again on Hannah's mugshot. She was a natural blonde with soft features and ice-blue eyes that seemed to connect with hers even from the page. Her date of birth was 10.10.79. Her last known address was on the outskirts of the market town of Morpeth, around half an hour away.

Kate looked up at Carmichael. 'Is this address still current?'

'No guv. She's been gone for months.'

'How many?'

'Five. The landlord tells me she cleared off sharpish, leaving a few belongings and without paying her rent.'

'Has he still got her stuff?'

'No, it was dumped at the local tip.'

'He must have a copy of her tenancy agreement that we can use as a handwriting comparison,' Jo said. 'She'll have signed that, surely.'

Intuitively, Kate knew where Jo was heading without

actually spelling it out. She was hoping to quash Hank's theory that the offender had written the note and not Hannah.

Carmichael was one step ahead of her. 'It's nothing more than a scribble. Ditto her custody sheet and fingerprint forms. The former address she gave the landlord when she signed her agreement is non-existent. He claims there was nothing of any value in the flat, a few clothes but no jewellery or personal items she might return for. You cover your back and travel light when you're on the run from a maniac.'

The tension in the room increased.

Kate tried not to think of what Hank had said before Lisa arrived but couldn't rule it out. If that letter was written by someone other than Hannah Swift, she'd need more than Garibaldis to sweeten the pill. The more Kate thought about that, the more she drifted towards his point of view. The reason she was leaning that way was staring her in the face.

Jo was uncharacteristically tense. She didn't think it possible that Hannah had been duped into writing the note. Neither did she think it had been written under duress. As she'd pointed out, handwriting could be used as an indicator of stress and there was no evidence of it. It begged the question, how could Hannah have penned such an emotive letter without a shaky hand?

Kate turned to face Hank. 'Find out which barrister represented her. Maybe they can shed light on the case. While you're at it, talk to the CPS. Maybe she had friends in high places. Jo thinks she knows the police, trusts them even. God knows what it all means, but I intend to find out.'

'I'm not sure I like where this is going,' Jo said. 'If Hannah wrote the note, she was terrified of someone.'

'If?' Carmichael's eyes shifted from Jo to the other two.

Kate sidestepped the question. 'Put your thinking cap on, Lisa. We need all there is to know about Hannah. Hank and I will pay her solicitor a visit when we've spoken to Chalky. Go! Let me know when he lands.'

# 13

There was a large amount of dried blood on Chalky's uniform shirt when he arrived half an hour later. In need of a shower and a warm drink, he was a walking history of his day. As he slumped down in a chair in Kate's office, he apologised for keeping her waiting and for his unkempt appearance. He'd come from a street attack on a young male, the injured party taken to hospital with life-threatening injuries. An arrest had been made, the offender charged with attempted murder.

'Welcome to my world,' Kate handed him a coffee and sat down. 'Was it a fight?'

'No, entirely unprovoked. According to witnesses, the IP was walking along, minding his own business when the offender went apeshit. He produced a knife, stabbed him six times before two members of the public intervened, holding him until our lot got there.' He shook his head. 'I'm getting too old for this job, Kate. I have four years to go and I'm off.'

'Will the kid make it?'

'Touch and go, last I heard.'

'This one wasn't so lucky.' Kate slid Hannah's file across her desk, then a crime scene image showing her lying on the floor of the caravan, eyes frozen in horror.

Chalky physically recoiled. 'Oh, Christ!' He placed an index finger on the file. 'Is this her?'

'Yes, though that goes no further than this room. There may be someone else in danger.'

'Understood.' He flipped open the file. 'What do you want to know?'

'As much as you can tell me.' Kate leaned into her chair. 'Right now, you're one of very few people I know of who had any contact with her.'

'Do I need a lawyer?'

'Not unless you have something to hide.'

After a heavy shift for both of them, police banter was light relief. On this occasion it fell flat. Kate liked Chalky. He was one of the good guys. They had worked together for a while before she joined the CID. With no interest in becoming a detective, he'd remained in uniform. He was a good officer with a sharp eye for detail and a memory to match, but his initial reaction gave her cause for concern.

'Do you remember who her brief was?' she asked.

'Terence Walker. He's a partner at Prentice, Lavelle and Walker.'

'I've come across the firm but not him personally.'

'You didn't miss much. He's a toad.'

'So I hear.'

Walker was no slouch. His reputation in court was legendary. He played to win and often did. Some heavy criminals had escaped justice by engaging his services, a clever interpretation of the evidence swinging the jury his way. A veritable Lincoln Lawyer but without the finesse of Michael Connelly's fictional attorney, Mickey Haller.

'They're not the most respected law practice in the city,' Chalky added.

'Yeah, I know . . . which is odd.'

'Odd?'

She meant for a woman who shops at Liberty for her pyjamas. 'Not important . . .' She changed the subject. 'Carmichael tells me that the charges were reduced before the case came before a judge.' She tapped the file in front of him. 'There's no record in there to indicate why. I thought you might remember.'

He gave a shrug. 'No idea. I was warned for court that day. When I got there, I was told that Hannah had changed her plea, that I was no longer required. The jury were dismissed. The CPS are the ones you should be asking. The case was sound, Kate. Hannah was caught red-handed. They probably gave way to pressure from her barrister in exchange for a guilty plea for a first offence.'

'Probably? You don't sound so sure.' It was happening more and more, but Kate had no time to debate the rights and wrongs of it. Her mind was sifting other possibilities she intended to keep to herself for the time being. 'What was she like?'

'Smart, classy, gave us no trouble.'

'How was she locked up?'

Chalky put down his coffee. 'What do you mean?'

'Question too hard for you? What were the circumstances of the arrest?'

'Anonymous tip-off.'

Kate was caught off balance. 'You knew where she'd be?'

A nod. 'And when she'd be there.'

'Interesting.'

What Kate found more riveting was the fact that Chalky, although unhappy that the charges had been reduced, had referred to an offender by her first name. Unheard of in police speak. She parked the thought for a moment.

'How did the arrest go down?' she asked.

'I don't think she had a bloody clue that the drugs were even there. I've seen enough dealers in my time to know one when I see one. She was an unwitting courier if you ask me, not a significant player—'

'She said that?'

'She didn't have to. It was written all over her face when we stopped and searched her vehicle—'

'The file said she was driving a Mercedes C-Class, a far cry from the wheels she has now. Was it confiscated at court?'

'No . . . it was a hire car.'

Kate's heart leapt. 'Hired in her name or someone else's?'

'Hers. Paid for with cash, a one-week rental.'

'Bugger! Processed though, yeah?'

Chalky nodded. 'Not that it took us anywhere. We found

her dabs and those of the staff at the hire company, that's all. None matched those on our database.'

Hannah's note was in Kate's head: *I'm not entirely innocent.* Time to play the Devil's advocate. 'A cash transaction, short-term car hire and a kilo of smack in her possession sounds like she was up to no good . . . and yet, you didn't think she was dodgy?'

'That's not how I saw it, no. She denied any knowledge of the gear.' Chalky held up a hand, fending off an interruption. 'I know they all say that, but she came quietly. What player do you know who doesn't start bawling for a lawyer the minute you lay hands on them? If Hannah had a role, it was a subordinate one—'

'In your opinion.'

'It's the only one I have. Besides, the anonymous tip-off bothered me.'

'If it smells like a set-up . . .'

'Exactly that. My supervision wasn't interested. He wanted her charged and processed.' He yawned. 'Sorry, Kate. I need to crash.'

'You and me both.' Or was there a reason he wanted to get out of there? 'OK, we're done. Get yourself home.'

Chalky stood. He made no move toward the door.

'Is there something else you'd like to tell me?' Kate asked.

A slight hesitation. Chalky bit his bottom lip, shifted his weight from one foot to the other, a sign of nervousness. Unusual for him. Kate had known him a long time. Nothing fazed him, except on this occasion it had. 'I gave Hannah the opportunity to tell me if she was being used, but she didn't come across.'

'Covering for someone?'

'Frightened of someone more like. When we stopped her on the street, her eyes were all over the place. She was terrified and only seemed to relax when she got to the nick. You'd think that she'd reached a place of safety, not a holding cell. Don't take my word for it. The custody sergeant even joked about it.'

Kate waited. He had more to say. She gave him a nudge. 'Get it off your chest, Chalky. It'll make you feel better.'

He wiped a hand over his face. 'Prosecution lawyers tend to get nervous when the arresting officer isn't convinced of guilt. I wasn't toeing the party line. The CPS didn't want me to give evidence.'

'Tell me you weren't screwing her.'

'No, but there's an outside chance you might come to that conclusion.'

'How so?'

He looked away, then at her. 'Kate, in all the time I've been doing this job, I've never given an offender my private number. For Hannah, I made an exception, so if you find it in her possessions, I want you to know that's all there was to it. It was a daft thing to do, but I figured she was in dire straits, in need of help . . .' He glanced down at the gruesome crime scene image on her desk, then at Kate. 'I guess I was right.'

# 14

The offices of Prentice, Lavelle & Walker were located in Milburn House on the corner of Dean Street and Side in the heart of Newcastle. Close to the city's castle keep and cathedral, the Grade II listed building commanded a fine position, a short walk from the Crown Court and the iconic Quayside. The interior was high-tech, a contemporary and prestigious address from which to do business. It was probably viewed by senior partners as on brand, a saying Kate detested almost as much as she did the dodgy firm who ran their operation from there, surrounded by legal firms whose reputations were well-respected. It was good cover for a brief whose raison d'être was to make as much money as possible defending people he knew or suspected to be guilty.

Right now, Walker was a lead, the only one Kate had.

En route to his office, she'd had a feeling that the meeting wouldn't go well and mentioned as much to Hank. Arriving with no appointment, the detectives were made to wait by a receptionist who informed them that the lawyer had someone with him and couldn't be disturbed. She picked up her mobile and sent a text. If she was warning her boss, Kate had lost the element of surprise.

When they finally got to see him, Walker was the objectionable "toad" Chalky had described, down to his sleazy suit, slicked-back hair and shifty expression they could just make out through his titanium eyewear. His office was large, the wall behind him displaying his credentials, expensive furniture, the best money could buy. He put the shutters up the minute they began asking questions about Hannah Swift. Kate took an instant dislike to him and had seen enough in her police service to recognise a person who had something to hide.

Walker asked for ID and was shown it, then made it clear that Kate had wasted valuable time, hers and his, turning up unannounced. He relaxed into his high-backed leather chair and spoke slowly and deliberately, a patronising tone. 'You should let your fingers do the walking, Detective Chief Inspector. We're so good at what we do, we even have an entry in the phone book.'

'Mr Walker, forgive me for saying so, but I find your attitude rather defensive. In fact, it's bordering on hostile. Ninety-nine per cent of the legal profession would be keen to help us with our enquiries. You, on the other hand, seem hell-bent on making our job more difficult. Is there more to your reluctance than meets the eye?'

The brief bridled at the implication but said nothing, a smirk spreading across his face. He was clearly enjoying himself.

'Your lack of cooperation is puzzling,' Kate continued. 'Detective Sergeant Gormley and I are here for background information on a woman we know you've represented in the past. It would help if we knew exactly how that came about, whether she was a cold caller, recommended by another client, or perhaps you were the duty solicitor on the night of her arrest—'

'Our junior staff cover that type of thing.'

'I stand corrected. Could you check to see if you'd acted for her before in a capacity other than criminal: house purchase, probate issue or such like?'

'You expect me to tell you?'

'I asked nicely.'

'Too bad. As you well know, my hands are tied by client confidentiality.'

'Then let me put your mind at rest. You'll get no complaints. Hannah Swift is dead.'

'I'm sorry to hear that.'

He acted cool. It wasn't working. His colour was rising as rapidly as the tide over the Holy Island causeway. Given his reputation as a big cheese, he looked far more worried than Kate had expected, and so it proved when he tried to fill the silence that had opened up between them.

He asked: 'Where, when and how did it happen?'

'You laid the ground rules, Mr Walker. Is this a one-way street or not?'

'Until I have official confirmation, by which I mean a signed death certificate, I'm unable rather than unwilling to help you. Now, if you don't mind . . .' He gestured toward the door. 'I have work to do.'

Kate stood her ground, considering where to go next. She'd been polite but it was time to take the gloves off. 'Your ethical code as a member of the Law Society is commendable, but let's not play games, Mr Walker. You have a reputation for defending scum and yet you won't answer a few simple questions on a first offender who got off with hardly more than a slap on the wrist when she appeared at court.' She shifted her gaze to her 2ic. 'I find that illuminating, don't you, Hank?'

Nodding, he eyeballed Walker and followed her lead, putting pressure on the solicitor. 'I'd be interested to know if you and Ms Swift have, or in her case had, a mutual contact you're trying to protect, sir. In the spirit of cooperation, perhaps you'd like to reconsider and give us his or her name.'

Walker switched his focus on Kate, glaring at her. 'Keep your bagman in check, Detective Chief Inspector. I object to his outlandish allegations, his tone – and yours too, for that matter. Now, this unscheduled meeting is over. I have nothing to add and I need to get on.' He gestured to a point over her shoulder. 'The door is that way. Close it on your way out.'

Wiping his face with his hands, Walker blew out a breath. Before the detectives were clear of the building, he told his secretary to hold all calls, then got up, closing the door Daniels had left open. He knew her by reputation only. She was trouble. Smart, successful, tough and uncompromising, on her way up. Of all the detectives in Northumbria Police, she was the one he was most frightened of, the one that he'd managed to avoid, until now.

Her involvement was not good news.

Scooping his mobile off his desk, Walker tapped a contact he didn't want to talk to, his stomach rolling over as the phone rang out at the other end. He'd been warned not to call but what else could he do?

This was an emergency.

As he'd anticipated, the call went straight to voicemail. Without leaving a message, he hung up, then redialled immediately, hoping that the man he was trying to contact would realise the urgency and answer.

His strategy worked.

The phone was lifted on the fourth ring. 'This had better be good.'

Walker didn't like being barked at. 'It's Walker—'

'I know who it is. What do you want? Don't tell me that one of mine is in the cells—'

'Not this time. We have a situation . . . potentially.'

'Well either we do or we don't, in which case why are you bothering me?'

Walker began pacing. The man on the other end was in a foul mood, his default position, a commanding voice guaranteed to strike fear into anyone he talked to. Theirs was a mutually beneficial arrangement but, from the moment they met, Walker had known that getting into bed with this particular individual was unwise. This client made 'dangerous' sound like a minor inconvenience. There was no telling what he'd do if Walker pulled the plug or suggested ending their long-standing arrangement.

He knew too much.

'Well, I'm sorry for disturbing you but I just had a visit from two of Northumbria's finest, DCI Daniels and DS Gormley.' He paused to allow that much to sink in before delivering news that he knew would send his 'client' over the edge. 'They were asking about my involvement with Hannah Swift.'

Kate's Audi Q5 was parked on double yellows. As she trudged through the snow towards it, she was angry with Walker's intransigence. It hadn't come as a shock, but she'd hoped for more, even from a lowlife like him. All she'd managed was to put his back up. Damned if she'd beg for information, she demonstrated her mood by slamming her car door, almost taking it off its hinges. Pulling her seat belt across her shoulder, she buckled up, turned on the ignition, indicating to pull out.

'He's nervous, isn't he?' Hank said.

'He should be . . .' Kate didn't look at him. 'I'm not finished with him.'

She checked her rear-view and side mirrors, waiting for a break in the traffic. Drivers were wary. They were crawling along, their tyres failing to maintain a grip on the steep bank, some drivers losing control, their vehicles fishtailing, seemingly in slow motion, narrowly missing the cars parked on either side of the road. Kate was grateful for her top of the range four-by-four – or would be if any of the buggers would let her out.

'Where's a blue light when you need one?' she said frustratedly.

'Don't be too hasty.' Hank placed his right hand gently on the steering wheel, preventing her from moving off.

A hint of pleasure in his voice made her look at him.

'Hold on.' He pulled out his mobile and began snapping away.

'What are you doing? We don't have time—'

He looked up at the building they had just vacated, cutting off her objection.

Kate dipped her head so she could follow his gaze through the windscreen. On the second floor, Walker was pacing up and down talking on the phone, a terrified expression on his face. Her mouth fell open. 'If he's tipping off an offender, I'll have the bastard struck off.'

The man in the flash office examined his manicure, waiting for Walker to stop rambling and get his shit together. He despised weakness in any form, and the brief had plenty. The only thing he had going for him was his expertise. He was a decent advocate, in civil and criminal cases, the best available outside of the M25. Skilled in make-believe, he was a man with the ability to turn a jury. He was also greedy and pliable, the way he liked them. Walker's desire for material wealth outweighed his morals, assuming he had any. The more cash he accumulated under their partnership, the harder he worked to keep it.

Money talked.

He couldn't argue with the cliché. It was his driver too. Always had been. Wealth had bought him every pleasure – and some. He was living the dream. Protecting his empire required a plan. Now he'd amassed a fortune, there were no lengths to which he wouldn't go to conceal his identity.

'What did you tell them?' he said.

'About you? Nothing. What do you take me for?'

Walker's tone displeased him. Who the hell did he think he was talking to? Others had tried the backchat. One of them was lying in the morgue. 'I'll ask again, what did you tell them?'

'Nothing, I swear.'

'That's the right answer.'

'I just thought you should know—'

'That's what your retainer is for and don't you forget it. Relax . . . I've not seen that bitch in almost five years and I have no intention of seeing her again.'

A relationship with her had been a mistake. A big one. In his world, unbiddable equalled disposable, until he realised that she was also indispensable. He was good at reacting to changing circumstances, an authority on improvisation. Using her as bait was a stroke of genius, as satisfying as smoking a good cigar.

'Walker, have I made myself clear?'

The brief didn't answer. Understandable. His alibi was bollocks. Walker's silence was proof that the message had reached its target. For now, he kept it civil.

That could change.

'If Daniels and her cohort revisit, leave me out of the conversation. My relationship with Hannah Swift didn't happen. Got it? You keep schtum and you have nothing to worry about. Mention my name and you will live to regret it. We both have a lot to lose. The only difference is, I have more. That puts you at a disadvantage, my friend. It would be wise to remember that.'

'You don't understand. Daniels and Gormley are murder detectives.'

'I know who they are.'

'Then you must know that Hannah Swift is dead.'

'So I gather . . .'

Walker was apoplectic.

As he continued to whine, the man tuned him out, glanced through the window at the driving snow. All morning there had been no let-up, for it or for him. The south lawn was covered, the carp lake frozen over. The boughs of the trees hung low, heavy with snow. Painted white, there appeared to be no horizon between land and sky.

Walker was still giving him earache. 'They're looking into her associates, past and present. It's only a matter of time before—'

'Before what? Keep your fucking mouth shut or there'll be consequences. Was my name mentioned?'

'No, but—'

'Then why are we talking?'

'I'd rather not be left in the dark if you . . .' Walker stopped talking mid-sentence, probably rephrasing what he was about to say, in case it came out wrong. 'What I mean is, do I need to stand by in case you require my services?'

'What I require from you is your silence. Do not fail me.'

The line went dead.

# 15

As Kate mounted the stairs, she told Hank to play along with whatever happened up there. His retort to 'be gentle' went over her head. He knew what was coming. She pushed through a set of double doors. The receptionist's hands froze in mid-air, two inches above her keyboard. She'd lost the sickly smile the detectives received the first time they entered. Kate barged straight past her into Walker's office, shutting out the echo of 'You can't go in there' as she closed the door behind her.

Placing both hands flat on Walker's desk, Kate leaned in, towering over him.

He protested in the strongest terms, ordering her off the premises. 'This is outrageous!'

'You took the words right out of my mouth.' Kate stood her ground, her tone level, eyes on the solicitor. 'If I were to ask who you were talking to on the phone just now, you'd tell me to shove off, right?'

'Absolutely.'

'That's what I thought.'

'Who in hell's name do you think you are? In case you hadn't noticed, there are letters on the door you just flung open. I'm a bona fide member of the legal profession and I will not stand for intimidation.' He was losing it, beads of sweat forming on his upper lip. 'You're not the only one with a job to do, Detective Chief Inspector. Who I was talking to is my business, so please leave and take your bagman with you.'

Kate glanced at Hank. 'What do you reckon? Phone records?'

A nod from Hank. 'Sounds like a plan.'

'Good luck . . .' Walker sneered at Kate. 'That would require a judge's signature. I don't fancy your chances of acquiring one.

If you intend to return to this office at any time, you'd better have a warrant.'

'Oh, we will . . .' Kate spat the words out. 'And we'll make damned sure it's for your arrest.'

They both knew she wouldn't get either. What she would get was an official complaint, an investigation by Professional Standards. A minor irritation. It wouldn't be the first time, nor the last. No copper could do their job without the occasional brush with a stroppy brief. Walker would have taken exception and kicked up a fuss, even if she'd given him the respect he thought he deserved. She made a mental note to give Bright the heads-up that trouble was brewing.

'We both know what went on here, Walker. You may make a living from defending the indefensible, but I'd be very careful if I were you.'

'Is that a threat?'

'From me? No, but I can't speak for the lowlife I suspect you're protecting. Hiding behind a cloak of respectability won't save you from him. I've seen his handiwork.'

'I have no idea what you're talking about.'

Kate gave Hank a nod.

He held up his phone, presenting Walker with the image he'd captured through the window.

The brief was unperturbed. 'I wasn't aware that using the telephone in one's private office had become a criminal offence, Sergeant Gormley.' He gestured towards a pile of well-thumbed legal journals on his desk. 'As you can see, I'm extremely busy. I spend much of my day on the phone. Some of those conversations are relaxed, others are agitated, not that it's any business of yours.'

'Nice try . . .' Kate's tone was serious. 'We'd like to see the file you have on Hannah Swift and we'd like to see it now, otherwise I intend to sit here until my 2ic finds a magistrate. A search warrant will do nicely. Your call, Mr Walker.'

The brief hesitated, in two minds, then thought better of

pissing her off any further. With a face like a smacked arse, he got up and left the room, leaving the door ajar. Kate watched him approach the woman she'd upset on her way in. Turning his back on the SIO, presumably so she couldn't lip-read, Walker spoke quietly, conspiratorially. The receptionist got up and rushed out, her heels clicking across the wooden floor as she disappeared from view, leaving him alone in reception.

Kate spied Walker's iPhone lying on his desk.

'Hank, check his mobile.'

He was out of his chair like a bullet from a gun. Kate kept one eye on him, one on the door to reception. Walker was getting impatient, about to retrace his steps. Quickly, she called the firm's number. He glanced at the phone. With no one to answer it, he lifted the receiver, buying her some time.

His voice arrived in Kate's ear. 'Prentice, Lavelle & Walker.'

She didn't speak.

'Hello? Terence Walker speaking. Can I help you?'

Using a thick Scouse accent, Kate said. 'Sorry, mate. Wrong number.'

She disconnected.

Walker slammed the phone down.

The receptionist reappeared, a manila folder in her hand.

Snatching it from her, Walker headed to his office, just as Hank replaced the iPhone and returned to his seat, slipping his own device into his pocket in the nick of time.

Walker rounded his desk and sat down. Flipping the file open, he stared at Kate over the top of his specs. 'I take it that the body being spoken about on the news this morning is my ex-client, Hannah Swift?'

'Would you mind?' Kate indicated the file. 'We're pushed for time.' She'd already got what she came for.

'I can't remember much about the case,' Walker said. 'From memory it was fairly straightforward. I'm sure you have all the details. We're a busy practice. We get thousands through the door annually.' He handed over the file. 'As far as the defendant was concerned, I can't say she stood out.'

Kate stared at him. For a brief who liked every T crossed and I dotted, the lie was unconvincing. Hannah Swift wasn't someone this piece of shit would ever forget. 'Why don't I believe that?'

'Believe what you like, it's true.'

The file was thin, just a couple of pages, nothing in it that Kate didn't have back at base. She looked up at Walker. 'Where's the rest? I asked for the whole file, not the watered-down version.'

'That's all I have. I'm afraid your time is up . . .' He stood, tripping over an excuse to get rid of them. 'I have a meeting I'm late for. See yourselves out.'

Kate was already walking away.

'By the way . . .' Walker called out after her. 'I'll be writing to your guv'nor forthwith.'

Kate paused at the door and spoke with her back to him. 'I'm quaking in my boots.'

'You should be.'

Slowly, she turned to face him, a wry smile developing. 'Given that this is the first time we've met, it's only fair to warn you that when I go after someone, I don't fail. You've been caught in a lie and I intend to prove it.' Due to Hank's keen observation, Kate had floated one in while the goalie was off his line. She was one up, but under no illusion. Walker would even the score just as soon as he was able.

'Nice going, Hank . . .' Kate climbed into the Audi for the second time, feeling much better than when she'd climbed out of it. Walker was a mouthpiece for the rich, however they had come by their money. On this occasion, whether his client had built his or her empire from legitimate means or from peddling misery to others, the brief had been unable to hide his anxiety and was now caught up in the ultimate crime. 'Not a word to anyone about his phone,' she warned. 'And I mean anyone, our lot included. The less people who know about your underhand methods the better.'

'Mine?'

'Don't panic.' Kate grinned. 'This is on me.'

'Sorry to disappoint you . . .'

'What do you mean?'

He grimaced. 'We have a number, no name. Walker may be a shit but in no way is he dim.' Pulling his phone, Hank brought up the image he'd taken of the solicitor's most recent outgoing call and turned the device to face her. The name tab at the top merely said: JC.

'Jesus Christ!'

'Probably not,' Hank quipped. 'And he won't help, unless you renewed your membership.'

Kate laughed, but was bitterly disappointed. 'Well, whoever he is, Walker won't want to become the meat in the sandwich between him and us. The least we should do is give it a whirl.'

'Why don't I trace the number first.'

Hank's anxiety was noticeable, so strong Kate could feel as well as see it.

He continued . . . 'This could go sideways, Kate. Remember Hannah's warning. If you go for him, he'll come for you—'

'When has that ever stopped us?'

'Do you really want to show your hand this early?'

'We have no choice.'

'Bollocks. At least take a moment to think it through.' He held up his mobile. 'As evidence goes, this is paper-thin. We saw him use the phone, that's all. We have no proof that JC has any connection to Hannah Swift whatsoever. On the other hand, if that were the case, you could be exposing yourself to danger.'

'We're detectives with a duty to follow up all leads,' Kate said. 'I concede that we have no hard evidence of a link, but

I'm following my gut on this one, Hank. A slim chance is still a chance.'

'It's a gamble—'

'Yeah, one I'm prepared to take . . . alone if necessary.'

'That's not happening.'

'Then make your mind up. One minute it's Hannah's note, then it's his, now it's hers. You need to decide which side of the fence you're on. By the way, if it turns out that the threat is heading in our direction, under no circumstances must Jo or the boys find out. We keep this between us. I don't want them worrying unnecessarily.'

'Shame you don't feel the same about me.'

'I do, Hank. Always.' She held his gaze for a moment. He'd planted a seed of doubt she could ill afford to let grow inside her. Even a short delay was undesirable if they were to get on top of the investigation into Hannah's death. The upper hand was theirs for the taking. 'Look, I appreciate your concern. It's good that you're nervous. It'll keep you alert should things go wrong.'

'You mean when we have to explain how we got his or her number?'

'Let me worry about that. Besides, who'd ask?'

'Professional Standards might.'

'And who will they believe: me or that utter scumbag Walker? He wasn't just rattled, he was bricking it. Did you see the sweat pouring out of him? Whoever he called is connected to Hannah somehow. I'm not sure how, but I am sure. It needs probing, for no other reason than to explore your half-arsed theory that I may be the target.' She smiled wickedly. 'This could be our first break. Who knows where it might lead? I might even get lucky and recognise the voice.'

'I still think we should check out the number first.'

'And let Walker tip off JC? No way. I'm not letting this fucker slip away from us. It could be the foundation stone on which we build our case. Besides, I want him to know we're onto him. Let's make him sweat.'

Before Hank could dissuade her, Kate hid her caller ID and dialled out, putting the phone on speaker, asking Hank to record the conversation so they could replay it later. The call was answered almost immediately.

'You're learning,' the male on the other end said, a malevolent tone. 'I told you when we began our association, never to contact me on your own phone. Make sure it doesn't happen again.'

Kate said nothing.

There was a tense moment, the man on the other end realising that it wasn't Walker on the line. The longer the silence, the more excited Kate became . . . until he knocked her for six.

'Well, well,' he said. 'If it isn't Kate Daniels.'

# 16

The smile slid off Kate's face. Either she'd come across JC before, or Walker had given him her name and he'd done his homework as soon as the phone went down on the first call he'd taken. She locked eyes with Hank. They both knew she'd not given the solicitor her first name. It didn't appear on her warrant card either.

Hank was urging her to hang up.

Kate stayed on the line. She didn't recognise the voice. The man on the other end sounded like he had a big ego. Unlike Walker, he wasn't easily rattled. Quite the opposite. There had been amusement in his tone, as if he was toying with her, letting her know that he was smart and untouchable.

He wasn't.

Kate held her bottle. If she had any doubt whatsoever that Walker had warned an offender, it had vanished now. That small victory was all she'd hoped for and more. 'Wherever you're hiding, JC, I will find you.'

'Game on,' he said.

He disconnected.

Hank said nothing.

Kate started the car and moved off.

The A1 north was clear. The gritters had done their job, but when two Traffic cars passed at high speed, blue lights and sirens engaged, Kate knew instinctively that she wouldn't get far. As she watched them disappear, the vehicles she was following slowed and the Audi's high-tech in-car system warned of diversions ahead. Decelerating, Kate swore under her breath. The absence of southbound traffic was an indication of a major RTA, a theory confirmed seconds later when the air ambulance appeared, hovering in the distance as it weighed up the situation.

Someone had asked for an emergency airlift.

She glanced at Hank. 'If they close the road, we might have to abandon our plan to interview Simon Shepherd.'

He gave a nod but remained silent.

'Stop festering over that phone call—'

'I'm not—'

'Aren't you?'

'No.' He looked away, not quick enough to hide the deceit.

'Hank, you and I have one similarity to the man or woman we're hunting. We both play to win. JC could be a middleman, the guy who does the grunt work. I don't think so somehow but, if the arrogant shit thinks he's untouchable, he can think again.'

'Any thoughts on who he might be?'

'None. I've been thinking about it non-stop. I don't recall anyone we've put away with those initials.'

'Me neither.' Hank fell silent.

Had it not been for the fact that their investigation was beginning to bite, the situation might have been depressing, but Kate was on a mission and had no intention of slowing down, unlike the long line of vehicles she was trailing. As she crawled along for another fifteen minutes, unable to turn around or get off the carriageway and choose another route, more blue lights were visible in the distance.

As traffic ground to a halt, she stopped the car and got out, telling him that there were four police vehicles, a fire and rescue appliance, one ambulance and personnel in high-viz jackets in attendance. A Traffic cop Kate knew well was walking the line instructing drivers to turn around.

Maybe all was not lost.

As cars and lorries peeled off, one by one, frustrated by the detour, she inched forward, hoping Inspector Andrea McGovern would let her through. Kate wound down her window as she arrived, drawing a circle with her finger to the driver of the car behind, a gesture he didn't like. She ignored him in favour of the two detectives.

'Kate, we're dealing with a fatal.'

'I figured. Any chance I can squeeze through?'

'Yeah, no bother.'

Using her radio, Andrea alerted colleagues that the DCI was on her way. An angry expletive was hurled at her from the driver behind. He'd overheard and was making his mouth go, complaining that he too was on urgent business. Ending her transmission, Andrea walked towards him.

Kate waited, checking her wing mirror to ensure the dickhead wasn't going to give her grief. She needn't have worried – Andrea was a pro.

'Turn around, sir. The road is closed.'

'Then why's *she* getting through?'

'None of your business. Have a nice day.'

Swearing loudly, he did a three-point turn, drove onto the verge, then floored the accelerator, deliberately spraying her with a fine powder of snow as he took off in the opposite direction. Walking to Kate's Audi, Andrea wiped snowflakes from her face, a wry smile developing. 'There's always one,' she said.

'Tosser,' Hank said. 'You want his number?'

'No, I got it. My oppo's stationed at the next junction south. That guy's delay just got a whole lot longer.'

'Nice one,' Kate said. 'Anything we can do to help?'

'Thanks, but I've got a full crew now.' Andrea glanced briefly over her shoulder at the tailback. 'I'd better go. Drive carefully.'

'Will do. And thanks for letting us through. I'll grab a takeaway coffee in case you're still here on the return journey,' Kate said. 'You look like you need it.'

'Great. You need an escort?'

'We'll holler if we do.'

# 17

Kate drove slowly past the RTA site. It was a mess, an upturned vehicle in the ditch at the side of the road, two others in bits, a lorry facing the wrong way, debris strewn across the carriageway. There were shocked casualties, five in total, up on the embankment, out of harm's way, each wearing a silver heat sheet, providing immediate warmth to those less injured.

Hank was still brooding.

Using the hands-free, Kate called the incident room. Carmichael picked up on the first ring, stating her name and rank. 'Lisa, I want you to do something for me.'

'Sure, what is it?'

'I want you to research all my cases for an offender with the initials JC, male or female. I'll explain later. Hank and I are on our way to see Simon Shepherd. Any news from the PolSA team?'

'If you're praying for more notes, you're out of luck, guv.'

Kate sighed. 'Do you have *anything* for me?'

'Most of the team are out conducting interviews. No sightings of Hannah or her car yet. Maxwell drew a blank with the local registrar but found her birth registered in East London. Father is named as Peter Swift. Mother, Marianne Briand.'

'French?'

'Yeah,' Carmichael said. 'She died four years ago. Neil did a further search and found her death certificate.'

'What about the father?'

'Still breathing. Lives on the Isle of Dogs.'

'Nice.'

'Shall I get onto the Met and have someone go over there?'

Kate had recent links in London but none who'd give her the time of day. She'd upset too many detectives down there.

An idea popped into her head. 'No, leave it with me. I want someone decent. I know just the man to find me an officer who fits the bill.' She paused. 'Did Maxwell find anything on Aaron?'

'He's still checking.'

'OK, is that it?'

'Yeah, actually no, boss. Forensics aren't finished examining the contents of the caravan yet, but they gave us the heads-up that Hannah's note was definitely written on a sheet of paper from the writing pad recovered at the scene. It's the only page missing and there are no indentations on the rest of it. Only one shop in Newcastle stocks it and they don't have her name on their database.'

'Doesn't mean she didn't buy it there,' Hank said.

'I thought that too, Hank. I asked the manager to check his records. No cash sales for that item in the past two years. The pen Hannah used to write the note only has her prints on it, ditto the Elmo rollerball, and there was nothing else concealed in her coat. Her missing shoe was in the van, as are the buttons from her shirt, so the killer didn't take them.'

Kate was impressed with the speed at which the information was filtering through and said as much to Lisa. 'What about the enquiries you were making on Shepherd?'

'His firearms certificate is current. He also has a permanent Yell.com entry advertising his campsite. I've just received his landline history from BT. I'm checking that now. Is there anything else you'd like from me?'

'As it happens, yes. Hank will send you a mobile number. Check it against Shepherd's phone record for me.'

'Whose number?'

Hank shot Kate a warning: For now, the less people who knew about JC the better.

It had occurred to her that Walker could himself be the killer. There was nothing in Hannah's letter that ruled him out. Paradoxically, there was more to rule him in. He was forensically aware and meticulous. And when he said 'You should let your fingers do the walking' it was a red flag, given that Shepherd's advert appeared in Yell. Was the solicitor taunting her? Maybe JC was a heavy, the man who'd step in to help if Walker required someone to do the grunt work.

All options were still on the table.

'Doesn't matter,' Kate said into the phone. 'It's a long shot . . . To be honest, I'm not hopeful it'll be on there. I'm covering myself, just in case.'

'Understood.'

'Hank sent the text,' Kate said. 'Did you get that, Lisa?'

'Yeah, that's received.'

'When you're done with Shepherd's call history, I want you to prioritise Hannah's social media accounts. Jo thinks she may have tried to communicate with us that way.'

'Will do.'

Kate disconnected, then redialled.

The call was answered immediately. 'Stone.'

'David, it's Kate . . . Daniels. I heard you were kicking your heels with little to do.'

'Yeah, unlike you. How's it going?'

'Slowly. I need a favour.' She explained what she wanted.

He agreed to help and rang off.

Detective Chief Inspector David Stone was another SIO stationed at Northern Area Command HQ. Though born and bred in the north, he'd done most of his policing in the Met before transferring to his home force. Kate had not seen that much of him, but his reputation was growing. Bright rated him, which was a big tick in her book. It took a lot to impress him.

Hank glared at Kate.

'What?' she said.

'I could've given Hannah's old man the death message.'

'So could I, but it must be done in person. I need you here. Swift requires a face-to-face with someone we can trust, someone with the sensitivity and experience to get the job done.

You heard Stone. He has someone in mind, a DS who'll put Swift on a plane north, assuming flights are available and able to land. Book him into a good hotel for a couple of nights and forward the reservation to me. I intend to meet him at the airport this end. Once he identifies Hannah's body, hopefully he'll have a lot to tell us about her. That's where you come in, so stop sulking.'

# 18

Despite the picture-perfect view through the windscreen, JC continued to occupy Kate's mind as she drove. On the phone, he'd sounded middle-aged. British. No discernible accent. Certainly no hint of the north. Jack Shepherd had described Hannah's speech as cosmopolitan. Kate wondered how and when she'd arrived in the region and if JC was still here.

By now, he could be anywhere.

It was a dispiriting thought she didn't dwell on. It would sap her strength, nullifying the progress she'd made. She had to hope that he was still around. He didn't strike her as a man who'd run. She'd detected no nervousness in him. In fact, if anything, the opposite was true. In spite of this, Kate had no doubt that she was on the right track.

A picture formed in her mind, an expensive suit, smart eyes, a Bright lookalike perhaps, a man on a mission with a lot to lose. Normally, a guy like that would delegate his dirty work in order to keep his own hands clean. On this occasion, she didn't think he had. Where was the fun in that? Kate had interviewed many men and women who enjoyed inflicting pain. They possessed that same threatening tone of voice, both fearless and ruthless.

A dangerous combination.

Kate had no hard evidence that Walker had tipped him off. She was convinced that he had, though why he'd gamble with his status and livelihood was mystifying. His motivation could only have been greed. What else was there? The lawyer had the clout to make waves for her involving Professional Standards. Would he risk it, knowing she'd be standing right behind him wielding a metaphorical chainsaw?

A charge of aiding and abetting an offender for a man in his position was curtains. He stood to lose everything, his home, his reputation – such as it was – and his family. He'd end up in jail.

Before leaving the office, Kate had googled a few of the big cases he'd been involved in, some in the north, others in the capital. There was more than one image of him on the steps of Newcastle Crown Court giving a victory speech to the media, a guilty client grinning at his side.

It made her sick.

There were a variety of reasons a so-called watertight case could fall at the last hurdle. After weeks, sometimes months of painstaking intelligence-gathering and hour upon mind-numbing hour interviewing suspects, she'd seen violent offenders walk free. It was gut-wrenching to observe a clever defence team destroy the credibility of eyewitnesses simply because they were elderly, or they normally wore glasses but didn't have them on that day, or because they themselves had previous convictions, a history of drug or alcohol abuse, or had been caught out in a lie in the past.

Then there were the police officers unable to articulate their part in an arrest of a murder suspect, who somehow managed to sound unsure even when the case against a defendant was rock solid. They all had to start somewhere but defence counsel could smell inexperience like a dog could sniff a rabbit. Planting the seed of doubt in the minds of a jury that these people, civilian or police, were unreliable was all it took to sway a decision against the prosecution, even in the face of hard evidence.

Give Walker his due, he knew how to pick the right barrister for his clients, but if it was revealed that he'd aided the offender who'd taken Hannah's life, he'd have a hard job finding a decent one to represent him if he ended up in court himself. He'd lose too. No judge would condone such behaviour from a legal professional.

Walker was screwed if he so much as opened his mouth.

Notwithstanding the many serious criminals he'd helped navigate the criminal justice system and avoid prison, he'd never cope if he was sent down himself. He'd have to drop his self-importance to survive. He might have the funds to pay for protection, but he'd always be looking over his shoulder, at risk of attack. Within weeks, he'd be begging for Rule 43: solitary confinement in a VPU, forced to eat, sleep and shit in a tiny cell for twenty-three hours a day. A grim prospect. His mental health would suffer. Sooner or later, he'd become depressed, unable to cope with the isolation. Before long he'd contemplate suicide. Tough. He'd been given every opportunity to cooperate and refused.

She had no doubt that he'd live to regret that decision . . .

Whatever JC was paying him, it wasn't enough.

For a brief moment, she considered deploying a surveillance team to watch and follow Walker. The thought vanished as quickly as it came into her head. Mounting such an operation was unlikely to reap rewards. Now she'd put the frighteners on, he wouldn't come within a country mile of JC, who Kate knew was using burners to avoid detection. That was how powerful men and women operated. No names. No contact. No paper trail.

She'd be wasting her time, tying up precious resources, physical and financial.

Hank was uncharacteristically quiet. She was about to ask him a question when she realised that he hadn't said a word for ages. A glance to her left confirmed that he was sending the zeds up, his chest rising and falling, head lolling to one side, lips parted slightly.

He was dead to the world.

She let him sleep. It had been a stressful week, especially the last day and a half. The coming days would be worse. Kate pressed on, keen to reach her destination, convinced that the only way she'd find JC was to find Hannah, figuratively speaking. The real Hannah. Not the victim she'd become. Something – or someone – had kept her in the north-east.

Kate was sure that someone was Aaron.

An alternative theory arrived in her head. Hannah may have stayed because it would give the impression that Aaron was here, when in reality he was elsewhere.

Simon Shepherd was a property developer. He lived on a fine estate, deep in the Ingram Valley, with the Cheviot Hills as a backdrop, way off the beaten track. It was jaw-droppingly beautiful, with far-reaching views, extensive lawns and a stable block. The Audi's tyres crunched on frozen snow as it glided to a halt at the front door, parking behind a high-end Range Rover with a personalised number plate. There were no tracks in the snow, to or from the front gate, proof that the vehicle hadn't moved for some time.

Kate waited a beat, enjoying the peace, then nudged Hank gently with her elbow.

He stirred, disoriented.

'Sorry to wake you.'

Blinded by the glare of sun on snow, he blinked, apologised for nodding off, aware that she needed a kip a lot more than he did. He looked up at the house, his mouth dropping open. 'Jesus! I wasn't expecting this, were you?'

'The clue was in the address,' she said. 'Anything with "Hall" after it is hardly going to be a hovel, though even "Hall" doesn't do it justice. It's like a scaled-down version of the Queen's House, Greenwich. Jo and I went there once. Tell you what, I wouldn't want to pay the mortgage.' She threw him a crooked smile. 'Are you good to go?'

He gave a nod.

They got out of the car.

The snow was deep here, the house sitting perfectly in its surroundings, an impressive Palladian façade, a columned portico across the centre of the building, flanked by symmetrical wings on either side.

Kate rang the bell.

The man who answered was dressed in outdoor gear, a full-length Crombie coat, woollen scarf and black leather gloves, a car key in his right hand.

'Simon Shepherd?'

'Yes.' He glanced over her shoulder, checking the driveway. 'I'm just on my way out.'

Kate held up ID. 'I'm Detective Chief Inspector Daniels. This is my colleague, Detective Sergeant Gormley. May we come in?'

'Yes, of course.' He stepped back, shaking both of their hands when they got inside. 'Actually, I was expecting you.'

# 19

Thrown by the comment, Kate's guard was up. The man standing in the doorway was like his father, only taller, leaner and a damned sight better off by the looks of it. On the back foot, she could find only find one explanation for the fact that he was anticipating a visit from the police. It prompted her to ask if his old man had been in touch.

Shepherd shook his head. 'If only that were the case. No, I caught an outside broadcast on the midday news about that unfortunate woman who was found dead last night. I recognised the location in the background. As you can imagine, it came as quite a shock. The presenter said the site had been sealed off. I've been trying my father's number ever since. I can't believe the old bastard didn't tell me. I understand even less why he's not picking up.'

Kate owned up. 'That might be my fault, sir. I specifically asked him not to speak to you until I'd had the chance.'

Shepherd was puzzled. 'Why would you do that?'

'That's what I've come to talk to you about.' She eyed the keys in his hand. 'Are you in a hurry to get somewhere?'

'I was about to drive over there to find out what's going on.'

'I'm afraid that won't be possible until the scene is fully processed. I can't see that happening today or even tomorrow. There'll be a lot of activity up there this week, a full search team, forensic personnel. I can get a message to your parents and ask them to call you, if you'd like?'

'That would be helpful.'

He swept a hand to one side, inviting the detectives to move through the hallway and on into a wonderful drawing room, professionally designed and with original features, beautifully preserved. It seemed too tidy for a man who'd recently become a parent. The very least Kate had expected was baby paraphernalia. Then again, in a house this big, there would undoubtedly be a nursery and probably a live-in nanny to go with it.

The house was very still.

There were fresh flowers and photographs – none of them featuring his parents, Kate noticed – but no cards on display to celebrate the arrival of a newborn. She decided to tread carefully in case there had been a complication. Shepherd took off his coat and scarf, threw it over a chair and pocketed his keys. With his back turned, Hank flicked his head toward the adjoining study door, which stood ajar.

Kate acted on his cue. 'Do you work from home, sir?'

Shepherd turned to face her. 'Most of the time. I have an office in the city but, technically, I'm on paternity leave.'

Kate relaxed. 'Is your wife at home?'

'She's been in hospital for a couple of weeks. Our child Abigail arrived six weeks early. She's in the neo-natal intensive care unit in Cramlington. Christina, my wife, refuses to leave. Fortunately, they have the facilities to cope with such a drama—' He stopped talking abruptly.

Kate could've sworn that he was about to add the word: queen.

Shepherd held her gaze. 'Excuse my bad manners. Can I offer you refreshments: tea, coffee, a soft drink?'

'That's kind of you but we're on the clock,' Hank said.

Kate agreed – she was keen to question Shepherd and go.

They all sat down.

Shepherd confirmed that he'd entertained his parents last evening. They had arrived at around four and left after dinner, not long after eight. At night, with clear roads and average traffic, it would take them around fifty, fifty-five minutes to drive from there to Craster, conveniently alibiing them for the time of Hannah Swift's death. When asked if he was aware that his parents had rented out one of the vans off-season to a woman they knew only as Helen, Simon Shepherd claimed he'd no idea.

'So you'd not met her?' Kate asked.

'No, I'm rarely there. My parents prefer to come here.'

'I can see why.' The job required Kate to stroke egos now and then. 'When was the last time you were there?'

'A month ago. And, before you ask, I saw no one, other than my parents.' He seemed overly anxious to tell them that. 'You can't suspect that they had anything to do with that woman's death?'

*That woman?*

Kate bristled.

Referring to Hannah Swift that way was an insult to the person she once was, reducing her to someone of little consequence, a minor irritation that had ruined an otherwise busy day, paying no regard to the family and friends she'd left behind. Kate would have forgiven him if he'd added the words poor or unfortunate to his description, but he was too busy listening to the sound of his own patronising voice.

'No offence,' he said, 'But that is a ridiculous notion. Did you ever see the seventies TV show, *The Good Life*? That's them to a T. I grew up there, I should know. My father was literally a pig in shit, until he keeled over one day and was airlifted to hospital. After that, he couldn't manage the livestock, let alone the heavy lifting or land management.'

'So he diversified.'

'Don't ask me why. He's way past retirement age, not to mention waiting for a heart bypass. You'd think my mother was trying to kill him off. The caravans were her idea. She once lived in a kibbutz – the old-fashioned type, not the modern equivalent. She believes in community and living off the land.'

'Sounds perfect to me,' Kate said.

'I can think of nothing worse. My father and I argued over their decision to invite the great unwashed onto their land. What happened last night was entirely predictable. I warned them. Would they listen?' The question was rhetorical. 'That land will be mine one day. I offered to buy my inheritance

from them. It would have afforded them a comfortable retirement, but they refused point-blank. Apparently, they want to
end their days there.'

'Understandable,' Hank said.

'It's nonsense. They can't cope. Last night proves it.'

With every word he uttered, Kate had to work harder to
suppress her contempt. She disliked him even more than
Walker – and that was going some. 'What do you propose to
do with the land?'

'I'd have thought that was obvious. It's a rare development
opportunity. Plans for a hotel with direct access to the beach
have already been drawn up. It would be worth millions to the
right investor. The caravan park is hardly adding to its charm.
The only upside is that it's been mixed use for seven years, lived
on and used for temporary accommodation. Coastal tourism is
on the up. If I get it through planning, I could clean up. I'm
talking millions, not the few measly quid my parents make
from it. If they're struggling, they brought it on themselves.'

Kate felt sorry for Jack Shepherd. He seemed like a proud,
independent man, not the type to ask for help or admit that he
was in financial straits, even to his son, a man who was obviously loaded and impatient for him to pop his clogs so that he
could benefit financially. The thought made her sad. There was
little to be said for getting old. She changed the subject, leading
her witness in another direction. His father's health might be
failing, but Shepherd Junior was fit and healthy.

'Can you recall when you were last up at the farm?'

'Yes. I'd been to Durham and called in on the way home.
I'll check my calendar.' Taking his mobile from his pocket, he
checked the screen, then looked up. 'It was the twenty-fourth
of last month. I'd gone down the night before for an early meeting the next day. It ended at eleven, eleven fifteen. I arrived at
their place at around twelve thirty and left around one. I was
worried about leaving Christina. Nothing about her pregnancy
has been straightforward.'

Another perfect alibi, exactly when Hannah Swift was, according to his parents, always out. From the look on his face, Hank thought so too. Again, Kate changed tack. 'Your father said he took Helen in because he thought she was in trouble. I gather your sister had been in similar circumstances as a young woman. Can you elaborate on that?'

Shepherd glared at her. 'What in God's name for?'

Kate chose her words carefully. 'We have to eliminate anyone who has a connection with the crime scene—'

'Do you?'

Kate couldn't read his expression.

'Inspector, I understand you have a job to do, but if you think Zoe is in any way involved, you're not only misguided, you're out of your bloody mind.' He was angry now, his eyes cold and unfriendly, like someone had flicked a switch. 'Why my father would even mention it to you is beyond me. If he'd looked after her better, she might not have run away.'

'You and Zoe are close?' Kate asked.

'Very,' he barked. 'Wait here.'

Shepherd got up, moving towards his study, pulling the door to behind him. Kate and Hank exchanged a look: what was that about? Kate dropped her head on one side, listening. It sounded like Shepherd was opening and closing drawers or cupboard doors. Whatever was going on in there it raised the hairs on the nape of her neck.

She needed eyes on him.

Hank was wary too.

She knew why.

A few short months ago, having allowed a suspect to leave a room alone, an inexperienced colleague had been badly injured when the offender returned with a gun and opened fire. It was a rookie mistake Kate was now repeating. She'd never have done that, had Shepherd not charged out of there so quickly, had *she* not been so distracted by the contents of Hannah's note.

Panic took her breath away.

An image shot into her head, transporting her to Jack and Peggy Shepherd's cottage, a firearm propped up in an unfamiliar hallway, a coiled leather belt, two loops where cartridges were missing. Their son was a landowner too, brought up on a smallholding. He'd be able to handle a gun.

Kate stood up, flicking her head towards the study door, pointing at her right eye with her forefinger. Receiving her unspoken message, Hank was on the move, positioning himself to one side of the door frame, back flat against the wall, body turned side on to protect vital organs, ready to take action if need be.

The door was yanked open.

They needn't have worried.

The only thing Shepherd was carrying when he returned to the room was a gilt-framed photograph and a separate snapshot that appeared old and curled at the edges. An explanation spilled from his mouth as he walked in. 'If you're looking to blame someone for a suspicious death, you should know that Zoe is a very different person now.'

'I don't look for scapegoats, sir.' Kate said. 'I prefer the truth.'

He came to an abrupt halt, his eyes on Hank's empty chair. 'Has Sergeant Gormley left us?'

'No, I'm still here,' Hank said casually. 'I was just admiring your artwork. What an amazing collection.'

Nicely done, Kate thought, the tension draining away. Hank had taken a bullet in the line of duty and she felt guilty for allowing a situation to develop that might have put him in the firing line once again.

Unaware of the narrative running through her head, Shepherd focused his attention on Kate. 'This is Zoe twenty-five years ago.' He handed her the curled-up photograph, waiting while she examined the image. The subject was young and blond, a carefree look in her eye. A big smile lit up her face. She had what looked like a spliff in one hand, a bottle of vodka in the other. No glass. The handsome, bare-chested male sitting next to her was wasted, his head lolled to one side, eyes almost closed.

Kate looked up.

'I can see you're confused by the relevance,' Shepherd turned the framed photograph to face her, a contemptuous expression. 'This is Zoe now. Does this override your contempt for my family, Detective Chief Inspector?'

# 20

Simon Shepherd was the right profile for JC. He was smart, or thought he was, an arrogant man who'd forgotten his roots and who'd shown little or no real interest in, or respect for, his parents – or his wife for that matter. The only person he seemed remotely concerned about was his sister Zoe. Once an able-bodied young woman, she was now a middle-aged paraplegic incapable of inflicting pain on anyone. According to her brother, she'd received life-threatening injuries in her early twenties when a mate who was stoned lost control of his vehicle on a blind bend, sending her hurtling through the windscreen into a drystone wall.

Shepherd's voice arrived in Kate's head. 'The resulting brain injury left her with complete paralysis. She's able to communicate only through a portable speech-generating device with eye-tracker capability.' He glared at her. 'I'd say an apology is in order, wouldn't you?'

Kate had stared at the image for a long while, making him wait, passing it to Hank as he arrived by her side. No explanation was required. The evidence was there in black and white. Eventually, she thanked Shepherd for his cooperation. He didn't deserve an apology.

Hank's voice broke through her thoughts.

'I like the way you planted doubt in Shepherd's mind that we might call again.'

'He can count on it. He wasn't very pleasant, was he? And he has a switch . . . That always bothers me.' Kate had thrown it out there, pausing to let the implication sink in, confirming that she'd be in touch with Shepherd if she needed to speak with him again. He didn't care for her attitude and it showed. 'The media reported the death as "suspicious", no mention of cause, yet he didn't even ask how Hannah had died. It's normally the first question we get at the start of an investigation.'

'Yeah, I thought that was odd.'

Kate gave him the side-eye. 'Maybe he already knew.'

'I was thinking the same. What did you think of his admission that he'd visited his parents' smallholding?'

'I don't know. Maybe that's all there was to it.'

'Or it was an attempt to cover his back. Maybe he asked them over for dinner to get them out of the house as a favour to a friend.'

'Seems unlikely . . . Then again, we're looking for co-conspirators, not one man working alone.' Kate sighed. 'We can't prove any of it. And he's not JC. If he had been, I'd have known as soon as he'd opened his mouth. I'm no voice recognition expert but he had a definite Northern twang, despite his best efforts to conceal it. He pretends that he's a cut above, with the provenance that a home like his suggests, but I wasn't fooled. He's new money, not old, Hank.'

On the return journey, Kate checked her satnav, relieved to find that the southbound carriageway of the A1 was now open. Before she joined it, she pulled into a garage to grab three take-away coffees – one for her, one for Hank and one for Inspector Andrea McGovern – who was still dealing with fallout from the RTA. Road and air ambulances were gone, most of the debris cleared away. Under arc lights, accident investigators were taking measurements on the road and images to back them up.

Keen to get to base, Kate handed Andrea her coffee and pushed on.

Arriving at Middle Earth three quarters of an hour later, an unsettling thought lingered in her mind as she made her way into the building, setting off in the direction of the MIR with Hank hot on her heels.

Using his ID to gain access, he opened the door and stood

back to allow her through, catching her eye, asking what was on her mind, a friendly show of concern she'd come to expect from him over the years.

'You hardly said a word in the car. You OK?'

'Sorry . . .' She turned to face him just inside the doorway of a room buzzing with energy, ignoring the team around them. 'I was miles away, mulling over our interview with Simon Shepherd.'

Hank took off his coat and slung it over his shoulder. 'What about it?'

Kate slipped her own coat and scarf off, draping them over her arm. 'He made no secret of the fact that he wants his parents off their land in order to make money. Despite his airs and graces, he's no different to Walker—'

'Except that dickhead is out of his depth and Shepherd clearly isn't.'

'Yes, but what I'm getting at is, both men are driven by an overwhelming desire for wealth. This is pure speculation, but we've been working on the assumption that JC is the boss, that he or someone working for him killed Hannah, ransacking her caravan in order to find something she had that they wanted. Either way, they don't go alone. Why not? Involving an accomplice brings enormous risks.'

'The killer needed a lookout—'

'Not if they knew the Shepherds would be out.'

Her comment floated in the air between them.

Hank said nothing but Kate could see the wheels turning in his head.

'Removing Hannah's car wasn't an afterthought, it was a move they'd anticipated. They had to be sure to remove anything and everything that might be incriminating: bag, laptop, mobile phone. I doubt we'll ever find them. We don't know whether they got what they were after, only that it was important enough and damaging enough to gamble on an accessory to murder. Hannah probably knew too much about

JC's operation, or whoever he's working for. Taking her out stopped her from sharing it.'

'Whoa, back up. You've lost me.'

'Greed is the link to whoever is in charge, Hank.'

'You think JC might be working for Shepherd?'

'I don't know, but his phraseology bothers me. He described what happened at the campsite as "entirely predictable". At the time, I thought he was talking about his parents bringing trouble to their door with their tourism enterprise, but it was vague and could be taken two ways. What if he was saying one thing but meaning something else? What if, indirectly, he was referring to Hannah's death being a foregone conclusion?'

# 21

They decamped to Kate's office and closed the door. Sandwiches, two bags of salt and vinegar crisps and KitKats were on her desk, a yellow Post-it note from Carmichael in her usual flamboyant scrawl: Enjoy! Having missed lunch, they appreciated the gesture – they were ravenous. Kate made coffee and sat down with Hank to eat. It was clear that Hannah posed a risk to JC – or his employer if it turned out that he was the go-between, not top dog.

Kate picked up her internal phone and made a call. 'Jo, Hank and I are in the building, my office. Have you got a moment?'

'Sure. I'll be there in five.'

Kate hung up.

Draining his coffee, Hank leaned into his chair. 'I think we should raise an action to look into Zoe's RTA.'

'Why?'

'Because we can. Because—'

Her mobile rang, cutting off the conversation.

Kate swiped it off her desk, lifting it to her ear. 'Daniels.'

'Kate, it's Stone.'

'All sorted?' She put the phone on speaker so that Hank could listen in.

'Yeah. An ex-colleague now has the lowdown on your investigation into Hannah's death. DS Kyra Thakur is experienced in dealing with the families of murder victims. She's completely trustworthy, someone I can vouch for. Rest assured, Peter Swift is in excellent hands. I passed on your number and have hers in case you need it. Got a pen handy?'

'Yeah, shoot.' Kate grabbed one and pulled a memo pad towards her.

Stone reeled off the number and she wrote it down.

'As soon as the job is complete, Kyra will let you know,' he said. 'Assuming Swift is willing, she'll book him a flight, make sure he gets on it and text you his ETA. I imagine it'll be to-morrow morning.'

'Good. I'll alert the morgue and update them on timescale later. Appreciate it, David.'

'Need anything else from me?'

'No, we're good now, thanks.'

'Good luck.' Stone disconnected.

Kate bit into her sandwich, eyes fixed on her 2ic. 'Sorry, Hank. You were saying?'

'I'll be honest with you. I don't like Simon Shepherd. I get the impression he's hiding something. We only have his word for how his sister's accident went down. I wouldn't be sur-prised if he was responsible, not one of her mates as he led us to believe.'

'Would he be stupid enough to be caught out in a provable lie?'

'He's arrogant enough to expect that we'd take him at face value.'

'Agreed, but what made you think of revisiting Zoe's RTA?'

'If he was lying then, he could be lying now. A guilty con-science would explain his concern for a sibling whose images he hides away in his office and why he flipped when you asked him about her. There were no photographs displayed in his fancy drawing room.'

'Well observed. Ask one of the team to look into it.' She thanked him for his vigilance. It was a good spot – one she hadn't picked up on.

He shrugged. 'Mopping up is what I'm here for.'

There was a second interruption, this time a knock at the door.

It opened and Jo stuck her head in. She'd put feelers out to domestic violence organisations in order to find out if Hannah had ever sought refuge in the region. 'They're on it and will be in touch,' she said.

'You want coffee?' Hank asked.

'No thanks. What's going on?'

'You'll get the full rundown at the briefing,' Kate said. 'But first I want to run something by you before I share it with the team.'

Jo took a seat.

Kate took a moment to gather her thoughts. 'When we spoke earlier we were in agreement that Hannah was somehow familiar with the police. A scenario popped into my head then, which grew when I later spoke to Chalky about her arrest on a drugs charge, the circumstances of which concern me.'

'Which were?' Jo had not been party to the discussion and they hadn't spoken since.

'The anonymous tip-off which Chalky's shift received and acted upon. As the officer in charge, he was convinced she'd been set up, that she had no clue that drugs were concealed in her vehicle. An "unwitting courier" he called her.' Kate paused, unsure of whether or not to divulge the next bit, then decided she would. She trusted Hank and Jo implicitly. 'There could be a potential problem,' she warned. 'Chalky gave Hannah his number because he perceived a situation where she might be in danger.'

'Well, he was right about that,' Jo said.

'Still, he should know better,' Hank said.

Jo shot him down. 'I've never met the man but, as far as I'm concerned, he did the right thing.'

'I couldn't agree more,' Kate said. 'Don't worry, I'm not about to throw him under a bus when he was trying to help, but that may not be the end of it. His actions, however altruistic, could land him in hot water if his name comes up in the enquiry.'

'And if it does?'

'I can't see how it can, unless we find a diary, laptop or mobile. Should that change, then he's on record as reporting his indiscretion to me and will face questioning, like any other person of interest. This conversation didn't happen, understood?'

Jo and Hank were nodding – a meeting of minds.

'Now, when we three met this morning, we agree that Hannah was murdered because she was in possession of information that could do someone harm, something her killer was desperate to retrieve. I need to chase this up through official channels but my theory is that she may have been registered as a police informant.'

# 22

Hank linked his hands behind his head, staring across at Kate. She never missed the opportunity to pump a theory if she had one. There had to be a reason for Hannah getting off lightly at court. The enquiries he'd made with court admin hadn't got past first base. If she'd been on the books as a registered informant – better acquainted with the police than they first imagined – Kate's idea made perfect sense.

'You'll meet resistance proving it,' he said.

'State the obvious, why don't you?' Kate was smiling, not snapping. 'Let's keep this to ourselves for the time being. Investigating the possibility is a task I'll take on myself. I want answers. I won't get them without diplomacy.'

'Why not?' Jo asked. 'A woman is dead and you're the SIO in charge.'

Kate wasn't sure how to answer. She chose the truth. 'It's not that simple, Jo. The use of criminal informants is a sensitive subject, an area of policing shrouded in secrecy. Running covert human intelligence sources used to be a breeze, dealt with at local level. These days, the handling of informants is no longer a matter for divisions. It's the remit of the FIB.'

'Who are they when they're at home?'

'Force Intelligence Branch.'

Hank added: 'Posh title for bureaucrats who know next to nowt about policing.'

'To some extent, Hank's right,' Kate said. 'The landscape has changed irrevocably in the past twenty years. Intelligence-gathering is more difficult for detectives trying to infiltrate organised crime groups or terror cells. It's chaos.'

'But if Hannah was recruited, it stands to reason that her killer was a big player, one worth catching, right?'

'Right, but I'll still have my work cut out persuading those on his or her trail to reveal an identity. If Serious Crimes are after him and Hannah's information was good – and I have no doubt it would be – they might now have an undercover cop on the inside who'll require protection. I doubt they'll know of Hannah's death yet, but if they do, they'll close ranks if she was compromised.'

Jo's eyes widened. 'You think that's possible?'

Kate bit her lip. 'I'd like to think not, but in a murky world fraught with danger, it happens. Someone may inadvertently have revealed her identity to another informant who passed it on. Or, God forbid, a clever offender, by which I mean our target, managed to gain insight into what she was doing for us by requesting information through the Freedom of Information Act.

'You said, us . . . Sounds like them and us to me.' Jo rarely raised her voice but she was getting more and more angry. 'I thought we were all on the same side.'

Before Kate could placate her, the door burst open.

Carmichael entered, in a flap. 'Guv, sorry to interrupt. I just had an interesting conversation with the landlord at Hannah's old flat. He forgot to tell me that there had been a break-in while she was living there. The neighbours opposite had come home from work and found her door ajar. They shouted for her but she didn't answer. They didn't have her number so they called the landlord. He went round and found the place had been turned over. Hannah freaked out when he told her.

'*Now* the idiot remembers?' Kate said. 'She's lying in a freezer!'

'He didn't know that,' Carmichael said. 'Still doesn't. When I spoke to him the first time, I merely said that I was making enquiries about a former tenant. To be honest, I don't know how, but I think he probably made the jump.'

'Makes you think that?'

'He was overly excited, mouthing off about police

accountability and public protection. I didn't confirm or deny it, obviously, and he didn't ask, but if that's what he was alluding to, Aaron could be in trouble. The guy wants press attention as the person who stood up for Hannah when we didn't.'

'Yeah, like we don't have a social conscience. Jesus Christ! This is all we need.' Kate dropped her head in her hands. Preservation of life trumped everything and she had no leads on Aaron's whereabouts; no clue if he was an adult able to protect himself or a vulnerable child. She raised her head, her expression harder than before, her focus on Carmichael. 'Hannah learned from her mistake, Lisa. That'll be why she changed her name when she approached Jack Shepherd. Check the burglary file. It may contain forensics—'

'There is no file, I already checked.'

'Why not?'

'The landlord reported the break-in. A uniform cop went round to investigate, but Hannah wasn't interested in reporting a crime. She said nothing had been taken, claimed that it was just kids out for what they could get. Though it wasn't the most salubrious area, the officer didn't buy it. He assumed that it was a domestic dispute, that there had been no break-in, just an ex letting fly, smashing up her stuff.'

'"Just?" When the fuck are we going to take men letting fly seriously?'

'The flat was tidy when he got there, boss. Hannah refused to cooperate.'

'Can you blame her?' Jo said. 'She wouldn't be able to get out the door fast enough.'

Kate kept her focus on Carmichael. 'The case was written off as NFA?'

'Yes, No Further Action,' Carmichael added, for Jo's benefit.

Jo locked eyes with Kate. 'Can we stop the landlord going to the press?'

'We can try. It's almost impossible to keep a victim's identity a secret for long. The more witnesses we speak to, the greater the chance of people inventing their own truth. If this is going to hit the press, we can't afford to waste a moment. Lisa, dig into the landlord's background. See if you can find a lever. If there's none, we need to appeal to his better judgement to buy some time.'

Kate paused a moment.

'Hank, take Lisa and feed this to the team. Put them on standby. Our priority has always been the boy, but we need to step up our efforts or he'll be joining his mum – assuming he is Hannah's kid. Jo and I will join you in a minute.'

As they left to gather the squad for the evening briefing, O'Brien slipped into Kate's office unannounced. Like Lisa had, a few minutes before, he came to an abrupt halt.

'Don't you people ever knock?' Kate said angrily.

'Sorry.' O'Brien glanced at Jo, then at Kate. 'Guv, I saw Hank and Lisa leave. I didn't realise you still had company. I'll catch you later.'

'No, as you were . . .' Kate swept a hand towards Jo, palm up. 'This is Jo Soulsby, Criminal Profiler.'

'Hello.' Jo smiled a weak greeting, still fretting over the threat to Aaron.

'Paul O'Brien, CSI.'

'I've heard a lot about you.'

'Likewise.'

Kate didn't have time for niceties. 'You have something for me, Paul?'

O'Brien approached her desk, handing her an inventory, the full contents of Hannah's caravan. 'The van has been stripped to the bone, guv. Just as well Shepherd doesn't want it. It's now in bits. We went over it one final time, like you asked. I'm afraid we lucked out. There were no more notes.'

'The way my day is going, that doesn't surprise me. Sit down while I take a look.'

The list made interesting reading. Hannah's coat was there, her PJs, shampoo and other disposable stuff. One thing was missing. O'Brien had highlighted it in his comprehensive report.

. She looked up at him. 'No other clothing?'

'Only what she was wearing, guv.'

Kate was piecing together the way Hannah Swift had been forced to live her life, always looking over her shoulder, taking steps to protect herself, as women had been doing since time began. 'Given that it's midwinter, the fact that we now know she'd been burgled before, this is gold. Looks like she kept everything in her car to facilitate a rapid exit. I'm guessing her mobile and car keys were grabbed by her attacker on his way out.' Kate switched her focus from Jo to O'Brien. 'Take a bow, Paul. The one thing the killer missed, you found.'

# 23

JC hurled Hannah's laptop across the room. It smashed against the wall, taking a chunk out of the plaster, fracturing the screen, sending parts of the keyboard flying off in all directions. He'd paid top dollar to have some jumped-up whizz kid hack into it – and for what? An easy job, he said. Too fucking easy. The fact that there was nothing on it was a major disappointment because, deep down, JC knew she'd have incriminating evidence hidden away somewhere.

It existed.

There was sod all in her vehicle or on her phone. The bitch was taunting him from the grave, as she had done the night before last, making him lose control. Even as she bled out, he'd seen defiance in her eyes, a look that said: *You'll get what's coming, eventually.* It was like locking eyes with the Devil. She had hung on for longer than expected. That split-second stand-off felt like a week.

Unsettling.

Still, he'd eliminated the chance that she'd be able to pass on what she knew . . . but, having taken care of one threat, another had emerged, then another and another. His fault, he supposed. Involving a third party multiplied the possibility of getting caught. He thought about that for a long moment, replaying the journey from the campsite, the thrill of having pulled off his mission without a hitch, a successful operation. In. Out. Job done, just as he'd planned it, though he hadn't managed to make her talk.

C'est la vie.

She was gone.

Give Hannah her due, she was gutsy, but therein lay the rub. The kid he'd hired to accompany him was far less courageous, except behind the wheel, with his foot to the floor. Then he had no fear. Nicknamed Mad Max, he was king of the road. He could shift through the gears at breakneck speed. He'd been selected on the basis of his reputation, having previously outrun police.

'Car chases are a doddle,' he'd said smugly. 'It's not a case of who's the best driver. It's who's prepared to take the risks. You think it bothers me if my driving puts others in danger? Think again. The law pull off though. They have to. Ninety-nine times out of a hundred it works. If it doesn't, head for the pavement.'

Max's laughter echoed in JC's head.

He knew all about aggression and what could be gained from it.

The problem was, Max now had detailed knowledge of that night: time, date and location. He was too thick to realise that in aiding and abetting the commission of an offence, he'd be equally guilty in the eyes of the law. He was supposed to take Hannah's car and fuck off, but who was to say that he hadn't hung around? Maybe even filmed JC in the act as proof that he wasn't responsible for her death.

Max was a liability, one JC couldn't afford.

Looking across the cityscape from his office window, he weighed up the odds. If any of that information fell into the wrong hands, living the dream was a thing of the past – for both of them. He couldn't trust Max. He couldn't trust anyone. If the kid was ever caught, he might cut himself a deal in exchange for a lenient sentence.

Hmm, well, trading was his thing too. It had brought him riches far beyond his wildest dreams.

His mind was made up . . .

The kid had to go.

Then what?

Finding Aaron was his only hope, but now someone else was out there looking for him. The good news was, he didn't have to pay her. The state was taking care of that. He smiled inwardly. All he had to do was be patient and let Kate Daniels find his target, then take him out. He'd have to be careful. Northumbria's most revered detective was the biggest threat of all. She'd cottoned on to Walker much earlier than JC had expected. He couldn't afford to underestimate her. She'd put him down and enjoy doing it.

Well, he'd see about that.

This was his game.

His rules.

She'd play nice or he'd kill her too.

# 24

'I have no doubt whatsoever that the victim's note is the key to our investigation.' Kate checked her watch and then focused on O'Brien. 'Would you mind sticking around, Paul. I'm about to brief the team. I appreciate you rarely come within a million miles of an incident room, but you were at the scene, which means you have insight my lot don't. That could be enormously helpful if we need to clarify anything.'

'Fine by me,' he said.

Kate added a warning. 'It goes without saying that anything you hear or see in there is strictly confidential.' She was about to add 'including victim ID', which he'd see posted on the electronic murder wall, but held her tongue. O'Brien knew the score. He'd never let a victim down before. He wouldn't start now. If anyone was going to blab, it would be Hannah's landlord.

'Let's do this,' Kate said.

Jo gathered her notes together and stood up.

Kate led the way down the corridor, Jo and O'Brien following close behind. At the door to the incident room, she paused, asking them to go on ahead while she made an important call.

The incident room was packed to the rafters when Kate walked in a few minutes later. MIT personnel had assembled. They were waiting to give feedback on individual progress, except Maxwell – the one person she was desperate to speak to.

Hank arrived by her side, a big yawn. 'The team are aware that Aaron is in danger of being exposed—'

'Including Maxwell?'

'Yes.'

'Then where is he?'

'No idea . . .' Hank scanned the room, stymied by the DC's absence, then turned to face her. 'He was here a moment ago. I told them all to stay put.'

'Find him for me, please, Hank. I haven't got the energy to run around after him.'

He moved away just as Maxwell hurried through the door, one side of his shirt hanging loose from the waistband of his jeans. He stopped dead when he noticed Kate standing there, his colour rising as he moved further into the room.

'Sorry for keeping you waiting, guv. I needed—'

'Spare me the details and tuck yourself in. You're up first. If Bright walks in here and sees you like that, he'll kick your arse.'

A ripple of laughter reverberated around the room.

'Settle down,' Kate told them. 'We're not in nursery school.'

Harry couldn't help himself. 'Neil thinks we are.'

Everyone laughed, including Kate when she followed his gaze.

Possessing few inhibitions, Maxwell hadn't bothered leaving the room to sort himself out. He'd just turned his back and was currently shoving a hand down the front of his jeans, it had to be said, with some difficulty. Having spent hour upon mind-numbing hour in the rear of a surveillance van, often as the only female detective among a load of men unable to hold their water, it was nothing Kate hadn't seen before.

Maxwell turned to face her, clothing intact.

'Tell me you have news,' she said.

Waggling his hand from side to side, a yes and no gesture, he rushed over to his desk, grabbed an A4 sheet from his out-tray. Retracing his steps, he joined Kate at the front, confirming that he did have something important to share.

'Take the floor and get on with it then,' she said.

They waited for everyone to stop talking.

Maxwell began his delivery by reporting that he'd found

no marriage certificate for Hannah, so he'd run her details through the birth register and found Aaron.

Kate's heart leapt. She hadn't expected that.

Maxwell checked his notes. 'The lad was born February twenty-eighth, 2009. Hannah registered the birth a week later at the Windsor and Maidenhead Register Office. Her address is on the certificate, a home that was in her name at the time and was sold on a year later—'

'And the father's name?' Hank said.

'Left blank.' Maxwell paused. 'Maybe she didn't know who it was—'

'Here we go,' Harry said. 'Another ignorant jump to the wrong conclusion.'

Kate gave him hard eyes, a hint to back off. He didn't. His mumbled retort included the words 'misogynist prick'. Kate refocused on Maxwell. 'Neil, before you go making assumptions, let's find some hard evidence. Has it not occurred to you that Hannah may have wanted a kid but no man to go with it? I know loads of women who've made a conscious choice to have a child on their own or, like me, not to have one.'

'The possibilities are endless,' Jo said. 'The father may have scarpered before Aaron was born. Or he's the man who killed her and she'd already begun to have misgivings about him. In either scenario, she wouldn't want his name associated with her son. I know I wouldn't.'

Maxwell looked shamefaced.

Witnessing his discomfort, Kate had a sense that he was beginning to crumble under the weight of criticism, even though it was part and parcel of being a cop in the MIT. Challenging one another's assumptions was how things got done but, now he'd been slapped down, she felt the responsibility to lift him up. His morale, or any other team member's, could not be allowed to slip at such a crucial juncture in the investigation.

'You've done a good job, Neil. Keep working on it. Harry,

have the Met canvass her former neighbours, find out what she was like and who her associates were.'

'Should I drop everything else and concentrate on Aaron?' Maxwell asked.

'Until further notice, yes. Though that may not be for very long. I've arranged for a Met detective to give Hannah's father the death message. In case she rings in, her name is Kyra Thakur. She was recommended to me by DCI Stone. I asked her to prompt Peter Swift gently for information about Hannah, what she did for a living, former relationships, kids. If he can shed light on where his grandson is, we're in business. He doesn't know it yet, but he's flying up here to ID his daughter's body – that's assuming he agrees.'

Maxwell looked at her. 'Aaron's middle name is Peter. Maybe they're close.'

'That gives me hope,' Kate said.

# 25

The briefing had been going on for well over an hour. The team were looking jaded but they had covered a lot of ground. Maxwell was on his feet again. 'Jack Shepherd was right about the colour and prefix of Hannah's vehicle,' he said. 'The full registration is: YA16 ABN. ANPR cameras registered it twice on the A1, north of Warenford last Friday and south of Alnwick the Friday before that. On each occasion, it was seen travelling either south or northbound, then the other way twenty minutes later.'

Kate narrowed her eyes. 'Alnwick, is what, eight or ten miles away? Warenford a bit more? If Hannah had arranged to meet someone, in either place, she didn't hang around for long—'

'She was making a phone call,' Carmichael said quietly.

Those sitting closest overheard.

All eyes shifted in her direction . . .

Including Kate's. 'You know something we don't, Lisa?'

'Maybe . . . I just finished checking Jack Shepherd's incoming call history. He doesn't use the phone much and one number stood out. Amy asked him about it but he was none the wiser, though he did receive the call at around the time he let the caravan to Hannah. I did some digging. It turns out that she purchased the number from an app specialising in protecting the owner's identity, allowing them to remain anonymous with multiple, disposable numbers.'

'You mean a burner?' Harry asked.

'Kind of, though in this case it's legit. Entirely justified by anyone who perceives a danger. It was a Pay-As-You-Go deal, so no contract. Hannah purchased a batch of these numbers at the same time and had a substantial credit on her account, almost two hundred quid.'

'How did she pay?' Kate asked.

'A one-time payment via an iTunes account. No verification or personal information required.' Lisa paused, a sad expression as she looked across at Kate. 'Guv, I believe in exercising caution, but Hannah took it to another level in order to protect herself. She switched regularly between these numbers. While she had the capability to send and receive calls, on each of the numbers she used there were no incoming calls.'

'None?'

'No, and every outgoing call was made to the same number, which I found out was purchased in the same batch. Given her plea for us to find Aaron, it wouldn't take a genius to work out that she sent him the SIM or SIMs so they could keep in touch safely. Any texts she sent would automatically delete after being read.'

'Sounds a bit James Bond to me,' Brown said.

Others agreed with him.

'I looked into it when a mate of mine got into internet dating.' Carmichael rolled her eyes. 'She's twenty-eight and drop-dead gorgeous. Why she'd even consider that as a viable way to find a boyfriend is beyond me. I was worried that she might end up with a telephone stalker if she used her real number and things went tits up. I persuaded her to get a second number and set up her subscription online. She's glad of the extra level of security.'

'I bet,' Jo said. 'I didn't even know there was such a thing.'

Kate thanked Carmichael for taking the initiative. 'Anyone else?'

DC Brown held his hand up. 'I managed to locate and interview the three customers from The Bull public house,' he said. 'Jimmy Nicholson, Robert Hall and Jeff Charlton remember the conversation with Jack Shepherd, though they all confirmed, independently, that he never mentioned the name of his new tenant. Shepherd mentioned in passing that he'd received an unexpected windfall after a terrible year financially. They all denied having discussed it outside of the pub. I have no reason to disbelieve them.'

'OK, that's it for tonight,' Kate said. 'Get yourselves home. I want you in here at six thirty sharp.' As the team began to disband, Kate approached Harry, dropping her voice to a whisper. 'A word before you go, please. My office.'

Harry joined her there seconds later. He looked wary, and had his coat on, a heavy hint that he'd rather not stay long. That suited Kate, but she had something to say that couldn't wait till morning.

'Shut the door, please, Harry.'

'I know what you're going to say, guv—'

'I thought you might.' Kate hadn't sat down, even though she was as keen as everyone else to get out of there. She leaned against her desk, feet and arms crossed. 'Lay off Maxwell, eh? I know you don't rate him but he's doing his best. By disagreeing every time he opens his mouth, you're undermining all I'm trying to do with him.'

'Guv, you've got to admit he asks for it sometimes.'

'He does and it's my remit to bollock him over it, not yours. I don't give a shit what you say to him privately, but you don't do it in my incident room. Is that clear?'

He didn't answer.

'I mean it, Harry. I'm asking nicely this time. If I have to ask again, I might not. I'm sorry, but I don't have time to play referee.'

'You won't have to. I'm the one should be apologising.'

'OK, then. Get out of here and we'll say no more about it.'

Kate followed him from her office, pulling on her coat. To her surprise, Jo was waiting in the incident room. Before they had a chance to speak, Carmichael called a collective goodnight to all three. They waved in response. Jo was about to say something when Kate's phone rang, cutting her off.

It was the number Stone had given her earlier.

Kate looked at Jo apologetically. 'It's the Met detective I've been waiting to hear from. Sorry, I'll have to take it. You go on. I'll see you at home.'

Jo nodded and walked away.

Kate took the call. 'Daniels.'

'Ma'am, it's DS Thakur.'

'Kyra, I appreciate the cooperation. Sorry to dump that on you.'

'It's what we do.'

Kate liked her already. Stone had chosen well. 'How did it go with Peter Swift?'

'Naturally, he's devastated, though he agreed to fly north to confirm ID. There's no one else can do it. Hannah was an only child. I couldn't get him on a plane tonight, so his Heathrow departure is 08.15 tomorrow; ETA Newcastle, 09.35. You'll be sent a scan of his passport when he checks in. Peter has been briefed that you'll meet him at the other end.' Kyra paused. 'Ma'am, I'm afraid you're not going to like what else I have to tell you.'

# 26

Kate arrived home to a warm, inviting house, the intense aroma of garlic and Italian herbs hitting her senses as she walked through the door. Finally, she felt ready to eat, even though Kyra Thakur had put paid to the possibility of getting a lead on Aaron or his whereabouts. That particular line of enquiry had evaporated when the Met detective fed back that Peter Swift had not seen or heard from Hannah for years. He was unaware of whether or not she'd since married or become a mother.

As instructed, Kyra had left it there.

Stone had been right, Thakur was a pro.

Though grateful to her and him, Kate was painfully aware that tomorrow's planned meeting with Hannah's father now had an added and very personal dimension. For many years Kate had been estranged from her old man because she didn't live up to his view of the ideal daughter. Relationships were complicated. It made her wonder what dysfunctional family dynamics were at play in Hannah's life.

Closing the front door, Kate leaned against it, pleased to be shutting out the world and the investigation for a few hours before returning to base. She stood there, taking a moment to shake herself free of the case, something she tried to do most nights before greeting Jo, not always successfully.

The haunting chords of one of Kate's favourite songs drifted along the hallway from the kitchen at the rear: Charlene Soraia, 'Wherever You Will Go'. At the top of her voice, Jo sang along. Her only audience – Nelson, her beloved Labrador – sloped out of the kitchen towards Kate, looking less than enamoured.

If he could've rolled his eyes, he would have.

She crouched down and gave him a hug. 'I completely agree with you,' she whispered. 'Your mum has many talents. Singing isn't one of them. Go on, in your bed.' As the dog moved away, Kate stood in the hallway listening. The song's lyrics seemed more apt than usual. At work, Jo had tried to guide her through one of her darkest days and been knocked back. Kate would have lost it if she'd let her in.

An apology was overdue.

Dropping her car keys on the side table, her bag on the floor, she shrugged off her coat, kicked off her boots and moved down the hallway. When she reached the kitchen, Jo was swaying gently to the music, putting the finishing touches to their meal, a glass of red on the bench beside her. She wore cut-off jeans, a raggy old T-shirt, frayed at the edges. Her feet were bare, wet hair hanging loose around her shoulders.

Unable to take her eyes off her, Kate was filled with a mix of emotions: guilt for having pushed her away earlier – the only way she'd have coped with such a grim day – deep love and a yearning for intimacy, the one thing guaranteed to heal her. She couldn't make it through this case on her own.

Sensing a presence, or maybe a change in atmosphere, Jo swung round, a big smile as their eyes met, an odd expression – part relief, part curiosity. 'Hey, you made it!'

'Was there any doubt?'

'Once you took that call, I thought I might have to eat alone.' Jo pointed over Kate's shoulder. 'Actually, I thought I heard you before. Did you come in and nip out again, or did I imagine that?'

'No. I arrived just in time to admire your moves.'

Jo laughed. 'How long have you been standing there?'

'Not long enough. Feel free to carry on.'

Turning down the volume on their Bose system, Jo held up her wine and changed the subject. 'I started without you.'

'So I see.'

Eyeing the open bottle on the kitchen counter, Kate walked towards it, picked up an empty glass and poured herself a small measure. Jo took a step forward and gave her a gentle kiss on the lips. They held each other for a long moment. There were times when words were useless, touch more appropriate. This was one of them. In Kate's exhausted state, Charlene's lyrics had got to her. She turned away and went upstairs to shower before dinner.

Jo was about to dish up by the time Kate arrived in the kitchen in her PJs, asking if there was anything she could do to help. There wasn't. Unlike Kate, Jo had everything under control. They took their meal into the living room to eat on their knees in front of the fire. When they had finished, Jo cleared away the dishes, returning with another bottle of wine.

'Not for me . . .' Kate waved it away. 'One more will tip me over the edge. I have an early start. More importantly, I'm meeting Hannah's father off the plane at nine thirty. I can't do that with a hangover.'

She updated Jo on the latest disappointing development.

'Swift has no idea he's a grandfather?' Jo's eyes widened when Kate shook her head. 'Oh my God, poor man. Hearing of Hannah's death must have been dreadful. Finding out that she kept that from him will break his heart all over again. You'll tell him?'

'When identification is complete, not before. I have no choice. As far as I'm aware, he's now Aaron's next of kin.'

Kate's eyelids were getting heavy. As usual, she fought sleep. For most people, it was a safe haven. For her it was a place where demons lay waiting to attack. It was only when Jo moved in with Kate that she realised the full extent of her nightmares. It was scary waking up to the sound of whimpering, witnessing a loved one fight off an imaginary foe.

She continued to listen as Kate talked, providing a sounding board, hoping that verbalising her thoughts before retiring might give her some respite when she finally went to bed. Jo soon realised that Kate was in trouble. She was obsessing about Hannah alone in that van. Waiting. Jumpy. Terrified of every sound outside in case it was the man who'd threatened to take her life.

Although Jo had once been married to a predatory male, a serial philanderer who couldn't have cared less about her feelings or those of their kids, try as she might she couldn't comprehend what Hannah's life must've been like. It wasn't only the brutality of her death that was tearing Kate apart. It was the inevitability of it – the fact that Hannah had nowhere to turn – that Kate found hard to swallow.

'We've got to stop this happening,' she said. 'These are mothers, daughters, sisters. No one gives a fat rat's arse about them—'

'You do, I—'

'Yeah, when it's too fucking late.' Kate apologised for snapping.

'No, I agree with you. We need to care when they're still breathing.'

Kate looked like a torn soul.

Jo knew she'd carry Hannah's note with her for the rest of her days.

'I need your help,' Kate said. 'You're the one with the expertise. I lock them up, I don't spend time with these vile men like you do. You engage with them, for hours on end. I need a pointer. Anything and everything you can give me.'

'I'm putting together a profile, but I need more time. It'll be counterproductive otherwise. I could be giving you a bum steer.'

'How long do you need?'

'As long as it takes. Kate, I know you're desperate, but it's not something I can rush.'

'Sorry, I'm just frustrated.'

'Me too.'

Jo poured herself another glass of wine. She'd worked extensively with dangerous offenders, much of it with lifers, during and after sentencing. She'd seen the whites of their eyes, questioned their motivation, given courts of law the benefit of that experience. And yet, like Kate, she was struggling when it came to JC.

*She had to give her something.*

'Based on the content of Hannah's note, JC is most likely highly intelligent, manipulative and successful. I could make inferences on personality type, but it won't narrow down a list of suspects. Had Hannah died at the hands of a serial killer, I'd have more to go on, like violence progression and state of mind during the commission of the offence. I have an inkling that he's been building up to this. What we need is his trigger, the thing that made him snap.'

A few restless hours later, Kate woke, aware of a presence close by. Disoriented, she sat bolt upright, strands of sweaty hair sticking to her forehead as her eyes adjusted to the darkness. A faint slither of light peeped in through a chink in the curtains from the streetlight beyond. She jumped as a hand touched her shoulder. It wasn't JC or any other monster lurking there. It was Jo, waking her gently, telling her that it was time to make a move.

Her bedside alarm glowed: 05.45.

Kate fell back, wanting to close her eyes, only vaguely aware of Jo taking her by the hand last night, hauling her off the sofa and up the stairs to bed, covering her with the duvet, wrapping a safe pair of her arms around her. That's when the lights went out, physically and metaphorically.

Rolling over, she kissed Jo's cheek. 'Go to sleep.'

'You want coffee?' Jo's voice was thick in her throat.

'No time. See you at the office.'

Kate was up, dressed and out the door in less than fifteen minutes.

The temperature outside had lifted overnight, though the snow hadn't yet melted. Kate moved gingerly towards her car. Few were up and about. Pre-dawn was her favourite time of day, a new day breaking, a city waking up, the orange glow of streetlights reflected off the pavement.

The gritters had cleared the roads and she made good time, arriving at Northern Area Command HQ at quarter past six. Walking briskly down the main corridor, she used her ID to gain access to a door marked: **MAJOR INCIDENT SUITE – NO UNAUTHORISED ENTRY**. Half the team had beaten her in and were heading to their desks as she entered. She greeted them before moving to her office, where she sat down to do some admin.

First, she checked the incident log to see if anything had happened overnight, something she did every morning. There had been various updates, telephone calls from Craster residents who'd been at work when the house-to-house team were knocking on doors. Hannah had been seen in the village on a number of occasions, but details and dates were sketchy.

She'd been placed at The Jolly Fisherman once or twice and was seen looking through the window of a former artist's cottage a few minutes' walk from the harbour, described by some as the perfect hideaway. Kate wondered if she'd been getting ready to move to somewhere more comfortable. Perhaps the isolation of the farm was getting to her, her motivation for moving fuelled by the fact that the campsite would fill up in spring.

There was an alternative: she was an informant who'd been advised to move.

Kate noted that Harry had it in hand to follow up on every sighting of Hannah from which the MIT would produce a timeline. Kate felt sad that Hannah hadn't made the move earlier. Neighbours offered a level of protection the caravan didn't. She might have survived had a passer-by heard her screams.

Kate's blood ran cold.

Pushing the thought away, though it continued to nag at her, she focused on her emails. Scrolling through them, answering those requiring attention, ignoring others, she e-signed a budgetary request for overtime, a priority no SIO could afford to neglect. In the coming days, her team would be working flat out. They needed paying, though there were those among them whose goodwill she could rely on if it was knocked back. Such professional integrity still existed within the CID.

Some things were more important than money.

In her peripheral vision, a note on the top of her in-tray caught her eye. Underneath was a report that wasn't there when she left. Kate picked them both up. The note was from Carmichael, short and sweet: *Hannah's ex-landlord has seen sense. I'm fairly certain he won't go to the press. Lisa*

Wondering how she'd managed to talk him round, grateful that she had, Kate binned the note and studied the report. Curiously, it was marked *For the Urgent Attention of the SIO: Hannah Swift Incident*. Intrigued, she pulled the document towards her, lifting her feet up on her desk, leaning back in her chair to read it.

Five minutes later, her office door opened.

Hank stuck his head in, asking if she wanted a brew. She held up a thumb and carried on reading. He disappeared, returning with a mug of steaming hot tea. Placing it on her desk, he sat down.

'What you reading?'

'Forensics report. One of the tyre impressions they took at the gateway to Shepherd's campsite was from a small car, identified on their database as a fairly new Pirelli Centurato All Season Plus. It had little wear – in all likelihood it had come from Hannah's Fiat. They found dark blue paint on Shepherd's damaged gate and a second impression from a much larger vehicle. A four-by-four is their best guess.'

'A best guess won't get us far.'

'No, but they think it's a Land Rover Discovery. They're awaiting confirmation from the manufacturer.'

'Simon Shepherd has one. I assume we'll be paying him another visit.'

'I told you he's not JC—'

'Doesn't mean he's not involved.'

'Doesn't mean he is either. Look, I know you don't like him, neither do I, but we have nothing on him.'

'Yet . . .' Hank put his tea down, crossed his arms and stared across at her. 'Kate, he has a connection to the crime scene and drives that type of motor. I'm sorry, but in my book, that alone bumps him up a list of suspects.'

Kate lifted her hand to her ear. 'Sorry, for a moment there I thought you said list.' Her sarcasm wasn't appreciated. 'Don't go pointing the finger is all I'm saying.' Bored with the conversation, she looked beyond him through the open blinds of her internal window into the MIR. No sign of who she wanted to talk to. 'Have you seen Carmichael yet?'

'Yeah, she just arrived.'

'Get her in here, please.'

Hank got up. From Kate's office door, he called out to Carmichael. She arrived a moment later and they both sat down. Kate shared the disappointing news from the Met before addressing the younger and less arsy of the two detective sergeants.

'If Hannah's father can't help, I'm hoping you can, Lisa.'

Carmichael cocked her head on one side. 'He's not coming?'

'Yes, he is, but we need a lead on the boy and he can't give us that. It's imperative that we throw everything at Hannah's online presence now. It'll give us insight into what she was doing in the days and weeks leading up to her death. I'd rather stick pins in my eyes than hang out with a bunch of strangers, but I'm hoping Hannah felt differently. More than that, I'm hoping her isolation drove her to create an online persona that allowed her to communicate with others, even on a superficial level. I gather it's quite addictive once you get going. If she engaged with anyone in a meaningful way, we need to find them.'

'You haven't found her yet?' Hank was looking at Carmichael.

Reacting to the implied criticism, she defended herself. 'No, because people behave differently online. You can be anyone you want to be. Hannah would hardly use her own name, would she? She was in hiding. The anonymity of social media would suit her. I don't suppose for one minute she talked about Aaron, but no one can exist in a vacuum. We all need someone, even you when you're less grumpy.'

'Lisa's right,' Kate said. 'Assuming Hannah has an account, of any kind, there must be something she wished she'd never said online.'

'We're all guilty of that,' Carmichael added.

Hank snapped his head around to face her. 'Not you, I hope.'

She narrowed her eyes. 'What's it got to do with you? You're no longer my supervision. Kate is.'

'You miss me though, don't you?' he teased. 'A word of advice. Whatever the boss tells you to do, run it by me first . . . She doesn't always play by the rules.'

'Careful,' Kate was enjoying the banter. 'Lisa's next in line as 2ic.'

'Not if she gives away secrets online,' he scoffed.

'It only happened the once. It was—'

Kate held up her hand. 'Don't tell me. I don't want to know.'

'It wasn't that bad.'

'Well, I hope you learned your lesson.'

'I did, and you're right. A slip of the virtual tongue online, a needy or drunken post, has spawned many a repercussion, including the sack. Once it's out in the ether . . .' Lisa left the sentence unfinished.

'Well, in this instance, that's precisely what I'm after,' Kate said. 'If she made a mistake, I'm relying on you to find it. I can't see her uploading images of her son, but we can use her images to track her geographical footprint. How far did you get with the original action?'

'Not very. Worldwide, there are thousands of Hannah Swifts on Facebook alone, some with her year of birth.' Carmichael shook her head. 'I have no idea why people do that, but they do. As soon as Maxwell discovered her date and place of birth, a Windsor address, I went back to my contact to ask them to refine the search criteria. They haven't come back to me.'

'Chase them up, now please.'

Carmichael made a move, pausing as she reached the door. 'Guv, if Hannah was inactive for a while, it makes our job more difficult, but if her old man has information about friends, schools she attended, websites she owned, former mobile numbers, that'll help a lot. The more keywords we can use, the greater the chance of finding her.'

'Hank and I will follow that up when we see him later.'

'Great. I'll do my best. Most account holders are lazy. They forget to alter bios, update personal information or state their preferences. Don't get me started with security or privacy. It's mind-boggling how much you can find out about a person online if you know where to look. If there's one tiny thread left hanging, I will find her.'

Hank was sceptical. 'I'm not convinced she'd be that sloppy.'

'Prove us wrong,' Kate said. 'JC found her somehow.'

# 28

Kate and Hank made their way to the Intelligence Unit hoping to confirm or rule out Hannah Swift as a registered police informant. It was a double-edged sword. Even though she was now deceased, they would hit a brick wall if she'd been involved in an investigation that was still ongoing – in other words, none of their business. All they were hoping for was confirmation that Hannah was passing on information. They knew they wouldn't get the name of her handler, even if they begged. There was no way the department would jeopardise an operation before criminals were lifted and put before a court of law.

An hour later, the detectives came away none the wiser, Hank grumbling all the way to the car. 'I was hoping they'd give us a hint. But no . . .'

'Stop moaning . . .' Kate picked up the pace, scanning the car park for her vehicle. 'It's not a case of being stonewalled. The integrity of long-running investigations has to be protected. We knew that before we set off.'

He spread his hands. 'So why bother?'

'Don't ask, don't get—'

'Yeah, well, we didn't get, did we?'

'How was I to know that the one person who might've given us something off-the-record had transferred to another force?' Kate aimed her key fob at her vehicle. The doors clunked open as they moved towards it. 'Stay cool, Hank. We'll crack our case without them. If we make an arrest and fuck up an important sting, they'll be the ones with egg on their faces.'

'Oh yeah? How d'you work that out?'

She met his gaze over the roof of her car. 'Think about it. Hannah's death could, potentially, discredit the force if it becomes known that she'd been working for them when she was brutally murdered by the man she was informing upon. Maybe it's their cash we retrieved from Shepherd. If they moved her because she was in danger, they should have provided round-the-clock protection.'

Hank reached for the door handle. 'What the—'

'What now?'

He was looking down at her vehicle. 'Bastards!'

She walked around to the passenger side. He stepped away, exposing a deep gouge down the entire side of her pride and joy. Someone had keyed it. A deliberate act. Kate looked around, feeling like she was under surveillance. Hank felt it too. He glanced up at the windows of HQ. Not all of her enemies lived outside of the force.

Kate followed his gaze.

No one visible.

'I'm going in,' he said.

'No, Hank. We don't have time. I'll have the CCTV checked later. Besides, it could've been done at home. It was dark when I left this morning. I wouldn't have noticed. We have one priority and that's to get to the airport.'

Kate took the A189 central motorway, heading north, away from the city centre. The atmosphere in the car was grim. Hank was still seething about the criminal damage to her Audi. If it had been minor, she'd have coughed up without making an insurance claim. For years she'd paid a premium after a fugitive rammed her previous vehicle during a car chase. Though there was less damage this time, it would cost a fortune to fix.

She tried not to think about it.

'We're not having much luck, are we?' Hank said.

She glanced into the passenger seat. 'It's a paint job. Forget it.'

'I wasn't talking about the car. I meant the investigation. We're swimming against the tide here, Kate. There was nothing broadcast on TV or radio that would have caused Hannah to pen that note. As you said, we don't know which Friday, or even how long the note had been there. We lucked out with arsonists. None were found with the initials JC.'

'Keep the faith, Hank. Our problems are nothing compared to those of the man we're due to meet. Can't say I'm looking forward to it.' She sighed, turning right at Cowgate, heading for the A696, the main route to the airport. 'Call the morgue. Make sure they're ready to receive us.'

'You did that already.'

'Don't argue. Just do as I ask.'

As he made the call, Kate didn't share what was on her mind, over and above the keying incident and the fact that lines of enquiry weren't paying off. The feeling that someone had eyes on her was growing stronger. Jo's voice suddenly arrived in her head: *Did you come in and nip out again?*

Such an innocent comment.

Or maybe not.

Was the noise she'd heard a figment of her imagination or had someone been trying to get into their home last night? Having seen the extent of Hannah's injuries, that was unthinkable. Kate checked her rear-view mirror. Traffic was heavy. She saw nothing untoward. Was Hank right? Was she the target? Was someone watching her, warning her to back off? Or was her mind also playing tricks?

# 29

His eyes fixed on the rear of the Audi. He kept three-car cover in case she spotted him. Assuming she'd got the message that he wasn't far away, she'd be looking for a high-end vehicle he'd already torched, not a boy racer driving a piece of shit. He laughed out loud, banging his hand on the steering wheel. Hiding in plain sight was his speciality. Besides, whoever had heard of a surveillance car with a noisy fucking exhaust?

Inside the vehicle, he could hardly hear himself think.

Mad Max had no need of his wheels now. Lured by the promise of another job, attracting a hefty remuneration of untraceable cash, they had agreed to rendezvous at dawn at a disused quarry, an isolated area shrouded in early morning mist. It was peaceful and still as JC took to the woods to await the kid's arrival.

The throaty thrum of the engine hit his ear before the car came into view, a few minutes earlier than scheduled. Max got out and sat on the bonnet, his breath visible in the freezing air, a beany pulled down tight around his ears, shoulders hunched in a coat made for warmer weather. He seemed not to have a care in the world as he lit a cigarette he had no idea would be his last. Checking his watch, he looked around, a big sigh, impatient to make the deal and be on his way.

Time to move in.

In a split second, Max's expression changed. Had he seen movement beyond the treeline? Yes, he had. He scanned the woods, peering uneasily in his direction. Time to put him out of his misery. JC emerged from the shadows, his shotgun locked and loaded, poised to finish him. There was a moment of confusion, then of clarity, as the kid realised that the man he'd come to meet was there to take, not give.

Another disposable asset.

Hannah had more balls.

Begging for his life, Max backed away precariously close to the edge of the deep ravine behind him, tears and snot running down his face. Where was his bravado now? His terror rose, eyes wide with uncontrollable fear. There was an impasse as he weighed up his chances. Decision made, he ran, stumbling over rough ground.

Mistake.

Taking aim, JC slowly squeezed the trigger. The blast sent the boy hurtling over the edge. A splash, then it all went quiet.

Sweet dreams, kiddo.

He'd served a purpose.

Protecting himself was something young Max hadn't understood. Fail to plan, plan to fail. This had always been JC's motto. Covering his tracks was a necessary evil. For his part, there was more at stake now than there had ever been. Late last night it had come to his attention that he'd been written out of his parents' will. They were planning to hand the lot to his bitch of a sister.

Anticipating such a possibility, and in certain knowledge the idiots always used the same weasel of a solicitor, JC had paid someone to let him know should his suspicions ever become a reality. It wasn't that he needed the money. What angered him was the principle of the thing. He was entitled. And if they thought they would get away with it, they could think again. Their new will would never see the light of day.

He'd made sure of it.

He was down but not out, with unfinished business to attend to. Kate Daniels was at the very top of that list. Her right indicator winked a warning to trailing vehicles that she was pulling into the outside lane, turning right. He maintained his position. As he passed her vehicle on the inside, he glanced to his right, getting an eyeful of her loyal wingman as the Audi slowed to give way to traffic exiting the airport, turning right toward Ponteland.

He'd have to be careful now.

Word on the grapevine was that Hank would go down fighting rather than let his esteemed boss come to harm. An experienced officer he might be, but he had no conception that she was on JC's target list. Even if he did, he couldn't protect her twenty-four seven.

JC smiled to himself.

Last night, he'd driven through a wealthy suburb, a leafy but trendy area on the fringes of Newcastle, dubbed 'the village' the city's answer to Notting Hill . . . a good vibe, lots of bars, restaurants and hotels nearby, but it was the interior of Kate's Victorian terraced home that he was really interested in.

Once inside, his eyes had prowled her living room like a movie camera. Lights were dimmed, candles lit, awaiting her return, shadows flickering across the walls and ceiling as music drifted out from a room at the rear. Very romantic. He had to hand it to the detective chief inspector. She had style. Being inside her home with the woman who shared her life gave him a thrill like no other. The dog he hadn't counted on. Fortunately, it was hungry . . .

They were both hungry.

# 30

In the short-term car park, Kate reversed her vehicle into a spot so that Peter Swift wouldn't see the damage to the Audi when they emerged from the terminal. She wanted him to be confident that he had the best team looking into his daughter's death, not a second-rate bunch of idiots who couldn't even look after their own transport. Intending to sit in the rear with him, she handed Hank her keys, asking him to wait in the car and drive them directly to the morgue as soon as they returned.

Understandably, Swift looked pale and drawn as he walked into the arrival's hall. Physically, he was in good shape, impeccably dressed, looking much younger than his sixty-seven years. He was a tall man, around six three, with a formidable presence. He had blue eyes and a good head of silver hair with an uncanny resemblance to Richard Gere.

Kate stepped forward. 'Mr Swift?'

He pulled up sharp. 'Yes.'

'I'm Detective Chief Inspector Kate Daniels. I'm so sorry we're meeting in such sad circumstances.'

It took a moment to find his voice. 'Is there no doubt?'

Kate chose her words carefully. 'Sir, I don't want to give false hope. You're the only person who can tell us that for sure.'

A nod of understanding. 'Then we'd best get on with it.'

On the journey into town, the atmosphere in the car was as grim as it was tense. For around fifteen minutes, Swift stared blankly out of the window as the car sped south. Until identification was complete, what was there to say? Small talk wasn't helpful in situations like these.

Kate was keen to go at his pace and take it gently.

She was there for a purpose: first and foremost to gain

formal victim identification. Equally important to her investigation was to elicit as much information from Hannah's father as she could, so she could locate Aaron, whom she still believed to be in grave danger. While the man sitting in the seat beside her didn't know of his existence yet, any information he could provide about his daughter's early life might reveal a clue to the child's whereabouts. Kate was prepared, willing and able to hold the man's hand during that difficult conversation.

Met detective Kyra Thakur had intimated that Swift was a private man who'd asked few questions when informed of the suspicious death of a young woman in northern England. Though devastated by the thought that his only child's life had ended prematurely, he'd declined the offer of a Family Liaison Officer. Kate had no intention of persuading him otherwise. In his shoes, she'd have felt the same way.

Was he in denial?

Failing to accept the inevitable wasn't uncommon in Kate's experience. She hoped that was not the case, though his first question made her wonder if it might be: *Is there no doubt?* There was no ambiguity in police circles.

It was Kate's job to warn Swift of injuries to the body before he viewed it, but there was a time and place to do it. She decided to wait until they arrived at the morgue. She didn't want him dwelling on it in the car. Naturally, his imagination would be in overdrive, but it would never match the reality of the scene facing Kate on the night of Hannah's murder.

Swift's voice interrupted her thoughts.

'It's a few years since I've been here,' he said. 'I used to come to this part of the world often, so I'm familiar with this route into the city.'

Kate turned her head in his direction, a half-smile. 'For business or pleasure?'

'Business. I retired from investment banking three years ago. You may not be aware of it but, as modern cities go, Newcastle's future is as exciting as its industrial past. It embraces change. That's always a good thing.'

It was also a good thing that he was talking, a diversion that suited them both.

Kate asked: 'Did you ever holiday in the area?'

'Sadly, no, though my late wife and I passed through it often en route to Scotland.'

'Then you'll have seen some of our wonderful coastline—'

'Are you fishing for clues, Detective Chief Inspector?' He never took his eyes off her. 'I may be retired but I'm able to use Google. I gather Hannah was found at the coast.'

'Yes, that's correct. I'm sorry. I didn't mean to offend.'

'Neither did I. As the SIO in charge of the investigation into my daughter's death, I expect nothing less than a thorough examination of the facts. Never apologise for doing what's required. I'm aware of how long a haul there may be in front of us, so let's drop the formality of rank, shall we? You have a name and I'm not a sir. May I call you Kate?'

'Please do.'

'If you have the time, I'd like you to show me where Hannah was found.'

'Of course.'

'I have nothing to rush home for. My wife died before I retired. I thought about staying on, but decided I might travel while I'm fit enough to enjoy it. Northumberland was not on my agenda, especially in such bleak circumstances. I didn't know Hannah was living here. So, go ahead . . . I won't break. Ask your questions. I'll do anything to assist your investigation.'

'Perhaps later.' Kate pointed to the morgue. 'We're almost there.'

# 31

Kate and Hannah's father sat in the small but comfortable family waiting room while Hank went to sign them in. He returned a few minutes later with Heather Gilbert, Tim Stanton's assistant, who had everything prepared and was keen to expedite the process of identification. She greeted Peter Swift with empathy and sensitivity, telling him she'd wait outside until he was ready.

Kate gave Hank a nod that was almost imperceptible, thanking him for giving Heather the heads-up that Swift had not yet been warned of the horrific nature of his daughter's death and that Kate needed more time to prepare him.

Hank escorted Heather outside.

Kate waited until the door closed before speaking. 'Peter, identifying a loved one is never easy. Before we go in, I must warn you that Hannah has substantial injuries to her head and face—'

'Are you saying I might not recognise her?'

Kate loathed this part of her job. 'It's possible.'

His eyes misted slightly. 'I understand.'

'Do you need a moment alone?'

'No, I'm ready.' He stood up, keen to get it over with.

Kate did likewise, leading him out to join the others.

He was very brave as they approached the viewing room. Once inside, the detectives stood discreetly to one side, allowing Heather a moment to settle the man's nerves. Swift had asked not to view the body through glass, but to be physically in the room with his daughter. As the sheet was removed, he showed no emotion.

That would come later.

Kate was relieved to see that Hannah didn't look quite as

bad as she'd expected now the blood had been cleaned away, though bruising and cuts were evident. Only her face was visible and one arm so he could hold her hand if he so wished. The fact that he didn't brought a lump to Kate's throat. He spent little time with his daughter, though he was given the option of doing so. Kate didn't judge him for it. Some people were tactile. Others couldn't bear to look, let alone touch. The process of identification was all over in a matter of minutes. There was no doubt in Swift's mind that it was Hannah.

Formalities complete, Kate explained that it wouldn't be possible to release the body for burial for some time, asking if he had any questions before leaving. There were none. Hank drove them straight to Craster, remaining in the car so that she could talk to Swift alone. Though the caravan was gone, he'd asked if they could walk for a while on the beach where Hannah had spent much of the past two months, the ancient ruins of Dunstanburgh Castle visible in the distance. Kate suspected that this remote headland was where he'd come to be alone with his memories of his daughter.

Kate had considered changing his hotel reservation to one in Embleton, a short distance away, a pleasant walk for those fit enough to make it. She discounted the idea. Hannah's murder would be on the minds of locals. Kate wouldn't want to risk the possibility of surrounding him with people talking openly about it.

She couldn't risk it.

As they walked, it began to snow again. Large flakes swirled on the wind, a magical sight that was incompatible with the ghastly reason that had brought them there. She'd like to think that the peaceful scene would remain with Swift when he returned home, not the image of a lifeless body in the morgue they had just come from.

Pulling up the collar of his overcoat, Swift slowed his pace, turning to face her. 'I didn't want to come north. In fact, I refused. Did your Met colleague tell you that?'

'No, she didn't mention it.'

'As Hannah's next of kin, I felt I had no choice.'

Kate was trying not to dwell on the fact that, in the eyes of the law, he did not fulfil that role. Despite his young age, Aaron was her nearest relative, the person who stood to inherit her estate.

Swift carried on talking. 'DS Thakur gave me reason to believe that I might regret it if I didn't come.' His gaze settled somewhere in the middle distance. 'Now I'm here, I think she was right. It's so beautiful, as was Hannah when, before . . .'

He couldn't say it.

'I'm so sorry for your loss,' Kate was finally able to say with confidence.

'You're very kind. Believe it or not, we were once insepar-able.' His bottom lip began to tremble, moist eyes locking on to Kate's. 'Though it pains me to say it, I lost Hannah a long time ago.'

Kate had an in and seized upon it. 'May I ask why?'

He hesitated. 'Do you happen to smoke?'

'Not often, I quit. But I always carry some for days like these.'

Wondering if he was trying to avoid the subject, Kate handed a new packet over and a lighter to go with it. Swift stopped walking, tore off the cellophane wrapper and took one out. Turning his back to the North Sea, shielding the flame in order to light it, he took the nicotine deep into his lungs. It seemed to calm him. He returned the packet, thanking her. Resisting the temptation to join him, Kate slipped them in her coat pocket.

The weather was getting worse. It was very nearly a whiteout now, the castle ruins like a ghostly shadow. The only sound was the waves crashing against the rocks below, sending sea-spray high into the air. Kate suggested they walk to the car before Hank sent out a search party.

They turned back.

'You would've liked Hannah,' Swift said, finally. 'She was smart. When she left university, there was no gap year, no aspiration to hang on to academia via a PhD. She went straight into business on her own. In five years, she'd built up a hugely successful global company, one of the fastest growing at the time.'

'What type?'

'One that began with me, I suppose . . .' For a moment, Swift stared out to sea, lost in his memories. Turning, he smiled at Kate. 'My work took us all over the world. By the age of five, Hannah could speak multiple languages fluently. As a family, we were invited to every corporate event imaginable: major golfing tours, World Cup football, horse racing and Formula One.'

'Perks of the job?'

'Exactly that. Hannah loved to travel. It was like a drug to her. It wasn't the celebrity lifestyle, more the cultural experience that attracted her. She studied geography and economics at Jesus College, Cambridge. The company she founded arranged personally designed packages to every sporting event imaginable, including tours and transportation, hospitality and exclusive, luxury accommodation. You name it, she could arrange it. She had a way with people, and they loved her.'

'You must've been very proud.'

He didn't answer.

Kate had heard the good bit. The downward spiral that led to Hannah's death was much harder for him to share. She gave him a gentle nudge. 'Peter, I can see how difficult this is for you to talk about, but I desperately need your help. I'm struggling to understand how Hannah got from there to here . . . and I must if I'm to catch the person responsible for her death.'

Swift didn't look at her as he spoke. 'You and Hannah have much in common. She was persuasive, a good communicator too. The last time I saw her was in 2009. In April of that year, she'd arrived home unexpectedly, asking for a bridging loan to tide her over. I hadn't seen her for ages. She'd been living the high life abroad. I saw quite a change in her.'

'In what way?'

'She was . . .' He paused, reaching for the right way to describe his daughter. 'Stressed out, I think is the current term. Totally out of character. Hannah was normally so full of life. Nothing fazed her. I should have known that something was terribly wrong. Deep down, I think I did, but she had big plans to expand her business and, stupidly, I put it down to pressure of work.'

'When she was living abroad, did she write?'

'Write? Who the hell does that these days?' Swift gave a half-smile. 'She'd text, occasionally she'd call.'

Kate had been hoping for a handwriting comparison with the note, the content of which she had no intention of sharing. The man had enough to cope with. Knowledge that his daughter had lived in constant fear would surely break him. When Kate found the perpetrator, it would come out in a subsequent trial, but that was for another day and she'd prepare him for it.

'Did you loan Hannah the money?'

'No. I gave her two hundred thousand.'

'Wow! That's generous.'

'I wanted her to have it. Though she didn't know, her mother had been diagnosed with cancer by then.' His eyes grew cold. 'The possibility of losing Marianne put a lot of things into perspective, wealth being one of them. As they say, you can't take it with you. Anyway, Hannah was an only child. She stood to inherit everything eventually. In June of that year, she returned home, begging for more. When I asked what it was for, or when she might repay me, she became evasive. When pressed, she said it was better I didn't know. As soon as it was out of her mouth, I could see she wanted to take it back. It was then I knew for sure that she was in some kind of trouble.'

Kate was doing the maths. Aaron was born in late February 2009 so he must have been four months old when she last saw her father. Was she trying to accumulate enough money to make a run for it, fearing for her own safety and that of her child?

'Did you discuss it further?' Kate asked.

'I tried . . . I told her that whatever it was could be fixed, that I'd front up the cash, on one condition—'

'Which was?'

'That she move in with us or go to our house in Bordeaux to sort herself out. Marianne is French. She inherited the property from her parents. It had lain empty for months while she was being treated. I told Hannah she'd be doing us a favour. She point-blank refused. We rowed. She left.'

'You didn't get to the bottom of it?'

Peter shook his head. 'When we didn't hear from her, Marianne and I became very concerned.'

'And yet neither of you reported her missing.'

'No. She was an adult. As I said, we'd argued. Realistically, what would the police have done?'

Kate didn't answer, though under the circumstances, she could've said 'very little'. She hadn't meant to sound judgemental – she was merely stating a fact – but commenting on his failure to report Hannah missing turned out to be the trigger for Swift to let go. As the relentless snow blew horizontally along the beach, the floodgates opened.

# 32

Carmichael left the archives office. It had taken her an hour to locate the file on Zoe Shepherd's road traffic accident. There was nothing in the paperwork to suggest that her friend hadn't been driving when it left the road and hit a tree. The thought depressed Lisa as she walked down the corridor heading for the incident room, her pace slowing as she passed Jo's office. She was alone in there, elbows on her desk, head in her hands, reading.

Carmichael walked on, then turned on her heel, retracing her steps.

She waited a beat and knocked gently on the door.

Looking up, Jo beckoned her in.

Lisa stepped inside. 'I'm not disturbing you, am I?'

'Yes, but you're a welcome distraction. I just made coffee. Help yourself.'

The detective sergeant did so, then sat down, a nod towards the handwritten note on Jo's desk. 'Still at it?'

'Don't remind me . . .' Jo took off her specs. Linking her hands together, she lifted them over her head and relaxed back in her chair, eyes on Lisa. 'I've been over and over it a million times trying to decide if I've missed anything. It's easy to read things into it that you think might be a hint. More difficult to interpret specifics. I have one or two ideas on what Hannah was trying to tell us. Have you seen Kate? I've been trying to call her.'

'I guess she's still with Swift. She'll have her phone off.'

'Of course, I'll catch her later.'

'I've not heard from Hank either. It's rare for one of them not to call in for an update, not that there's much to tell them at the moment. Hopefully, they've made more headway than we have. They left the morgue some time ago, I know that much. Hannah's dad made a positive ID.'

'Poor man. Is there something I can do for you, Lisa?'

'You already did.' Carmichael raised her coffee mug, both hands cupped around it. 'I just spent an hour and a half in the archives. No heating. No window on the world. The cells are more inviting.'

When Carmichael re-entered the MIR, Harry greeted her with a big smile on his face. The weather had changed and so had his mood since she'd gone to investigate the RTA that put Zoe Shepherd permanently in a wheelchair.

'What's going on?' Lisa said.

'You know Sandy Laing?'

'The court reporter?'

'Yeah. She just gave me an interesting tip-off.'

'About what?'

'Walker . . .' Harry made Carmichael wait, teasing her with the fact that he knew something she didn't. 'Lawyers are generally well-paid, but rumours have been circulating for months. It seems Walker has been living way above his means: taking time off, booking luxury holidays, buying up property, hiring high-class hookers. Apparently, his wife rarely sees him.'

'The guy's a snake. I'm surprised she hasn't left him.'

'According to Sandy, she's young enough to wait for a better offer. Why would she leave if he's rolling in his ill-gotten gains? The boss is right. He's on someone's payroll. He's the bridge between us and Hannah's killer, no doubt about it. If we could only nail who he's working for, we'd be sorted.'

'That's good intel, Harry. Shame we have no access to his bank account.'

'There'll be no audit trail. It'll be a cash-only deal.'

'Well, I hope the dodgy git gets what he deserves.'

'Keep the faith.'

'It's hard to do that when we're wading through treacle.'

'Shit morning?'

'You could say that. I've scanned months of newspaper ads looking for a cryptic clue from Hannah. There are none. The Met have spoken to her old neighbours. That led nowhere. She was pleasant, smart. "Kept herself to herself" was the consensus. And as far as Hank's theory on Shepherd goes, I just found out that he wasn't behind the wheel of the car that left his sister so horribly disabled.'

'I've lost count of those I've locked up for swapping places following an RTA.'

'So have I, but that's not the case this time. Emergency services were on the scene within minutes. The driver was trapped in the car and had to be cut free. He was hospitalised and later charged with driving under the influence of drugs and banned from driving for three years. Zoe sued for damages. Though the payout she received was substantial, it'll never compensate her for the extent of her catastrophic injuries.'

## 33

The hotel was situated in the heart of the city. Its once shabby interior had been transformed, having undergone a total refurb. The enforced closure had given the owner the time to increase its value threefold. Kate was impressed. It was money well-spent, turning a rundown boutique hotel into something quite special with clean lines and a contemporary feel. Hank knew someone who'd worked there and had chosen well.

Swift checked in at reception, collected his key and told Kate he'd freshen up and join her shortly in the bar. After identifying his daughter, he needed a stiff drink. So did Kate, though she didn't verbalise the thought and wouldn't have one while on duty. Well, she would, but not in these circumstances.

She watched him enter the lift before instructing the receptionist where to send his invoice. At the bar, she ordered a double espresso and took a seat near the fire. Her feet were frozen. She stared into the flames, deep in thought. Swift had painted a picture of his daughter that would aid the investigation, creating lines of enquiry that might lead to Aaron. Keen to update her team, Kate turned her phone back on, checking emails while she waited for him to return. Jo and Harry had both been trying to get in touch.

Jo had not left a voicemail.

Harry had – no detail, but his tone was upbeat.

Hoping for positive news, she called him.

He answered immediately, as if he'd been waiting for the phone to ring. 'DS Graham.'

'Harry, sorry I didn't pick up. After Swift identified Hannah at the morgue, he asked to visit the scene . . . yeah, I know, but he insisted. I think it helped. I hope it did. Listen, I'm at his hotel now. I might be tied up for some time but Hank's on his way to give you a hand. I was going to leave him here to do some male bonding, but Swift seems to have taken a shine to me. He's talking, so I'll stick with him.'

'So where is he?'

'Upstairs, dumping his bag. Make it quick.'

'We need round two with Walker. Thought you might like to handle it while you're out and about.'

'No can do, I don't have any wheels. Hank has mine. What's the story?'

'Well, it seems Walker's—'

Kate heard the lift ping its arrival. 'Hold on a second . . .'

She swung round just as Swift re-emerged, heading for the bar.

'Harry, it'll have to wait. Hank will sort it when he gets there. I'll call a cab and join you as soon as I'm done.' She disconnected, keen to resume her conversation with Hannah's father. He'd already filled in some blanks but she needed more from him. The name of the company Hannah had once owned would do for starters.

Swift scanned the room, looking for her.

She waved to attract his attention.

He moved towards her with what looked like a double whisky in his right hand. 'Apologies, I didn't see you. I thought you might have stepped out for a moment.' He put the drink down. 'Can I get you something?'

'I'd love one, but I have loads to do.'

He sat down facing her, awkward in her company, more than he had been initially. Kate suspected it was because he'd let go of his emotions on the beach. He struck her as a man who, under normal circumstances, would be in total control. From the short time they had spent together, Kate had formed the impression that he was more likely to take his grief home than wear it on his sleeve. Still, the situation was far from normal – and everyone had a breaking point.

'Peter, if I upset you earlier it was never my intention.'

'No need to apologise. It didn't even cross my mind. It was an obvious question. One I knew you were bound to ask. You're not the first person to raise an eyebrow because I never reported Hannah as a missing person.'

Kate liked this man. He was calm, polite and kind.

Unprompted, he began to talk. 'I fully expected her to land on my doorstep and confess all. I couldn't bring myself to involve the police. She was the CEO of a global enterprise. Doing brilliantly, by all accounts. Imagine the stigma if all was well and it became known that she was being treated like a teenage runaway. Families fall out sometimes. Name me one that hasn't.'

Kate nodded. She could relate.

'For around four years we kept tabs on her progress,' Swift added. 'She was often in the media, winning some award or other. She seemed perfectly happy, living her life, though Marianne saw through her smiles. My wife was in a bad way. I didn't know how long she had left and decided to look for Hannah before it was too late.'

Kate was nodding. This was breaking his heart.

'We went to her home, but she'd moved out. We'd lost track of her friends. Those her mother could remember hadn't heard from her either. I got nowhere. The following year, I engaged the services of a private eye to discreetly look into her affairs. If you need to verify that, talk to Alex.' He took a business card from his pocket and handed it over.

**Alex Hope: Collingwood Surveillance and Close Protection**

Kate noted a Greenwich address. 'This is him?'

'Her. She's ex-military intelligence, the best there is. I trust her implicitly. She's done corporate work for me over the years, at home and abroad. I had hoped she'd give me a handle on what Hannah was up to and advise me on what to do next. Sadly, despite her best efforts, that didn't happen.'

'Why not?'

'You can't follow someone you can't find. Hannah had been so careful to cover her tracks, it quickly became obvious that she didn't wish to be found. That's not to say I didn't worry about her. I did. So did her mother, every single day. Alex told us that Hannah had dropped out completely, cut all ties and moved house three times in the intervening years.' He paused, guilt flooding his face. 'If Hannah had been your daughter, I'm guessing you'd have done things differently.' His voice broke mid-sentence. 'I assure you, given another crack at it, so would I.'

Kate felt sorry for him. He'd made a fatal mistake. One he'd have to live with for the rest of his life. The raw anguish in his eyes was proof that he blamed himself for not making Hannah's disappearance a police matter. A parent's first duty is to protect a child. Age didn't come into it. Swift had failed miserably.

Kate had no inclination to rub it in.

'Property wasn't the only thing Hannah disposed of,' he added. 'At the end of 2015, she sold her business on, which worried me even more. The money went offshore, I know that much. I had a forensic accountant look into it. The trail went cold. If you've accrued enough money to live on, it is possible to disappear without trace, but you know that already. A change of name, bank accounts set up with a false ID and you're flying. As good as she is, Alex found sod all.'

Kate thought about that for a moment.

If Hannah had gone to such lengths to disappear, why had she given her real ID when arrested on a drugs charge? Was it a cry for help? A way of touching base with the authorities in case something happened to her – her only link to a past life? If she'd confided in Chalky that she was in danger, she might still be alive. He'd have helped her. God knows he'd tried, despite the risk to his reputation if she was ever re-arrested in possession of his private number. Kate mulled that over in her mind. Hannah could have called him at any time. So why hadn't she? Had JC found and destroyed that lifeline? Was it JC who'd masterminded her disappearance, obliterating all trace of her, confounding a seasoned pro like Alex Hope?

'What was the name of her former company?' Kate asked.

'Unique Sports Packages.'

'USP is a cracking acronym.'

'She was clever with words.'

Kate knew that from Hannah's note, which was still being analysed by Jo. Nothing could be gained from letting him see it. Father and daughter were estranged. Had been for years. If Kate shared the content with him, all he'd dwell on was Hannah's terror. That note was now an exhibit, damning evidence that would be made public when the perpetrator faced trial.

Swift had enough to cope with and Kate needed him to focus.

She asked: 'Would it be fair to say that Hannah's clients were mostly affluent?'

'Yes. Throughout university she canvassed high-profile figures with a view to getting them to endorse her service when it was up and running. She could pitch her business like a pro.'

'Any takers?'

'Many, including government ministers, pop stars, TV personalities and, of course, sportsmen and women. You name it, they were desperate to get on board . . .'

As Swift continued to talk, Kate tuned him out, a cold hand resting on her shoulder, a warning to pause for thought. Those at the top had the most to lose. Was JC one of Hannah's sponsors, one of her clients?

Swift's next sentence drew her back into the room.

'Hannah was paranoid that cyber criminals might access their details. When she first incorporated, she came to me for advice and took appropriate steps to protect her database. She knew what she was doing. By the time she was set to go live, her security rivalled any financial institution.'

'I don't doubt it, but we both know that online fraud costs

financial institutions billions globally. Cyber theft is big business. Just when we think our security is watertight, crooks find a way to breach it.'

'You're right, but they did not attack Hannah's business, if that's the prelude to a theory. The company was sold on for a tidy sum, more than even I thought it was worth. Check it out at Companies House.' Swift drained his glass and was silent for a long moment. 'I can accept that people want to disappear sometimes, especially if they're in trouble, but I've never understood why Hannah would turn her back on me and her mother. We adored her . . .' He cleared his throat. 'Marianne never saw her again and neither did I, until today.'

*Tell him.*

Kate hesitated, wishing she hadn't hogged the fire. She was burning up. 'Peter, you look exhausted. I'm sure you'd like some time alone, but I have questions and something to say that might shock and upset you. I can arrange a meeting room if you'd prefer to go somewhere more private.' She meant somewhere cool.

'Relax, there's nothing you can say now that will make matters worse.'

Kate wasn't convinced. Having lost a daughter, she wasn't sure how he'd feel about finding a grandson. She indicated his empty glass. 'Before we start, can I get you another?'

'No, just spit it out. I don't need Dutch courage or a private room.'

Kate didn't want to spook him, but he had a right to know. 'I have reason to believe that someone else may be in danger.'

A deep frown pinched his eyebrows together. 'I'm sorry, I don't understand.'

Kate leaned in. There was no way that she could drip-feed what she knew. She had to come right out with it. 'DS Thakur asked you whether Hannah had any children.'

'That's right.'

'I now have confirmation that she did. A boy, Aaron. He

was born in 2009.' She paused a moment, giving Peter time to digest the information. 'Hannah was living in the south of England then.'

'I've changed my mind. I will have that drink.'

Catching the eye of the bartender, directing her attention to Swift's glass. The girl gestured that she'd bring over a refill, then held up a coffee cup. Kate shook her head. When she turned to look at Hannah's father, he was wiping his face with both hands.

'Is the boy with his father?' he asked.

'I don't know.'

'Who is he?'

'I don't know that either. He wasn't named on the birth certificate.'

As they sat there in silence, staring at one another, Kate saw no anger, just unmitigated sadness. What Swift said next felled her emotionally. Marianne had once told him that the worst thing about dying was that she wouldn't live long enough to see grandchildren. The jury was still out on whether he would.

# 34

JC was untouched by the sentiment. If Marianne was such a sicknote, what possible use would she have been to a kid? Facing the wall, he kept his eyes trained on the mirrored tiles that gave him a good angle on the table Kate Daniels and Peter Swift were sitting at. Why the miserable faces? It wasn't as if either of them had met Aaron. In fact, he was the only one of the three who had.

His mobile lit up on the table.

Lowering the newspaper he was hiding behind, JC dragged it towards him, glancing at the screen: Jeffery McDougal, Stockbroker, a man he couldn't afford to ignore. He got up and wandered away until he was out of earshot. Daniels had heard his voice. He didn't expect that she'd have forgotten it.

'Jeffery, is this urgent? I'm with someone.' He was nothing of the kind.

The man had a US southern drawl. 'It is if you want to make a killing.'

JC glanced across the room at Daniels. 'Always.'

'Good, because the share price of your biggest competitor took an unexpected dive when the stock market opened this morning and is currently in a tailspin—'

'That's market forces for you.'

'Frankly, I'm staggered. The stock was moving up, gathering momentum, then it fell off a cliff. Rumours are circulating that the board of directors were trying to force through rapid growth and it's tipped the scales. This could be true or just a whispering campaign. No one seems to know where the information came from. Either way, investors are backing off.'

The thoughts in JC's head were louder than McDougal's.

The news wasn't unpredictable. It was well-planned. *His*

*doing.* Except the dealer didn't know that he'd lit a match and left nervous capitalists to fan the flames, neither would he ever suspect it. These kinds of transactions were best kept private They were not to be shared with the men and women who could legitimise his business dealings, those who would step up and swear on a bible that he was on the level.

McDougal was still talking. 'I take it your instructions remain the same.'

'One man's misfortune . . .' JC left the remainder of the sentence unsaid.

'Indeed. I'll keep you posted.' McDougal disconnected.

JC sat down, tuning into the conversation going on behind him. He'd never met Swift, though he'd heard a lot about him when he and Hannah first met. The man was a legend in her eyes, something JC had used to his advantage. Another opportunity to twist the virtual knife and make her more compliant. Hannah's estrangement from her father was his doing. He'd made it clear that if she didn't break all ties, if she didn't get in line, he'd carry out his threat to murder her parents. In one fell swoop, he'd broken her spirit and the bond that existed between father and doting daughter.

The man JC was looking at would blame her, not him.

A waitress approached Swift, delivering a Scotch on ice. She caught JC's reflection in the mirror tiles, hovered for a moment, then took a couple of steps towards him. 'Can I get you anything, sir?'

Her attention was unwelcome.

What she could do for him was get lost. Having just returned to his seat, he could hardly get up and walk away again, ignoring her. Unable to speak, he shook his head, his eyes travelling down her body in admiration, a wink as they completed the return journey. His actions could go two ways: she'd feel intimidated and take umbrage – he was, after all, old enough to be her father; or she'd respond positively to the hint at post-shift fun and extra cash. Either way, she'd sling her hook.

Glowering at him, she did just that.

Her loss.

He resumed earwigging the conversation between Daniels and Swift, though for the time being it had stalled. Grandpa was far from happy. He was giving the detective a hard time for no apparent reason. What the fuck was wrong with him? He'd lost one and gained one. As far as JC was concerned, he was quits. He felt like tapping the ungrateful bastard on the shoulder, telling him to get a grip.

JC knew what was coming . . .

The good detective would defend her victim, her sole purpose in life.

Swift: 'Why in God's name would she keep Aaron a secret from us?'

Daniels: 'To protect you and Aaron, I suspect.'

*Tick.*

Swift: 'Against what?'

Daniels: 'Not what, who—'

*Tick.*

Swift: 'You're saying the boy could be in danger?'

Daniels: 'That's exactly what I'm saying.'

*Tick.*

JC had to hand it to the DCI. She appeared to have her finger on the pulse of this murder investigation. Pity she didn't have a clue that he was listening to every word. Plan A was working. Hiding in plain sight was his favourite game. In a few minutes' time, he'd have what he came for and be on his way.

Swift: 'Forgive me for saying so, but if the boy is in danger, that's down to Hannah. She could have told me. Should have. I'd have moved mountains to help. Instead, she ran away, breaking her mother's heart and mine. You can dress it up as much as you like but I'll never forgive her for that. She didn't care about us.'

Daniels: 'You're wrong.'

Swift: 'You can't possibly know that.'

Daniels: 'Nor, with respect, can you. Why name the boy after you if she didn't care?'

Swift: 'What?'

He was taken aback by that, no more so than JC.

One to add to the long list of things Hannah hadn't shared with him.

Daniels: 'Aaron's middle name is Peter. Look, I'm going to level with you. At this moment in time, I have no idea where he is. I'm hoping you might help locate him.'

Swift: 'How? Until a few minutes ago, I didn't even know he existed.'

As Daniels studied him, JC studied her. She had an intense look on her face, pleading with Hannah's father to help her find the boy before *he* did, though she had the good sense not to use his initials.

JC stifled a grin.

Why would he care? They weren't real. Just a little joke between him and Walker. Any minute now, she'd ask the question that would deliver Aaron on a plate without his old man having to lift a finger.

JC was almost home and hosed.

Daniels: 'Are there relatives that might have taken him in?'

Swift: 'No.'

Frustrated, JC almost slammed his fist down on the table. C'mon, you idiot. Think! Swift was shaking his head, an expression that suggested the question was laughable. JC held his breath, waiting for the detective to give him a shove. She didn't disappoint.

Daniels: 'There must have been someone Hannah was particularly attached to growing up.'

Swift: 'Plenty. I told you, she was very popular. Everyone loved her, friends and family. There's not one among them who wasn't as shocked as we were that she'd lost contact, but I can't think of one who'd collude in such a contemptible deception and keep it from Marianne and me.'

JC glared at Swift's reflection in the mirror, urging him to do better, urging her to carry on with this line of questioning until he came up with an answer. JC needed that information. Not next week or next month. He needed it now. Finally, Daniels upped the ante, keeping her voice low and level, her eyes on the prize.

Daniels: 'I can't go into detail, but I have reason to believe that Hannah was involved with someone who took advantage of her, someone she was trying desperately to get away from. If I could have kept this from you, believe me I would, but this man is dangerous and I'm in a race against time to find him.'

JC chuckled to himself: *Over here*.

Daniels: 'Will you at least give it some thought?'

A nod was all the answer Swift gave.

No! This was Daniels' fault. The stupid cow was treading too gently, dancing round him like he might break. She wasn't there to hold his hand. She was there to squeeze information out of him. In her case, metaphorically speaking. In JC's, well, he was happy for her to do the squeezing. Only he could see that she was done. He'd heard enough. Like Hannah, the detective hadn't lived up to expectations. She'd disappointed him, failing to utilise her brain and bleed the fucker dry. Well, if she wouldn't, JC would take it from here.

# 35

The minute Hank got to base, Harry collared him, sharing the tip-off he'd received regarding the exponential growth of a certain lawyer's lifestyle in comparison with his estimated average earnings. It had been a long and stressful day. Hank was in the right frame of mind to have a go at someone. Anyone would do. The fact that Walker had been lined up as the target of his frustration was an added bonus. By the time Hank had finished conning him into thinking that he'd been, and still was, under surveillance, the obnoxious prick would be forced to slam on the brakes. His spending spree would be over until the heat died down.

*That would wipe the supercilious smile off his face.*

Grabbing a coffee, Hank checked the murder wall for updates, then used Kate's office to make a call, finding out that Walker was defending a well-known villain in court, but that the case had unexpectedly been adjourned and would resume tomorrow at 10 a.m.

The detective's luck was in.

Hank dialled out on the landline, waiting as it rang out, lifting his feet onto Kate's desk. He took them down again as Carmichael tapped lightly on the open door, then entered, a gloomy expression on her face.

'Eurgh!' He put the phone on mute and looked past her. 'What have you done with Lisa? You know: young lass, big smile, loadsa cheek—'

'She bunked off . . .' Carmichael slumped down in the chair opposite, thoroughly fed up. 'Or would have if she'd had the opportunity.'

'Rough day?'

'I've had better. I've been kicking my heels with nowt to do but wait for others to get back to me.'

'You'll get no sympathy from me. I've been driving Miss Crazy all day.'

The hint of a smile from Carmichael, a nod toward the phone. 'Either they're not in or they know it's you.'

A woman's voice hit Hank's ear. 'Prentice, Lavelle & Walker.'

Hank drew a finger to his lips to silence Lisa, before unmuting the phone and putting it on speaker so she could listen in. 'Oh, good afternoon,' he said. 'My name is Joseph. I tried catching Mr Walker before his case folded. In relation to his other case, could you let him know that the judge in Court 4 signed a bench warrant for his non-attender, Ms Charlotte Elisa Marshall.'

'That case wasn't listed for today. Hold the line please . . .'

Hank covered the handset. 'Works every time.'

Lisa was grinning like a loon, her mood lifted by his subterfuge. 'Where d'you get the name from?'

'That's for me to know and you to find out.'

The line clicked and the female said, 'Joseph, I think you've got your wires crossed. I just spoke with Mr Walker. Ms Marshall's case has already been dealt with.'

'Really? That's not my understanding.'

'Well, take my word for it and check your facts next time.'

The line went dead.

'Friendly,' Lisa said.

'See my problem? I'd never get past the Rottweiler on reception.'

'No, but I might—'

'And spoil my fun? What do you think the chances are? Besides, in your current mood I doubt that. I'll bypass the guard dog and catch Walker as he leaves the office.'

'Can I at least tag along?'

'It's not a job for two.'

'Oh, go on.'

'Nope.'

She tipped her head back, eyes fixed to the ceiling. 'I'll die of boredom if I don't get out of here soon.'

'Aren't you up to your eyes in Hannah's social media?'

'That's part of the problem. Without more background information I'm totally screwed. Any idea how the boss is doing with Swift?'

'I guess he must be playing ball. She wouldn't hang around if he wasn't.'

'Will she be here for the six o'clock briefing? Will you?'

Hank nodded. 'But you'll need to spread the word. Kate wants the whole squad here. No excuses.' He hauled himself out of his chair, shrugging on his coat, checking his pocket for car keys. 'I'll leave it with you then. And you'd better be wearing that smile when I return or there'll be trouble.'

# 36

As days go, this one had been short but lousy, one step forward, three back – and some. Not to worry, Walker thought. If the juror who'd thrown a wobbler today wasn't in tomorrow, the trial would continue without further delay. The presiding judge would rule on it. Come to think of it, the absence of that particular juror might turn the case on its head. Walker didn't like her sour face. She was far too conservative for his liking, the type who'd convict a man because he was wearing the wrong expression, the type who'd rock the boat during deliberations trying to sway others to her point of view. Walker didn't give a shit if the case was settled by unanimous or majority verdict, so long as his client walked.

He left his office, turning left out of Milburn House, heading up the steep hill on Dean Street. His vehicle was sitting in its pre-paid designated parking spot on the top floor of the multistorey car park. He considered his trek up there as his daily exercise. Who was he kidding? He was out of shape and short of breath by the time he arrived at the top of the concrete stairwell.

It took him a moment or two to recover.

The temperature was sub-zero, the air rank with the stench of gallons and gallons of beer-laden piss. Keen to avoid the rush of late-night shoppers and those heading to the city's restaurants, theatres and bars, he took off in the direction of his car, then stopped suddenly, with the distinct impression that he was not alone.

Walker turned, racing toward his vehicle, grabbing his keys from his pocket, pointing the fob at the car with urgency. He pushed the button once, twice. Nothing happened. He was too far away. He tried again. The doors clunked open and the lights flashed once. He blew out a breath, finally heading for a place of safety, a glance over his shoulder.

No one there.

He swore loudly, cursing himself for being stupid. From an early age, he'd possessed an overactive imagination, scaring himself to death at the slightest thing, but you could never be too careful when you worked with criminals. In an instant, any one of them might take offence or go overboard at something he said or didn't say in the course of their defence.

Oversensitivity was a common trait among the guilty.

One particular individual sprung to mind. JC was switched wrong. He wouldn't fit the legal definition of a psychopath, but he wasn't far off. He was unpredictable and volatile, with a temper on him that was something to behold. More often than not, there was no trigger for his mood change; he went from calm to frenzied without warning and for no apparent reason.

Thinking about that shook Walker to the core.

Telling himself to stop being paranoid, he pulled up sharp, then listening to the squealing of wheels as they ascended the ramp onto the floor below, and the booming bass of a car radio, its volume up too loud. Doors opening. Doors slamming. Male voices talking in hushed tones. The unmistakable smell of nicotine.

He couldn't work out if that meant safety in numbers or a greater threat.

Unwilling to wait around to find out, he fumbled with the car door. The locks were open, but the handle wouldn't move. It was frozen solid. Panic rising, he pulled and pulled, and still it wouldn't budge. It was then that a figure emerged from the shadows. Like an old-fashioned, B movie character, it didn't move an inch. All Walker could see was a powerfully built silhouette.

Nothing more.

If this was an attempt at intimidation it was working.

Unable to make out who it was, Walker backed away with a

glance over the edge of the concrete railing. It was a long way down. In that moment, a plan formed in his head. He would end his association with JC, though this was neither the time nor the place to do it. Tomorrow. He'd do it tomorrow from the safety of his office.

Walker relaxed, thoughts of being free calming him. He too had friends in high places. JC wasn't the only powerful man in town. What could he possibly do? If he touched one hair on the head of someone in the legal profession it would be counterproductive, attracting the kind of attention he was trying so hard to avoid. For too long, Walker had shown deference. JC didn't deserve it – and wouldn't get it from now on. The thought died in Walker's head as he recalled the last time they had spoken: *Keep your fucking mouth shut or there'll be consequences. Do not fail me.* When he looked again, the figure was gone.

# 37

Kate faced the team with renewed enthusiasm even though the briefing was set to be a lengthy affair. Her day had consisted of a fruitless trip to the Intelligence Unit, a distressing airport pickup, a grim task at the morgue, a visit to the crime scene with a bereaved family member, then to Swift's hotel to deliver a heartbreaking revelation. Despite all this, she no longer felt jaded. This morning the MIT had little to go on. This evening they were flying.

The amount of background information supplied by Hannah's father about her education, the business she once owned and her personal life prior to 2009 was everything Kate had hoped for and more. Having shared it with the team, she began issuing instructions, raising actions in order of priority.

While she spoke, Carmichael entered the most salient points into her computer keyboard, including the name of Hannah's former company, a contact at her Cambridge college and the address of her late mother's home in France, all of which popped up on screen as she typed. By the time she'd finished, the electronic murder wall was in better shape than it had been twelve hours ago.

She stopped typing. 'All done, boss.'

'Great, let's crack on then. That note you left me yesterday. How certain are you that Hannah's landlord won't big himself up by claiming we failed to protect one of his tenants?'

'Very. I told him that it would be counterproductive for him to speak out should the press learn that his entire portfolio is made up of properties that are unsafe places for women to live in.'

'Nice one.' Kate scanned the faces of those assembled. 'The next few days are crucial. Your efforts could save the life of a kid. It's that simple.' A pause underlined the seriousness of her words. 'I'm convinced that during the period 2008 to 2009 – perhaps when Hannah was living abroad – we'll find the link to her killer. That's when her life changed, when she changed, according to her father. That's when Hannah met her tormentor. I'm relying on you to find and apprehend him.'

Looking around the room, it was clear that her words had hit home. Every single face was solemn, their eyes filled with conviction. This is what they were good at. They would not let her down. 'Before we knock off for the day, is there anything you want to raise that we've not yet covered?'

'I have a question.' Jo's hand was in the air.

Kate was intrigued. Whatever she was about to say was important for the team to hear, otherwise she'd have discussed it at home over dinner. 'The floor is yours.'

'Was there a key on O'Brien's inventory?' she asked.

'Only for the caravan. Why?'

'Hannah's note is driving me insane. She writes, quote "I'm in no doubt that you'll find the key to what went on here" unquote. We all know that finding the key to anything is a common enough phrase but, my question to you all is, should we discount it on that basis when it could equally be a subtle hint that she left a key for us to find? I'm sorry, guys, I don't want to keep you, but it's been lingering in my mind all day.'

'Don't be daft, you're right to query it.' It was the first time Hank had spoken. He'd arrived a few minutes late for the briefing. With every chair taken, he was standing in the entrance to Kate's office, his right shoulder leaning against the door jamb, feet crossed at the ankles, hands thrust into his pockets.

'Hank's right,' Kate said. 'With Aaron's life at stake, we need to question everything . . . and I mean everything. We know the van was searched, Hannah's possessions removed. Whoever did that was looking for something. We have no idea what it was, or if it was found. In my opinion, Hannah was too smart to leave incriminating evidence on her computer or her mobile phone for someone to steal—'

Brown cut her off. 'Guv, if that's true, why delay the search for her son by leaving such a cryptic note?'

'Because if she'd written down anything specific, including where to find him, Aaron would already be dead. Hannah had the sense to realise that the likelihood of the note falling into the wrong hands was high. As we've already discussed, she was trying to communicate with us and may have used other ways of doing that, in the press and online. Now that Lisa has her magic keywords, she's confident that she'll track down her social media accounts.'

'I'll do my best . . .' Carmichael turned to look at Jo, a thoughtful expression on her face. 'Jo, please don't think I'm rubbishing your idea, but when you were speaking it occurred to me that Hannah might already have given us a key in the metaphorical sense by pleading with us to find Aaron. Might that also be a signpost? Perhaps he's the one in possession of the incriminating evidence we suspect the killer was trying to find.'

'Good thinking,' Jo said. 'If that's the case, we can only pray that he's as resourceful as his mum. But I still think there might be a physical key we've yet to find. Surely it's worth another look. I'm not talking about the caravan – far be it from me to suggest that crime scene investigators haven't done their jobs properly—'

'It's happened before,' someone muttered.

'Not on O'Brien's watch,' Kate said in his defence.

'I was thinking more of the surrounding area.' Jo's eyes landed on Kate. 'Kate, this is not an either or situation. My theory and Lisa's could carry equal weight. There is a physical key or Aaron is holding vital information, in which case we need to get a shift on. Collectively, we'd never forgive ourselves if anything happened to him and it turned out that we'd over-looked something that might have prevented it.'

Kate took a moment to consider all that had been said.

Jo and Lisa trusted their instincts.

Kate trusted them.

# 38

The MIT were restless for home. It was getting on, ten to eight showing on the wall clock behind them. It might be a complete waste of time setting so much store on one or two words of Hannah's note, but Kate was taking no chances. Applying solid logic, Jo had made a good case for pursuing a course of action that simply couldn't be ignored. Lisa's idea was also valid. The team were in agreement. A further look around the scene was worth a shot, for more reasons than one, in Kate's opinion.

'Harry, don't bother the search unit. Put the action down to me and Hank.'

'Why?'

'Since when do I need to justify my decisions? I asked nicely. Will that do?'

The DS put his hands in the air, backing off. His expression was sullen and Kate knew why. After reprimanding him for having a go at Maxwell in public, she'd done the very same to him, setting a lousy example. There had been a definite edge to her tone, though she'd stopped short of saying *because I said so*. She could let him sulk but his role was pivotal. She needed him onside.

She climbed down, explained her rationale. 'They didn't find a key on first inspection. I'm not saying we'll do any better, but you know as well as I do that it's not beyond a savvy offender to keep a close eye on a crime scene to see the comings and goings of a Murder Investigation Team.'

'Fair enough.'

'Good. Today, we were able to fill in the missing blanks of Hannah's life. We now have a number of lines of enquiry to follow. We're finally getting somewhere. I don't want to jeopardise that by drawing unwelcome attention to the campsite if it holds vital evidence or the key to it. Sending a PolSA crew up there for a second search will flag up the fact that there's something still to be found, evidence we don't yet have in our possession. Shepherd's place is by no means secure. We have no personnel to guard the perimeter round the clock.'

Harry nodded his understanding.

'Besides,' Kate said. 'Hank and I are heading there tomorrow.'

'Are we?' Hank grimaced. 'I was hoping to hop on a plane to Bordeaux.'

'In your dreams,' she said. 'If anyone is going there, it'll be me. That's what rank is for.' Everyone laughed, including Harry. Kate had won him over. 'For now, we concentrate our efforts locally. I'd like to see if the Shepherds remember anything they didn't tell us the last time we spoke to them. Hank and I will take a look while we're up there. Jo, would you like to come along? You've not been to the site. A clean pair of eyes might be useful. Cops don't always get it right. You'll bring a different perspective.'

'Sure, if you think it'll help.' Jo didn't often attend crime scenes.

'OK, let's wrap it up. Go home and tuck your kids in. I want you all in here early doors.'

As the team disbanded, Hank grabbed his coat and wandered over to join her. 'Sorry I was late.'

'Harry told me where you were. Anything to report on Walker?'

'He got the message.'

# 39

Kate looked sideways. Across the room, Carmichael and Brown had their heads together, arranging a quick drink at a local pub. Neither had family ties. Just then, Andy's mobile rang in his hand. His mildly irritated expression altered when he viewed the home screen. He said something to Lisa. Intrigued, she shuffled closer as he answered the call and held the device between them. They both listened. Thirty seconds later, Andy hung up. He stared at the phone, before glancing in Kate's direction.

'Fuck!' she said under her breath. 'There goes my dinner – and yours, if I'm not mistaken.'

Hank called out. 'Did you have to answer the damn phone, Andy?'

'The house-to-house team found a witness, Sarge.' Reacting to the exchange, the majority of the team hung back. Coats were on, but no one moved. 'Her name is Gemma Munro. She owns a café in Craster. She recognised Hannah when uniforms were doing their rounds with her photograph. The duty sergeant had the foresight to secure CCTV, inside and out, though the tapes only cover a week or so. Munro changes them over every weekend, though she has been known to forget.' He held up his phone. 'I have them here. Want me to upload them?'

'No, you get off. Forward them to me. I'll take a look . . .' Kate glanced at Hank, his coat half on. She didn't need to spell out how significant the next few hours might be. This was one witness, one sighting, but if they could pin down Hannah's movements in the days leading up to her death, it would push them closer to a resolution of the case. 'You OK to stay on for a bit?'

'Can I get takeaway?'

Kate made a face. 'Must you?'

'I'll drop if I don't eat soon.'

'Be quick then. The rest of you stand down.'

Hank and the MIT were gone before she had time to change her mind.

Kate walked into her office.

Jo dragged her coat off her chair and followed her in, giving her a pointed look as she walked through the door. 'Did it not occur to you that Hank might have had plans for the evening, what's left of it? You could have asked me to stay.'

Kate sat down. 'It's fine. Julie's out tonight and so is Ryan.'

'You make it sound like you're doing him a favour.'

'You know Hank. He'll do anything for a bucket of noodles.'

'OK, if I'm not required, I'll be off then.' Slipping her arms into her coat, Jo wrapped a plaid blanket scarf around her neck, tucking it in. 'I'll think of you when I'm in a hot bubble bath with a pink gin.' Checking that the incident room was truly empty, she gave Kate a peck on the cheek before heading for the door. Without looking round, she called out. 'I won't wait up.'

'Fine,' Kate called after her. 'Make sure you lock up.'

'Yes, Mum.'

'Jo, wait!' Kate's internal phone rang. It was Bright, asking for an update. When she looked up, the profiler was already gone.

# 40

'Can I call you back, guv? I'm tied up at the minute. House-to-house found a witness and I need to follow it up . . . No, it's too late to drive up there now. She lives and works in Craster. I have CCTV. Hank and I are about to watch it—'

'What are you really doing?'

'Guv?'

'Never mind,' Bright said. 'I'd rather not know. Keep me posted.'

He rang off.

Keen to catch Jo before she left the building, Kate raced from her office, through the incident room and down the stairs, two at a time. Witnessing her urgency, two uniformed officers coming the other way parted to let her through. She called out her thanks, crashing through the back door and out into the frozen car park at the rear of the building. Out of breath, she stopped dead, scanning the area. A number of vehicles were queued up at the exit barrier creating clouds of visible vapour from hot exhausts as they warmed up in the freezing air.

None of the waiting cars belonged to Jo.

Just when Kate thought she'd missed her, headlights were switched on near the perimeter fence. Jo's Land Rover Discovery was parked next to her own vehicle. In her panic to get down there, Kate had forgotten that. Raising a hand to an approaching police vehicle, Kate dodged between two cars, arriving at the driver's side of Jo's four-by-four seconds later. She was breathing heavily, exhaling white clouds of her own.

The window slowly opened. 'Are you insane?' Jo glanced at the temperature gauge. 'It's minus five.'

'I need to talk to you.'

Jo splayed gloved hands. 'I have a phone.'

'It wasn't appropriate.'

'Well, if a call won't do, get in. You'll catch your death.'

Kate didn't argue.

Standing out there in a thin shirt was likely to invite a bout of pneumonia. She ran round to the passenger side and climbed in, grateful that the car had warmed up while Jo scraped ice from the windscreen. Kate was suddenly all choked up, moved by the music coming through the speakers. Like Lady Gaga, she couldn't find the words.

Jo silenced Spotify. 'Kate, what's wrong?'

For a long moment, she kept her eyes front, staring at the defrosting windscreen, before swivelling in her seat to face Jo. 'I wasn't joking when I asked you to lock the doors when you get home. I want you to deadlock them, windows too.' When pressed for a reason, Kate made light of it, pointing out the damage to her Audi. 'If there are undesirables hanging around, it's better to be safe than sorry. There's been a few break-ins lately.'

'Thanks for the bedtime story but I'm under no illusions as to who might come calling. I'll be fine, Kate. I have Nelson—'

'Oh, c'mon. What's he going to do? Lick an intruder to death?'

Jo laughed.

'Don't you dare make light of it.'

'You said it!'

'To demonstrate that he won't be able to protect you against a dangerous and unstable maniac. Look, I have no proof that we're a target, but we must assume that we might be. When dealing with people like JC, cops can never be too careful, nor can anyone associated with them.'

'I'm not just anyone.'

'No, you're not. You mean the world to me, which is why—'

'Kate, did you forget that I'm a pro too?'

'No,' Kate took her hand, squeezing it gently. 'I just worry about you . . .'

'Relax. I heard you the first time. I made light of it upstairs because I didn't want you to worry the team or do this.'

'Do what?'

'This!' Jo's eyes flashed in the darkness. 'Worrying on my behalf isn't helping you do what's required. We have no idea what JC is up to, but neither do we know what might happen to either of us on any day we're on duty. That's the truth of it. It's what we both signed up for. You can't protect me either, so please stop trying. It'll drain your energy and wreck your concentration. Get your arse in there and do your job. I'll be vigilant, I promise.'

# 41

Kate watched Jo drive off in the dark, trusting her to take the necessary precautions, feeling only slightly more confident now that she'd hammered home the message to take care. It wasn't as if the house was vulnerable. They were security conscious, with a state-of-the-art alarm fitted. Even so, her mind wouldn't rest completely.

Back in her office, Kate made coffee and sat down at her desk, wishing that she too was on her way home. Sliding her ID card into a slot on her desktop, she logged on, accessing her inbox, clicking the first of two emails Brown had forwarded from the house-to-house team, the one that included two attachments: interior and exterior CCTV footage.

The sender was Sergeant Laurence Wood, an officer she didn't know but took an instant shine to. He'd had the sense to indicate the time Hannah Swift had entered Munro's café on her last visit – arriving at 12:10 and leaving at 13:45 – saving Kate the bother of trawling through a whole day's footage to find her.

Clicking on the interior link, Kate fast-forwarded to the relevant section, feeling tense. Observing any victim alive when you'd already seen them lifeless always produced a strange sensation, an emotional pull she couldn't quite explain, even to herself. The bond between the living and the dead seemed all the more poignant in this investigation.

Hannah had made sure of it.

As the counter skipped forward, Kate was in that grim caravan, reading Hannah's note, the last line urging her to find Aaron. It underlined the fact that since Kate and Jo had moved in together, she'd inherited a ready-made family. Like Hannah, Kate now had reasons to be fearful. It was one thing being responsible for your own fate. Having to consider the safety of others was a different thing entirely.

Jo was in her head again.

Overlaid on that image were handwritten warnings that began to scroll before Kate's eyes like movie credits. They seemed to radiate, drawing her attention, before fading away, only to be replaced by another and another, all from Hannah's note: I'm begging you ... take care ... If you go after him, he'll come for you ... watch your back. The thought of Jo heading home alone was scary.

Kate was relieved when Hank entered, though the aroma of his Chinese carry-out made her even more nauseous. She could hardly complain that he wanted to eat. Refreshment breaks hadn't been on the agenda all day. It was unreasonable to expect him to work late on an empty tank, though knowing his eating habits, he'd have been grazing at every opportunity.

Dragging a chair towards her desk, he sat down so they could watch the CCTV together. 'What did I miss?'

'Not much. You eat, I'll talk.' She didn't have to persuade him. He attacked his carry-out like the last meal of a condemned prisoner. 'Wood's email is quite detailed. He spoke to Munro personally. According to her, Hannah was a regular customer. She went into the café most days, except Fridays, always between twelve and two.'

'Corroborating Shepherd's statement.'

Kate gave a nod. 'She definitely followed a routine. Craster is minutes from the campsite by car, not much further on foot if she'd used the beach to get to there.'

'I hope she enjoyed those walks.'

Kate's heart missed a beat. She shared the sentiment but couldn't look at him. It was a toss-up to see which one of the so-called murder squad elite was the biggest softie underneath. She was grateful that Hank was there with her. Late at night, when the lights were dimmed and everyone had scarpered, the Major Incident Suite felt eerie with the ghosts of victims, past and present, wandering around. She didn't believe in the spirit world. It was just memories playing tricks with her psyche.

Hank picked up on her unease. 'What did I really miss?'

'What do you mean?'

'We're alone now, Kate.' He looked over his shoulder to check through her office door. 'The coast is clear. No need to pretend. I want the truth this time.'

'Nothing . . . OK, if you must know, I'm worried about Jo.'

'I'm worried about you.'

Kate said nothing.

'What about her?' he asked.

'I gave her the benefit of my wisdom before she left. Told her to lock herself in and not open the doors.'

'You did right to warn her.'

'She brushed it off, but I could tell it scared her.'

'Your security is good, isn't it?'

'No system is unassailable, Hank.'

# 42

Jo knew that Kate and Hank would be hard at it but texted Kate to put her mind at rest. **Home. Doors locked. See you later. x** Jo shivered. It was freezing in the living room. Too late to light the fire. No point doing so with Kate still out. Pouring herself two fingers of gin, adding a splash of tonic and a slice of lime, she took it to the kitchen at the rear of the house, popped an ice cube into it and sat down in the chair closest to the Aga, a constant source of heat at any time of year.

Nelson opened one eye and closed it again. He had the right idea. He'd dragged his bed so close to the oven, it was almost touching. Jo checked her phone. An email had pinged in as she arrived home. Keen to get inside and shut the door, she'd ignored it. She opened it now. It was from a close contact who worked for Women's Aid. She was halfway through reading it when her phone rang in her hand. She answered without checking the screen.

'Hello?'

'Mum . . .' was all she heard.

'Tom? Is that you?'

'Yes . . . Take the phone away from your ear.' He raised his voice in case she hadn't heard. 'Did you get that? We're on Facetime.'

Feeling like an idiot, Jo looked at the phone. Tom was on screen, laughing. She hated Facetime, Zoom and Skype, which he was well aware of. That made her instantly suspicious. 'Did Kate put you up to this?'

'What? No, why would she?' He couldn't lie to save his life.

Now she knew why they were on a videocall and not plain old-fashioned audio. Seemingly, Kate required proof, even in her private life, but it was good to talk to someone, other than the detectives Jo worked with. It had been a rough couple of days at Middle Earth. Morale was flagging due to lack of progress, though it was set to improve – at least, she hoped it would.

The horrific murder of Hannah Swift was taking its toll on everyone.

Pushing that thought away, she smiled at her son.

It had been a while since she'd touched base with him at his Tyneside flat in Heaton, in what was ostensibly a lad's pad, all he could afford when he bought it. Kate and Jo had asked him to move in with them, but he was happy in his own space and fiercely independent. Working freelance suited his lifestyle. He didn't have to adhere to anyone's clock but his own.

*Heaven.*

'Isn't Kate home?' he asked innocently.

Jo played along. 'Not yet, no.'

'You still working?'

'No, I'm done for the day, but you look swamped.'

Tom was at his desk, the whiteboard behind him covered with concepts and Post-it notes associated with a busy IT professional, including a list of recommendations on software. To help him focus, the idea of organising big contracts with visual cues had come from Kate and her murder wall.

He adored her.

'I'm just about to log off too,' he said. 'I'm knackered. That client I mentioned keeps changing his brief. Still . . .' He yawned. 'He's paying me shedloads. I have no complaints.' He drew a can of BrewDog to his mouth, took a swig and left his desk, heading for a comfy chair. Jo knew it faced the screen of a huge smart TV, his own private cinema. Since he was a kid, he'd always loved the movies. 'By the way, Mum, tell Kate, dinner's on me when I'm done.'

'We'd love that.'

'Yeah, you can come too if you like. May as well, given that you're joined at the hip.'

Jo smiled, wishing that was the case. She didn't jump when

the doorbell rang. It was Nelson growling that put the wind up her.

'Hey,' Tom said. 'What's wrong?'

'Nothing,' she lied. 'I'm just worn out.'

'Mum, you're acting weird. Is that someone at the door?'

She glanced towards the closed kitchen door, her turn to bluff. 'Just Kate, darling. She'll have forgotten her key again.' She stood up. 'Better let her in before she breaks the door down. I'll call you tomorrow.'

'Night, Mum.'

Disconnecting, Jo turned off the kitchen light, pulling the door ajar so she could see along the hallway. Dogs were as susceptible to danger as humans. Some would turn and run, others would stand their ground. Fight or flight was the universal reaction of all beings. Nelson leapt from his basket, rushing past her before she could prevent him from doing so, barking at the indistinct shadow standing outside. Whoever was there, it wasn't Kate.

## 43

Kate had been worrying unnecessarily because Jo had insight into her world. Unlike a member of the public, with no real clue how stretched the police were, the profiler was aware that response times were down, that officers were so thin on the ground she could scream all night and no one would come running. Knowing that she might get the shit kicked out of her – or end up like Hannah while waiting for the emergency services to arrive – was terrifying. She replied to Jo's text with a smiley face: ☺

With Jo safe at home, Kate put the device on silent mode and was finally able to focus. In view of the time, Hank agreed that they should concentrate their efforts on the date of Hannah's death when she was inside the café, as highlighted in Wood's email. What went on before and after was equally, if not more important, as it had the potential to pinpoint specific times and locations when the victim was last seen alive, an update on the information gathered from Jack and Peggy Shepherd. But that relied upon the presence of CCTV, public or private, which in a tiny fishing village like Craster could not be guaranteed.

As well as the time of day, the on-screen display showed the date in the bottom right-hand corner. Keeping a close eye on the counter, Kate stopped the video a few seconds before Hannah walked through the door.

She took a deep breath. 'Ready?'

'As I'll ever be.' Hank stopped chewing, the hand holding the chopsticks freezing in mid-air. He pointed at the remainder of his meal. 'Mind if I finish this while we work?'

'Go ahead.' She pressed play.

Due to the ambient lighting conditions, the video was better quality than either detective expected. Watching Hannah made the hair on Kate's head stand to attention, tightening her scalp, sending a chill right through her. Munro wasn't wrong. Though Hannah's hair was longer than in the photograph supplied by her father – the only image available for use as a comparison, other than the one taken at the time of her arrest – it was undeniably her.

Kate's hands felt clammy. She didn't dare look at Hank. He'd clock her emotional reaction immediately. She was transfixed, watching Hannah choose a table away from the window with a view of the door and the street beyond, a good move for a woman in fear for her life.

Slipping her arms out of her backpack, she placed it on the table.

Kate paused the tape, rewound slightly, paused it again and zoomed in. 'Make a note of her bag. It wasn't on O'Brien's inventory. I'd like it traced.'

'Good luck with that.' Hank listed the item, adding the time beside it for future reference.

They studied the image closely. The backpack was entirely black with a flap over the front that spanned the whole width of it. There was a small light-coloured strip in the centre near the bottom.

Kate zoomed in on the brand name: MOLESKINE.

Smiling at Hank, again she pressed play.

On screen, Hannah took off her coat and hung it on the seat opposite, something Kate had done a million times when she wanted privacy, to give the impression that the seat was already taken. As they watched, Hank drew her attention to other customers in the café. There were only two, both women, neither of whom was paying Hannah any attention. Without prompting, he took a photograph of the screen and made a note on his pad to raise an action to trace them.

At this time of year, with any luck, they'd be local.

A third woman Kate assumed was Gemma Munro or one of

191

her staff walked into shot, approaching Hannah's table. They spoke briefly, then she disappeared as quickly as she'd arrived. Hannah sat down, only her left side visible to the CCTV mounted high above her head. She opened her bag and slid a space grey laptop out of it, together with a notepad, a pen and a mobile. She lined the items up, very precisely, as if they were exhibits being shown to a judge and jury.

Perhaps they were, Kate thought, but didn't say.

Stopping the tape, she dropped her head in her hands and shut her eyes. The flashback arrived without notice: the oblong shape on the caravan seat, the only area of flowery fabric free of blood.

'Kate? You OK?'

'Yeah, sorry.' She looked up at him. 'It's the pad and pen Hannah used to write her note.'

'Could be.'

'Is,' Kate said emphatically.

'I'm sorry, you lost me.'

'Hannah is telling me it is.' Kate ran the tape again. 'Now watch how she lines the items up on the table, in a precise order. She's doing that for a reason, laptop first, then the notepad. That laptop . . .' Kate jabbed at the item on the screen. 'Is a MacBook Pro.'

'You sure?'

'Positive, you're looking at one.' Kate flicked her eyes towards the device in front of him. 'I don't need a degree in maths or a tape measure, Hank. That's a thirteen-inch laptop, diagonally. I know the dimension like the back of my hand. Measure it if you like. It's a foot wide and eight inches deep.'

'I'll take your word for it.'

'According to O'Brien, that's an eight by six notepad.' She nodded toward the monitor. 'Now take a look.'

He stared at the image. The depth of the laptop and the length of the pad were practically the same. 'You could be right.'

'I am right.' Again, Kate pressed play.

On screen, Hannah pulled the laptop towards her, flipped the lid open. The device was password protected. Hannah used her fingertip to wake it. The angle of the screen was oblique to the camera, the worst possible shot. Hank swore under his breath. What happened next shook Kate to the core.

Turning her head slowly, Hannah deliberately looked into the camera lens, earnestly and with an intense expression.

Kate wasn't expecting it.

Neither, it had to be said, was Hank.

Kate's stomach rolled over at the sight of her victim's ice-blue, intelligent eyes. Though Hannah was looking at both detectives, it felt like she was communicating directly and very personally with only one of them.

# 44

Jo had been watching the door for a good five minutes, in two minds as to whether she should dial 999. The indistinct shadow of a male had gone. The question was, was he waiting outside for her to check the street, a chance to grab her? He could think again. That was not going to happen. She was about to turn away when the growling resumed. Backlit by a streetlight, the hooded figure reappeared. The door rattled as he tried the handle, then rang the bell.

He must've heard Nelson, so why persist?

Jo panicked.

What if he knew she was inside? What if he'd seen a slither of light from the gap beneath the kitchen door? It had appeared shortly after Jo moved in, when Kate decided to replace the old carpet that was once there with wooden flooring. Had the man gone away to find a jemmy in order to break in, a weapon he could use against the dog and her?

In the dimly lit hallway, Nelson turned and walked towards her, his adrenaline returning to normal, the hackles on his back disappearing.

The hooded man had gone.

Jo blew out a breath, an idea occurring. Kate was desperate for JC's description. In case that was who had come knocking, Jo crept along the hall into the living room and peeped through the curtains. The figure was facing away from her, a heavy coat, the hood up, tracksuit bottoms, training shoes, a bag on his back. If he'd come equipped for burglary, he'd decided against it.

Maybe Nelson had put him off.

The man checked up and down the street, his face still

concealed by the hood, then walked around the side of the house. Jo froze, holding Nelson back by his collar, trying her best to placate him. She considered her options. Stay put or leave via the front door? Was this his plan, a trick to get outside and then pounce? If Jo knew one thing about dangerous offenders it was never to underestimate them.

Back in the kitchen, she scooped her phone off the table where she'd put it after speaking to Tom. On her keypad, she jabbed at the number nine three times. Before she could speak, an elbow crashed against the small pane of double glazing in the rear door. The glass fell inwards and shattered onto the floor. A hand reached in and turned the key. Jo dropped the phone into her pocket. It would trigger an alarm at the control room.

Nelson's growl got deeper and more threatening.

Jo took a step away. How could she have been so stupid?

The intruder switched on the light and screamed, shocked by the sight of her.

'Fuck! James, what the hell—'

'Sorreee . . . I thought you were out?' He took down the hood of his coat and sweatshirt, revealing his blond hair and the noise-cancelling headphones she'd bought him at Christmas. 'Why didn't you answer the door?'

'Why didn't you call me?'

'I lost my mobile.' He bent down to stroke Nelson.

The dog licking him made Jo sob. 'Why didn't you use your key?'

'I lost that too. Mum, I'm sorry. I didn't think.'

'You broke in!'

'I've been evicted. I need to doss here for a while. I'll pay for the window.'

'I don't give a shit about the window. The police will be here any second.'

'What? Why?'

'Because this is Kate's house, because I called them, you

idiot! What did you expect?' She pulled her phone out and lifted it to her ear. 'Hello? I'm sorry, please cancel this call.'

The control room was busy as always, loads of background noise, calm voices, clipped dialogue, some colleagues asking for information, others giving advice. 'Madam, what service do you require?'

'None.' The caller sounded shaky. 'I'm fine. I apologise for wasting your time.'

The controller adjusted her headset, the epitome of calm. 'Did you intend calling 999?'

'Yes, but I don't require any assistance.'

Jo was well aware that, having dialled the emergency number, and then not spoken, her call would be treated with the utmost seriousness. A car would most probably have been dispatched to the general area immediately, and so it proved.

'There's a vehicle en route to your location. What is your address?'

'Really, there's no need.'

'I'm afraid there's every need if someone entered your premises illegally. I heard the yelling. You sound upset.'

'I am, but not in the way you might think.' Jo threw James a dark look. Had he shouted through the door, this embarrassing situation could have been avoided. 'I'm perfectly fine. It was a misunderstanding.' She knew how ridiculous those words must sound to the woman on the other end, a woman who will have received hundreds, possibly thousands of calls just like this one since she'd taken on the job of a control-room operator. Many of them from terrified females who were being threatened, forced to deny a problem.

'You're getting a visit anyway,' the controller said.

Expecting a patrol car to rock up at any moment, Jo sighed. 'Well, if you insist on logging this call and wasting valuable resources, please contact Detective Chief Inspector Daniels in the MIR. This is her home. I don't want her viewing the incident log and thinking that I'm in danger, because I'm not. Look, you sound busy. Don't bother, I'll do it myself.'

# 45

Kate didn't answer her internal phone when it rang. She wanted to finish up and get home before midnight. Fat chance of that happening. On a split screen, making sure that the timing was in sync, she ran through the video again, with the exterior CCTV video running simultaneously, pausing every now and then to make notes independently of Hank.

'No sign of anyone outside looking in,' she said.

'That day,' he reminded her. 'This is only one day's footage. It'll take forever to go through the rest.'

'I'll put a team on it tomorrow. I want to take one last look, not of the whole thing, just one bit.'

'Why?'

'Just to be sure I haven't missed anything. Get yourself home. I can manage.'

'If you're stopping, I'm stopping. Wanna cuppa?'

'No, it's too late. I'd love a glass of water though.'

'I'd prefer a pint.' He got up.

Kate closed down the external video, rewinding the interior footage to the moment where Hannah looked up at the camera. Kate had viewed thousands of CCTV images during her police career. Some shoplifters, armed robbers, even fugitives on the run seemed incapable of avoiding closed-circuit television cameras. So many looked up, a sane person could be forgiven for thinking that they wanted to be caught.

Even from the observation room downstairs, Kate had witnessed murder suspects make aggressive gestures toward the camera, knowing she'd be watching their every move, a form of intimidation, reminding her that, even though they were going down, they had mates who could take her out. On this occasion, however, there was no threatening look, no fingers drawn across a neck, no hands holding an imaginary noose. Hannah's fixed expression was a tactic to hold the SIO's attention, not deflect it. Something in that expression struck a chord deep within her . . .

It was like flicking a switch.

She said quietly. 'We're on the same wavelength—'

'I always thought so.' Hank put her water on the desk and sat down, stifling a grin.

As tired as Kate was, she laughed. He knew she was referring to Hannah and her, not him and her. Pointing at the screen, she said: 'See what she's doing? This is what she does, Hank. More importantly, how she does it. The old-fashioned way. She's tech savvy, her father said so, but she writes in longhand because she knows it can't be traced digitally, because some cyber-creep might be looking over her shoulder.'

'That's a bit of a leap—'

'No, it's not. Hannah knew we'd find her here. That's why she frequented the same café, day after day. Why she's using eye contact to make us sit up and take notice. What she's saying is, I'm here and so is another clue.' To demonstrate, Kate replayed Hannah arriving. 'See that? She makes straight for the table. There's no fannying around. Shall I, shan't I sit near the window or closer to the counter where it's warm? Shall I sit close to others for a chat or keep my distance? She's already worked out in advance where she wants to be—'

'In relation to the CCTV, you mean?'

'Exactly that. I told you, she's controlling the situation.'

'Big mistake then. If she thought we could read what's showing on her laptop, she miscalculated.' Hank disposed of his meal carton in her wastepaper bin and dragged his water closer. 'Look at the screen. It's hopeless. We can see fuck all. There's no way we can enhance that—'

'You couldn't be more wrong.'

He stared at the screen, none the wiser. 'Give us a clue then.

I should be wearing my PJs. I can't be chewed to sit here all night if you've worked it out already.'

'See the touch bar?' She indicated the narrow strip that ran along the top of the keyboard. 'This means her laptop can't be more than five years old. The feature was only introduced by Apple in 2016, which is when I got mine and when I suspect she got hers.'

'How d'you work that out?'

'I'm guessing, but it makes sense if you think about it. Hannah's Fiat is a sixteen plate. Maybe that's when she began making plans to leave the bastard who took her life. And if you're binning your old life, trying not to leave a footprint, the first thing any sensible person would do is buy a new car, new tech, new phone and SIM.'

'Which we'll never see again. Chances of recovery are slim. In fact, they're non-existent. JC's not someone who'll leave crumbs for us to follow, Kate. As soon as he's searched her stuff, it'll be torched, along with any useful information it contains—'

'Were you even listening at the briefing? I'll bet you my life savings that Hannah's tech would be clean. That's her way of giving him the middle finger. I suspect it's causing him a lot of anxiety. He might sound like he's in control, but my guess is he's far from it, if he's who I spoke to and not some middleman brought in to do the grunt work. We have to find a way to get ahead of him.'

'Yeah, with a lot of legwork.'

'Bring it on. We're good at that.'

'This has been a bit of a waste of time, hasn't it?' Hank took off his glasses and threw them on her desk, rubbing at his eyes with his fingertips, exhaustion setting in. 'All we know is what bag she carried, what laptop we're looking for.'

Kate beamed at him, a convincing sparkle in her eye.

'We know a damn sight more than that, Hank.'

# 46

Kate sat back in her chair, hands clasped on top of her head. Thirty minutes ago, she felt totally drained. All she wanted to do was to go home, kiss Jo goodnight and crash. Now, she felt alive, rejuvenated, with the energy to work all night if she had to. What she'd seen in the past half hour had triggered a feeling of euphoria. Without writing anything down, Hannah Swift had cleverly used non-verbal communication to talk to her. In the weeks leading to her brutal death, she'd been building a rapport with the SIO who'd investigate her murder.

'You spotted something I didn't.' It was a statement from Hank, not a question.

'It's fucking genius!' Kate said. 'We may not be able to see Hannah's screen, but she's using her laptop to get across her message in ways I could never have imagined.'

'Go on then, tell me.'

'Hold on a second, I need to change the playback speed of the video.' She wanted to create a slow-motion version of the original to aid the next steps. Making the adjustment, she left the still on Hannah just seconds before she looked up at the camera. 'OK, all set. I want to show you something.' She handed Hank his specs. 'Keep your eyes peeled.'

Pushing her desktop keyboard away, Kate replaced it with her laptop, woke it up and then closed Mail, Calendar and Music, leaving only Safari open, explaining to Hank what she was doing and why. He wasn't great with computers and didn't own a Mac, so it was necessary to talk him through it. With the benefit of hindsight, Carmichael – a computer geek – would have been the better choice for this particular task.

Clicking on Safari, Kate brought up a page of sites she'd

bookmarked, with a sideways glance at Hank. 'You know what favourites are, right?'

'Yeah, I'm one of yours . . . You used to be one of mine before you decided to treat me like a halfwit.' He made a sarcastic face. 'I may not be tech savvy but I'm not totally thick . . . You're forgiven, in case you were about to apologise.'

'Just checking.'

'Yeah, well don't.' His gaze shifted to her laptop screen. 'You're kidding!' He pointed at a blue icon with the scales of justice picked out in white, the initials of the Crown Prosecution Service underneath. 'You have the CPS as a favourite? How fucking sad is that?'

She laughed.

'Actually, some of these are redundant. They needed deleting. As it happens, the CPS site has its uses. Tell anyone I said that and I'll break your arms. Now, watch and learn. As you can see, some of these icons are made up of brand logos, the CPS being a good example. Others are just letters, but that doesn't matter because, as you can see, they all have a mini-description underneath.'

Kate looked at him again.

His eyes were fixed to the screen.

She could tell that because it was reflected in each lens of his glasses. 'Now for the good news. Remember I mentioned the touch bar earlier?'

'Yeah, what about it?' Hank dropped his gaze, looking straight at it. Finding the top line of Kate's favourites replicated there, he made the jump without the need for an answer. Raising his head, he examined the image of Hannah's touch bar on Kate's desktop, just as she increased the magnification. 'Jesus Christ!'

He sat back in his chair, bowled over by the find.

The clues were all there: Hannah's bookmarked favourites, some easier than others to identify. Reading from left to right, the first icon bore the distinctive red logo of the Santander

Bank, a big clue as to where she kept her money. The second was a hand, palm up, holding the word **Refuge** drawn in pink on a white background. Underneath, written in black, were the words: *For women and children. Against domestic violence.*

'These next two are a little trickier.' Kate was pointing at the third and fourth icons. They were merely capital letters: a deep pink W in a white box; a white G in a black box. The fifth one was easy. On a yellow background, the familiar walking fingers of Yell.com where Hannah had found the advertisement for the Shepherd's Gate Caravan Park.

'I've seen number six somewhere.' Kate stared at the logo, a shield with a pair of arms wrapped around it.

'Another refuge, maybe?'

'Possibly. Jo and I were discussing them yesterday. I'm sure I've seen it recently. Sorry, my mind is a total blank.'

'It'll come to you.'

'In the morning, I'll get Lisa to trace the ones we can't easily identify. We may not have Hannah's computer, but she's telling us where to look.'

'D'you think it's possible that she left evidence in a refuge safe?'

'Given the sacrifices she made in relation to her family, the steps she took to avoid bringing JC within a million miles of her old man, I'm inclined to think not. Hannah would never put other women in danger.'

Hank locked eyes with her. 'You're inside her head, aren't you?'

'I suppose I am. When we started this investigation, I didn't want to go there. Now I do. If I think like her, we'll catch her killer. She's leading us right to him. There's more. I haven't shown you the good bit yet. Watch how she looks up again, stares at us for a second time, then see what she does with her right hand. Hannah places her middle finger on the trackpad drawing down, shifting the cursor to the bottom of the screen to make the dock appear, then draws it across. Keep watching.

See here! She gives the trackpad one tap, opening another application, then turns to camera, another stare. She's telling us to concentrate.'

'I get that, but how does it help us?'

'Concentrate. She turns back, places her hand on the keys like a touch typist and voila!'

'What? I didn't see anything.'

'Oh, for Christ's sake. Watch her left hand.'

'You said, right.'

'That was then, this is now.' Kate ran it again. 'There! Did you see it that time? She used her left pinky finger to make one keystroke on the letter A. Then . . . wait for it . . . she looks up again . . . and raises her right hand to close the laptop. All done.' Hank waited patiently as Kate rewound one final time, only this time, as Hannah raised her hand to end her session, Kate paused the screen. 'Now look at the touch bar.'

Hank's eyes widened. 'You're shitting me.' The icons he'd been looking at before had been replaced by three email addresses, the first of which was: aaron.usp.09@hotmail.com. 'Well, the kid's buggered now if JC has her laptop—'

'Not if Hannah is as sharp as I think she is.'

'Even if she deleted it, won't it remain in the background?'

'Not if she wiped the whole thing, no. She'll have erased the hard drive and reinstalled macOS. Remember the lengths she went to purchasing disposable telephone numbers that weren't linked to a contract to protect herself and her son? A woman who does that isn't fucking about, Hank. She wouldn't leave anything to chance. I reckon she'll have gone through the process we just saw every time she visited Munro's café. If we could pull last week's tapes, I guarantee Aaron's email would be different. Like I said, genius. As Carmichael hinted at, there's such a thing as exercising caution, then there's Hannah Swift.'

'Yeah, well he still found her, didn't he?'

Kate didn't bite. 'I have an email to write.' She glanced at her watch. 'It's quarter past twelve. Go home and get some kip. I'll leave Carmichael a note, write this up for Harry and pick you up at seven. Jo and I will search the scene for the key she thinks might be hidden there. I want you to interview Munro while we do that. If she's half as smart as Hannah, she'll know a lot more about her than we do. Munro is now our star witness.'

# 47

Kate wrote to Aaron asking him to get in touch urgently. The chances of a reply were negligible. She expected it to bounce back undelivered within the hour. It took less than a minute for the "mailbox unavailable" message to ping into her inbox, dissolving her triumph, plunging her into exhaustion once more. She swore loudly, her eyes drifting through her open office door to the ugly images on the murder wall. In protecting her son, Hannah had made it difficult for anyone to find him, including the police.

Kate typed out a long list of actions which she attached to a message to Harry, copying it to Carmichael, asking her to take the reins in the morning until she returned from Shepherd's Gate with Hank and Jo. She then forwarded Sergeant Wood's email to both – outlining exactly what she'd discovered – asking them to discuss and delegate the work among the team, adding a note at the bottom . . .

**Prioritise the rest of the CCTV, inside and out. I want eyes on it asap. Any updates – call me immediately. K**

Before she logged off, Kate noticed that Sergeant Wood had included his mobile number at the bottom of his email. She hesitated, but only for as long as it took her to put on her coat and scarf, grab her car keys and dim the lights.

*If I'm up, he's up.*

She left Middle Earth via the rear door, giving him a bell as she walked towards her car. Introducing herself, she apologised for the late call, acknowledging the contribution he'd made to the investigation. Thanks to him, the MIT finally had something to add to the timeline. It took a moment for him to wake up. It was obvious to Kate that he'd been dead to the world when the phone rang.

'Ma'am, how can I help you?'

She'd rather he drop ma'am for a start. She answered to guv, boss, Detective Chief Inspector or plain old Kate, but now wasn't the time to be picky. 'Talk me through your discussion with Gemma Munro.'

'Yes, of course. What do you need to know?'

'Everything.'


An email popped into Jo's inbox. She poured herself a glass of red and sat down to study it, then logged on to a site she hadn't used in a very long time. As she began to type a reply, she heard footsteps approaching. Quickly, she closed the lid of her laptop.

'Still at it, Mum?'

She swivelled in her seat to find James standing there. 'Yeah, I'm helping Kate.'

'Eyes Only, eh?' Her son was sharp. Nothing passed him by.

'Something like that.'

'Well, if you're throwing an all-nighter, I'm off to bed. Just wanted to say sorry for that.' He thumbed toward the badly repaired rear door. 'I didn't mean to scare you.' He bent down, kissing the top of her head. 'Am I forgiven?'

She smiled. 'What do you think?'

'Don't stay up too late.'

'I won't.' Reaching up, she squeezed his arm gently. 'Goodnight, love.'

She waited until the coast was clear, until he was upstairs with his bedroom door closed. As a woman who'd been psychologically abused by his father, Jo had the women's refuge survivors site open and didn't want him to see what she was looking at. Her profile was out of date. She wasn't even sure if the organisation deleted old contacts or left the virtual door open in case users needed help.

Logging on, she expected disappointment.

Success – she was in.

Sergeant Wood had been silent for too long. He was probably nervous, might never have spoken to a busy SIO and wouldn't want to fuck it up. Kate told him to take his time. What she really wanted to say was: get a wriggle on, I've been up since yon time and I'd like to get to bed. Restraining herself, she followed up with a prompt to get him started.

'Was there any hesitation when Munro was shown the IP's image?'

'No, none. I wasn't there, but the PC who was said her mouth practically dropped open. She had the foresight to let me know immediately and I took over from there. Munro obviously knew why we were in the village. You can't keep a secret in a place that small for long. She also knows the family who own the caravan park. I gather Mrs Shepherd regularly pops in for cakes and pastries.'

Kate wondered if Peggy had recommended Munro's café to Hannah. More importantly, if she'd ever popped in while she was in there. If that had been the case, why had she failed to mention it when first questioned? Had both been on the premises at the same time, they would surely have spoken. Kate was hoping Munro would have been party to that conversation.

'What's Munro like?'

'Friendly.'

'Sensible?'

Wood was experienced enough to realise why that was important. A mind reader too. Or he'd just woken up to the terminology of the twenty-first century. 'Guv, she'll make a good witness if that's why you're asking – assuming you need her.'

'Oh, I'll need her . . .' Kate climbed into her vehicle, strapped herself in and fired up the Audi, continuing their conversation over Bluetooth on the ten-minute journey home along the A1058 coast road. On her instruction, Wood and his team had been working blind. All they had was an image of a woman they knew had been brutally murdered, not her identity.

'Did Munro know the victim by name?'

'She didn't – and nor did I. No names were ever mentioned. She described the IP as a complete loner. Every time Munro tried to strike up a conversation, the woman shut her down politely. Munro was curious about her for sure. Only natural, I suppose. We all take notice of the quiet ones rather than the gobshites, don't we? Well, I do.'

Kate smiled.

She felt much the same. The less people told her about themselves, the more she wanted to know. It was in her DNA to be curious. 'Did she say anything about the time the IP was in the café? I'm hoping she was nosy enough to have taken a peek at what she was working on, to find out whether she was a mature student, a gamer or whatever.'

'Funny you should say that. The IP kept her head down mostly, either on her computer or scribbling away, occasionally reading the *Northumberland Gazette*. Given that she went in so frequently, Munro had this romantic notion of her being a writer who'd set aside a couple of hours around midday and had chosen to work in her café. The idea tickled her, but she was too embarrassed to ask.'

Kate moved out to allow another vehicle to enter from the slip road.

The driver raised a thumb as she passed by.

Kate went back to her call. 'They didn't ever chat?'

'Only when Munro took her order,' Wood said.

'OK, leave it with me. My 2ic will interview her first thing tomorrow.'

'He'll have a job, guv. The café is only open ten till four in the winter . . . Munro does live above the premises though.'

# 48

Kate pulled into Holly Avenue and parked the car, surprised to see the lights still on in her home, in the hallway and in the attic room that no one used. She found Jo in the kitchen, a load of work spread out in front of her, Nelson sitting on her feet. Kate stopped dead when she noticed the boarded-up window.

'Don't panic, everything's fine. I tried calling to warn you. You didn't pick up.'

'Sorry, I was swamped. I don't understand. You were at home all evening, weren't you?'

Jo explained what happened. 'You said not to let anyone in.'

'I didn't mean James!'

Handing her half a glass of wine, all that was left in the bottle, Jo added that they now had a lodger who couldn't afford to pay bed and board. 'His employer was forced to let him go, Kate. He wasn't going to tell us, then he lost his flat and had no choice. Tom doesn't have room for him. He can stay until he finds his feet, can't he?'

'Of course. Does he prefer to smash his way in, or would he like to use his key next time?'

Jo laughed, then grimaced. 'He can't find it.'

'You mean he's lost it. Bang goes our security, such as it is.'

'Don't be cross. It'll be in his flat somewhere. I'm collecting the rest of his stuff tomorrow. If it isn't there, I'll change the locks.'

'Is that why you're up? You could have left a note. It's almost one.'

'No, I have something to show you.'

'I need sleep. Can it wait?'

'I'm afraid not.'

'What is it?'

'It's the Women's Aid survivors' forum.' Jo opened her Mac-Book, tapped a few keys and turned it to face Kate. 'All the posts on here are moderated to ensure that women don't give anything away to their abusers. The site carries useful information on how the abused women can protect themselves. I have to warn you, it makes grim reading.'

Kate put a hand to her mouth. 'Oh God!'

'What?'

'Can you save that as a favourite?'

'What? Why?'

'Here, let me.' Kate slid Jo's laptop across the kitchen table, saved the site, then sat back staring at the icon that appeared on the favourites screen. That same deep pink W symbol on a white background, exactly the same as the one she'd found on Hannah's laptop, only this one had added content because she was viewing it on the screen as opposed to a touch bar. It simply said: *This is my abuser* . . .

# 49

For a long moment, Kate lost the ability to speak, stunned by the fact that she and Jo had come to the same place via a different route, driven on by a mutual need to resolve the case and bring a dangerous man or men to justice. It was as if it was meant to be. She looked up at Jo, her voice breaking as she spoke.

'Hannah was using this very site.'

'I know she was.'

'Clearly, but how?'

Jo hesitated. 'I had a conversation with a Women's Aid contact earlier. You don't know her. Something she said jogged a bad memory, a very low point in my past.'

Kate could see this was difficult for her.

Jo exhaled. 'When I was married to Alan, I created an account on the site.' She rolled her eyes. 'Don't judge me, Kate. I may be a psychologist, but I'm a woman first. Not all doctors can treat themselves.'

'You never said.'

'Don't take it personally. It's part of my past I'd rather forget. The site content made me ill. I became obsessed with it. I went to bed at night and dreamt of it. It was full of stories much worse than my own. In the end, I bottled it. I didn't have the guts to share my own experience. Anyway, as you probably guessed, I found a post I firmly believe is from Hannah.'

She pushed an A4 sheet across the table.

Kate began to read.


Hello again,

I'm not good today, a bit desperate to tell you the truth, but I want you to know that it wasn't always this bad. HE was the one

I'd dreamed of meeting, funny, attentive [content removed by the moderator] and single.

It was lies.

We met on [removed by the moderator]. I remember [removed by the moderator] the excitement, the hint of possibility. HE arrived [removed by the moderator] totally out of the blue. It was all too much to be honest. Now I think of it, it seems like a lifetime ago. The heat was relentless that summer. [removed by the moderator] Even now, in spite of everything, I felt safe in his arms. I still remember the buzz [removed by the moderator]

Thinking back, even then I had doubts about him and [removed by the moderator] Things didn't seem right to me. Let's just say, life had its ups and downs. As the years went on, [removed by the moderator] Then the controlling began . . . It changed every aspect of my life: how much I spent, where I was allowed to go. [removed by the moderator]. He took over [removed by the moderator] If it hadn't been for [removed by the moderator] . . . well, let's just say, I'd have topped myself.

I came to recognise the triggers that preceded the violence. I bear unimaginable scars, mental and physical, as I know you do. I may not be able to run my finger over all of them but they exist internally. He threatened to kill [removed by the moderator] if I left him. I stayed. No brainer. What was I to do? I was stuck.

No place to go.

No way out.

No hope.

Well, YOU know what it's like, don't you? You've seen all this before. You've tried to help others in my situation. You know you can help me as I'm trying to help you. Tell [removed by the moderator] not to be angry. None of this was my doing, nor his. I couldn't rely on others for protection. I have no regrets at the actions I took. You see that, don't you? There was no other way.

Signing off now.

Thanks for reading.

Knowing you are there means everything to me.

1lastrequest

Kate stared at the username at the bottom of the post until it became blurred by the tears in her eyes. She blinked them away, revealing the macabre handle, a repeat of Hannah's plea that whoever found the note she'd left in the caravan must find Aaron. Kate could feel Jo's hand on her back, rubbing gently, calming her, supporting her, a moment of anguish for both of them.

Kate never took her eyes off the screen. 'This is definitely Hannah. Well done for finding her. Just look at the replies . . .' She scrolled through two dozen supportive messages, including two from the moderator urging Hannah to call 999.

Jo said, 'Hannah doesn't respond to any of them.'

'Yeah, and we know why. This is a public forum with more regulations than HOLMES, warning users not to give too much away in terms of their kid's names, workplaces, locations, any details that that might expose a mother or child to their abuser. Women's Aid know that no system is unassailable, hence the need for a moderator. JC could be hiding behind any one of Hannah's cheerleaders. If he wants in, he'll find a way.'

Jo's expression was forlorn. 'You expect me to sleep now?'

Now Kate met her gaze. 'I didn't mean—'

'Relax, I know what you meant.'

'Yeah, well, the idea that he might assume the persona of an abused woman is equally sick.'

'Thankfully, Hannah didn't play ball. Did you notice how she capitalised HE and YOU, echoing her original note. She's communicating with you, Kate. It's as good as a signature.'

Kate rubbed at her temples, feeling under even more pressure to find Aaron. Jo didn't yet know that she'd found his email address, or that Kate had sent him half a dozen messages to get in touch. She wasn't about to share that before they went to bed. Besides, each one had bounced back, an outcome which was as depressing as it had been predictable.

'There must be other posts here,' she said. 'Look, it's really late. You go up and get your head down. You look exhausted and we have a busy day tomorrow. I'll carry on searching for a bit.'

'Don't waste your energy. I've been over it a hundred times. There's nothing there.'

'No further posts from 1lastrequest doesn't mean there are none. I know she's dead, but I will not let this woman down. I'd like to try different combinations.' She took out her phone, scanning the original note, picking out words that Hannah might have adopted as a username. Her eyes homed in on one possibility. Keeping the same format as 1lastrequest, Kate said, 'How about 1redmist?'

Jo typed it in. 'No matches.'

'Try redmist1 or redmist on its own.'

Jo hit the keyboard. Each suggestion produced a negative result.

'Fuck!' Kate returned to the note. 'OK, give 1notlikethis a go. Failing that notlikethis1 or notlikethis.'

One by one, Jo typed them in. 'Nothing. How about darkness? she suggested. Didn't she write "Darkness isn't new to either of us."

'It's worth a shot.'

Jo entered darkness1. 'Nothing found.' She entered two other choices, 1darkness and darkness on its own, then shook her head.

Kate reread the letter over and over, highlighting another possibility. Jo repeated the action one last time with the same result. 'Kate, stop! It's like trying to guess someone's password. The computations are infinite. Also, I'm not trying to teach my granny how to suck eggs, but there are other sites like these, loads and loads of them.' She held up the A4 sheet containing Hannah's post. 'We need the unmoderated text for this. I'll set up a meeting.'

Finally, Kate admitted defeat.

# 50

Breakfast was a quiet affair, with not much eaten and even less said. Kate had hardly spoken two words, beyond reminding Jo to call the survivors' forum, only to find that she had dashed off an email to her Women's Aid contact when Kate was in the shower and received an immediate reply. Vicky, the contact, had confirmed an appointment for three o'clock and would ask the moderator to attend.

'Kate, you look tired.'

'I am, Hannah's post knocked me for six last night. I didn't sleep.'

'Actually, you did, the minute your head hit the pillow.'

'Doesn't feel like it.'

'What do you expect on four and a half hours? I feel like death warmed up too.'

'Only you don't look it.' Kate smiled widely. 'Better?'

'Marginally.'

'Well, it's all I have.' Kate checked her watch. 'We must go . . .' She sent a text to Hank letting him know they were on their way and drained her coffee. She was out of her chair, grabbing her keys. 'We'll talk in the car.'

Hank lived in Fenham, an area to the west of the city, eight minutes away. They took Kate's Audi. Traffic was light and the roads had been gritted.

Halfway there, she turned to Jo and said, 'That's odd.'

'What is?'

'No reply from Hank. Hope he hasn't slept in.'

'No chance. He's too much like you.'

'Ha! That's why I like him.'

Kate concentrated on her driving, checking for pedestrians as she approached traffic lights at the top of Osborne Road.

They switched from red and amber to green. Having almost come to grief at this very junction early one morning, Kate head-checked the road before turning left.

'This case is getting to Hank, isn't it?' Jo said.

'Him and me both.'

'More than any other?'

'I think you know the answer. When we thought you'd perished on the way to New York he was as frantic as I was. But, in answer to your question, yes. This case is right up there. Every victim counts and all cases are distressing. It's not just the level of violence that makes this one stand out. It's the fact that Hannah had been looking over her shoulder for so long, trying and failing to escape her abuser. For all her money, intelligence and high-profile contacts, we're struggling to understand how she never made it.'

'Don't judge her, Kate.'

'I'm not!'

'Aren't you? I've come across women who'd been terrified for longer and I've worked with men who made their lives a misery for decades—'

'Yeah, and I've come across many more who ended up on a cold slab way before their time.' Kate gave way to traffic negotiating the busy Blue House roundabout. She stared at Jo while stationary. 'For the life of me, I just cannot understand what possessed them to allow it to go on unchecked.'

'Allow?' Jo exploded.

Kate felt her disapproval, even as she said it. When she spoke, her tone was harder than it had been. 'I didn't mean it like that. Look, if what I said makes me sound judgemental, I apologise. I've never been abused—'

'No, but you have been controlled by a vindictive officer who almost ruined your life – and you did sod all about it. I'd have thought you of all people would understand.'

'Thanks for reminding me.'

Even though it was true, Jo took it back. Kate had spent

217

her late teens, twenties and thirties hiding something that she should have been open about. Then she said something that riled Jo even more.

'Anyway, that's different.'

'How is it different? Go on,' Jo pushed. 'How's it different?'

'Look, I don't want to argue with you. My first duty is to preserve life. It bugs me that women like Hannah don't feel supported enough to come forward and speak up.'

'That's an organisational issue you need to change from the inside.'

'Believe me, I've tried . . . and failed—'

'Then fail better. You can't have it both ways. You were quick enough to tear a strip off Andy for being unrealistic when he asked the very same question—'

'Yes, and I also said that women were dying as a result. You think I don't care?'

'No, of course not. I don't know anyone who cares more—'

'Look, can we not do this now?' They were approaching Hank's home. Kate stopped the car. There were lights on inside the semi-detached house, but no sign of her 2ic. 'Hank usually waits outside when we're double, or in this case, triple-crewed. Where the hell is he?'

Jo checked her watch. 'We're early.'

Kate tapped her fingers on the steering wheel, on a short fuse, keen to get going.

Jo was impatient for another reason. 'Kate, I'm sorry but I need to get this off my chest. Coercion is a gradual thing, the men who use it as a method of control highly manipulative. Hannah will have been tricked into thinking that any rows were her fault, in her head even. That if she ever plucked up the courage to tell all, she wouldn't be believed. Even reading the redacted post, it sounds like JC was waging psychological warfare, making threats to kill, stripping her of her independence, her assets, her dignity and probably the means to get away.'

218

Kate turned to look at her. 'Presumably why she asked her father for money, cash JC wouldn't know she had. I think that's what she's been living on since she managed to escape.' She shook her head. 'I once worked on a case where, in order to protect himself, a wealthy landowner put everything in his wife's name without her knowledge or consent. Insurance against prosecution.'

'Let me guess, he exposed her as the deviant one?'

'Correct. She was remanded in custody on multiple fraud charges before we found out the truth. Imagine how disastrous that scenario would've been for Hannah, someone who'd want to begin again. No bank would touch her, even if she was once a celebrated entrepreneur almost from the minute she graduated. I can't begin to imagine the humiliation of losing that status. If only she'd told her old man.'

'What's he like?'

'A lovely bloke. He'd have helped her—'

'He did, by giving her the means to exist—'

'So why not go the whole hog and tell him what was happening?'

'For the same reason she didn't tell you. Maybe the prospect of divulging her mistake to shareholders, clients, friends and family was too much to contemplate. People are cruel and unforgiving, Kate. If she'd been honest about what was going on, what response would she have got? You can just hear them, can't you? The silly bitch should've known better than to drop her knickers for a guy who was as dodgy as fuck. Would they have understood? Would they hell.'

'Having met him, I think her father would have.' Kate checked her watch, then Hank's living room window. No sign of him. 'If Hank doesn't show himself soon, we'll get caught in the rush hour. I was hoping to avoid it.'

'Like this conversation?'

'No.' Kate reached for Jo's hand.

'Good, because, for the record, I'm as angry as you are.'

219

'I know that. I also know that Hannah may not have had a choice in all this.'

'That's where you're wrong,' Jo said. 'I know that sounds like a contradiction, but it's not meant to. I think Hannah decided that looking over her shoulder for the rest of her days was not for her. She did have a choice, Kate. We all do, even if we sometimes don't recognise or act on it. More than that, I think Hannah had a plan to gather enough incriminating evidence to annihilate JC. She wanted revenge and she's relying on you to deliver it.'

# 51

It wasn't Hank who walked down the garden path two minutes later. It was Julie, his wife. She had a coat on over her dressing gown, Ugg boots on her feet, bed hair and something in her hand. She smiled as Kate wound the window down and waved at Jo.

'Morning,' Kate said. 'Is Hank ill, Julie?'

'No. He left already. I thought you knew—'

'Would I be sitting here if I did?'

"Spose not.'

Julie took Kate's Northern bluntness in her stride. No offence was meant and none was taken. They went back years and were the best of friends, two women married to different halves of the same man. Kate had the better part of the deal. It hadn't passed her by that Hank's vehicle was parked on the driveway.

She made a face. 'What did he do, jog in?'

Julie laughed, wrapping her arms around herself to keep warm. 'A Traffic car turned up without warning at six thirty. I assume Bright sent it. And so did Hank, I guess.'

'What the hell's he playing at? That's not how things are done, and he knows it.'

'When has that ever come into the equation? Hank follows your lead, makes the rules up as he goes along. He grabbed his coat, said something about another murder and left—'

'Linked to our investigation?'

'No idea.' Julie shivered. 'I handed him a bacon butty and off he went.'

'No worries. I'll sort it out when I get in. Get yourself inside. If I were you, I'd crawl under the duvet. It's too early to be up.'

Julie handed another bacon butty through the window.

'Sorry, you'll have to share. I didn't know Jo would be with you. No one tells me owt.'

'Thanks,' Kate said.

Eating was not on her agenda. As soon as Julie walked away, she handed the sandwich to Jo, telling her to fill her boots. Julie went inside and closed the door. The light went out in the living room and on in the hallway. It looked as though she was taking Kate's advice. Kate had no feeling that she'd been lied to. Raising her window, she did a U-Turn and sped off towards Newcastle and the Coast Road.

'Something's wrong,' she said.

'So I gather.'

'I don't mean another murder.' Kate looked sideways. 'Why would the guv'nor call Hank and not me?'

'I'm sure he had his reasons.'

'Yes, but Hank knew I was collecting him. Why did *he* not call me?'

'No idea.' Jo swallowed what was in her mouth. 'This sandwich is delicious. I should travel with you more often.'

Ignoring her, Kate called Hank. When he didn't pick up, she called Bright. No reply there either. Halfway to Middle Earth, she couldn't help herself. She rang Control for the heads-up on any major incidents that had been logged overnight. 'There were none on the incident log when I left the MIR in the early hours,' she told them.

'A body was found at two a.m.,' the controller said. 'Some disused quarry in the Shire.' He was a Northumbrian with a broad accent. He meant Hexhamshire. 'Locals have been complaining about undesirable goings-on for a while now, camping illegally. Parties, drugs . . .'

'An overdose wouldn't involve the MIT.'

'You're right, the kid had been shot.'

'Anyone we know?'

'ID confirmed as Max Gilroy.'

'The twocker: young, cocky, no off switch?'

'Not anymore, guv.'

The slang term for car thief was as good as any. The kid Kate was referring to had been in and out of trouble forever. The first time he was caught behind the wheel, he was eleven years old, driving a stolen E-type Jag. Consequently, he was known throughout the force as the kid with the big E-go.

'Incidentally,' the controller said. 'His vehicle was found burnt out twenty miles away. The SIO on the shooting thought he might've been killed there, dumped later, but that wasn't the case. The quarry was definitely the crime scene for the shooting. That's been confirmed.'

'OK, thanks.' Kate said.

'Anything else I can help you with?'

'No, yes. One last question. Who sent a Traffic car to DS Gormley's home?'

'Not me. I'll check . . .' She heard the controller typing. 'Nowt to do with us, guv.'

# 52

Kate asked Jo to wait in her office while she went to find Hank. He wasn't in the incident room when she arrived and neither was anyone else from the MIT. Their desks were as they had left them, a mess. Kate noted that there was no update on the murder wall. No indication that she was now working a double-hander. If Gilroy's murder was being touted as a linked incident, where the hell was Hank? Why hadn't he summoned the team and put them to work? Why hadn't he contacted her with the lowdown on this major development?

The MIR should've been rocking.

She checked her mobile. No messages or missed calls. For a moment, she stood there, scratching her head, unable to make sense of it. Her morning, it had to be said, was not going according to plan, or anywhere close. She swung round as the door opened. Carmichael wandered in without a care in the world and a cheery smile on her face. She had no coat on, which meant that she was not just showing up for work.

Clocking Kate's sullen expression she pulled up sharply. 'Boss?'

'Where were you?' Kate said.

'Locker room. Is everything all right?'

'You tell me.' Kate bit the inside of her cheek. 'What the hell's going on?'

'Not a lot.' Carmichael blushed. 'I only got your email a minute ago. Harry's not in yet—'

'Did I wake up in a parallel universe or am I still asleep? I meant with Gilroy.'

'E-go?' Carmichael seemed flummoxed, not only by the interrogation but the subject matter. 'Sorry, I don't understand. What about him?'

'He was found dead last night. Gunshot wound.' Kate could see that her confusion was genuine. Carmichael had no clue what had triggered such a raft of questions. Kate walked away, then turned, hands on hips. 'Lisa, there's a rabbit off. When I went to pick Hank up at seven, Julie said he'd been hauled in early to deal with a murder. There has only been one overnight.'

'Gilroy?'

'Yes. Control confirmed that the Home Office pathologist has been and gone, that Gilroy's body is now in the morgue and that all detectives have left the crime scene.' Kate spread her hands. 'So where is he?'

'I thought he was due in Craster with you.'

'Change of plan . . . what about Bright?'

'I've not seen him.'

Kate covered her mouth, fear arriving in her eyes.

'Boss, what's wrong?'

Kate stared at Carmichael for a long time, her thoughts in turmoil. 'I haven't told anyone this, not even Hank, not even Jo, but I think someone might have been in my home the night before last. I also think . . . know . . . that someone keyed my car yesterday. I can't prove that it was done here or at home, but would you check our CCTV when you have a minute? I want to rule out whether I'm being watched and warned to lay off. More importantly, I want to make sure that Hank isn't now a target.'

'Sorry?'

'My first thought when I heard about Gilroy was that he was JC's accomplice, that he was murdered to keep his mouth shut. His body was found in a remote location west of Hexham. Julie said a Traffic car picked Hank up at six thirty, but Control know nothing about it. I assumed Hank would have come straight here, but I'm now wondering if he was dropped at the scene, arriving too late to get a lift. JC is a devious and dangerous man. What if—'

'Kate, don't say it. Don't even think it.'

'How can I not? Find out who called it in, who was dispatched to the scene and which SIO is dealing with Gilroy. It should be me, but clearly it's not. Whatever you do, don't go away. I'll need you later. By the way, Jo's in her office. She's bound to come looking for me. If she asks, tell her I won't be long, but please don't mention what we just talked about.'

'Where are you going?'

'To find the guv'nor.'

# 53

Kate practically ran all the way to Bright's office, ignoring the greetings of detectives arriving for duty, none of whom was Hank. The only person she was interested in speaking to was the Detective Chief Superintendent. Bright rarely followed convention, but he'd never cut her out of the action. He liked her across everything. That suited her too, so why had he acted differently today?

He didn't answer when she knocked at the door.

She pushed it open, poking her head in, in case he had someone with him and wanted privacy. He was alone, lights dimmed, blinds closed. There were signs that he'd been in a while, a used coffee mug, work spread out in front of him, a newspaper and the faint smell of last night's alcohol. His shoulders were hunched, his head hung low. If she didn't know any better, she'd think he'd pulled an all-nighter.

Maybe he had.

He was the force legend, the most senior detective who, ordinarily, looked the part: greying hair, smart clothes, a touch of class. She felt an unexpected stab of sorrow as she stood there looking at her mentor and father figure. Intellectually, he was as sharp as ever, but as each day passed he was ageing before her eyes, reminding her that at some point in the not-too-distant future he'd retire, leaving a huge hole in her life that would be impossible to fill. Already emotional, very worried about Hank, the thought made her want to weep.

Bright acknowledged her with a nod but didn't speak.

She held his gaze, detecting a sadness behind his eyes. There was an awkward moment between them. Unusual. She remained calm, though she was incensed at being sidelined. She wanted to know why. More importantly, she wanted to find Hank and wasn't quite sure how to begin that conversation without sounding like she too was losing her edge. Before she had time to decide, he stood up to open the vertical blinds, affording her the opportunity to check out the whole room, not just the bit she could see, a quick scan of what was on his desk.

She was none the wiser.

When she looked up, he still had his back to her. Kate focused on his reflection in the glass, anxiety etched on his face as he stared out at the dark streets beyond. That made her nervous. Whatever was going on in that head of his, she wasn't going to like it. He turned to face her, remaining on his feet.

'Sit down, Kate. I need to talk to you.'

'Likewise.'

'Why don't I go first . . .' He sat down, rigid in his chair. He leaned forward, resting his forearms on his desk, one hand gripping the other, eyes fixed on Kate . . . and finally he spoke. 'You're aware of yesterday's suicide on Dean Street?'

'Vaguely.'

'He's known to us.'

'Known to' had many connotations, but instinct told her that he didn't mean an offender on this occasion. She hoped it wasn't someone close to him or her. Losing Robbo felt like yesterday. It was still raw. A colleague taking his own life would be too much for them to bear. Sadly, as in all walks of life, it happened.

'His name is Terence Walker,' Bright said.

'The Terence Walker, partner at Prentice & Lavelle?' Of all the things she was expecting, it wasn't that. 'Oh, I get it. You heard we had the gloves off—'

'You think this is a wind-up?'

'Is it?'

'Do I look like I'm joking?'

She refrained from backchat. Right now, she was staring into the eyes of a man whose expression said: Don't fuck with me. She was beginning to understand what it might feel like to face a firing squad.

'Nothing to say?' He studied her reaction.

'What do you want me to say?'

'He didn't jump, he was thrown.'

'Well, if you're looking for suspects, you'd better add my name to the list.'

'Kate, stop pissing about. In what circumstances did you have the gloves off?'

She looked away, then at him. 'Look, you're going to find out anyway . . . I attended his office without an appointment. It was an acrimonious meeting. He probably shot off a complaint to the Chief as soon as I left him. Just giving you the heads-up, in case there are any awkward questions now he's dead. I meant to tell you earlier. It slipped my mind.'

'Did it?' He locked eyes with her.

'Am I in trouble?'

'Did you do anything wrong?'

'Yeah, I pushed him, as hard as I bloody could, metaphorically speaking. He's not . . . he wasn't the most pleasant man I've had the misfortune to interview, but he came a close second. Let's just say I was getting negative vibes—'

He cut her off. 'In what context did you interview him?'

'He acted for Hannah Swift in her one and only court appearance. She got off lightly. Either she was working as a police informant, which I've yet to establish, or she had friends pulling strings. Walker's reputation for working with shady characters isn't fictional, Phil. It's real. Anyway, he wasn't playing ball. Hank and I were shown the door. As soon as we left him, Walker was on the blower. With reason to believe that he was covering for another of his clients, we returned to the office and I pressed him for a name.'

'And he wasn't forthcoming?'

'No.'

'Well, before he took a swallow dive, he was seen arguing

with an unidentified man by a witness who works in the building across the road. She's adamant that he was shoved over the barrier. I put Stone on it.'

'Why?'

'Don't push it.'

'I'm not! But I am stretching to find the rationale for involving another SIO. If Walker didn't off himself, then potentially it's a linked enquiry, or should I say another one. You heard about Gilroy?' Bright didn't answer. Of course he had. 'You need to reconsider and hand Walker to me.'

'I can't—'

'You mean you won't. Stone will understand. Even if he doesn't, you're the boss, right? As you've reminded me many times, you say jump, we ask how high?' Kate wondered why he wasn't coming across. She waited for a response. It didn't arrive. They were locked in a stand-off across the desk. 'Well, it must be serious if Stone is in and I'm out.'

'You're a piece of work sometimes—'

'I'm fighting my corner, like you taught me—'

Bright slammed a fist on the desk, yelling at her. 'Do not play the innocent with me! It won't wash. There's more to this than meets the eye and we both know it . . .' His expression was overtly hostile, his jaw set like a vice. 'This is as serious as it's ever likely to get for someone we both know. Walker's mobile was found in his pocket. Hank's prints were all over it *and* he fits the description of the man seen helping him over the edge. Your wingman is our prime suspect.'

## 54

David Stone stood up as Kate flung open the door to his office without bothering to knock, registering her outrage. He'd been expecting it. And would have felt the same way had the roles been reversed. It didn't surprise him when she went straight for the jugular. A seductive mix of ambition and vulnerability, Kate never held back when she had something to say, especially, though not exclusively, in defence of her team. When it came to protecting her wingman, nothing and no one would stand in her way.

'I've just come from Bright's office,' she said. 'If you want to question any of my officers, now or in the future, have the fucking courtesy to run it by me first.'

'I tried,' he said calmly. 'You didn't pick up.'

She checked her mobile, her eyes flashing as she looked up. There was no apology. No climb down. She slipped the phone into her pocket. 'Where's Hank?'

'Shall we sit?'

'I'm fine as I am.'

'Suit yourself.' He sat down, crossing his arms, then uncrossed them, a less confrontational posture. The desk between them was barrier enough, hindering any opportunity to build rapport. He didn't want her reading anything into his body language that wasn't there.

'Where is he?' she repeated.

'At home most probably. I'm sorry, Kate. I had no choice but to suspend him.'

'On what evidence?'

'Bright didn't tell you?'

'A print on a mobile phone. Are you mad? It's a fucking set-up!'

'There's more.' David wasn't too happy that their guv'nor had only told her half the story, passing him the buck. Maybe he hadn't. Despite his rank, David wouldn't put it past her to have walked off in a rage before he had the chance. With a reputation for acting first, asking questions later, Kate hadn't quite lost control of her temper, but it wouldn't be long before she did.

'What possible motive would Hank have to assist Walker to backflip onto a concrete slab?' she asked. 'That's more my style than his.'

'Careful . . .' David smiled, unable to help it. 'That was almost an admission of guilt.'

She softened slightly. 'Have you met Walker?'

'Only at the morgue. It wasn't pretty.'

'Better than the pavement.'

'Marginally . . . I take it you didn't care for him.'

'That's an understatement.'

'I have plenty of evidence, Kate. What I don't have is motive—'

'Because it doesn't exist. C'mon, David. Hank's no fool. If he'd topped Walker, he'd have made damn sure he didn't do it in the eyeline of a witness. And he'd have wiped his dabs off that phone.'

'Would you like to close the door?' he said politely, looking past her. 'My squad can hear every word you're saying. Along with my credibility, their jaws are dropping.'

'I don't give a toss.' Retracing her steps, she kicked the door closed, rattling the glass and the detectives beyond it. She turned to face him. 'Who's your witness?'

'You know I can't tell you that.'

Kate gave him a knowing look. 'You think I can't find out?'

It was like a game of blink first that David wasn't going to win.

'C'mon, man, we're on the same side here.'

'That we can agree on.'

'Look, I'm sorry for yelling. I admit, I was seething when I heard you were questioning Hank. Of course I was. You'd have been too, in my position. My current case has been difficult from the outset. It just got personal. The guy I'm up against is ruthless. He'll crush anyone who stands in his way – or, worse still, wipe them out. There can be no other explanation for Walker's death.'

'You sure about that?'

'Absolutely. Hank has nothing to hide. I need to interview your witness.'

'Not going to happen.'

'The fuck it won't. Hank isn't the one you should be chasing, David. If Walker and Hannah Swift were murdered by the same man, then this is part of my investigation. These incidents are linked.'

'Not yet they aren't.'

'Mark my words, they will be by the end of the day.'

'Ordinarily I'd tell you to knock yourself out, but Bright isn't going to let you within a hundred miles of this.'

'You think that'll stop me?'

David gave a little shrug. 'Maybe we should pool resources.'

'No way! I'm warning you, do not queer my pitch.'

Stone had never seen her rattled. The idea that her trusted DS was in trouble had shaken her. He said: 'Maybe when you stop mouthing off, you might consider how investigating your wingman feels from my perspective. For the record, I'm as capable of interviewing witnesses and maintaining an open mind with suspects as you are.'

'Hank is not a suspect. He was under my orders when he checked Walker's phone—'

'Not the way he tells it.'

'I don't give a shit how he tells it. He's protecting me. Frankie Oliver would do the same for you.' The DS she was referring to was a third-generation cop who had a sharp brain and tongue to go with it. She was to Stone what Hank was to

Kate, a formidable second-in-command with a reputation to match. 'You know that or Hank would already be under arrest.'

'Are you finished?'

'Not on your life. You and I don't have a family. Hank does. If he's implicated in ending another man's life, he has more to lose than his liberty.'

'You're emotional, I get that.'

'Damn right I am, but my feelings for Hank won't compromise my role as a murder detective, so you can cross that off your list for starters. I'm not asking, nor do I want you to pull any punches just because he's one of us. I know you have more integrity than that. Go after him. No holds barred. I can live with that, but I'm telling you he's innocent. Just so we understand each other, I intend to do everything in my power to prove it.'

'I'd expect nothing less.'

'Have you considered that your witness may be on a killer's payroll?'

'The witness is clean, Kate. She's been working in that building for thirty years. Now, I'm putting you on notice that I need to interview your team. I appreciate that their loyalty extends to one SIO, which happens to be you, but I'm counting on you to play ball.'

'Done. Come with me!'

# 55

Word of Hank's suspension had already leaked out by the time they reached Kate's incident room. Jo was there, sporting full-on consternation. Carmichael too, though she was doing her best to hide it. All she knew about policing had come from Hank. He'd been to her what Bright had been to Kate: an inspirational tutor, a confidant and friend. Now Lisa knew that Hank wasn't in the kind of danger she'd been led to believe he might be, she'd cope. Kate wasn't sure about the rest of them. She wasn't even sure about herself. All she could think of was Hank's apology for coming late to last night's briefing and his reply when she'd asked him how it had gone with a certain solicitor.

*He got the message.*

Pushing that ugly thought away, she stood in front of the murder wall and called the team to order. 'Listen up! For those who don't know, this is Detective Chief Inspector David Stone. He's the SIO for the suspected murder of Terence Walker. I want complete transparency between our teams. Give him anything he wants.'

David's phone rang as he thanked her. 'Sorry, I've got to take this. Are you free at one?'

Kate nodded. 'Here?'

'I'll text you.'

She watched him walk away before scanning the room.

Detectives' heads were down. There were rumblings of discontent. She had to lift morale and lead by example. 'I can see you're unhappy with what I just said but I want you all to pitch in for Hank's sake. DCI Stone is not the enemy, so put that out of your heads right away. No detective wants to destroy the career of another, especially one who's liked and respected throughout the force. Through no fault of his own, Stone has made enemies today, even though he's acting under orders. Some in the CID will be queueing up to shaft him. You will NOT be among them.' She paused without taking her eyes off them. 'We work together or we don't work. Have I made myself clear?'

There was a collective, 'Yes, guv.'

Stone's caller had rung off before he pressed to answer. He'd lingered outside the MIR, waiting for the reaction to Kate's instruction. Having heard what she'd said, he wanted to go back and thank her. He was touched by her words. Instead, he made his way down the corridor before anyone clocked him earwigging the rest of her impromptu pep talk. He liked her. It was hard not to.

Kate was glad to have got that off her chest. It was the right thing to do. No one should have to work in a hostile environment. She knew only too well what that felt like. She scanned the faces of her team. 'It's good that we understand each other. Remember, we have nothing to hide from Stone. Same goes for Hank.'

'Without him we'll struggle,' Harry said.

'Tough,' Carmichael glared at him. 'We'll have to up our game then, won't we?'

Kate agreed. 'With three murders on the cards, two teams running them, there's little chance of drafting in help, even with an increased budget – which I'll have to beg for. All we can do is try. And if that doesn't work, we try harder.'

In her office, Kate ran through the priority actions with Harry and Carmichael. Content that they knew what they were doing, she levelled with them. 'Keep it to yourselves, but Hank's prints were found on Walker's phone. I'll explain later.' She focused on Carmichael. 'Remember the number I asked you to check against Shepherd's phone record?'

Carmichael was nodding.

'It's the number Walker called the minute we left his office the first time around. I want you to find out anything you can about it and keep me updated about its use. If it pings, I want to know immediately.'

'Yes, guv.'

'So what happens now?' Jo asked as Kate drove away from Middle Earth.

'We visit Shepherd's place as planned. If there is a physical key, I want it found. I'm seeing Stone later. He'll have his work cut out proving innocence or guilt. I may not be part of that, but I want to keep him close while he does it. If I'm to make that rendezvous and hook up with you in time to meet your Women's Aid contact at three, we'll have to be quick.'

'That's not ideal with so much at stake.'

'You're right. We can't afford to rush it. If we don't find anything in the time we have available, I'll revert to plan B and send in a search team. I've asked Amy Heads to speak with Shepherd so that's one less problem for us to deal with.'

'Would it help if I look for the key while you nip into the village to talk to Munro? I'm not sure I'd know where to start. I don't have your skill, but I'm willing to give it a go.'

'Not on your life. It's too risky.'

Jo swivelled in her seat to face her. 'You think JC's still around?'

'Don't you?'

'That's why I need to lock the doors, right?'

Kate felt guilty for sharing a suspected trespass of their home with Carmichael but not the woman she lived with. Jo deserved to know of her suspicions, all of them, but there was a fine line between warning her and terrifying her. Was it wise to get into it on the way to the crime scene? Jo was becoming impatient, speaking Kate's name, ever so gently, as if through a blanket, pulling her back into the car. 'All I'm saying is we can't discount it,' Kate said finally. 'I'm convinced JC threw Walker off the top floor of the Dean Street car park. It sure as hell wasn't Hank.'

# 56

Kate drove through the pretty village of Denwick. Not wanting Jo to dwell on JC, she changed the subject. 'I need to call Hank again. According to Stone, he made a statement and handed over his mobile. He wasn't picking up his landline earlier. He might now he's had time to process this idiotic nightmare.'

She used her vehicle's voice activation to make the call.

While she waited for an answer, anticipating a difficult conversation, Jo gave her a weak smile of encouragement. The call cut to voicemail. It didn't surprise either of them that Hank wasn't in the mood for a chat. He'd be completely devastated that his precious warrant card was lying on Stone's desk.

Kate kept it light.

'Hey, is that Strangeways?' She was hoping he'd respond to humour. She was out of luck. 'Since when does my bagman slope off without telling me? Hank, we need to talk. You've had my back more times than I care to remember. In case you're in any doubt, I have yours now. You're at home because of me. You tell Stone that when you see him. If you don't, I will. You have nowt to worry about, so stop crying into your beer and call me.' Kate hung up, keeping her eyes on the road. If she so much as looked at Jo, she'd be in chunks.

They often lapsed into a comfortable silence, especially in the car as the miles flew by: a chance to unwind and let their minds wander; an opportunity to solve problems without interruption. It was a sign of intimacy, not irritation. A strength, not a weakness. They hadn't said a word for a good half hour. On this occasion, it was Jo who spoke first.

'So what evidence does Stone actually have?'

Kate shook her head. 'I don't know the full extent of it. I'm hoping he'll fill me in later.'

'Well, if you want that to happen, don't wind him up.'

Kate moved to the inside lane. 'I think it's a bit late for that.'

'You didn't—'

'Might have.'

'When will you learn to back off?'

'Hardly my style, is it?'

'Well, there are ways to get people onside. Having a go isn't one of them. Didn't they teach you that at training school?'

Kate snorted. 'You wouldn't want to know what I learned at training school.'

Jo thumped her left arm.

'Ow!' Laughing, Kate turned off the A1 and onto the B1340. 'Unlike you and me, Stone and I happen to speak the same language. If I had to describe him, I'd say he was more concerned than angry.'

'All the more reason why you should cut him some slack.'

'You're right. Who'd want to be in his shoes? His situation is beginning to resemble his name – he's between a rock and a hard place. That doesn't concern me. Bright didn't choose Stone by accident. Since he arrived from the Met, he's proved how good he is. Privately, I happen to think that he's the only DCI on the force who can get Hank out of the mire.'

## 57

A bell tinkled as Kate and Jo entered Munro's café. It was gone ten, so the place was open for business. Fortunately for them, not so for the owner, there were no customers inside. A woman appeared from a small preparation area out the back, behind the counter. She was wearing a lilac blouse and purple bistro apron with wide pockets and a big smile on her face.

She picked up a pencil and an order pad. 'What can I get you, ladies?'

Hoping to boost her daily takings – Kate couldn't imagine she'd get busy on such a freezing day – she ordered two lattes, then held up ID. 'I'm Detective Chief Inspector Kate Daniels, this is my colleague, Jo Soulsby. Might we have a word?'

'Yes, of course. The name's Gemma. Take a seat. I'll bring your drinks over.'

As Jo moved away, Kate grabbed her arm, leading her to Hannah's favourite table, glancing up at the camera and yet seeing the image in reverse. Jo had no idea why Kate was dragging her away from a table with a view. When she explained, Jo shivered, as if a ghost had walked over her skin.

Kate didn't react, though taking Hannah's chair felt very personal.

Munro was extremely cooperative, unfazed by the attention of police. Sergeant Wood had warned her to expect another visit. Kate asked her many questions: did her customer always carry a backpack? What is it heavy or light?' Did she ever see what was inside?'

'The usual: laptop, phone, pen and pad, a newspaper occasionally.'

Kate had come prepared. She showed her a photograph of the Moleskine backpack. 'Was it this bag?'

'Yeah, that's it.'

'Do you happen to remember what newspaper? That may seem like an odd question, but it could be vitally important to us.'

'The local one.'

'*Journal*, *Chronicle*?'

Gemma smiled, as if it had been a daft question. '*Gazette*.'

Before Kate could resume her questioning, the doorbell rang again. A man walked in. Munro asked if she could leave a moment to serve him. He was a takeaway customer collecting an order. As she walked away, Kate pulled her phone, and searched the net, trying to find out how often the *Northumberland Gazette* was published. Wiki told her it was a weekly issue, but her eyes were drawn to the paper's own website below, a white G in a black box, one of the sites in Hannah's favourites.

'Did you find something?' Jo whispered.

'Yeah,' Kate flicked her eyes left. Munro was about done. 'Tell you later.'

Munro approached and sat down. 'Sorry.'

'Don't apologise,' Kate said. 'Gemma, did your customer arrive by car or on foot? I'm trying to establish where she might have parked.'

'That I don't know. As you saw, we have double yellows outside.'

'You told Sergeant Wood that she was a very private person, kept herself to herself. Did she ever have a conversation, however short, with anyone while she was here?'

'Not that I'm aware of . . . Well, obviously, my back was turned some of the time. I go into the kitchen to prepare stuff, even if customers are in, but I'm never away for long. I'm pretty sure not. The café is a meeting place for some folks. If they'd spoken to her once, it would have happened again. And if she'd brushed them off, I'd have heard about it. There's not a lot to do round here but gossip – though, if anyone asks, I'll deny I ever said that.'

Jo smiled at her. 'Your secret's safe with us.'

'Did Mrs Shepherd ever come in when she was here?' Kate asked.

'Oh, yes. Sorry. I thought you meant anyone Helen didn't know. Peggy did come in one day. It was nice to see them engage.'

Kate registered the name Helen and let it ride. It can only have come from Peggy Shepherd, or one of the three guys Jack Shepherd allegedly told of his lucrative arrangement in The Bull public house.

'Was Mr Shepherd with her on that occasion?'

'Yes, he was.'

Kate moved on, wondering what the Shepherds were playing at. 'How did Helen pay when she came in?' Kate knew the answer to that. Munro confirmed it was cash. 'And where did she sit?'

'Right here.'

'Always?'

'Always.'

'One last question,' Kate said. 'Did Helen's behaviour change in any way between her first and last visit?'

Munro looked sad. 'Actually, yes. In the past couple of weeks I noticed her looking at the CCTV a lot. If it had been anyone else, I'd have been suspicious. Put it this way, I'd have made the assumption that they were getting ready to rush the till.' She rolled her eyes. 'Not that there's ever much in it, but Helen didn't give off those vibes. She wasn't the type.'

'Thanks, I'm done for now, but I may return when my team have reviewed your CCTV.' Kate wanted to tell her that the footage had already helped enormously, but it would only provoke questions she had no intention of answering. 'In the meantime, if you remember anything you think might be important, any detail, however small, would you give me a call?'

Kate handed Munro her business card.

The café owner plunged her hand into her pocket and

reciprocated. 'I hope you catch the person responsible. Helen was so nice. Very polite, even though she made it crystal clear that she wanted no chit-chat . . .' Munro looked down, then up again, eyes flitting back and forth between Kate and Jo. 'I only wish I'd tried harder.'

'This is not your fault, Gemma. You provided the premises in which Helen felt safe. If that wasn't the case, she'd have stopped coming. There was nothing more you could have done for her.'

'Are you going to be OK?' Jo said.

'Yes, I'm fine. Sorry.'

'Don't apologise,' Kate said. 'You've been a great help.'

She stood up. Jo followed suit. They moved towards the door. As they reached it, Munro called out.

'May I ask why you asked about Mr Shepherd?'

Curious, Kate retraced her steps. 'It's important to establish any contacts Helen had while she was here, whoever they might be. Is there something I should know about him?'

Munro stalled.

'Gemma?'

'It's probably nothing.'

'Let me be the judge of that, eh?'

Silence.

Kate had to give her the confidence to say what was on her mind. 'Gemma, anything you say to me is confidential. If you have information, I need to hear it.' She paused . . . and still the witness didn't speak. She'd have to find another route. 'Out of interest, was the Shepherds' visit before or after Helen seemed to take notice of your cameras?'

'It was a while ago. A month, six weeks maybe. I don't think the two things are connected. Look, Mrs Shepherd is a good customer, a kind lady, the type to lend a hand to anyone in need. Her husband is the same. It didn't surprise me that they'd given Helen a place to stay.'

'You knew about that?'

'It was common knowledge that they had someone living there. You can't keep secrets in a place like this. We've got sod all to talk about. When Peggy spoke to Helen in the café, I put two and two together.'

'She hadn't mentioned it before?'

'No, never.'

'You're absolutely sure?'

'Certain.'

'Do you employ anyone else, Gemma?'

'On my takings?' She snorted. 'I'm a sole trader with no staff and even fewer days off. Peggy came in on her own that day, I remember that. I guess her son was parking the car.'

'Her son?'

'Yes . . .' Munro looked confused. 'Sorry, I assumed you knew. I thought that's who you meant. Clearly that's not the case. The thing is, Helen seemed totally fine with Peggy, but she was uncomfortable when Simon arrived. Between you and me, I don't care for him either. The guy's a total sleaze.'

# 58

'He lied to me. He looked me in the eye and fucking lied.' Kate slammed the car door, pulling her seat belt across her chest. Securing it, she took out her mobile, prompting Jo to ask if she was about to call Hank. She'd guessed wrong. 'No,' Kate said. 'I'm sending Amy a text. I want the Shepherds questioned about their son's contact with Hannah.'

Jo looked at her. 'Do you think she's up to it?'

'She'd better be. I have one pair of hands. With Hank suspended, I have no choice but to trust my personnel, however inexperienced. I expect Amy to pull her weight like everyone else—'

'And if they become suspicious?'

Kate stopped typing. Jo's warning had given her pause for thought. 'You know what? You're absolutely right . . .' She deleted the text. 'I was about to warn her to be subtle, but I don't know what I was thinking.'

'You weren't. You rarely do when you let your anger get the better of you. The last thing you need is his parents tipping him off that you're on to him. You'll lose the element of surprise when you question him.'

'That's me told . . .' Kate smiled, calmer now. 'On a scale of one to ten, it's hardly a priority. They alibied each other for the night Hannah was killed. I happen to believe that's true, even though I disliked Simon Shepherd from the moment I set eyes on him.'

'So why lie about having met her?'

'I don't know, but I intend to find out.'

Kate took off at speed, heading downhill past the kipper shop Craster was famous for. She drove past the harbour, wishing they had time to get out of the car and take in the colourful boats and sea views on offer. Instead, she turned left out of the village, passing the RNLI lifeboat station, arriving at Shepherd's Gate a few minutes later.

As the Audi passed through the now ungated entrance, Kate glanced at Jack and Peggy's cottage but didn't stop. Amy had been instructed to alert them that she was coming. She proceeded along the bumpy dirt track into a clearing where the caravans were parked, each with their own electric hook-up and water supply.

With the sun out, and the CSIs gone, Kate could see the attraction for those wanting a peaceful holiday close to the Northumberland coast. She parked beside the concrete slab on which Hannah's static caravan had once been pitched, a sad reminder of where her life had come to a premature end. In her head, it resembled a giant tombstone, blown over in a stiff wind.

Scooping her phone off the dash, Kate accessed an image of the van in situ, handing the device to Jo. She stared at it for a long time before pinching her fingers together, then spreading them across the screen to expand the photograph. Her expression hardened as she saw the vast amount of dried blood on the windows.

'Ugh . . .' She shivered. 'I don't know how you could walk in there, Kate.'

'It wasn't easy.' Grabbing her hand, Kate squeezed gently. 'Try not to dwell on it. I only showed you to refresh your memory. I thought Hannah might have chosen a van of the same make or colour, something that'll make it easier for us to find a key, if one exists.'

They got out of the car, taking their time to examine each caravan, beginning with those parked closest to the one Hannah had been renting. On the night of her murder and into the following morning, the PolSA team had established that the doors and windows of all the vans on site were locked and secure, confirming also that nothing had been attached to the underneath of Hannah's van or anyone else's.

In difficult and dirty conditions, Kate and Jo searched around rubbish bins, behind the LPG cylinders, in unlocked storage containers, anywhere and everywhere where a key might have been secreted. Kate normally had people to do the grunt work.

An hour later, she gave up. Exhausted and frozen to the marrow, she blew on her hands. 'It's no use. We're wasting our time. We could be here all week and not find anything. I'll have to organise a proper search team.'

Jo didn't answer.

Kate swung round, expecting to see her standing there, nodding in agreement. Jo was nowhere to be seen. Panic seized Kate instantly. She called out. No reply. She looked around. No sign of her. Finally, she ran to the car.

Jo wasn't there either.

Kate's phone rang.

Fumbling it from her pocket, ready to give Jo a piece of her mind, Kate stared at the screen: JC. She'd saved the number to her phone for such an eventuality. Something cold slithered down her spine. Choking down a sob, she tapped to answer, lifting the phone to her ear. The line was open, but no one spoke – and neither did she.

The caller hung up.

*No!*

Scanning the scene, just yards from where Hannah took her last breath, Kate saw what looked like a red coat lying on the ground in the distance, surrounded by the bright colours of the rainbow. The sea sounded muffled in her ears. Gulls flew overhead in slow motion. The onshore breeze seemed to die, sucked off the land, creating a vacuum around her in which time stood still.

Unable to make sense of what she'd seen, Kate looked again, trying to shake the image away, feeling like she was under the influence, hallucinating in the worst way possible but . . .

What she was looking at was all too real . . .

Railings. A child's playground: slide, roundabout, see-saw . . . swings gently rocking back and forth . . .

Jo's coat!

Kate ran, screaming her name . . .

As she got closer, she took in the shape of a body lying face down on the ground. She saw legs, an arm outstretched, head twisted to one side. Suddenly, the body moved. Jo got up onto her hands and knees, head turned in Kate's direction, her expression morphing into one of alarm.

'What's up?' she said as Kate finally reached her.

'You're shitting me!' Kate bent double, hands on knees, trying to get her breath back. 'What part of we stick together did you not understand?'

The danger wasn't over. Kate's eyes shifted round the site, from van to van, anywhere that JC might be hiding before he made his move. She didn't think he'd take them both on at the same time. Still, Walker had been thrown from a great height during rush hour in the city centre. That took some balls. Gilroy had been shot. As confident as she was in her ability to fend off an attack, Kate could do nothing against a firearm.

'Jo, hurry. Get in the car.'

'Kate, stop it! You're scaring me.'

'Car, now! He just called me.'

Jo didn't ask who. The meaning was clear. She sprinted like an athlete to the car, Kate following, scanning the scene as she ran. They were breathless as they climbed in. Locking the doors, Kate reversed at speed, her wheels kicking up dirt and gravel as the Audi sped away.

'So what happens next,' Jo said.

'I didn't mean to frighten you. I have no proof whatsoever that JC is here. The timing of the call may just have been a coincidence, but I wasn't taking any chances. We'll find out soon enough—'

Right on cue, her phone rang. 'Speak to me, Lisa.'

'JC just called your number.'

'I know. Where from?' Kate stopped the car.

'Would you believe about half a mile from Walker's office? Bottom of Grey Street. The device has been turned off again. We're doing a scan of the cameras to see if we can see anyone.'

'Good. Keep me posted.'

'Will do.'

Disconnecting, Kate blew out a breath, her focus on Jo. 'It's fine. He's miles away. Or should I say, his phone is.'

Jo blushed, ashamed for having gone AWOL. 'Sorry, I didn't mean to worry you.'

'You're safe, that's all that matters. Why did you wander off?'

'I saw the playground at the bottom of the pasture.'

'And you fancied a slide?'

Jo laughed.

'It's not funny, Jo. What the fuck were you thinking?'

'I figured Hannah might have spent time there reminiscing about Aaron. It's what I'd have done if I was missing Tom or James. Then I remembered what she said in her post on the survivor's site about her life being full of ups and downs. I just ran. I found this attached to the underside of the see-saw — a metaphor for her life, no?'

With forefinger and thumb she held out an object, a small black box made of hard plastic, about three inches long, two wide. Kate didn't touch it. Instead, she photographed it still in Jo's hand, then took an evidence bag from the glovebox, asking her to drop it in. A potential exhibit, it should have been photographed in situ but Kate wasn't going to argue. When she knew the coast was clear, she'd go and do it.

She looked at Jo, a smile developing. 'You amaze me every single day.'

Jo's eyes were on fire. 'I do get it, y'know, Kate.'

'Get what?'

'How this job drags you in. How fixated you have to be to keep going.'

'You just had your first eureka moment,' Kate said.

# 59

A gold label on the front of the box identified it as a product made by Polco, a company that Jo hadn't heard of but Kate definitely had. Her father had one just like it in his garage, a throwback from the sixties, a classic car accessory at the time, probably a collector's item now. The label had three lines of lowercase text written on it: **never locked out – keep-a-key – hidden magnetic box.**

Instinctively, they knew there was a key inside.

Kate sent the box for forensic examination, raised an action for someone to go out and reinterview Simon Shepherd, then summoned Carmichael. She reported that Hannah had thrived at Jesus College. An exemplary student, she was well liked by her peers. 'I approached three of her closest friends, boss. All confirmed that she suddenly dropped off the planet around four or five years ago without warning, just as Swift told us. All said there was no man in her life at university, ruling out the possibility that she may have met JC during her studies.'

'I know that already.'

'Since when?'

'Last night. Jo found a post Hannah had put up on a Women's Aid survivor's website. She talks about having met someone out of the blue. Sounded like a whirlwind romance, not a drunken grope in a halls-of-residence. With all that was going on, I didn't have time to feed it to the team this morning. Besides, much of the post had been redacted. Jo and I are meeting aid workers at three. I'm banking on them having kept the original.'

'They must have, surely.'

'Hope so. I can't tell you what it did to me, reading the posts on that site. So many women, some with kids, trapped in relationships and terrified for their lives. It's sickening. I couldn't help thinking of how many more might end up like Hannah before we take violence against women and girls seriously. It'll be on the agenda for tonight's briefing.'

Kate checked her mobile. 'Anything else for me?'

'French Police have been in touch,' Carmichael said. 'The Bordeaux house is shuttered, the garden overgrown. They say it doesn't look like anyone's been there for years. The neighbours confirmed that the family used to use it often until around 2007/8. Hannah was there around that time.'

'With or without an escort?'

'Without.'

'Right.' Kate nodded. 'Swift said she's been living abroad pre-2009 and that the house had been empty since his wife became too ill to travel. After her death, he couldn't bring himself to go there. Too painful, I expect.'

'Talking of his wife, I gather Marianne Briand's family are well known in the local community, well-connected too. Her brother is a celebrated judge, her nephew the commune's mayor. They were none too happy that Peter didn't have his wife interred in the family plot. I'm not sure he'd be welcome.'

'OK, how you doing with Hannah's social media?'

'She's not on Facebook, Instagram or Twitter. There's an old account on Linkedin, but it's years out of date, a throwback from when she was in business. You should see her bio. It's very impressive.'

'She's not on any other platforms?'

'No. It seems that every time we open a door, Hannah slams it in our face.'

'How's Maxwell doing with Munro's CCTV?'

'He's been through the footage. Whenever Hannah visited, she chose the same seat, went through pretty much the same routine every day. Andy double-checked everything. He agrees with Neil. It looks like she was rehearsing for show day. Absolutely nothing deviates from the last day's playback you and

Hank viewed last night. No sign of anyone hanging around outside and nothing to suggest she was being watched.' Carmichael paused. 'Shame the same couldn't be said of you, guv.'

'I'm fine,' Kate lied. 'You didn't say anything to Jo about our conversation?'

'Hell, no. I requested CCTV as per your instructions. You're sure your car was keyed yesterday?'

'No, it could have been done at home the night before. Still, it's worth checking.'

'I'll do what I can.'

'Thanks, Lisa.'

'Any news of Hank?'

Kate shook her head. 'He hasn't returned my calls. Probably still sulking, only this time he's forgiven. I'll call in on my way home.' She glanced at her watch. 'Out of interest, has Stone asked to see anyone since I left?'

'No, but I was hoping he'd pick on me.' Carmichael gave a wry smile. 'Put it this way: I would if he would.'

It was rare that Carmichael made personal comments. Though she was best mates with Andy Brown – they had arrived in the same intake – it had never developed into anything more. 'I'm seeing him soon,' Kate teased. 'I'll put a word in—'

'No.' Carmichael was horrified. 'Please don't—'

'Relax: I was joking.'

'You like him too, don't you?'

'I'll like him even better when he clears Hank. Stone gives as good as he gets. If I need to find his weakness, are you prepared to wear a wire?'

Lisa burst out laughing.

A text arrived from Stone. Kate tapped to read it. **Tell me you've not eaten. Table booked in the canteen. One o'clock. My shout.** ☺ Grinning, she passed the phone to Lisa. 'Here's your chance—'

'Really?'

'No, you idiot. Get to work.'

# 60

Stone was waiting when Kate arrived. He stood up as she approached the table. She was beginning to think there was something wrong with him. She'd never known a detective, let alone one of his rank, with such impeccable manners. Officers on nearby tables were sniggering, wolfing down food like there was no tomorrow. Abandoned Formica tables were littered with dirty plates, smelly takeaway cartons and used coffee cups.

'Nice lunch venue,' Kate said.

Stone grinned. 'I thought so.'

Kate kept a straight face as she eyed the vending machine. 'Have you ordered?'

'Thought I'd wait for you.'

'Nice manners. Hank never would.'

They moved toward the machine. Kate went first, opting for ham and cheese and a bottle of water. Stone put his money in, pressed a few buttons and waited for his to be spewed out. The grab arm stuck. He kicked the machine hard. Eventually, it dropped his lunch in the tray at the bottom.

'Have you spoken to him?' he asked as he collected his food.

'Not yet.'

She didn't need to tell him that she'd been calling Hank all morning. He'd probably worked that out for himself. Some-times, the relationship between SIO and 2ic was a pain in the arse. Kate and Hank had been lucky. Professionally speaking, they were made for each other. Partnerships like theirs were hard to find. Everyone knew it, including Stone.

'I thought you wanted to question my team. So why aren't you?'

'We were meeting. I thought I'd get what I require from you.'

They sat down. While they ate, Kate gave Stone a brief run-down of the investigation into Hannah's murder. She wasn't sure if he knew that Hank had been to see Walker yesterday. For now, she kept that to herself.

'What's your strategy?' he asked.

'To find the truth. What's yours?'

Stone's hand froze halfway to his mouth. 'What do you think? Bright didn't put me on it by accident. He's as keen as I am to get to the bottom of Walker's death as quickly as possible. Whatever the outcome, he knows I'll do it properly. No loose ends.'

'How was Hank when you took his ID?'

'Use your imagination.'

Kate shrugged. 'What did you expect?'

'Not what I got. Being told "fuck you" twice in one day by colleagues is a first for me.'

'If you want to improve on your personal best, push harder.'

Stone grinned.

Kate didn't apologise for her earlier outburst. 'I know what you said about Hank's dabs being on Walker's phone, but if you'd talked to me first I'd have explained that to you. You had no need to put my wingman on indefinite leave—'

'I had every need. My witness took a photograph, Kate. The guy Walker was arguing with has his back to the camera so I couldn't make a positive ID—'

'So it could be anyone.'

'On the other hand, it could be Hank. Kate, it was Hank. He admitted that he was there and that they'd had words.'

Her whole body tensed. 'Isn't that what we do?'

'Hank went to ask Walker about his finances. You knew that, right?' He took in her nod. 'Well, the fourth floor of a multistorey is an odd place to do it, don't you think?'

Kate sidestepped the question. 'He's a good bloke, David.'

'I know. He asked for no representation and gave a voluntary statement.'

'Can I see it—' She held up a hand. 'Forget it, I shouldn't have asked.'

'Drop by my office later. You can see it, so long as you let me do my job and I have your word that there'll be no interference. I need to show you something.' He took out his phone, tapping on a short video showing CCTV of the car park at Middle Earth. 'That's Hank, right?'

'Yeah, so what?'

'I took possession of his coat. Walker's DNA was found on the right-hand pocket and on the back, along with animal hair we matched to Walker's dog.'

A memory stirred. 'That's easily explained. I have no idea what Hank told you, but he sat in Walker's chair when we visited his office.'

'Why would he do that?'

'Because I asked him to.' Kate rolled her eyes. 'I'm explaining because Hank's well and truly fucked unless I do. We made more than one visit to Walker's office on Wednesday. After we left the first time, he made a call. Hank spotted him through the window. We went back in, fearing that he'd tipped someone off. On that occasion, he left us alone, leaving his mobile on his desk.'

'And you couldn't resist—'

'No, I couldn't. We needed that number. I appreciate that technically it wasn't playing fair, but potentially it was our only link to the man we think cut Hannah's throat. There was no other way to get it.'

'Wipe the prints next time.'

Kate looked away, then at him. 'This is all my fault. Hank didn't off Walker, JC did.'

'With the evidence I've got, others might disagree.'

'It's true.'

'I'm inclined to believe that.'

'So what are you doing to prove it?'

'Patience isn't one of your strengths, is it?'

'Not when Hank is languishing at home, no.'

'Give me a break, the enquiry is only hours old. I made a start by seizing CCTV from Walker's office. I also have a good contact with his mobile provider. I know for sure that the call you referred to is the only one he ever made to JC's number. You must've really spooked him if he didn't use a burner.'

'There you go then. You see now why I was angry? I have nothing against you, but it's not enough to charge Hank with—'

'You're wrong, Kate. There's a lot of evidence: prints, DNA, eyewitness testimony of an argument between Hank and Walker, means, opportunity. Hank admits he was there. He came late to the briefing . . . which he's yet to explain. I've seen juries swayed by less.'

'Who told you he was late?'

'I have my snouts.'

'In my team?'

'Did you ask him why he was late?'

'Nice sidestep. No, I didn't. It was the arse-end of rush hour. Why would I?'

'Fair enough. I'll do it myself.'

The atmosphere between them was tense. 'You know this is utter bullshit, right? I'd stake my reputation on it. Manipulation is JC's speciality. He's the one you should be looking for, the one we're both looking for.' Her eyes fixed on his like lasers. 'This goes no further. Only Carmichael knows. I think JC has been in my house, keyed my car and now he's framing Hank for a murder he didn't commit. Yet again, he's demonstrated his power. We cannot let him get away with it.'

## 61

JC wondered how Daniels was enjoying the game. He was degree-standard at feeling smug. Finishing his lunch, he dabbed at his mouth with a white linen napkin, then folded it carefully and placed it on a side plate, writing an imaginary cheque on his hand to summon the waiter. He may not have got what he was after from Daniels and Swift, but what came after their meeting turned out to be perfect in every way.

He'd made it into the city in time to lie in wait for Walker, making minor adjustments to the solicitor's vehicle before he arrived. They had met in Dean Street car park many times in order to do business, except on this occasion the rendezvous was not pre-arranged. An impromptu meeting was the best way to communicate his wishes, to reinforce the hierarchy in their relationship, to remind him that a parting of ways was unwise . . .

Unless he was prepared to make it permanent.

The solicitor was a creature of habit. He arrived and left his office at the same time every day. You could set your watch by him. Big mistake, one that JC exploited to the full. He'd waited in the shadows, arms crossed, eyes trained on the lawyer as he entered the top floor from the stairwell, his antennae working perfectly. It was obvious to JC that he'd sensed a presence.

Pity he had no bottle.

Eyes wide with uncontrollable fear, he'd swung round, scanning every recess, row upon row of vehicles parked there. Frozen to the icy concrete beneath his feet, he'd looked again and again, his focus shifting from car to car.

So many vehicles . . .

A hundred places to hide.

JC had read his mind. Hunkered down inside any one of

them, with only dim light available, someone with murder in mind would be hard to spot. Then Walker did something unexpected. Placing his briefcase on the deck, he dropped to his knees, his head turned sideways, almost resting on the floor, trying to spot an imagined adversary. The idiot had been watching too much TV.

*It was comedy gold!*

JC had been forced to cover his mouth to stop himself from laughing out loud.

Walker heard the key that dropped to the ground as JC got out, teasing his gloves from his pocket. He froze, fearing that he'd given himself away. The sound of the metallic object bouncing on the solid floor seemed to echo round the cavernous space. Walker jumped up, terrified, looking and listening.

Nothing.

There was no one to see or hear.

And still he was spooked.

Knowing someone was there, he turned and ran to his car.

Pulling on his gloves, JC was about to approach him when he heard footsteps on the stairwell. They were moving toward him, not away, though Walker seemed not to have noticed.

JC took cover.

It was then that providence struck.

DS Gormless appeared at the top of the stairs. His presence, just a few feet away, was as scary as it was exhilarating to JC. The air around him was suddenly charged with electricity, a tense moment. Just thinking about it now made his heart race. Some things were meant to be. Fate had dealt him a lucky break. If Hank had arrived any earlier, it would have resembled synchronised swimming.

JC had never been impulsive. He was normally methodical, planning every next move, checking and double-checking, leaving nothing to chance, but the opportunity was there and he took it. He hadn't gone there to kill Walker, but it would've been remiss not to with the good detective offering himself up as a suspect. It wouldn't take long for police to place him at the scene. Two birds, one stone, was a delicious combination. JC had seen the potential to dispose of Walker and put Daniels' minder out of action.

He chuckled.

Now he had, she was his for the taking.

## 62

Kate had spent around an hour updating Bright on where she was at, adding that Hank's suspension wouldn't dissuade her from pursuing JC if that's what he was hoping for. Paradoxically, it would compel her to keep on his tail with as much firepower as she had in her armoury. He'd underestimated her feelings for her professional partner. The bond was strong and would never be broken. Her guv'nor understood . . .

He'd taught her that.

Kate was racing along the corridor to collect Jo and head off to Women's Aid when Carmichael caught up with her. She had news on Gilroy, AKA E-go, AKA Mad Max. Kate stopped outside Jo's office door. Their eyes met through the glass, a smile passing between them. Kate held up a hand, fingers splayed out, indicating that she'd be another five minutes.

Jo nodded.

Kate swung round. 'Make it four if you can, Lisa.'

'I'm sorry, but it can't wait.'

'OK, be quick.'

'The quarry where Max's body was found is off the beaten track. ANPR clocked his vehicle hoofing along the A69 heading west at six forty-five a.m. yesterday. He was driving. No passengers. This tallies nicely with the pathologist's findings. He reckons he'd been dead for around eighteen to twenty hours, give or take, so seven or eight a.m. approximately. The report is on its way to you, but I thought you'd want to know before you disappear again.'

'Was that a hint?'

'No, guv.'

'Hey, I'm pulling your leg. Promise I won't leave you alone all day tomorrow. I appreciate how much there is to do. Keep it up, you're doing a great job.' She reached for Jo's door handle, then turned round, with an extra word of encouragement for Lisa. 'Hank will be so proud when I tell him—'

Carmichael cut her off, ignoring the compliment. 'The thing is, Max's vehicle was seen after the estimated time of death.'

'Well, it didn't drive itself away from the crime scene, did it? Whoever shot him took it.'

'Correct. I checked the tape myself. It's impossible to make out the driver.'

'Disappointing, but hardly unsurprising. Anyway, we all know who he is.'

'Yeah, but not what he looks like.'

'True. We'll catch him, Lisa.'

'I wish I had your faith. It won't surprise you to learn that the car was spotted en route to the place where it was torched. It had to get there somehow and it's miles from the quarry where Max's body was found. You'd assume, however, that a driver fleeing a murder scene would take the quickest or most covert route.'

'You're saying he didn't?'

'That's exactly what I'm saying. The car was seen travelling in the opposite direction, on the A696.'

'What time was this?'

'Nine fifteen. Kate, he was following your Audi when you went to pick up Hannah's dad.'

Kate let go of the door handle – she wasn't expecting that. She swore so loudly, Jo came out of her office to investigate, her eyes shifting between the two detectives, trying to gauge their mood. It wasn't combative. It was deeply troubled.

'What's wrong?' Jo asked.

Lisa didn't know where to put herself.

Kate knew why. 'It's OK, Lisa. This changes things. Jo needs to hear it now.'

'Now?' Jo looked at her. 'What have you been keeping from me?'

262

Kate told her of her suspicions, the intruder at their home and the fact that she'd been followed. 'You're not going to believe it, but on the way to the airport I had a feeling that I was under surveillance. I even checked the rear-view a few times but didn't see anything untoward.' She tried to picture it, but it was useless, then it came to her. She eyeballed Carmichael. 'Couple of cars back there was a red Ford Focus. Please tell me that wasn't him.'

Lisa didn't have to say it for Kate to get the message.

'Fuck!' She slammed her hand against the wall, then pinched forefinger and thumb together. 'I was this close. Get hold of Peter Swift. As quick as you can.'

'Already taken care of, boss. I called him as soon as I realised he might be in danger. Fortunately, he took an early flight home.'

'Did you warn him?' Jo said.

'No need. If JC had his home address, he'd have shown himself before now. Besides, we picked up Swift's hotel bill. It had already been paid by admin. I called the manager to make sure Swift hadn't left an address or anything that might ID him. He hadn't.'

Kate praised her for taking the initiative, then made a suggestion, without making it sound like she'd missed something important. 'Call DS Thakur just in case. Explain the situation and leave it with her. She'll know what to do.'

'Will do.'

'Now, assuming you don't have any more surprises up your sleeve, Jo and I had better head off.' Kate saw a look of panic flash across Carmichael's face before she had time to conceal it. Without moving her head, she flicked her eyes in Jo's direction, prompting a response from Kate. 'Whatever it is, just say it.'

'In view of what I told you and what you said earlier, I examined our own CCTV.'

'And?' Kate was giving her the go-ahead to open up in front of Jo.

Lisa held up a USB flash drive. 'You really need to see this.'

The three women watched the footage together in Jo's office, Carmichael explaining for Jo's benefit that several cameras covered the car park at Northern Area Command HQ. 'The first part of the tape covers the gate.'

They watched until Kate's Audi came into view. The video jumped where Carmichael had switched to another camera. Kate parked her vehicle close to the perimeter fence and got out. The lights flashed as she locked it, then she moved towards the rear door of the building, disappearing inside. Carmichael moved the tape on. A figure wearing dark clothing, a hat and a hoody walked into shot.

When the figure bent down beside the Audi, she paused the tape, meeting Kate's gaze. 'JC was and probably still is following you.'

Kate urged her to keep watching.

'I have,' she said. 'Several times. He doesn't reappear.'

'How is that even possible?' Jo said.

Carmichael said: 'He's gone underneath, I reckon.'

'He's audacious, I'll give him that.' Kate held up her car keys. 'Have my vehicle and every other car being used on this enquiry checked for a tracker device, including your own and Jo's. Put the word out. Until we get the all-clear, if any of the team leaves this building, they're to use a pool car.'

# 63

Kate collected a police vehicle and set off for the city centre. Jo commented that the car had been freshly valeted. It was sparkling. Kate kept her face straight. That was never a good sign. She'd much rather have had one that smelled of last night's fish and chips than one that needed decontamination for any number of gross reasons.

She didn't share that thought.

Jo was quiet in the car.

Kate suspected that she was brooding about being left out of the loop regarding the possibility that an intruder had been in their home. Before she could raise the matter, Kate did it for her, offering a grovelling apology. 'There was no proof,' she said. 'And I wasn't prepared to worry you or anyone else over what was nothing more than a hunch at the time, however sinister it may now seem to you.'

Jo didn't answer.

Kate looked at her. 'Look, I was out of order, but I could do without the guilt trip.'

Jo kept her eyes front. 'You found the time to tell Carmichael.'

'Only this morning when, incidentally, I had another hunch that turned out to be a mile wrong.'

'Nice to know where I stand in the pecking order.'

'C'mon, that's not fair. Jo, Hank doesn't even know.'

'That I believe . . . You know why?' Jo turned her head slowly. 'Because if he'd known, he'd have warned me. You don't mind if I call James to let him know that he should exercise caution and not to open the door to strangers, do you? He's important to me.'

'Oh, for God's sake. I'm a pro, you said. You can't protect me, you said. Anything could happen when we're on duty, you said.'

Jo had already tapped his number into her phone.

Jo's Women's Aid contact was waiting in reception when they arrived at the pre-determined location. The two women embraced one another. It was obvious from their conversation that they hadn't seen each other for many years, though the first thing the aid worker said to Kate confirmed that they had kept in regular touch.

'You must be Kate. I'm Vicky . . .' The woman was softly spoken with vivid green eyes and red hair, tied up, wisps of which fell loose around her oval face. She stuck out a hand, a big smile for Kate, enthusiasm overflowing. 'This feels far too formal. I've heard so much about you.' She thumbed in Jo's direction. 'I hope you know how very happy you've made this one.'

The connection was instant.

As Kate followed her along a wide corridor into a small office, far away from her normal place of work, she threw Jo a supportive smile. She'd mentioned Vicky before, but only in passing. It was only last night that she'd added the context behind their relationship, how long it had lasted, how it came about. In a bad place at the time, it was a period of Jo's past she had no intention of dwelling on. The man who'd given her grief was now dead. Still, Kate worried that meeting Vicky again might bring some of those dark emotions flooding back.

Anticipating her guests' arrival, Vicky had arranged a pot of coffee and a plate of Viennese whirls. As she was pouring the drinks, the moderator arrived, a much younger woman with spiky pink hair and red cheeks from the freezing temperature outside. She took off her long Superdry coat, revealing skinny jeans, an oversized rainbow jumper that complimented her Acid Pink Doc Martens.

Vicky introduced her to Jo and Kate, using first names only.

The newcomer was Eden.

Kate felt a chilly vibe from her.

Jo felt it too and took charge, leaning forward, trying to get her onside. 'Eden, I'm so sorry we're not meeting in happier circumstances. As Vicky told you, Kate and I have reason to believe that a post written on the survivor's forum by someone with the username 1lastrequest may be our murder victim. I'm a criminal profiler, helping Kate. She's the Senior Investigating Officer assigned to the case.'

Without warning, Eden took a thin file from her bag, handing it over. Kate and Jo looked at one another and the room fell silent. The document inside made grim reading . . .

Hello again,

I'm not good today, a bit desperate to tell you the truth, but I want you to know that it wasn't always this bad. HE was the one I'd dreamed of meeting, funny, attentive, older than me, in good shape, a big-shot financier like my dad – or so I was led to believe – and single.

It was lies.

We met on a yacht in Monaco on the eve of the 2008 Grand Prix. I remember the noise, the excitement, the hint of possibility. HE arrived by air taxi, totally out of the blue. It was all too much to be honest. Now I think of it, it seems like a lifetime ago. The heat was relentless that summer. We ate in the best restaurants, drank the finest wine money could buy, danced till dawn. Even now, in spite of everything, I felt safe in his arms. I still remember the buzz, a gentle hand on the nape of my neck, his lips kissing my shoulder, his urgent whisper.

'Let's get out of here.'

Thinking back, even then I had doubts about him and his business dealings. I didn't want to believe them. Everyone thought he was so charming. They were also drawn to him, so convinced that he was who he was pretending to be, I started to doubt myself. Things didn't seem right to me. Let's just say, life had its ups and downs. As the years went on, it occurred to me that he had an ulterior motive for choosing me. Then the controlling began . . . It changed every aspect of my life: how much I spent, where I was allowed to go. Our friends were his friends. Mine were unimportant. He took over my business and my life. If it hadn't been for my child . . . well, let's just say, I'd have topped myself.

I came to recognise the triggers that preceded the violence. I bear unimaginable scars, mental and physical, as I know you do. I may not be able to run my finger over all of them but they exist internally. He threatened to kill Aaron if I left him. I stayed. No brainer. What was I to do? I was stuck.

No place to go.

No way out.

No hope.

Well, YOU know what it's like, don't you? You've seen all this before. You've tried to help others in my situation. You know you can help me as I'm trying to help you. Tell Aaron not to be angry. None of this was my doing, nor his. I couldn't rely on others for protection. I have no regrets at the actions I took. You see that, don't you? There was no other way.

Signing off now.

Thanks for reading.

Knowing you are there means everything to me.

1lastrequest

Kate's heart was aching as she reread the unredacted post. She glanced up at Eden, Vicky and Jo. For a moment no one spoke. It was as if they were taking a moment to pay their respects to Hannah, a woman none of them had met in person, but who they all felt they knew intimately. Hannah was skilled at drawing people in.

Kate broke the silence. 'This is so chilling.'

'And also intriguing,' Eden said, matter-of-factly.

Jo looked at her. 'In what way?'

'Did you notice how she began with "Hello again"?'

'What about it?' Kate said.

'This is her first post.'

Eden was staring at Kate, waiting for a response. The DCI remained silent. Hannah's first note was in her head. Momentarily, she was back in the caravan reading it, as lost for words then as she was now. She opened her mouth to speak, but nothing came out. This was one of those harrowing moments when she wished she could let go. Hannah Swift was talking to her from the grave.

# 64

'If Helen is your victim, it's clear that her life had been turned upside down, then cruelly cut short by the bloke she considered to be the one who'd make her happy,' Eden said. 'Well, surprise, surprise. Prince Charming turned out to be a fucking monster.' She was looking directly at Kate, with an accusatory expression. 'I'm sorry if it offends you, but I think much more could be done and needs to be done. It can't be left to charitable organisations like ours to support these women and children or to educate those whose duty it is to protect.'

That last sentence cut Kate like a knife. 'I completely agree and you both do an amazing job—'

'We don't want your gratitude. We'd like your help. We can't shift the power dynamic on our own.'

'Eden, that's enough.' Vicky had noticed Kate stall a moment ago.

'No, she's right,' Kate said. 'For what it's worth, I've had this conversation many times—'

'Words aren't enough. We need action.'

'Eden, let it go or leave us.' Vicky apologised to Kate. 'She gets emotional sometimes.'

'And I'll keep doing it until someone listens, until there's no need for #MeToo hashtags or anonymous forums to provide safe spaces for women to support each other, until violence against women and girls is no longer a thing.' Eden turned her dirty look on Kate. 'Can you imagine anything more stressful than invigilating on this site, wading knee-deep in other women's misery? You never ever get used to it—'

'I know.' Kate remained calm, though she was seething underneath. Not only because of the young woman's outburst – every word of which was true – but because she knew what it was like to be a lone voice in the dark. 'Arriving at bloody crime scenes isn't pleasant, neither is delivering the death message to grieving families. Eden, I'm not here to debate the rights and wrongs or argue whose job is more onerous. Neither do I need or have time for a history lesson. I'm on the clock, trying to find a man who I believe may kill again if I don't stop him. The quicker we get on with it, the greater the chance of that happening. Please, I need your help.'

Eden climbed down, her time to apologise . . . to everyone. 'I'm on shift in thirty minutes, so if you have any questions, feel free to ask.'

'Thank you. I understand you have to create an account in order to post on the forum, is that correct?'

'Yes, but it's an easy process. Is— was her real name Helen Peters?'

'I can't tell you that. There are reasons we're not releasing her identity to the public.'

'So it's not then?'

Kate ignored the question. 'When did she join?'

'Two weeks ago.'

It hadn't passed Kate by that this was around the time that Hannah started to take an interest in the Munro cafe's closed-circuit TV camera. Had she formed the impression that her end was near? If so, why hadn't she found a new place to hide? She'd moved on before at short notice. Kate wondered if she'd tried to communicate with Aaron through this safe site. 'Did she send or receive any private messages on the forum?'

'No, she didn't.'

'May I have her email address?'

Eden wrote it down and passed it over. 'I must admit, Helen's username worried me when I first read it. Does the content of the post mean anything to either of you?'

Kate played dumb.

Jo followed her lead.

Kate was there to gather information, not share it. That may

271

seem selfish to some, but that was the way it was. The way it had to be. As she'd told Jack Shepherd just a few days ago, letting something slip was dangerous – in Hannah's case, fatal. 'I have one last question, or should I say three. Of the users who replied to Hannah's post, can you tell me if any registered recently; if any have yet to post anything of their own; if any only ever commented on Hannah's post and no one else's?'

'Not off the top of my head,' Eden said. 'But I'll look into it.'

# 65

'Monaco?' Carmichael's eyes widened.

'Yeah, race day was twenty-fifth of May 2008. I looked it up. She met JC the day before. Of all the things I expected, it wasn't this.' Kate pointed a finger at her computer monitor. 'I thought JC might have been loaded, I was convinced he'd be flash, but even I didn't imagine he'd hang around with the most well-off people on the planet.'

'Wow! Take a guess at how much a bottle of fizz costs there.' Carmichael made a crazy face and didn't wait for an answer. 'Thousands. I watched a programme about it on TV. It was fascinating, a different world. If Hannah met her killer there, then she must've been rolling in it too.'

'Not strictly true . . .' Kate sat back in her chair. 'There's room for the rest of us. My old man is a petrol head. It was a dream of his to go. I decided, what the hell, I'd take him as a birthday surprise. He thought we were having a few days away in Nice. The morning of the race we took the train to Monaco. We didn't watch from a private terrace or hotel balcony. I couldn't afford that. We were perched on a hard stone wall, away from the track in the scorching sun, with a bottle of wine and a pair of binoculars, marvelling how the other half live.'

'How Hannah lived if she was on a berthed yacht with a first-class view of the race.'

'Exactly.' Kate remembered her own trip like it was yesterday. It was the best day she'd ever spent in her father's company, before he went all weird on her. Thankfully, he was over that now. She forced herself to concentrate, a glance at Carmichael. 'She lost her business after meeting JC, quite a long time after according to her father, so either she was the host offering corporate hospitality to others, or she was invited there by someone who was.'

'What a come down.' Carmichael took a step towards Kate's desk. 'Can I see the post?'

'Help yourself. When we're done, I want you to print it out and distribute it to the team before we begin the briefing. Everyone needs to see it.'

Carmichael dragged a spare chair to Kate's side of the desk and sat down.

Kate reread the post over her shoulder. The saddest thing about it was Hannah's vivid memory of meeting the man Eden had described earlier as "a fucking monster", the one who'd swept Hannah off her feet initially. How quickly feeling safe and protected dissolved into feeling threatened and vulnerable, destroying Hannah's self-esteem, her life and the business she'd built up from nothing. That toxic relationship was the beginning of a nightmarish journey for herself and her son.

'It's clear they had never met before,' Carmichael said.

'Yes. I wonder if "big-shot financier" means he was or is into counterfeit currency. How ironic would that be? The Grimaldi principality is one of the most secure places in the world in terms of criminal activity. Every time anyone moves they're captured on a zoom lens in case they're a somebody . . .'

Carmichael eyeballed Kate. 'Could work to our advantage.'

'With two hundred thousand people there on race day? I doubt it. It's crammed, an area no bigger than Hyde Park. Even if we're able to ID which yacht Hannah was on, the owners would likely refuse to divulge any photographs. These are not minor celebrities who like to pose for the camera, Lisa. They're billionaires who keep their faces out of the press, especially if they're dodgy like our target.'

'I'll do some digging. Hannah may have been able to disappear and cover her tracks when she was ready to leave JC. What she couldn't do was take down anything she posted historically, linked to the 2008 Grand Prix. Once it's out there, it's out there.

Google yourself sometime. There's stuff on there from when you made it into the CID at such a young age, the first time the Detective Chief Super pushed you into the limelight.'

'I didn't know that.'

'Hmm . . . nice hair too. You suit it short.' Carmichael giggled. 'I'm not cyber-stalking you, guv. It's a thing to google mates. It's amazing what's on there, even stuff people might like to bury.'

'I'll take your word for it.'

The smile slid off Carmichael's face. 'Yeah, well remember, some voyeurs are more sinister than others. I'm not trying to rub salt into the wound, but you need to watch your back. JC will have been all over your internet history.'

Kate said nothing.

Lisa turned her attention to the screen. 'I'll research from the eve of the Grand Prix onwards, see if I can find any photographs linked with her company and her name, see if she was photographed with any men who might be our target. I'm not saying it'll be easy. We only have initials, not a name.'

'No, but we have a partial description.' Kate paused. 'How did Hannah put it? In good shape, older than her? That could describe 90 per cent of the beautiful people gracing a yacht in the harbour, but it's a start.'

'We'll have to be careful to cross-check everything. Net images are often tagged incorrectly. Every punter named may not be who we think he is. Bright will be wading in lawsuits if we get it wrong. Leave it with me.'

Carmichael looked at her watch, asked Kate to send a copy of the post to her printer and headed off, closing the door behind her. With reasons to be cheerful, Kate called Hank, but still he wasn't answering. Her office seemed empty without him. She stared blankly out of the window, then opened up her emails, one in particular catching her eye. It had been sent by a DCI Jean Cassel, North Yorkshire Police. She wasn't known to Kate but the subject line intrigued her:

**We need to talk about Hannah**

# 66

Kate pulled her keyboard towards her. She emailed North Yorkshire Police to check on whether Jean Cassel was a bona fide officer and not an imposter taking the piss. It hadn't passed Kate by that Cassel shared the same initials as her target. Only an egotist would think she might not notice. JC was a man who liked playing games. Knowing that Hank was out of the way, was he getting off on the drug of intimidation?

Ordinarily, if witnesses came forward with information, Kate would suggest a face-to-face meeting, away from her office, so she could see the whites of their eyes and talk in private. Having seen what her nemesis was capable of, and with her 2ic suspended from duty, there was no way she was taking chances.

An email arrived, confirming that Cassel was genuine.

Kate sent thanks, then replied to the DCI: **11.00 a.m. tomorrow. N'bria Northern Area Command HQ?**

Almost immediately, she received a reply. **Timing is tight for me. Meet halfway, somewhere off the A19? If that suits, I'll text you an RV point.**

The words 'game on' entered Kate's head. JC had her number. Cassel didn't. Just because she was genuine, didn't mean that her email was. An immediate risk assessment was required. Arriving mob-handed might catch a killer. It might also backfire if she was wrong. The intelligence officer would dine out on her paranoia for the rest of her days.

Exercising caution, Kate began to type: **If you want to meet in person, I'm free 11–11.30 but it'll have to be here.** She paused, adding an alternative she knew JC would never agree to, if this was him messing with her mind. **Or I can set up a conference call.** When no reply arrived, Kate sent an urgent request to

**North Yorks force: Email Cassel's ID to Northumbria HQ for my immediate attention now please.**

The briefing began in earnest at six o'clock. First up, Carmichael informed the Murder Investigation Team that JC's phone was a burner, and therefore untraceable, that it hadn't been used since it called Kate when the person on the other end said nothing – another attempt by JC to shake her up. 'While I'm on the subject of our target, technical support have confirmed that our vehicles are all clear. No devices found. Your car keys are in my desk drawer, so you can stop carping about how you might get home.'

There was a collective sigh of relief.

'And, for my next segue . . .' Carmichael was on a roll. 'I'm still working on the key Jo found at the crime scene. The consensus is that it fits a safe or safe deposit box. I figured that Hannah was pointing us in the direction of Santander, but the bank say not.' She looked at Kate. 'I'm sorry, boss. They can't even find an account for her—'

'Jo and I might be able to help there,' Kate interrupted. 'Has anyone not read and digested Hannah's post yet?' No hands went up. 'Good, because we had a very interesting conversation with the Women's Aid workers who've been helping with that. Eden, the moderator of that post, told us that Hannah registered on the site as Helen Peters.'

'With what date of birth?' It was a good question from DC Andy Brown.

'Her own,' Kate confirmed. 'Lisa, you have enough to do with the Grand Prix and associated research. Seeing as he's volunteered, Andy can pick up the bank baton and run with it.' His face was the colour of his strawberry blond hair when she turned her focus on him. 'Get on to Santander with those details. If you get a negative result for Helen Peters, try other surnames Hannah might've used, Briand for example, with Helen or Hannah as a first name.'

'Or even Briand Swift, Briand Peters,' Jo added.

'Yes, or any combination you can think of. Get inside Hannah's head and use your imagination. And while you're at it, check to see if she changed her name by deed poll.'

Andy was nodding.

'Harry, how are we doing with completed actions?'

'The favourites on Hannah's computer have now been accounted for, bar one. As Lisa just alluded to, we already knew about Santander, not that it's taken us anywhere yet. The second one – the one with the hand holding the word refuge, is in fact the National Domestic Abuse Helpline. Then there's Women's Aid, the *Northumberland Gazette* and Yell—'

'Has anyone been in touch with the *Gazette*?' Kate asked.

Harry glanced at Maxwell.

'Hannah hasn't posted anything in their personal ads,' he said.

'Maybe she was just scanning the local news for anything JC related,' Kate said. 'If he's as well-connected as her post suggests, he might be a celebrity for all we know.'

'But why buy a physical copy if she had the digital version saved?' Amy Heads said.

'Digital tends to lag behind hard copy. No good for Hannah if she was looking out for an indication that he was in the vicinity. Or maybe we're overthinking this. Maybe she liked doing the crossword. She had a lot of time to kill.' Kate shifted her gaze to the receiver. 'Was there anything else, Harry?'

'Only that the last of Hannah's favourites is proving problematic. I was wondering if you'd remember where you'd seen it, guv.'

'Not until you asked, I didn't. Don't move!'

Kate rushed out of the briefing room and into her office. Her coat was hanging on the peg behind the door where she'd left it. Slipping her hand inside her right-hand pocket, she pulled out a business card. In the top left-hand corner was a distinctive logo: a shield with a pair of arms wrapped around it.

'Yes!' She almost punched the air.

Retracing her steps, Kate held it up to the team, bolstered by thoughts that yet another clue had been revealed. 'This card was given to me by Hannah's father. It's the business card of Alex Hope, who runs a surveillance and close-protection operation out of Greenwich. Swift used her company to find his daughter, unsuccessfully as it turned out, so why on earth would Hannah have Hope's website saved to her MacBook?'

## 67

It was Julie who opened the door. She didn't seem surprised to see Kate standing there. She looked worried, though she put on a brave face, trying not to get emotional. Kate gave her a hug on the doorstep, a few wise words that Hank's problems would all come to nothing. Unconvinced, Julie beckoned her inside. As Kate walked into the hallway, Ryan arrived, slipping a protective arm around his mother. He was mid-twenties, tall and blond, with piercing blue eyes.

'What's going on?'

'Just checking in on your dad,' Kate said.

'He's in the living room, spoiling for a row.'

'He might get one for not calling me.'

Ryan grinned. 'I'll be upstairs if you need backup.'

'I'll give you a shout.'

Kate loved Hank's only child as if he were her own. His father's police career hadn't made life easy for him or Julie over the years, any more than it had Kate's relationship with Jo. Detectives worked long hours, sacrificing much in pursuit of justice, often spending more time with each other and with the families of the bereaved than they did with their own loved ones. A work-life balance was a myth for emergency service personnel permanently on call.

She watched Ryan mount the stairs, then turned to Julie. 'The older he gets, the more like you he looks.'

'Like he wants to punch someone's lights out, you mean?'

Kate laughed. 'Not mine, I hope.'

'Not this time.' Julie made off towards the kitchen, making herself scarce so that Hank's 'other wife' could talk to him in private. Kate found him watching TV, a squashed beer can on the floor by the side of the sofa, a fresh one in his hand. Taking off her coat, gloves and scarf, Kate sat down opposite.

'What's a day off feel like?'

'Crap.' He killed the TV, no smile forthcoming. 'What's going on?'

'Plenty . . . I had the gloves off with Stone for not telling me he'd questioned you over Walker's death. I made it clear to him that he was out of order, that it was a ridiculous accusation.'

'To be fair, he didn't accuse me of anything.'

'Good to know he's our kind of copper.'

'What about the enquiry?'

'Jo and I went to Craster as planned. I had a good chat with Munro. She claims Shepherd the younger had met Hannah, so I'm having him reinterviewed to find out what he has to say for himself.' She didn't mention the email from North Yorkshire. 'Oh, and Jo found Hannah's key. Well, that's not strictly true, she found a magnetic box. I just got word that it holds a key.'

'You're joking!'

'Don't get too excited. We don't yet know what lock it fits.'

'Yeah, but it's a start.'

'We think some sort of safe deposit box. And I remembered where I'd seen that missing logo on Hannah's computer. It was Hope's—'

'The surveillance company? Why would she have saved that?'

'The way I see it, there can only be two reasons: either JC was also a client, or Hannah was.'

'Genius,' Hank said. 'What better way to cover your tracks than to employ the services of a pro who's skilled in finding people and, conversely, laying false trails to ensure they cannot be found?'

Kate was nodding.

'When Swift told me that Hope was ex-military intelligence, but hadn't found Hannah, even though he'd hyped her up as the best in the business, I caught the contradiction. Maybe he was misguided in putting his trust in the woman who'd carried out corporate work for him.'

'Maybe Hope did find Hannah.'

'Yeah, and maybe she told JC.'

# 68

'It's all kicking off without me then.' Hank toasted her with his beer, taking a long pull on the can, wiping a dribble off his chin with the back of his hand. 'Don't tell Bright, whatever you do. It's taken me twenty years to make him believe that I'm indispensable, to him and to you. Unless he already knows I'm not and you've come to give me my marching orders. Do I need to run out and buy a pipe and slippers?'

'Don't you dare, I need you.'

Hank looked away, realising that he hadn't pulled off a good mood. She offered no sympathy. He wouldn't thank her for it. Instead, she concentrated on what she'd come for, telling him that Stone had shown her his statement.

'That was good of him.'

'Lose the sarcasm,' she said. 'He did it as a favour to me. So stop sulking and tell me everything you told him.'

'What for?'

'I want to make sure your statement is accurate and as comprehensive as it needs to be. I'm not telling you it isn't, but you'd have been in shock when you made it. I'd like to walk you through it again.' Kate was good at that. Cognitive interviewing was her thing. She took a pen and a copy of his statement from her pocket. Unfolding it, she waited for him to begin.

He moaned, showing his frustration. 'Do we have to?'

'Yes, start talking.'

He blew out a breath. 'I left the office around four fifteen—'

'Anyone see you leave?'

'Carmichael.' Hank frowned. 'Actually, she asked to come along. I told her no. If I'd known I needed a witness, I'd have taken her with me.'

'Go on.'

'I was held up getting into town.'

'Where did you park? It's not in your statement.'

'Grey Street—'

'Where on Grey Street?'

'About halfway down. I nipped into Greggs for a pasty—'

'Also not on here.' She scribbled it down.

'As I was walking down the hill—'

'Hold on, did anyone see you in Greggs – apart from the person who served you?'

'No, the shop was empty. I bumped into Drew Dickinson and his lass as I left though.'

'Did you speak to him?'

'For a few seconds. They were in a rush.'

'Go on.'

'I walked on, downhill. When I got to the Mosley Street junction, I saw Walker coming up the hill on Dean Street. The lights were against me. I couldn't get across the road. He turned into the multistorey car park. I followed.' Hank rolled his eyes. 'That'll look good on CCTV, won't it?'

'Stop deviating. It may surprise you to know that I have a home to go to.'

'Walker was acting strange when I got there.'

'What do you mean? I want a blow-by-blow account.'

'He was jumpy—'

'Because he knew he was being followed?'

'No, there was more to it than that. I stood for a moment watching him. He was facing away from me, a few feet from his car, close to the edge of the top level.'

'What was he doing?'

'Nothing. It crossed my mind that the fucker was going to jump. I approached. He almost lifted off the floor when I tapped him on the shoulder. He swung wildly, a right hook. I sidestepped the blow. Punching fresh air, he lurched forward and crashed headfirst to the ground, losing his glasses in the process.'

Kate interrupted. 'Did he touch you as he went down?'

'No, but I almost lost my bait. I told him that separating a detective from the only thing he'd eaten since breakfast was a hanging offence. He didn't take the joke. He started yelling, trying to retrieve his specs.'

'And did he?'

Hank nodded. 'Half of one lens was missing. I don't know who he was expecting but it wasn't me. He was sweating buckets.'

'Did you ask him?'

'Of course. He said, no one. I asked him why so nervous then. He said I startled him. I'm telling you, there was more to it than that, Kate. He was petrified.'

'That's what happens when you associate with scum.'

'That's what I told him, almost word for word. I mentioned that we knew about the hookers, holidays and luxury homes, the over-the-top expenditure. I asked him to reconsider his position vis-à-vis the phone call he made following our visit to his office. I told him dirty money wouldn't sit well with the Lord Chief Justice, that he'd better start making up the truth.'

'He denied everything?'

Hank nodded. 'He thought I was bluffing. He told me he wasn't born yesterday. I told him it wasn't his birth that worried me. He said I was talking bollocks, that he wasn't mixed up with the guy who killed Hannah. I said I didn't believe him, told him he had two choices. Tell us who he called. We'd get the collar. He'd get to play hero. The windfall would stay put. Or he could keep looking over his shoulder. Go into hiding. JC would find him. Cut his throat. Recover his money. Problem solved.'

'What did he say to that?'

'Nothing for a while, but I could see he was shit scared. He was swaying, weighing up the odds. For a minute, I thought he was going to come across, then he said, quote, "Daniels doesn't make deals" unquote.'

'I would've made an exception in exchange for information.'

'Exactly. I told him he wasn't important to you. That all you wanted was justice for Hannah. I gave him a final nudge . . .' Hank apologised for the pun. 'I told him that he was out of his depth, a dead man walking. Kate, he looked like he wanted to top himself. I directed him to the Tyne Bridge, told him to take a left up Suicide Alley—'

'You didn't!'

'He was putting me off me pasty.'

'Well, let's hope Stone doesn't get himself a lip-reader.'

'Since when did you become telepathic?'

'It's not funny. Then what?'

'I left. And, before you ask, I didn't happen to see a dead man in the street below or a crowd of pedestrians rubbernecking or anything else untoward when I reached ground level. Walker was alive when I left him, Kate.'

'You saw no one else in the car park?'

Hank shook his head.

'Your conversation with Walker can't have lasted long.'

'No, it was all over in five, six minutes.'

'And yet you came late to the briefing . . . which Stone knows about.'

'You told him?'

'No! What do you take me for?'

'Sorry. Why is it relevant?'

'Fuck's sake! If you were interviewing a suspect who'd disappeared for a while after a suspicious death, you'd be hanging them out to dry, accusing them of getting their ducks in a row before being picked up.'

Hank ignored the dig.

Kate heard movement in the hallway. She wondered if Julie was earwigging at the door, getting angry or upset. Hank didn't seem to have noticed. Kate wasn't finished with him yet. 'Do not underestimate Stone, Hank. He's no slouch. You need to amend your statement before he asks for an explanation.'

He didn't answer.

'Where were you?'

'I nipped into Fitzgeralds, washed off incriminating evidence and sank a pint of High Level. How's that?'

She laughed, even though it wasn't funny. 'What were you really doing?'

'All of the above, minus the incriminating evidence. If I tell Stone that he'll think I'm taking the piss.'

'How long were you there?'

'Not long. I got stuck in traffic on the way back. That's it in a nutshell. I was with you till after midnight. When the traffic car arrived this morning, I honestly thought you'd sent it. The driver was vague when I asked. Said he wasn't about to deny the request of an SIO. Stone was waiting like the Grim Reaper as we drove in.'

# 69

The grandfather clock in Kate's hallway chimed nine times as she entered the house. Jo and James were in the kitchen, her clearing the table, him stacking the dishwasher. Apologising for not getting home in time for dinner, Kate declined what was on offer, telling Jo she wanted to go for a run first and maybe grab a slice of toast before bed.

'I didn't eat much either,' Jo said. 'I'll come with you.'

Kate met James's eyes across the room. 'You coming?'

'Not if it requires moving my legs. I hiked up Helvellyn with a couple of mates today.'

'Blimey, you're fit for a treat in this weather.'

'It was a hairy descent, right enough. We practically slid down to Grisedale Tarn across tightly packed ice. Ask me next month or, preferably, next year. Anyway, I don't want to cramp your style.'

'Oh yeah?' Kate said. 'In a race against your mum, you'd lose, mate.'

James grinned. He knew she was right. 'I'm meeting Tom for a pint. I'll be back around eleven.'

Jo opened her purse, handing him a twenty-pound note.

He kissed her and left the room.

Two email alerts arrived in quick succession.

Kate checked her mobile. One was from North Yorkshire Police with a warrant card image of Cassel, the other a personal one from the officer, including a mobile number. Kate tapped on it, telling Jo she wouldn't be long. Before she made it to the living room, the DCI answered, making it clear that talking on the phone was reckless, a word Kate found intriguing. They agreed an RV point, about halfway between their two bases. Disconnecting, Kate ran upstairs to change.

JC stared out through the windscreen at the quiet street beyond. Daniels had chosen well. It wouldn't do for him, but the area was pleasant enough. He'd spent most of his day scheming, wondering if the police had lifted Gormley yet. According to his lookout, there had been no sign of him at Northern Area Command HQ. Unlike Walker and Mad Max, JC trusted Stilts implicitly. He was someone who recognised the value of keeping his mouth shut. He'd never let JC down, in all the years he'd known him.

JC slid down in his seat as a young man left Daniels' house, pulling the door shut behind him. He turned the handle, checking the property was locked and secure, then took off in the opposite direction.

One down, one to go.

JC was hoping that the woman Daniels lived with would take the dog for a walk, leaving his target alone. Probably a little too optimistic. Still, he was feeling lucky. When the door opened a second time, he thought he might get his way. Sadly, that was not to be. Both women emerged, lingering on the pavement, stretching, warming up for a run, then setting off down the road at a gentle pace.

Hmm . . . there were possibilities here.

Should he lie in wait or take immediate action?

Kate didn't see it coming. There was no awful feeling that she was under surveillance, no warning of imminent danger. One second she was running along the road, telling Jo of her upcoming meeting with Frenchman Cassel, laughing about the fact that she'd mistaken him for a female, the next there was movement from the shadowy doorway to her left.

The shoulder charge knocked her flying off the pavement into the path of an oncoming car. She saw the eyes of its male driver widen as he pulled hard on the steering wheel in order to avoid her.

He wasn't going to make it.

The rear end of the vehicle slewed sideways on the icy road, a payload of around fifteen hundred kilos of metal heading straight for her, the car's bumper at eye level. It took her a split second to register that she was roadkill, then her survival instinct kicked in.

She had one chance.

Only the one.

On autopilot, Kate scrambled to her feet, launching herself into the air in order to save her legs. The thump as she collided with the hood was as nauseating as it was excruciating. She bounced off the windscreen, rolling sideways as the car came to a sudden stop, the wind knocked out of her as she connected with the tarmac.

White noise in her head.

Then the lights went out.

Job done, JC glanced over his shoulder as pedestrians rushed to Daniels' aid. He'd caught her just right, when she was in full flight and off balance, chatting with her running mate without a care in the world, taking little notice of her immediate surroundings. Keying her car hadn't made a blind bit of difference to the way she conducted her life.

This one was like Hannah, not easily intimidated.

The thought riled him.

Still, now he'd taught her a lesson, she might recognise the error of her ways, assuming she still had the brain capability for identification and perception. He wasn't sure if the thump he'd heard was her body or her head hitting the windscreen. When he was far enough up the street, he turned, watching events unfold. Daniels was lying on her back, one arm stretched out, the hand palm up.

She looked like a drunk, begging for change.

A woman screamed for someone to call an ambulance.

'Oh my God! Did you see that?' a passing girl said.

'Let me through, I'm a doctor.'

Cars were taking avoiding action, the drivers inside craning their necks to see what was going on, all eyes on the casualty – and still she hadn't moved. It was absolute chaos. Seconds later, JC heard a siren in the distance, getting closer, saw blue lights flashing beyond the frozen figure lying on the tarmac. A police vehicle came into view, weaving in and out of the traffic.

Time he was away.

When she came to, Kate was dazed and disoriented, struggling to focus. As the fog cleared, a cloudless sky emerged. She saw stars, literally and metaphorically. Bizarrely, it passed through her head how beautiful they were. Warm liquid seeped into her ear. She turned her head an inch as lights rushed towards her, horns blasting angrily. Amid the horror going on around her, Kate heard a police siren playing her song. She'd never been so grateful to know that colleagues were on their way.

Kate was conscious of a woman kneeling beside her, checking her pulse, a medic of some sort. And Jo, flushed from running, her skin glistening with sweat. She was horrified and tearful, but her voice was calm.

'You're going to be fine, Kate. Lie still, don't move. Ambulance is on its way.'

Kate hoped it wouldn't be long. She felt strange, out-of-body strange, like she was on the ceiling looking down on a crowd of strangers who in turn were peering down at someone who looked exactly like her. Was this her mind playing tricks? She had no time to answer her own question. She was floating away, the crowd getting smaller and smaller.

'God, she looks poorly. Her head's bleeding.'

'Poor lass. Is she going to make it?'

*Was she?*

# 70

Hank's distress reached Kate from beyond the curtain of her A&E bay. Given that she was not related or next of kin, it had taken long enough to persuade medics to allow Jo in. Until Kate lied to the doctor treating her, Jo had been made to wait outside. There was zero chance that a half-cut detective – who no longer had a warrant card to flash in the face of the member of staff denying him access – was getting in. The more he made his mouth go, the more chance that outcome diminished.

Kate exhaled, showing her frustration. 'Why did you call him?'

'Are you kidding?' Jo looked at her, incredulous. 'Because he'd never have forgiven me if I hadn't.'

'I told you I'm fine.'

'Kate, you heard the doctor, she wants to keep you in overnight for observation.'

'Yeah, well I'm not stopping.'

'Why d'you always have to be so stubborn? She said it's in case of internal bleeding. That's a big deal and I'll not stand by while you make light of it. And don't you dare pretend that your dice with death was accidental. If it had been, the guy would've stopped to help and not run off.'

'I'm glad you recognise the fact that if I stay I'm a sitting duck.'

'Fine! If you want to tell Hank that you're "not stopping", you can damn well tell him yourself. That's why I called him—'

'To protect me while I'm in here?'

'To talk some sense into you—'

'I never asked you to.'

Jo looked hurt.

Before Kate could apologise, a slurred expletive was uttered from the waiting area. 'For God's sake, listen to him. He couldn't fight his way out of a paper bag, let alone protect me. Jo, do something. He needs a public order allegation like a hole in the head, never mind a D&D charge. Please go and explain to the staff that I need to see him.'

'And say what?'

'Tell them he's here to take a statement.'

'In his condition? Do me a favour—'

'Tell them he's my ex then.'

'Yeah, that'll work. You just told them you like kissing girls—'

'Just get him in here before he decks the jobsworth he's arguing with.'

In the early hours, Hank hailed a cab, escorting Kate and Jo to their place. He slept in the spare room. After a restless night, he'd insisted on driving Kate to Middle Earth, leaving Jo at home with James. Over breakfast, Kate had argued against him escorting her, until he pointed out that, if she drove after being advised not to by a physician – not to mention discharging herself against medical advice – her insurance would be null and void.

He knew she wouldn't risk that.

Kate chose the armchair in her office.

Hank sat on the edge of her desk, facing her, feet and arms crossed. As a murder suspect who'd also been suspended from duty, he was banned from entering police premises. He'd be for the high jump if caught within a mile of the Major Incident Suite. Even so, Kate couldn't bear to ask him to leave a second time. She wanted to tell him that he was valued, that her job was twice as hard without him and half the fun. She said neither, knowing that articulating how much he meant to her would make her emotional when she needed to be strong.

Hank pulled himself from his trance, glancing into the incident room, the place where he'd hung out with Kate for so many years. The reality of being locked out of the investigation was bad, the prospect of having everything he'd worked for taken away even worse, but the thought of losing her bloody near killed him.

She yawned, wincing in pain.

He stared at her. 'Can I get you anything? Gin, painkiller, cut-throat razor?'

'No thanks.' She hardly cracked a smile. 'You didn't have to come up with me. I'm not an invalid.'

'And I'm not stupid. You're in agony. A blind man on a galloping horse could see that. Besides, it's not as if I have anything better to do, is it?'

'Listen, I got you into this. I'll get you out of it.'

'Is that a promise?'

'Absolutely.'

He valued their friendship above any other. Kate was so popular within the team, it had taken almost ten minutes to get through the incident room to her office door. The MIT were shocked to see her in the building and appalled at the state she was in. There was extensive bruising to one side of her face, a bald patch on the side of her scalp where staples had been applied to a nasty head wound.

Trying not to look at it, Hank glanced out through her internal window, just as the double doors to the MIR were flung open.

'Shit!' he said. 'Bright incoming.'

'Heading our way?'

'What do you think?'

# 71

Seconds later, Kate's office door burst inward.

She attempted to stand.

'Sit the fuck down,' Bright barked.

Walking round her desk, he took a seat, ignoring Hank as if he were invisible. For a long moment, the Detective Chief Superintendent stared at Kate, exploring her injuries as well as his options. 'Kate, listen very carefully to what I have to say. If you insist on working, that's fine by me, but when you're not in this building I want you in a safe house.'

'That's not necessary.'

'You don't get a say in it. You're going, end of.' Now he eyeballed Hank, pushing Kate's laptop towards him, sliding a flash drive across her desk. 'Show her . . . And while you're at it, take a look yourself, then you can invent a valid reason for being here.' Bright knew that with Kate in mortal danger, Hank wouldn't leave, even if ordered to do so. As her 2ic, he took his job of watching over her seriously.

'I'm seeing Stone at ten,' Hank said.

'Do not lie to me! I just saw him leave the building.'

Absolutely nothing got past him. No matter how careful they thought they had been over the years, he kept catching them out. Busted, Hank exchanged a worried look with Kate. The movement of her eyes toward the door was almost imperceptible. Receiving her unspoken message, he was on the move.

'Where the hell do you think you're going?' Bright said. 'I'm not finished with you yet.'

Hank's expression bordered on insubordination. 'Weren't you suggesting that I have no business here, or did I pick that up wrong . . . guv?'

'Cut the backchat. I appreciate your loyalty and I know Kate does. I assume you've checked every single collar she's made since joining the MIT as a detective sergeant for this JC character?'

'Carmichael has . . . and I double-checked it.'

'What about earlier, the shite she put away when she was in the drug squad?'

'No joy there either.'

'Which means he's an unknown quantity.'

'Totally.'

'Right, I've heard enough. I'm moving the goalposts. This maniac we're hunting is unpredictable and out of control. There's no telling what he'll do next. Now watch the video clip.'

Hank attached the flash drive to Kate's laptop and handed it to her.

She opened it with her fingertip, then pressed play.

They viewed the footage together, the blood drained from the face of her wingman as the tape ran on. It caught the moment that she was shoved into the path of an oncoming car that could so easily have killed her. Hank flinched as her body collided with the windscreen of the vehicle that hit her.

'Was that necessary, Phil?' Kate's hackles were up and it showed. 'I was there, remember?'

'Then you know perfectly well that it was deliberate. That fucker has a target on your back. You think it was a happy accident that CCTV caught the unfolding incident so perfectly? Think again. He chose his spot. He's giving us the finger, demonstrating his superiority.'

They locked eyes.

'How could he possibly know that I was going for a run? I didn't decide until I got home.'

'He was watching you. When you ran out onto Osborne Road, he followed in a vehicle nicked off someone's drive an hour earlier. By the time you reached Acorn Road he was waiting to make his play. And, before you ask, the answer is no.

We didn't see his face. The car was found torched on the road leading to Baker's Yard Industrial Estate. Whoever this guy is, you can't fault his organisation. He's done his homework. Now we need to do ours. Are you in or out?'

Kate didn't answer quick enough.

'Was there something you wanted to add? Because I'd like nothing better than to order you to take sick leave. As you keep telling everyone, Walker's murder is a linked incident, so it's no skin off my nose if I hand the whole lot to Stone. So, what's it to be, the safe house or your house?'

No one could ever say that Kate's reaction was out of character. If she had something to say she said it, no matter who she was talking to. 'Look, I appreciate your concern, really I do. Believe me, I get it, but my safety isn't our only worry, it's Jo's. She's compromised. Whoever shoulder-charged me off the pavement, whether JC or one of his henchmen, they saw her at close quarters. She's family . . . to all of us. I've made arrangements for her to move out temporarily. James has been staying with us. He'll go with her. When I'm certain they're safe, I'll go wherever you want.'

'I'm coming with you,' Hank said.

Kate turned to face him. 'I don't need a babysitter.'

'The hell you don't,' Bright said. 'So here's the deal. Hank, as of now, I'm lifting your suspension and will square that with Stone. You've not been charged with anything and I don't consider you a flight risk. This is now down to me, so don't fuck up. Until Stone has completed his enquiries, you'll take no further part in any investigation. What you will do is shadow Kate wherever she goes – but no one, and I mean no one beyond this office door finds out about the safe house. We saw what JC did to Hannah Swift. If he gets hold of Kate, we all know how this ends.'

## 72

The phone on Kate's desk pierced the silence. Bright stood up and left Hank to answer it. Kate could see how relieved he was to be on duty, though the novelty of being her personal protection officer would soon wear off. And it didn't mean his problems were over. Far from it.

He covered the speaker. 'Someone called Eden? Says you're expecting her call.'

Kate hauled herself up with great difficulty, aware of Hank watching her as she hobbled around her desk and lowered herself into her swivel chair. 'Eden, hi. Do you have anything for me?'

'Yes and no. I've searched our system to see if Helen had more accounts than the one we looked at and I can't find her anywhere. That's not to say that she isn't posting on other sites. Of the women who responded to her post, all have been around for a while. Apart from one, they're regular contributors I've spoken to personally. The other is something of a wallflower.'

'You mean they don't join in?'

'It's not unusual. Some users are shy. They wait on the sidelines for many months until someone else's post mirrors their own experience, triggering a response. I can't tell you which of the users I'm talking about—'

'What can you tell me about the account?'

'I thought you'd ask, so I analysed the browsing history. This user is not one who dips in and out. Whoever it is seems tethered to more than one device and is drawn to women who are in hiding, not those who haven't yet managed to get out. Up until very recently the person behind this profile accessed the site every day—'

'Until when?'

'The day you found Helen's body. Call me a suspicious cow, but I'm tempted to shut down the account—'

'No, Eden. I'm begging you, please don't do that yet. You said yourself, this user isn't posting anywhere. Keep an eye on it by all means, but if this is who I think it might be, we can't afford to tip him off. Under no circumstances should you make contact with him. If you do, two things will happen. He'll come after you and dispose of crucial evidence. If you do as I ask, and we can link him to the woman you know as Helen, you'll help convict this moron when we find him. Are you willing to do that?'

'Bring it on.'

# 73

Jean Cassel was late. Not his fault. Kate had rearranged their meeting to take place at Middle Earth. He was OK about it when she explained that she'd been involved in an accident. Hank gave him the once-over before allowing him inside, then took a seat outside the door, like a security detail protecting a US president. If laughing wasn't so painful, Kate would've been rolling on the floor, only she'd done enough of that lately.

Cassel had smoky eyes and dark wavy hair. He winced when he saw the state of her. As he made himself comfortable, all the scenarios of what he was about to tell her went through her head, official or unofficial informant being on top of that list. Introductions complete, refreshments offered and declined, she leaned into her seat, meeting his gaze across her desk.

'Tell me why you and I need to talk about Hannah,' she said.

'I've not come to say that I'm her handler,' he said. 'Though I can see why you might think it.' He was quietly spoken, completely fluent in English, a soft European accent, so unmistakably French it passed through her head that it was put on slightly to endear him to others.

As an intelligence officer, it was his job to detect, disrupt and prevent serious and organised criminal activity. Foreign nationals were perfect for the National Crime Agency, due to their language skills and exhaustive cultural know-how. French was particularly useful.

No doubt Cassel would be aware that she'd been onto his home force asking questions. What he didn't know was that Kate had mates there. Apparently, he was the proactive golden boy, getting good results, providing a steady flow of intelligence, which prompted her next question.

'So if Hannah wasn't an informant, what was she to you?'

'That's a good question—'

'I know, that's why I asked it.'

'You could say she was the exact opposite. What I mean is, she recruited me, not the other way round.'

Kate had no idea what he meant by that and didn't immediately rush to find out, which was exactly what he'd expect her to do. Any games they would play would be to her rules. Deep down she had the feeling that the man she was facing had been very close to Hannah, her 'go-to' copper perhaps, the man she trusted, one she'd potentially used as a confidant in the past.

So where was he when she was killed?

Keen to find out, Kate had no intention of pulling her punches. 'Maybe we should start at the beginning. Where, when and in what circumstances did you two meet?'

'Paris, 2004, in the run-up to Le Tour de France.'

'Was this a trip Hannah organised?'

'And directed. She was the best, a wonderful host. Beautiful inside and out. Classy, funny, switched on. We became good friends. I guess we were a natural fit. You do know she's half French?'

Kate was nodding. 'And after the tour?'

'Nothing. I didn't see or hear from her again for eight years, another sporting event, UEFA European Championships in Poland. Sport and travel are my passion too.' A flash of anger sparked in his eyes. 'I've never seen such a dramatic change in a person. Hannah had lost her joie de vivre. She was withdrawn, in a very bad place, doing her best to hide it. I was very concerned for her.'

'Did she confide in you?'

'Not then, no . . . but we kept in touch.'

'Did she know you were a detective?'

'Yes.'

'In the UK?'

'Yes. I married a Brit when I was very young. My wife couldn't settle in France so we returned to her place of birth. I joined up, loved it, allowed the job to take over.' He shrugged. 'Yeah, I know, I'm a walking stereotype. Only it's not such a cliché, is it?'

'You've been checking me out too?'

'Of course . . .' His lips were smiling though his eyes were not. 'I came home one night. My wife had cleared off with an auctioneer who lived close by.'

Kate was about to ask another question when two others popped into her head. Had he been screwing around with Hannah? Was he Aaron's father? No, the timing was wrong, assuming he was telling the truth. Was he though? Kate thought about that for a moment. He'd come forward voluntarily. She had no reason to doubt him.

Still, she tested his reaction. 'Any kids?'

'Me? No,' he scoffed.

'You don't like young 'uns?'

'On the contrary, I like them very much. I just don't think people should have them if they're not prepared to provide them with two parents.'

'Living with a divorcee who has children, I don't share that opinion. People change—'

'Yeah? Well, if you were an orphan brought up in a kid's home, you might think differently.'

Touchy. 'So why stick around when your wife left?'

'As I said, my background was difficult and unstable. There was nothing to go back for. I had friends and a home here, but I'm here to talk about Hannah, not me.'

# 74

Bored watching his colleagues working, Hank got up. After a quick check on Kate and Cassel, who were deep in conversation, he wandered through the MIR to see if he could find out what was going on. Carmichael was engrossed in her work. She looked up as he reached her untidy desk, smiling up at him.

'Nice to see you back.'

'It's good to be here.'

'How's the boss?'

'In worse shape than she's prepared to admit to. Pushing herself too hard. Always has. Always will. She'll crack one of these days.' He stood there like a spare part, eyeing Carmichael's computer screen. It was full of celebrity images including, he noticed, one of Danish actress Brigitte Nielsen and another of former tennis champion Boris Becker. 'She's not too ill to kick your ass if she catches you reading glossy magazines.'

'I'm not. Didn't she tell you?'

'Tell me what? No, forget it, Lisa. I don't want to get you in trouble with the Super.'

'What are you on about?'

Hank did a quick recce of the room, then turned to face her. He chewed at the inside of his cheek, withholding his outrage, buying himself time to calm down. 'If you see Bright, I was never here.'

'Why?'

'For the foreseeable, I'm Kate's heavy, no longer part of the investigation, no longer part of this team. I'm not even supposed to be talking to you.'

'Sorry? I assumed, well I thought Stone had cleared you.'

'Not yet he hasn't. Look, if you don't want to tell me, I can handle that.'

'Don't be daft . . .' Carmichael turned her attention to her screen, scrolled down, stopping on the sexually provocative pose of a woman draped across the grab rail of a superyacht. Next to it were several images of British racing driver Lewis Hamilton, on and off the podium. 'These photos are of the 2008 Monaco Grand Prix. It's where Hannah met JC. I'm looking for him, or should I say them.'

'We know what he looks like?'

'Not exactly, but in Hannah's post she described him as fit. Jo concurs. She couldn't give a facial description of the man who shoved Kate into the road yesterday, but she said he was powerfully built, fit legs, muscular thighs, a competent runner. CCTV gave us approximate height. If I can find Hannah, I might find him. That's the plan anyway.'

'The term long shot springs to mind.'

Lisa threw him a dirty look. 'I just spent three mind-boggling hours on this.'

'Have you found her yet?'

'Despite my best efforts, no.' Carmichael hooked a hair away from her right eye, a grim expression on her face as she looked up at Hank. 'Not one fucking sighting . . . with or without a murderer in tow.'

'Then I rest my case.'

'Thanks for the motivational speech. I'll bear it in mind for the rest of the day. What the boss wants, the boss gets. And, as you continually remind me, a long shot is still a shot.'

'Hey, c'mon! I'm not knocking you. I'm trying to help.'

'Well, I'm all out of thanks.'

Hank sat down on the edge of her desk, facing her. 'Lisa, when she was in business, Hannah ran a first-rate operation. According to her father, she blew away the competition. A host who's the real deal would remain in the background while their VIP guests mingle and grab the limelight. She wouldn't push herself in front of a camera. She'd more likely shy away from it.'

'That's true, but she might unknowingly appear in the background.'

'I agree, but you have to be selective or this action will drive you mad . . .' Hank gestured towards her computer. 'Look at the images you have up on screen. Most are of the F1 paddock or the pit lane where the paparazzi tend to hang out. Yacht parties are different. They're all the rage if you're minted. If, as we suspect, Hannah had organised or was a guest on the one where she met JC, then that's where you'll find her.'

# 75

Having got the measure of Cassel, even though she was keen to move on to his relationship with Hannah, Kate decided on a short break. She was dehydrating fast, in need of liquid. Hank was no longer guarding the door. She'd noticed him wander off a while ago, though she couldn't see further into the MIR, even with her specs on.

'Are you OK?' the Frenchman said, a concerned expression on his face.

'Yes . . . actually no. Would you mind asking my 2ic to get me some water, please? I'd get it myself, only I'm a bit stiff from my accident.' In reality, she had a raging headache. Her vision was seriously blurred. She was struggling to focus on her witness. If she shared that with him or any one of her crew, she'd be in an ambulance on the road to A&E before she could say stretcher.

Cassel got up and left the room, returning with her drink a few moments later.

Kate drank greedily from the bottle, telling him she felt better for it. She could see he wasn't buying it. He got up, opened the window and stood there looking out. She exhaled, a not-so-subtle hint that she was keen to crack on.

With his back turned, she asked: 'How much did Hannah tell you?'

For a moment, he didn't answer. He stood, immobile, shoulders rigid. Then he turned, leaning against the windowsill, a relaxed stance. 'Enough to raise my antenna. She made it clear from the outset that she wanted to know how she could shaft the man she once adored. Single-handedly, he'd destroyed her life. Treated her like dirt, like he owned her. She told me he'd been robbing her blind over a prolonged period of time. One night, early 2015, she challenged him over money he'd filtered out of her business. That night he went too far. He flew into a rage, slashing her across her back.'

'Why?'

'He didn't like the backless gown she was wearing.'

Even though Kate was aware of the injury, which had been listed in Stanton's post-mortem report, she felt physically sick hearing of how it was inflicted. 'He made sure she didn't wear another.'

Cassel nodded, though he showed no emotion. 'Ask me, he didn't like the accusation and was making sure she didn't repeat it. He tied her up, took a shower, got dressed and left her in their apartment. She got loose and fled to A&E.'

'Didn't the triage team call it in?'

'Hannah was smart. She used a false name and walked before our lot got there. I saw the scar. It was horrific, stretching from her left shoulder to the right side of her waist, deeper at the top than the bottom.'

The staples on Kate's head wound seemed to dig further into her skin. She wondered if his description indicated that the person responsible was left rather than right-handed. Was Cassel shagging Hannah? Had JC found out about it and flown into a rage? In Kate's opinion, no woman would show a friend, even a good one, such a hideous injury.

'You two were close?'

'Our relationship was platonic.'

'And yet you saw her scarred back.'

'She asked me to check that her wound wasn't infected.'

'Are you a doctor?'

'You know I'm not.' Cassel stared at her for a long moment. He didn't like her line of questioning. 'Look, we were not in a relationship. Hannah was in a state, physically and mentally. Instinctively, I knew that was the tipping point. There was no longer any doubt that she'd execute her plan.'

'Do you know where the apartment was, what hospital she was treated in?'

'No, it was in the city, I think.'

'What do you know about the guy who slashed her?'

'Only that he's a crook and a conman, heavily into money laundering.'

'Was he on your radar?'

'How would I know? She never revealed his identity.'

'Oh, c'mon. You must've checked your caseload to see if anyone—'

'Kate, we have hundreds of cases. They all fit the bill. These powerful men terrorise others. That's what they do: wives, girlfriends, the competition, us . . . anyone who gets in their fucking way. Hannah was careful never to name or describe him. I had no clue—'

'Did you ask?'

'Frequently. She said he'd kill us if he found out we were conspiring to bring him down. She said she wasn't having that on her conscience. There was no doubt in her mind that he was capable of offing anyone who got in his way.'

'Nationality?'

'British . . . I assume.'

'Oh, for fuck's sake!'

'No, wait, he was.' Cassel ran a hand through his hair. 'When I met Hannah the second time in 2012 she was still with him. He hadn't travelled with her because England had been knocked out by Italy in the quarter-finals.'

'That only means he's bad loser.'

'No. You're wrong. There was more to it than that. Hannah said he was more parochial than most travelling fans. He didn't see the tournament as a celebration of international football. Winning was everything. Nothing less would do. He had a deep-seated hatred of any other team. She said that he viewed competition, in any area of his life, as the enemy.'

'You just said she didn't describe him.'

'I meant physically. In 2015, when he put her in hospital, she described him as deranged. That's when I knew for sure that she'd leave him. I told her if he was the criminal mastermind she thought he was, and had intel to prove it, I'd take it to my guv'nor.' He paused. 'Let me make myself clear. That wasn't an attempt to recruit her as an asset, merely the offer of help, a suggestion that I could protect her while we did a job on him.'

'Using the intelligence system?'

'Yes . . . Hannah was having none of it. She said it was too dangerous for either of us. She was only interested in picking my brains.'

'Exactly what information did she want?'

'Everything . . . how I went about gathering intelligence, how she could finish him. I didn't violate regulations or part with trade secrets—'

'I don't give a shit, so long as you tried to help her.'

'I did.'

'So, let me get this right. Hannah was working to build a case alone?'

'I told you, she was clever.'

'Not clever enough to keep herself alive.'

For the first time since Kate had begun questioning him, Cassel bit. 'No need to be so casual about it.'

Kate checked herself. 'I'm not apportioning blame, Jean. I'm grateful for the background and I'm sorry for the loss of your friend, but the sad fact is that Hannah underestimated the man who killed her . . . and so very nearly did I. If you weren't who you are, I wouldn't be telling you this . . . I have three dead.' She lifted a hand to the staples in her head. 'This wasn't accidental. Last night, Hannah's killer almost made it four.'

# 76

Bright had been waiting for the knock. His penetrating eyes stared at the door as Stone appeared through it. The DCI showed no emotion, though Bright had heard rumours that he'd come to a decision to rule Hank in or out of Walker's murder. If only suspects in every investigation could be arrested or released as quickly.

'David, take a seat.'

'Thank you, sir.'

'Before we begin, I want to commend your effort. I gather your team have worked round the clock on this.' Bright exhaled. 'Hank has been in the CID almost as long as I have. He'll appreciate your haste. No doubt you're aware that Professional Standards are breathing down my neck, giving me earache for lifting his suspension.'

'How's Kate?' Stone asked.

'A pain in the arse, as usual.'

Stone grinned.

Bright didn't. 'I need a full debrief and I need it now.'

Stone flipped open a notepad, thumbing a few pages before he found what he was looking for. 'Hank left the MIR at four fifteen and was seen doing so by Carmichael. He's in Greggs on camera buying a pasty at four forty. CCTV picks him up on Grey Street a couple of minutes later, talking to a retired detective and his wife. The exchange was brief. They rush off in the direction of the Monument. Hank continues down Grey Street alone.'

'They've been spoken to?'

'The couple? Yes, they were in a hurry to get the airport Metro to meet their daughter off her flight. I secured proof of them getting on and off the train.'

'Where was Walker at this point?'

'He left his office at four forty-five on the dot, arriving at Dean Street car park at four forty-nine. At the same time, Hank's seen running across the junction of Grey Street and Mosley Street, as per his statement. He enters the car park after Walker. It takes them both a couple of minutes to get to the top floor, Walker arriving at four fifty-two, Hank a minute and a half later.'

'Presumably, their encounter was also captured on camera?'

'No. This is where it gets interesting. The car park's CCTV is pointing away from where Hank claims he caught up with Walker. There's evidence that it was tampered with.'

'Not by Hank, if he'd just arrived.'

'Not unless he did it earlier, no. He claims he was with Kate up the coast—'

'He was. She told me. So we don't get to see the exchange between Hank and Walker?'

'No, sir. But pastry crumbs were found on the floor where Hank stood, right where Walker went over the edge. The witness who works across the road saw two men arguing. Hank claims there was a misunderstanding in which Walker ended up on the deck. The heels of his hands were scuffed, but the pathologist said these scratches could not have been caused by the fall, and Walker's secretary confirmed they weren't on his hands that afternoon.'

'Go on.'

'Walker's specs were broken, one lens shattered, yet no glass was found on or near the body. Glass was, however, found beside Walker's car. We've identified it as part of his prescription lens, proving that he didn't lose it in the fall. Again, this substantiates Hank's claim that the specs flew off and had been smashed four floors above ground level.'

Bright wasn't any more relaxed than he'd been when Stone started talking. 'Is that all you've got?'

'No, sir . . . When CSIs arrived at the scene, the locks were open on Walker's car, but the doors were shut. The handles were frozen solid, or so investigators thought. In fact, they were superglued to prevent the solicitor from leaving. I reckon he was for the high jump that afternoon and Hank just wandered in by accident, wrong time, wrong place—'

'Why am I not reassured? You need something more.'

'Forensics lifted a silk fibre off Walker's coat. We can't presently identify its source. What I can say is, it didn't come from any clothing we took from Hank or anything we found at his home.'

'Fuck's sake, David. His prints were on Walker's phone.'

'Kate has given a statement that she ordered Hank to check Walker's phone when they were in his office, suspecting that he'd tipped off a serious offender who might go to ground if they didn't act immediately. In order to do that, Hank sat down in the lawyer's chair, which could account for the dog hair on his coat.'

'Could? That's not good enough. This is a copper we're on about. I want no ifs, buts or maybes . . .' Bright was practically snarling. 'First of all, Kate would lie through her back teeth to alibi him and smile while she was doing it. You know it, I know it, every fucking barrister from here to the capital knows it. Police versus the legal profession will be the scandal of the season. They'll be queueing up to prosecute. Second, nothing you said proves he didn't argue with Walker and then lob him over the edge. Do better.'

'I agree, it doesn't rule him out, but I have something that does.' Stone paused, a smile developing. 'Hank left the car park at four fifty-nine, turned right, heading towards Mosley Street. Walker's digital watch stopped at three minutes past five. Hank was in Fitzgeralds by then. What's more, he has a receipt to prove it. Stopping off for a half, buying a bottle of red for his missus, saved his arse. It's open and shut, guv. He's in the clear.'

# 77

A ringing mobile. Kate glanced at the screen. Bright was the caller. She wasn't even tempted to answer. Cassel had more to tell and she was keen to hear it. She muted the sound but her guv'nor was persistent. The screen lit up as he tried again. Opening her desk drawer, Kate threw in the device, hearing only the muffled sound of it vibrating as it rang a third time. Bright was almost as impatient as Cassel. He was checking his watch.

'Sorry,' she said. 'When did you and Hannah last meet?'

'Two, three weeks ago—'

'Well, which was it. Two or three?'

'Two. I sent her a pre-determined code—'

'Bit cloak and dagger, isn't it?' Kate suspected this had come from him. She watched his colour rise. He remained silent, his expression doing the talking for him. She'd hit a nerve. 'Where did you meet?'

A beat of time turned into a sidestep. 'Our usual rendezvous point.'

Without taking her eyes off him, Kate pushed a pad across her desk. 'I want the code and the RV.'

Cassel wrote them down and slid the pad towards her. He looked embarrassed. A glance at what was written there gave Kate the reason why: **STSP**. For Kate's benefit, he'd written the place name too: **Waren Mill**.

'Really?' She stifled a grin. 'Same Time, Same Place was your pre-determined code?'

'She's . . . she was an amateur.'

She wasn't the only one. No self-respecting intelligence officer would use social media shorthand. On the other hand, Cassel had filled in a blank for Kate. Warenford was in the system already, which wasn't far from Waren Mill. Hannah's vehicle had been spotted by ANPR on the A1 north of the village last Friday. Kate had suspected that she was meeting Aaron. Carmichael had suggested that she drove there to call her son on one of her many disposable numbers. Now it made sense. She was in fact meeting Cassel, possibly doing both at the same time.

'You sure your RV wasn't more recent?'

'Positive.'

She didn't challenge him. 'Did you meet at the mill?'

'No, in the long lay-by on the B1340 Links Road overlooking the bay and nature reserve. It was a waste of time. For the hundredth time, I begged her to part with what she had. She said the guy she'd been living with was so devious that only a person on the inside would be able to mount this kind of operation.'

'And you believed her?'

'I did, yes. Kate, I ask informants to take risks every day. You know that.'

'Sounds like she was playing you, Jean. Picking your brains would be like asking me how to commit the perfect murder and avoid detection.'

'When you put it like that—'

'How else would I put it? From where I'm sitting, she sucked you dry and spat you out.'

'Do you want this intel or not?' Cassel bit again, staring at her across the desk. 'Look, if she'd killed him, she'd have got off with voluntary manslaughter, no question. That wasn't enough though. She wanted to see him suffer the humiliation of losing everything, including his status.'

'Wasn't she afraid?'

'Of him? Sure. She'd tried leaving before. Called the domestic abuse hotline several times, begging for help. They found her a refuge in Middlesbrough. A couple of months later, he found her. Some heavies went over there, mob-handed. Broke down the door, attacked the refuge manager and hauled her out. Police were called. The mob wore balaclavas. Staff were unable to ID them. You can guess the rest.'

'She wouldn't grass on him when spoken to?'

'No, even though she suspected her days were numbered.'

His words hung in the air, the silence underlining them. Kate asked, 'How did you find out about her murder?'

'How do you mean?'

'It's a simple enough question.'

'I read about it.'

'And what, put two and two together?'

'I've kept my eye on Northumbria murder stats. That's how I knew you were the SIO.' Cassel checked his watch. 'Look, I'm sorry, I'm going to have to run.' He stood up, looking down on her. 'I hope some of what I've said helps you understand Hannah and her state of mind. When you put it all together, just remember she came to me, not the other way around. I warned her that her plan was fraught with danger.'

'You can say that again.'

'What could I do? Wherever that piece of shit is hiding, good luck finding him. Hannah saw finishing him as the only way she'd ever reunite with her son.' Cassel moved toward the door, turning as he reached it. 'By the way, where is Aaron?'

# 78

Kate managed to stand and shake his hand. Sometimes, there are tiny idiosyncrasies that put you off a person, a phrase or word they use, an inappropriate touch, a look, a mannerism that makes you doubt their credibility. Sometimes it's not even a thing. It's a feeling, instinctual, a hint of something being off.

This was one of those times.

As she watched Cassel walk away, a sinister thought occurred, one Kate didn't wish to acknowledge. To date, the MIT had found no other person Hannah had kept in touch with once her life took a turn for the worse. One by one, she'd let her relationships lapse until she was alone. Even after she'd left JC, she'd kept everyone at arm's length, including her family. What was so special about Cassel? Why risk keeping in touch with him if she wasn't willing to share? Was it, as he alluded to, because he was a cop whose brains she could pick?

Kate's head swam.

Did she buy Cassel's story?

She'd gone to great lengths to ascertain his identity as a police officer. She'd seen his warrant card. Unless . . .

*Jesus!*

She scooped up her mobile and summoned Hank. He arrived in less than thirty seconds. She stared at him, her thoughts all over the place. 'Quickly, go in the incident room and take note of Cassel's vehicle before he leaves.'

'What for?'

'Just do it!'

Hank rushed out, catching sight of the Frenchman as he walked towards his vehicle, a Merc C-Class Coupé. Lifting his iPhone, Hank took several shots of Cassel getting in, and of the registration plate as the car stopped at the red-and-white exit barrier, then a few more just in case. Pocketing his phone, ignoring the inquisitive, some might say suspicious stares of his colleagues, he returned to Kate's office. Having already made the jump, he pulled the door closed behind him and dropped the blinds.

'Fuck's sake, tell me I'm wrong.'

That, in case Kate was in any doubt, was Hank's personal shorthand. He was asking her to confirm her suspicion that Cassel might be the imposter she first thought he was, that she may just have spent two hours in the company of a killer.

'Calm down,' she said. 'It's just a precaution.'

'The hell it is. You'd have been out that door like a whippet had you not been bruised from head to foot. We both know it.'

'OK, it's not then.' Kate looked away, then at him. 'I want to know where his wheels were last night and the night Hannah died.'

'You cannot be serious—'

'I am—'

'Kate, a rational DCI would've remembered that Cassel's vehicle is probably blocked, assuming he uses that car for work.' He meant by the Driver and Vehicle Licensing Agency; it was standard procedure to protect any officer's identity if they used their private vehicle in connection with their work.

'So unblock it.'

'Why?'

'Since when did I need to justify a request—'

'To me? You don't. Have you forgotten that I'm in exile?'

'Forget that—'

'I can't . . . you know I can't. I have no authority. Even if I had, d'you think if I ask nicely the DVLA will play ball? You're wrong, Kate.' Hank was aware that he was pushing his luck. 'Last I looked, you and Cassel were having a cosy enough conversation. What the fuck did he say to trigger such a bad reaction? It must have been something pretty dire.'

Kate hesitated. 'It's what he didn't say that interests me, plus he held on a bit too long when we shook hands.'

'He's French! I'm surprised he didn't stick the lips on while he was at it.' Hank's focus was her head. 'Though you're not quite looking your best this morning, if you don't mind me saying so.'

'Thanks. I feel so much better now.' She wasn't laughing. 'And don't make light of it either. I'm not talking bollocks. His God's gift smoky eyes locked onto mine like a fucking cruise missile. Hank, some men have a thing they do that makes women feel uncomfortable. Yes, even someone like me. You can see it, feel it, hear it in their voices. It's designed to intimidate, to undermine. Fortunately, my spot-the-creep radar is fine-tuned and in full working order—'

'Seriously? You're suggesting a cop did it.' He made a crazy face. 'It's a bad trope in fiction. In real life, it'll get you laughed out of the MIR in a straitjacket.'

'Except we both know that it happens, in and out of uniform—'

'Rarely.'

'Yeah, well, in my book, one is too many.'

'I agree, completely. Kate, you don't need this—'

'Need what?'

'Slandering a fellow officer without an ounce of proof. What you need is a medic. I was joking before, but you don't look good.'

'I'm fine.' She wasn't.

'Well you'd better make damned sure you're right if you're going to rubbish the reputation of a DCI from another force. Why not sleep on it? You're tired, still in shock. That's obvious to everyone. You should be at home, resting.'

'In a safe house?' she scoffed. 'No, and I don't care if you're exiled. You can listen while I talk this through, can't you?'

Hank made coffee, placing a steaming mug in front of each of them, helping himself to a digestive before he sat down, an expression of disbelief still present.

'What?' Kate glared at him.

'I never said a word.'

'You didn't have to. It wasn't just that handshake. Give me *some* credit.'

'OK, I'm listening.'

'As you might expect from an intelligence officer, Cassel was very clear in his delivery. On the one hand, he gave me stuff we're already aware of. On the other, stuff we didn't know, details that have not appeared in the press.'

'Well, he would do if he was Hannah's prop. I assume she told him everything—'

'What if she didn't?'

Hank didn't reply.

'Exactly. There's only one other person who'd know all of this . . . the killer himself.' Kate paused. 'Cassel claims to have had a rough start in life. He was in care, or whatever the French equivalent is. When I asked him how much Hannah had confided in him, he didn't answer for ages. Didn't move or look at me. At first I put that down to upset over the cold-blooded murder of his friend – hold that thought, for a second – but maybe he was playing for time, being cautious, formulating a response.'

'And maybe you're a mile wrong.'

'That, I accept . . .' Snippets of her conversation with Cassel reverberated in her head, as if shot from the plunger of a pinball machine. She was wishing she'd taped their chat. 'Look, he went into a long-winded football-related explanation on JC's Britishness.' She explained exactly what he'd said. 'An attempt at misdirection perhaps. He also spoke in graphic detail about the old injury to Hannah's back, more than was necessary. Hank, there was no emotion. None whatsoever. I want you to find out . . . sorry, I want *someone* to find out if Cassel is left-handed. Actually, I know just the man to do it.'

'Who?'

'Ron.'

'Naylor's in North Yorkshire?'

'He is . . .' Ron Naylor was their old boss, a detective super-intendent they both rated and liked. Kate had gone to training school with him. 'We keep in touch and meet up occasionally. He's our shortcut to finding out about Cassel.'

'Yeah, well maybe he'll talk some sense into you. I sure as hell can't.'

'Humour me . . . I'd like nothing better than to rule Cassel out, but I'm telling you there was something that raised the hairs on my arms when we shook hands. At his own admission, he met with Hannah two weeks ago in Waren Mill, which means he's familiar with that area of the coast. For all we know, he could've been keeping obs on her for weeks. And another thing. Throughout our discussion, he displayed none of the emotion you'd expect from the friend of a murder victim. Not sadness, frustration or anger.'

'Maybe he's made like that.'

'Make your mind up. First he's a man of passion, now he's not. Hank, you know cops, they're nosy by nature, and yet he didn't once ask how Hannah had died. Tell me that's not odd.' Though he didn't speak, Kate could tell he was reassessing, at least giving her opinion due consideration. 'Actually, now I come to think of it, the whole time he was in here, he asked only one question—'

'Which was?'

'I'll give you three guesses.'

Hank shrugged.

Kate swallowed down the bile in her throat. 'He wanted to know where Aaron was – the one piece of information we know the killer is desperate for. Cassel knew about the boy and yet he didn't mention him until he was heading out the door. When I asked why, he said it hadn't occurred to him. He said Hannah had moved Aaron, that he knew the lad was safe. All perfectly plausible . . . or a complete fabrication.'

## 79

Things had not quite gone to plan. A pedestrian colliding with a car usually meant curtains. However, due to her agility training and quick thinking, Daniels had defied the odds and survived. There was only one place paramedics would take an RTA casualty, Northumbria's specialist emergency care hospital in Cramlington. Following the drama he'd created, there was no need for JC to engage in ambulance chasing.

He'd made his way there at his own pace and with time to spare.

He'd been sitting in the waiting area among the sicknotes, minding his own business, when her second-in-command arrived, trying to sweet-talk his way past reception. Unable to swing it without a warrant card, he was told to sit and wait like everyone else. Unimpressed, he'd taken a seat just yards from JC, so close they were almost within touching distance.

JC was used to taking risks, but this took things to another level. As they sat there, it riled him to think that Gormley was still around and not languishing in a cell for Walker's murder. Predictably, the DS was a man impatient of bureaucracy, and when the next approved visiting family member was buzzed into the treatment area, before the automatic door closed behind her he'd slipped in sideways with the stealth of a Royal Marines commando but, arguably, less finesse.

Nicely done, JC remembered thinking, though it hadn't worked.

He'd caught muffled voices through the door as Gormley was told to leave, the exchange getting louder and more heated with every passing second, an unfortunate occupational hazard for the medical profession these days. The detective should have known better. However, it all went quiet eventually. Either they had taken him out the rear exit – to avoid a scrap in full view of the waiting public – or someone had acquiesced, allowing him access for no other reason than to shut him up.

Two long hours later, he'd emerged, pushing an out of sorts, and it had to be said, pale DCI in a wheelchair. Daniels was down but not out. She looked like she was ready to rip someone's head off.

*His, most probably.*

The woman walking by her side was her housemate and running partner, whose shapely body was still dressed in sculpted reflective leggings and a thin running top. Her hair was scuffed tightly back from a face that laid bare her exhaustion. JC had thrown her a sympathetic smile as she walked by . . .

*I hope your friend's OK.*

She half-smiled, not a flicker of recognition.

Why should there have been? To her he was just another of the walking wounded waiting to be seen. As the group reached the door, a doctor followed them out. Less than impressed, he'd made a final attempt at persuading Daniels not to discharge herself. She told him she'd sign a disclaimer if it made him feel any better.

JC chuckled.

*You simply couldn't knock her down – no pun intended.*

Just as he was initially drawn to Hannah Swift, JC felt an affinity with Daniels. He liked nothing more than a formidable opponent, especially, though not exclusively, if that person happened to be female. She had awakened his appetite for a fair fight, where only fools underestimated one another. By now, she'd understand the rules of engagement. He'd become so obsessed, he'd almost forgotten what the game was.

Touching her had given him such a thrill.

# 80

Kate left Bright's office with a big smile on her face. She wanted to hug him when told that Hank was in the clear. There was no hard evidence to connect them yet, but two murders had now been merged with Hannah's: Gilroy's, due to the fact that, after his death, someone had followed her to the airport in his car; Walker's, because he was Hannah's solicitor. There was a strong suspicion that he'd been killed to stop him incriminating JC. Stone and his team were assisting.

Kate headed for his office.

Stone was on the phone when she stuck her head around the door. He beckoned her in, pointing to a seat. Whoever he was talking to, or laughing with, was someone special. Kate could see it in his eyes as he listened to the caller. She couldn't hear what was being said, but it didn't take long to work out who it might be.

'I've got company. Gotta go . . . yeah, yeah, I'll call you.' He hung up.

'How is she?' Kate said.

'She, who?'

'Frankie.'

Stone said, 'I assumed you were here about your 2ic, not mine.'

'Where is she anyway? I've not seen her around – or heard her either.'

Stone smiled. 'She's on leave this week.'

'She has withdrawal symptoms already?' Kate stopped teasing. Rumour had it that Stone and Oliver spent a lot of time in each other's company outside of work. 'Bright just passed on the good news, David. I don't know what to say.'

'Don't thank me. If Hank had been guilty—'

'I know,' she said. 'I won't forget this. Seriously, I owe you.'

'And I intend to collect, with interest.' He leaned back in his chair. 'So, how do you want to play it?'

Kate was impressed that he deferred to her as the officer in overall charge. Many SIOs would squabble over it, whingeing at being relieved of a case. Stone was bigger than that. Scoring points wasn't his style. She felt bad for giving him a hard time when she first discovered that he'd interviewed Hank without consulting her. It wasn't sneaky or disrespectful. It was a question of urgency. The first few hours of any investigation were crucial, with little time for debate. If the circumstances had been reversed, she'd have done the same. He didn't hold a grudge, and that made her decision on strategy an easy one to make.

'I'd like you across the lot,' she said. 'Both teams with access to everything.'

'HOLMES will give us that.' The acronym was in general use. It stood for the Home Office Large Major Enquiry System on which all murder investigations were run. 'We need to tie these incidents together with more than circumstantial evidence. Bright told me earlier, in no uncertain terms, that I need to do better.'

'He likes to hear the sound of his own voice occasionally.'

Stone was pensive. 'He misses being hands on, doesn't he?'

'Can you think of anything more boring than driving a desk all day?'

'Now you mention it.'

'Anyway, he's right. We all need to up our game. From my point of view, it's not important who does what, so long as both of our teams have a breadth of what's happening. From what he told me just now, it sounds like you have Walker covered—'

'But nowhere near cracked,' he warned. 'On the guv'nor's explicit instruction, my first line of the enquiry was to implicate or eliminate Hank. Now that's out of the way, my team are concentrating on everyone else. In need of witnesses, we're prioritising foot traffic at the multistorey. No one lying in wait to off Walker would be daft enough to park his or her car there, though all vehicle movements will be checked as a matter of routine.'

Kate swore. 'It'll take an age to trace everyone.'

'Maybe not . . .' David gave her reason to believe otherwise. 'Apart from the designated permit bays on the upper floors, the car park was almost empty. The Alive after Five brigade hadn't arrived.' He was referring to a scheme that allowed free parking after five o'clock to encourage shoppers to utilise the city centre in the evenings, including the many bars and restaurants.

Kate grinned. 'Thank goodness for cheapskates.'

'Indeed. Pedestrians are our best bet: who they saw, what they can tell us.'

'I agree.' She hesitated. 'Look, I hate to ask when you have so much on, but could your team also handle Gilroy? We know he was out with mates the night before he died. None of them are talking to us. We've established that his own vehicle was not on the road the night Hannah died, but it's possible he was JC's accomplice, knocked off for his trouble. My lot are knee-deep in actions. Just say if you—'

'Consider it done.' He eyed her injuries. 'Anything I can do to take the weight off you. How are you feeling?'

'Crap, but not a word to Hank. I want to finish this. I need to finish it.'

Stone nodded his understanding. They were two of a kind.

# 81

When Kate got to the incident room, her office was empty. Harry said he'd last seen Hank sulking in the men's locker room. Kate burst through the door, grabbed his upper arm and hauled him out, ignoring the stares of male colleagues in various stages of undress. His face lit up when he heard that he'd been given the green light to return to work. 'Stone stepped up for you, Hank. Anyone else might have dragged their feet.' Kate slid her hand in her pocket, withdrawing the buff envelope. 'He asked me to give you this.'

Hank's hand closed around hers and gave it a squeeze. He didn't speak, though he never took his eyes off her. He didn't need to look inside to know that it was his warrant card. Feeling it through the paper, he almost choked up.

Kate said, 'Fizz on me later, given that we're spending the night together—'

'Sometimes your timing is totally rubbish.' He explained: 'Probationer. Your six. Heard every word.' Playing to their audience, he raised his voice slightly. 'Kate, of course I want to see you, but there are only so many nights I can leave the wife without her getting suspicious. Oi!' He caught the arm of the young copper as he walked by. 'Were you just earwigging a private conversation?'

He almost stood to attention. 'No, Sarge.'

'For your sake, I hope not. Go on, get out of here.'

'I missed you,' Kate said to Hank, pulling a ringing mobile from her pocket: unrecognised number. Curious, she took the call. 'Hello?'

'Detective Chief Inspector Kate Daniels?'

'Depends who I'm speaking to . . .' Kate covered the speaker, addressing Hank: 'Go and share your news. I'll catch up with you.'

'My name is Alex Hope. Someone left a message to call you.'

'Thanks for getting back to me. Can you hold for a second? I'm in a public area and I'd like to take this in my office.' Kate followed Hank along the corridor, getting there in double-quick time. She sat down at her desk. Time to lob a grenade into the conversation. 'Ms Hope, just so you know, I'm a murder detective in Northumbria force and this call is now being recorded.'

There was a long pause before Hope answered. 'How did you find me?'

'Hannah sent me a clue. You know which Hannah I'm on about, right? Her father told me that he'd engaged your services to find her, something you were unable to do because she'd been careful to cover her tracks.' Hank's voice was in Kate's head. 'Isn't it more a case of you laying a false trail so that she could avoid detection, even by her frantic family?'

There was a beat of time when neither woman spoke.

'Yes,' Hope said. 'But I assure you there's a valid reason.'

'I doubt that.'

'Hannah and I were friends, Detective Chief Inspector. Whatever you think you know, I can assure you, you know nothing. We conspired to keep Peter and Marianne in the dark for their own safety and hers.'

Already, Kate liked this straight-talking woman. 'Don't you people have a code of conduct?'

'Sorry? I don't understand.'

'I think you do. Swift was paying you, wasn't he?'

'I didn't take a bean from him. I told him that, unlike corporate work, I operated on a No win, No fee basis for missing persons. It wasn't strictly true, but he didn't know that. Ask him if you don't believe me.'

'I will. For now, Aaron is my priority—'

'I don't know where he is,' Hope interrupted. 'By the time I found her – it took some doing, believe me – the kid was a day pupil at a prep school where he'd board as soon as he was of age. Hannah couldn't wait to get him to a place of safety, though I gather she had plans to switch schools without telling his father in order to protect the boy. She'd have moved heaven and earth for Aaron.'

'Did she tell you which school?'

'No. It was a question of need to know, she said. She wasn't taking any chances, even with me.'

'Shit.'

'I'm sorry, I appreciate that's a bitter blow.' Hope was silent for a moment. 'I'm sure you have many questions. I'm happy to help, but I think it's best if I do that in person. As it happens, I'm in Edinburgh. I have nothing on tomorrow. I'll jump on a train and come to you. Let you know when I land.'

The line went dead.

Kate sat back, relieved to have caught a lucky break. Greenwich was a long way from her Northumbria base. She was in no condition to make the trip and didn't want to entrust the Alex Hope interview to someone else, even Thakur.

# 82

There were moments in every investigation when it was necessary to regroup and prioritise. Having Stone and his team on board was a bonus Kate hadn't expected. Additional personnel would help raise the morale of a squad already at full capacity. Detectives were collapsing under the sheer weight of their workload. Fresh eyes would bring new ideas, a different perspective. While there were reasons to be hopeful, Kate still had a mountain of outstanding actions, many more than she could cope with, of which Simon Shepherd was one. He'd been playing hide-and-seek, it seemed, giving uniformed personnel the runaround, and he'd ignored all approaches from DC Amy Heads.

Kate was on her way there, Hank driving.

As the miles flew by, the sun came out. Kate reached up, unhooking her sunglasses from the visor. Slipping them on, she shut her eyes, thinking about Jo and James and how they'd cope living temporarily with Kate's father in Northumberland while she was at the safe house.

Not ideal, but they'd be safe there.

Bright had suggested that Jo work from home until things died down. That would be harder than it ought to be. Ed Daniels had reacted badly when Kate first told him about her relationship with Jo. To say that he disapproved would be a gross understatement. He'd behaved appallingly. That didn't change until Kate very nearly lost Jo and he finally came to his senses. The two women had since come to realise that the only way he could cope was to ignore the intimacy between them. He insisted on referring to Jo as 'Kate's friend', unable to bring himself to utter the word partner. That was as far as he was ever likely to go.

Kate could live with that.

She was sick of fighting.

On the plus side, her father adored Jo's sons. He'd taught them both to ride a motorcycle, just as he'd taught Kate. Right now, she'd like nothing more than to climb on her own freedom machine and head out into the countryside to think. Riding was her passion, the only thing that could stop the images that haunted her.

A one-letter text arrived from James: **K?**

Kate replied: **Yeah, how are you guys?**

**Great. Does anything ever happen in the countryside?**

**Not much. LOL.**

**Mum and I miss you.**

**Miss you too. X**

**Take care. ☺**

Kate threw her mobile on the dash.

Hank looked into the passenger seat. 'Who was that?'

'James. Every couple of hours he texts. What the hell is that about?'

'Want to know why he does it?'

'I know why. He's checking I'm still breathing. You might have warned me.'

'About what?'

'That grown-up kids make you feel your age.' Hank chuckled. Kate looked at him. 'Seriously, it works. It's one thing when your parents worry about you. That's what they're supposed to do. But when your kids start doing it . . .' She exhaled. 'Not sure I'll ever get used to that.'

Hank laughed.

The motion of the car and the warmth through the windows was sending Kate to sleep. She yawned. 'Actually, the lad might have a point. I can hardly keep my eyes open. Mind if I get my head down for five?'

'Go for it.'

Drifting off, Kate fell into a deep sleep, dreaming of an

isolated dirt track in the middle of nowhere, surrounded by trees. It was dark and damp. She couldn't find a way out. Lost and alone, she picked her way through a surreal landscape, a ghostly journey that took her past Jack and Peggy's cottage. As she knocked on the door, ivy grew out of the ground in fast motion, swallowing it whole until there was nothing left to see. No door or windows. No smoke coming from the chimney.

Disoriented, Kate pressed on, then stopped in a clearing.

A child's playground. Rainbows. Empty swings moving back and forth. A revolving roundabout. A see-saw going up and down. Jo appeared, handing her a key. As Kate looked at it in her open hand, it dissolved before her eyes, passing through her fingers like sand. When she looked up, Jo was gone, though the moving play equipment was still there. No children. No laughter. No Aaron.

'Aaron!'

## 83

Kate could feel a hand on her arm. Forcing her eyes open, she looked down and then up, meeting Hank's gaze, aware that she'd cried out in her sleep the second she saw the expression on his face. He said nothing as he turned into Simon Shepherd's gravel driveway. Bathed in winter sunshine, the house and grounds looked very different now, with lush green meadows stretching toward Cheviot.

The Range Rover on the drive suggested that the property developer was at home.

As they mounted the steps to the front door, Hank glanced at a vintage pram that was parked beneath the portico, then at Kate. 'Family heirloom or eBay?' They'd already had the old-new money conversation.

'Perception is everything,' she said.

The housekeeper who opened the door proved Kate's point. She matched the unflattering, stereotypical description of a domestic who'd been 'in service' for a lifetime, a woman who knew her place. This timid, overweight, middle-aged woman with hollow eyes and sallow skin was no fresh-faced Maria, any more than Simon Shepherd was the inimitable Captain von Trapp. You'd think she'd been selected on the basis of her fawning deference.

'Can I help you, sir, madam?'

'I hope so.' Kate held up ID. 'I'm Detective Chief Inspector Daniels, Northumbria Police.' She thumbed toward Hank. 'This is my colleague, Detective Sergeant Gormley. We'd like a word with Mr Shepherd, please.'

'I'm afraid he's not at home.'

It was clear that she'd been told to say that.

'Is that so . . .' Kate glanced over her shoulder at the

four-by-four. Rather than challenge the woman, she made a suggestion guaranteed to bring Shepherd out of hiding. 'Then perhaps Mrs Shepherd might help us. We're not fussed, either way. Tell her it's about the victim found murdered on her father-in-law's smallholding.'

'Ma'am, please wait here.'

Kate rolled her eyes at Hank as the door closed in their faces.

Thirty seconds later, the woman returned, showing them into Shepherd's study, offering tea, which they declined. When she left them, Kate wandered around the room, inspecting the impressive collection of books. If she was a betting woman, which she was not, she'd wager that half of them had been bought for show and had never been read by the present occupants.

She turned as the door opened.

Shepherd walked through it, an irritated expression. 'DCI Daniels. How can I help you?'

Kate feigned confusion. 'Sorry, I was expecting Mrs Shepherd. We were told you were out.'

'Apologies. Had I known it was you . . .' He let the sentence trail off. 'As I told you, I'm on paternity leave. Bonding with one's offspring is important from a young age. Please, take a seat.'

Kate hadn't come to get pally. She remained standing, as did Hank. 'Sir, last time we were here you stated that you were unaware that your parents had rented out one of their caravans off-season.'

'That's correct.'

'You also said that you'd not met the young woman in question.'

'Yes, that's also correct.'

'Mr Shepherd, is it right that you sometimes accompany your mother to Craster for her shopping?'

'No, why would I do that?'

'To pick up an order, to be a good son?'

He bristled. 'Why are you asking?'

'Please answer the question,' Hank said.

'I may have helped out once or twice, but it's certainly not a regular arrangement. Whoever said it was mistaken.' He scoffed. 'I'm a very busy man. I don't do my own shopping, let alone my mother's. The idea is preposterous.'

'This is no laughing matter,' Kate said. 'Mr Shepherd, I have a witness who saw you in a Craster café talking to our murder victim. It doesn't get any more serious than that. Do you or do you not recall an occasion when you spoke to a young woman in those premises?'

Shepherd shook his head.

'Maybe I can help you out. On the day in question, I believe you'd dropped your mother off at the front door of the café and went to park your car. Your mother was talking to a young woman when you arrived to pick her up, and you were party to that conversation. Do you recall it now?'

His mouth turned down and he shook his head. 'No.'

'You didn't pick her up, or you weren't party to the conversation?'

'I recall picking her up, but I wasn't aware of anyone else being there. Detective Chief Inspector, I'm not saying it didn't happen. You've met my mother. She's the sort to pass the time of day with anyone. She's elderly. Lonely. Her life is mostly mundane. Chatting to strangers is what old people do, isn't it? If I spoke to anyone, I don't recall it. Why would I? I'm not interested in her friends, let alone her tenants.'

Kate met his gaze.

He remembered all right.

# 84

As they drove back to base, a weather presenter reported that freezing conditions were set to return to the south and west of the county. Hank killed the radio, grumbling. His discontent had nothing to do with another snow dump. He could spot a liar from a mile off and was curious as to why Simon Shepherd was hiding the fact that he'd met and spoken to Hannah Swift. 'If there was nothing to it, why cover it up?'

Kate was in two minds. 'There was some truth in what he said, Hank. I've been in the same boat when my old man has stopped to talk to someone I don't know. Even though he couldn't stand the sight of me half the time, he'd be all sweetness and light, proudly introducing me as his daughter, a senior police officer. I've smiled and said hello. Secretly I was sticking my fingers down my throat. Patronising is too weak a word for it. Would I remember those people weeks later? Probably not, because they didn't mean anything to me.'

'So what you're saying is, I'm reading something into it that isn't there—'

'I'm saying that it's possible. Helping us isn't top of his agenda. The selfish prick doesn't give a toss about his parents or anything else that won't benefit him. Some people are like that. They can't be arsed to be involved, never mind appear as a witness in a case that has nothing to do with them.'

'I thought Munro said that Hannah reacted badly when he arrived in the café?'

'She did, but that's easily explained.'

'Is it?'

'Shepherd isn't a likeable character, is he? He looks down his nose at people, unless they can do him some good, then I bet he's a different personality altogether. He'll be charming and generous. That's the way guys like him are. Munro described him as a sleaze. If there was an atmosphere between Gemma and Shepherd, Hannah may have picked up on that and given him a wide berth, especially if he reminded her of JC. Victims of physical and emotional abuse are wary, Hank. It could be that simple.'

It wasn't often that Kate allowed Hank to take the wheel of her private vehicle. Driving was one of life's pleasures. She was never happier than when she was on the road. Today, her right hip was playing up where, last night, wrapped in thin leggings, it had connected with a strip of tarmac. She stared out at the sunset as the countryside gave way to industrial estates and social housing.

Hank turned off the A19, taking the Coast Road, heading west.

'I wish we didn't have to go to the safe house tonight,' she said.

He pulled out to overtake a slow-moving vehicle. 'Well, we do, so get used to it.'

'Bright would never know if we sneaked off home.'

'Don't even think about it. I've been charged with protecting you. I've only been out of the shit two minutes and I'm not jumping back in, even for you.'

'Fuck's sake, JC is trying to intimidate me—'

'He nearly killed you . . . And he set me up.' Hank left the road at the first exit. Traffic ground to a halt at the next junction they came to. He looked at her while they were stationary, a stony expression. 'Kate, if you don't go to the safe house, I'll tell Bright myself and he'll hand the case to Stone.'

'You won't do that.'

'Watch me.'

'Hannah is—'

'Dead . . . She's dead, Kate. And you're alive. I want to keep it that way. Since the moment you got your hands on her note you've been pushing yourself too hard. While you were doing that, you weren't on your toes, were you? If you had been, you'd have seen that bastard coming from a thousand yards away. The fact that you didn't scares me. It should scare you too. You need to focus. To do that, you need to sleep. And I mean real sleep, not the fucking horror show I witnessed earlier. Yeah, I know all about them. Jo told me . . .'

'Did she? Are you done?'

'Not even close.' He moved off, taking the underpass towards their base on Middle Engine Lane. 'Kate, I'm worried that he'll find Aaron before we do.'

'Watch out!' she yelled.

Hank was forced to take evasive action as a child ran into the path of the Audi. A pregnant woman with a fag in her mouth ran out, giving the boy a hard clout for his trouble, even before they reached the safety of the pavement. The kid didn't know what he'd done to deserve it.

'Look at her,' Kate said. 'He's barely school age.'

'Some people shouldn't have kids.'

'Cassel said the same thing to me earlier.' The sight of the boy screaming at the side of the road made Kate's blood boil. The Audi began to move forward. 'Stop, stop!'

Knowing what was coming, Hank hit the brakes, resulting in the blast of a horn from the driver behind. In spite of her aching bones, Kate was out of the car before it properly came to a halt. She remonstrated with the mother of the child, receiving a mouthful of abuse in return until she showed her warrant card.

'What you gonna do? Arrest me?'

'Don't tempt me,' Kate said.

'Conor's a twat, just like his old man.'

'Yeah, well you're hardly a role model.'

'Fuck off.'

Kate couldn't take her eyes off the woman's bump, another victim in the making. The poor bairn didn't stand a chance, any more than Conor did. The smacking had stopped, though Kate was in no doubt that it would continue, if not today, then tomorrow or the day after, ad infinitum. Before long, he'd be the one doling out the violence and would probably end up in the cells.

'Keep hold of him in future.'

On her way to her vehicle, Kate ignored the fact that her actions had caused a traffic jam on a road that was highly congested at the best of times. For Kate, this was the worst of times. She wondered just how much violence Hannah's child might have witnessed during his lifetime. Kate imagined her shielding him, doing her best to keep his life as normal as possible. As she climbed in, words tumbled from her mouth that were not intended for Hank.

'She was planning to send him away to keep him safe.'

'What? Who?'

'Aaron. Get going. I have an idea.'

# 85

Andy Brown was so excited to see Kate enter the building, he began talking to her as she moved at snail's pace along the corridor toward the MIR. 'Boss, I found Hannah's bank account. She was born here in the UK, but she had dual nationality. At the end of 2015, she changed her surname by deed poll to Briand. Two months later, she applied for a Santander account in that name while in France, using her Bordeaux address. She was a very wealthy woman.'

Kate gave him the side-eye. 'Andy, unless you can find posh boarding school fees on her list of expenses, I'm not fucking interested.'

She limped off, leaving him affronted in the corridor.

Hank followed. 'Did you learn your management style from the mouthy cow in the street? I think you hurt his feelings.'

'He hurt my ears. And if he's that sensitive, he's in the wrong job.'

'He is.' He held the door open for her. 'He works for you.'

She smiled at him as she walked past. 'Too harsh?'

'Just a tad.'

'OK, when we're done, find him and tell him I'm sorry.'

'I think it should come from you—'

'Don't push your luck.'

Hank laughed.

On a mission, Kate passed through the incident room towards her office, fending off all attempts to draw her attention. Door closed, blinds down, she picked up the internal phone, pressing nine for an outside line, then adding a number that was already open in her mobile contacts.

Peter Swift picked up on the fourth ring. 'Hello?'

Kate put the phone on speaker. 'Peter, it's Kate . . . Daniels.'

'Have you found the boy? Please, tell me you have.'

'I'm afraid not, but that is why I'm calling. I need your help.'

'In what way?'

'Certain documents written by Hannah have emerged in the course of our enquiries. I have reason to believe that she is dropping hints about the man who killed her. I think that she used your first name as Aaron's middle name as a signpost, one she anticipated that I might pick up and run with. Might she have sent her son to be educated at a boarding school that has some special connection with you or your past?'

'My father's job took him all over the world. I only ever went to one school.'

Kate exchanged a hopeful look with Hank. This could be the breakthrough they had been hoping for, or it could lead to nothing. Mentally, they were crossing fingers.

'Which is?'

'Haltonghyll, North Yorkshire.'

'Can you spell that for me?'

As he did so, Kate entered it in Safari.

The homepage loaded with an impressive image of a fine building set in acres and acres of idyllic countryside. It was an independent preparatory school taking only boys, boasting academic excellence, promising cultural and social development for every child. Kate pulled up another page, typing in a start and finish point. The school was just over two hours away by car.

Peter's voice brought Kate into the room. 'Would you like me to make enquiries?'

'No,' she said. 'I'll do it.'

'I doubt they'll talk to you without first consulting with the board.'

'My warrant card opens many doors, Peter. If your grandson is boarding there and staff are notified of a potential security breach, they'll see that time is of the essence.' Kate chose her next words carefully. 'Hannah stayed away to protect you. For the same reason, I believe she may have sent her son away, so please leave this with us. On no account should you discuss my suspicions with anyone or take matters into your own hands. If you do, all Hannah's efforts will be for nothing. It could have dire consequences for you and the child. Remember, when we find him, Aaron is going to need you.'

'You have my word, Kate.'

'I'll keep you posted.'

# 86

There was nothing to be gained and everything to lose by calling the school. A personal visit was required. Trying to find a child whose life was in peril – suspecting that she might be under surveillance – Kate decided that there was only one safe way to leave Middle Earth. She and Hank ducked down in the rear of a police vehicle, blues and twos engaged, sirens blaring as it sped out of the car park.

Hiding in plain sight could never be underestimated.

Receiving the all-clear from the driver, they spent the rest of the journey discussing strategy. If Aaron was a boarder at Peter's old prep school, Kate would take him into her care for his own safety. If not, she had no idea where to turn. It wasn't as if she even knew what the boy looked like, or who his friends were.

They reached Haltonghyll in under two hours, the arrival of the Traffic car causing quite a stir. Within seconds of pulling up in front of a building, described on the net as Grade II listed Victorian Gothic, the faces of adults and children appeared at the mullioned windows, at least fifty pairs of eyes staring out at them.

Leaving their driver in the car, Kate and Hank got out.

The front door opened as they climbed the steps. A smartly dressed woman introduced herself as the school's matron, Mrs Pearson. A slim lady with greying hair and sharp green eyes, she ushered them into a large study. When Kate asked to see Aaron, she was told that she was too late, a crushing blow she'd known was a possibility before setting off, but one she'd hoped wouldn't become a reality.

Aaron was registered as a boarder, but he was gone.

Kate was bereft, trying not to show it. 'Gone?'

'Temporarily,' Pearson said. 'Forgive me, but what is this about?'

'It's a police matter . . .'

'Yes, I'd worked that out.'

It was all Kate was prepared to say for now. 'Aaron obviously didn't just walk out of here. When you say gone, was he collected? If so, by whom?'

'Not exactly.'

'Either he was or he wasn't,' Hank said.

Pearson switched her attention from him to Kate. 'We received an urgent email from his mother to say that there had been a family bereavement. She's regularly in touch. She asked us to arrange a taxi to take him to the station in Settle—'

'Train or bus?'

'Train. She said his ticket would be there for him to collect and that she'd emailed him with instructions. I gather she intended to meet him at the other end.'

'The other end?' Kate queried.

'She didn't specify a destination. Why would that be our business?'

With a sinking heart, Kate moved on. 'When did you receive the email?'

'Yesterday . . .'

'At what time?'

Pearson consulted her inbox. 'Six forty-three . . . Aaron confirmed that she'd been in touch to explain that she needed to take him out of school for a few days.'

'And he left when?'

'This morning, after breakfast.' Pearson showed no signs of distress but what she said next felt like a justification for what, in Kate's opinion, was an almighty fuck-up. 'Aaron is a very sensible boy, Detective Chief Inspector. A star pupil, in and out of the classroom. He wasn't upset when spoken to, other than the fact that he'd miss the chess tournament we're holding tonight. He even joked about his absence having an upside. He meant someone else could win for a change. His housemaster saw him safely into a cab.'

'I need to search his room,' Kate said.

'Well, there are other boys to consider.'

'Mrs Pearson, my sergeant and I have been on the premises for five minutes and you've yet to ask for ID.'

'You arrived in a police car.'

'Which could have been stolen. As it happens, it wasn't, but you can't possibly know that.' Having put Pearson in her box, Kate held her warrant card in front of Pearson's face. It showed her image, certified her as K DANIELS, rank as Detective Chief Inspector with Northumbria Police. She put it away. 'My ID doesn't show that we are murder detectives. Please feel free to check with our HQ. Now, this is delicate and highly confidential. Aaron's mother was murdered on Tuesday in Northumberland, which means she couldn't possibly have sent you that email.'

## 87

Kate and Hank had split up. He went off to secure a copy of the email and to view and take a copy of the day's CCTV. It was crucial to get a handle on the cab driver who'd driven Aaron to Settle railway station. Kate followed Pearson through the building to the East Wing. A sweeping stone staircase, the treads worn from generations of footfall, took them to the second floor. The matron turned right, leading Kate along a wide corridor past door after door of student accommodation.

It was a toss-up as to which one of them was the most distressed.

Acting in loco parentis, the school owed a duty of care to all boarders. If word got out that the head or key staff were failing to provide an appropriate level of security for the children in their care, parents would be falling over themselves to remove their offspring and recoup the extortionate fees they had paid upfront.

Trying to push away the thought that JC had got to Aaron first, Kate wondered where all the children were. There was the odd snippet of conversation behind closed doors, the sound of a violin being played, but the corridor was deathly quiet otherwise, not a child in sight. Pearson stopped walking, knocked twice on an ornate mahogany door, then pushed it ajar, calling out to see if the occupants were decent.

The sing-song chorus of 'Yes, Mrs Pearson' came from inside.

She opened the door to reveal a four-bedded, wood-panelled room with huge floor-to-ceiling windows. Each bed had a set of drawers on one side, a small bedside table on the other and large blanket box at the foot for storage.

Three youngsters were sitting on the floor playing cards.

'Boys, could you leave us for a moment?' Obediently, they

got up. 'Don't go far, this lady is a detective. She may need to talk to you. Wait in the hallway.' Without questioning why, the boys moved past Kate, one of them smiling at her, clearly intrigued and more than a touch excited that he'd be talking to police.

Kate worked quickly, searching the drawers first, removing each one completely, checking that nothing was taped to the underside or around the edges. The deep bottom drawer held sports gear, cricket whites, gym clothing. The next, school uniform on one side, ordinary clothing on the other. The top drawer, pyjamas on the right, socks and underwear on the left. She'd searched a lot of boys' bedrooms in her time – some she wished she hadn't – but this was a new experience.

Everything was clean, pressed, neatly stacked.

Replacing the drawers, Kate turned her attention to the bed-side table. Underneath was a stack of textbooks on a variety of subjects. She flicked through each one, fanning the pages, giving them a shake to see if anything fell out.

Nothing did.

She did the same to a neat stack of notebooks she found in the table drawer. Placing them to one side, she tipped the rest of the contents out onto the bed, pausing to study an academic timetable for a long moment. The school day at boarding school was a damned sight longer than it was at a conventional school, she noticed. Adding this to the pile of notebooks, Kate turned to Aaron's pencil case, which revealed the usual paraphernalia, nothing she didn't expect to find in there.

Returning the drawer to its casing, she lifted the lid on the blanket chest at the foot of the bed, finding that it held everything else: personal reading matter, board games, a pair of well-worn boxing gloves, an ancient Swiss Army knife. Athletics medals too. There were pastels and artist's sketch pads, all of which were full, a mixture of still life, landscapes and portraits – one self-portrait and another of the boy who'd smiled at her when he left the room a moment ago.

Aaron, it seemed, was talented and thriving at Haltonghyll.

Comforted by the fact that he had mates and appeared to be having fun – and, more importantly, that he was alive that morning – Kate got down on her hands and knees to look under his bed. She found a suitcase there. Hoping it would reveal a hidden gem, she pulled it out. Nothing inside. Disappointed, she shoved it away and stood up, looking around the room. There was something odd here.

It took her a moment to realise what it was.

She turned to face Pearson, pointing at the items she'd placed on the bed. 'I'm going to have to take these.' She paused. 'Aaron's section of the room appears bland compared to his peers. There's a distinct lack of junk. The other beds are surrounded with personal stuff, including family photographs, some taken here, others at home. There's no iPad, laptop or mobile phone, all of which I presume Aaron owned.'

'I imagine he took them with him. Children, even those in our care, can't do without technology.' Clearly, she didn't approve.

'Can you see anything that's missing?'

Pearson took a cursory glance around Aaron's bed. 'I don't think so.'

Kate held on to her irritation. 'Please, look carefully.'

Pearson eyed the bed and surrounding area, pausing on his bedside table. 'Actually, yes. Aaron had a small, framed photograph of his mother. It sat there beside the lamp . . .' Her voice faded out of Kate's head, replaced by her own. She knew then that the boy wasn't planning to return.

# 88

Kate was properly exhausted but her brain wouldn't rest. She'd got nothing from Aaron's roommates and hadn't formed the impression that they were hiding anything. If Aaron knew that his mother's life depended on his silence, he'd have kept schtum for sure. With the stakes that high, who could blame him? His private life was no one's business but his own.

Hank had fared better than Kate. CCTV had provided a clear image of Aaron's cab leaving the school, its registration plate easily identifiable. He'd copied the footage and got hold of photographs of Aaron, who, it turned out, was the double of his mother.

Where the hell was he?

From Settle, he could travel via Leeds to anywhere, in any direction. Or north via Carlisle, then east to Newcastle or across the Scottish Border. Kate might as well stick a pin into a map and cross her fingers. She was clinging to the belief that he was following his mother's instructions. Was she keeping him safe, even from the grave?

It was 9 p.m. before the Traffic car dropped them off at the safe house.

In the hallway, Kate rolled her eyes at Hank. 'No expense spared,' she said sarcastically.

She hobbled to the sofa. This dreary flat was not where she wanted to be. She wanted to be home with Jo, not hiding in the shadows from JC, whoever he was. She wanted to be feeling his collar, slapping the cuffs on.

In the kitchen, Hank put on the kettle, then switched it off again. He checked the fridge. Some generous soul had filled it with goodies, including a few beers and a bottle of fizz that had a note attached.

**Boss, this was all I could get.**

Hank smiled. With all that was going on, Kate hadn't forgotten. Just then, his mobile rang. Pulling it from his pocket, he pushed the fridge door shut before answering.

'DS Gormley.'

'Hi, my name's Martin. I work for Rees Taxis. I've been asked to give you a call.'

'Yeah, thanks for getting back to me so quickly.' Explaining why they needed to talk, Hank looked out of the window. Unfamiliar with this particular safe house, he was impressed that the rear wall of the yard had a coil of razor wire on top should JC come calling. 'Do you remember the fare?'

'Course I do. I drop off and pick up from Haltonghyll all the time. It's a "nice little earner", as the saying goes. He was a good kid. They all are. I assume he's done a runner—'

'Why would you say that? Was he anxious?'

'No, but you wouldn't be involved if he was on the level, would you? If he's gone missing, it's nowt to do with me. I'm fully regulated, mate, no CRO number, same as you. I'm not into kids, even my own. Them running away is no biggie. Ask me, it's a rite of passage. Need a description of what he was wearing?'

What Hank did need was a beer. He took one from the fridge. 'No, I have it on tape,' he said. 'Can you recall what time you dropped him at the station?'

''Bout nine.'

Hank opened the kitchen drawer, finding a corkscrew, a T-shaped one, not the type with a bottle opener on the end. Just his luck. Who'd buy bottles when cans were a thing? He shut the drawer.

'Did he chat in the car?'

'Not really. When it's kids I tend not to engage, unless they do. You can't shut some of them up.'

'It's a twenty-minute drive. He must've said something.'

'I asked him where he was off to. He said a funeral. That killed the conversation dead, know what I mean? I gave the kid my condolences. He said thanks. Seemed OK. After that he was on his phone.'

'Talking?'

'Texting . . . or surfing. I let him be.'

'Was the fare pre-paid?'

'Yeah, by the school secretary. I asked the lad if he needed a receipt. He said no, got out, and away he went.'

'Thanks for the call, Martin.'

'It's Paul . . . Martin's my surname.'

'My mistake. Appreciate the help.'

The guy rang off.

Hank called British Transport Police asking if there was CCTV at Settle Station. He explained why he was asking. As soon as they knew a kid was missing, they offered to make enquiries with Northern Rail to see if they could identify Aaron getting on or off a train in either direction. Grateful for their assistance, Hank gave them as much detail as he was able, texted them an image of Aaron.

Disconnecting, he wandered into the living room to tell Kate. She was lying on the sofa, coat still on, eyes closed. His head went down. 'So much for celebrating my comeback.'

'I heard that.' She sat up straight. 'I wasn't asleep, I was thinking.'

'About what?'

'If Aaron was lured from the school, why would he take the photograph of his mum?'

Hank sat down. 'He wouldn't—'

'Is the right answer. We already know that Hannah was in the habit of calling or texting him on a Friday between midday and two. It's now Saturday, which means he didn't get a call yesterday. I checked Aaron's timetable. He has a free study period on a Friday from one till two thirty. His academic day ends at six, and spookily an email comes into the school forty minutes later.'

'You think he sent it?'

'Who else could have?'

'Good point.'

'The only way this works for me is if Hannah and Aaron had some kind of plan whereby, if he didn't hear from her at a designated time, he was to fuck off without raising the suspicions of anyone at Haltonghyll. By extension, that means that JC hasn't found him yet, but there's a downside.' Kate paused, meeting Hank's eyes across the unfamiliar room. 'If Aaron is on the fly, he's extremely vulnerable, out there alone in the certain knowledge that his mother is in trouble and may be dead. I can't even begin to imagine the heartbreak. The kid will be terrified.'

# 89

Kate called Hannah's father to update him, promising to keep in touch. Hanging up, she discarded her mobile on the arm of the couch, glancing up at Hank. 'He's worried sick. I'm going to have a bath, assuming there is one, then we'll have that drink. I need one. Afterwards, if you can get that going . . .' She pointed at the small TV in the corner of the room. 'The choice of viewing is yours, so long as we don't have to pretend we're mister and missus. I had enough of that in Spain.'

The last time they had spent the night together they were on a big job, posing as a married couple to blend in, while searching for a dangerous fugitive who'd fled to the continent to escape arrest. 'I'm still haunted by the Hawaiian shirt, pink shorts and Jesus sandals . . .' Kate said. 'Although it was the black socks, white legs combo that really cracked me up.'

'Hey, don't knock it. I take undercover work seriously.' He picked up the remote, bringing up the TV Guide, handing it to her. 'Choose what you want, I'll open the bubbly.'

'Just a small glass for me, Hank. I have work to do.'

'Tonight? C'mon, take the weight off for a bit.'

She stood up, finally removing her coat.

Her mobile rang.

Turning to look at her, Hank exhaled frustratedly. 'Don't answer it. You need to chill, Kate. Drink, bath, bed, in that order. Everything else can wait. Whatever work you were planning, we can pick up in the morning.'

Tempted to take his advice, Kate peeked at the screen. 'It's Carmichael. She wouldn't be calling if it wasn't urgent.'

Hank didn't argue. 'Suit yourself.'

Kate scooped up the phone and took the call. 'Hi Lisa—'

'Oh, thank God! Where are you?'

'Lisa, what's wrong? Why d'you need to know?'

Hank was about to say something. Like her, he was instantly suspicious.

Kate put her finger to her lips, silencing him. She covered her free ear, straining to listen. Something was obviously going down. Whatever it was, Kate could feel a sense of urgency. Removing the phone from her ear, Kate tapped on speaker. They could hear Lisa weeping. Neither of them had ever seen or heard her so distressed. Kate's stomach rolled over. From the look of him, Hank was thinking the same atrocious thought.

JC had her.

If not her, then Jo.

Kate's bottom lip quivered as she tried to stem a wail. Words deserted her.

'Boss, you need to come now!' There was an ominous pause. Carmichael was breathing hard, running by the sounds of it. 'There's been an explosion. It just came up on the incident log. Emergency vehicles on the scene. Sounds serious. Kate – it's your house.'

The scene was grim. Dense smoke hung in the air in an area that flashed blue from fire tenders and police vehicles that had rushed to cordon off the street and keep the public from getting too close. Even on this cold night, Kate could feel the heat from where she was standing. The flames were almost under control, but there was a gaping, jagged hole where the front door and half of the bay window used to be. Chunks of masonry and bits of Victorian brick littered the quiet tree-lined avenue.

The windows of neighbouring properties were out, as were some across the road. Concerned for the occupants, Kate sent Carmichael to liaise with the officer in charge. Lisa looked relatively optimistic as she walked back towards Kate a few minutes later, though as always, neither of them would take anything for granted. Whatever you heard at a crime scene could change in a matter of hours.

'All occupants accounted for, boss. A few minor cuts and abrasions, but miraculously no hospitalisations. There's a guy with a dodgy ticker refusing to leave home. His wife thinks he should. I might go and stick my oar in.' She placed a hand on Kate's arm. 'Hey, you're shivering. I wouldn't have called if I'd known that Jo and James were safe. You shouldn't be here. It's not twenty-four hours since you were wheeled out of A&E.'

Kate said nothing.

She could've added that if Hank hadn't insisted on the safe house, threatening to grass on her if she didn't play ball, she might have been lying in the morgue now. Keeping that to herself, she looked on as a small pocket of fire reignited around a pile of twisted metal, the remains of her beloved motorcycle.

When the tank exploded, it had blown the bike to bits.

From her position on the street, only the top half of the stairs was visible where they disappeared onto the first floor, one charred tread hanging loose, the tip of it breathing fire. The bottom half of the staircase was gone, along with part of the kitchen wall on the ground floor at the rear of the house.

Everything was black and smouldering.

'Did the OIC give any indication on method?'

'You can probably guess.'

'Accelerant through the letterbox?'

'Yeah, she's busy with the investigator just now, so I didn't hang around. He said there are no witnesses he could find in the properties closest to yours. That's not to say there aren't any. They just haven't found them yet.'

'Don't hold your breath, Lisa. We know who's responsible and he won't have taken any chances. They're good people round here. We look out for one another. If JC had been seen, he'd have been reported.'

Kate glanced over her shoulder, wondering if the perpetrator was in the crowd of onlookers, hiding among local journalists and camera crews, enjoying another victory at the home she shared with Jo, everything she'd worked for up in smoke. A last glance at the house made her well up. She hung on to her emotions, damned if she'd give the smug bastard the satisfaction of seeing her weep.

Turning her back on the observers beyond the tape, a warm feeling crept over her that had nothing to do with the smouldering building behind her. Did JC really think she was that stupid? Not one but two murder investigation teams were hunting a triple murderer. Kate wasn't fucking around. She had spotters in the crowd and a crew taking video from a friend's house across the road.

Kate used her call sign. 'Mike 7824: how's it going, guys?'

Hank responded. '3459: We have eyes on everyone, boss.'

'Including Amy?'

'Yup, she's looking good with her press pass on.'

Amy came back: '2845, I heard that.'

Kate caught the rookie mistake and shot off a warning: 'Maintain radio silence, 2845. If the target is there, we don't want to tip him off.'

# 90

Kate and Hank left the scene in a marked police vehicle, switching to a pool car at an agreed rendezvous to ensure they weren't followed. Kate took the wheel, insisting on paying Jo and James a personal visit before returning to the safe house, hoping and praying that they hadn't seen the late evening news by the time she got there.

It was snowing gently in Northumberland.

On the brow of a hill, she turned into a narrow lane where the snow was pristine, trees and drystone walls on either side. The vehicle moved through an open five-bar wooden gate, its headlights illuminating a single-storey stone cottage that sat alone in blissful isolation, at one with nature, much like Jack and Peggy Shepherd's place.

This evocative wintery scene always aroused an emotional response in Kate, reminding her of her childhood living there with her family. Happy times. Now she had a family of her own, but no home to go to. She stopped the car, cut the engine, staring out at the tiny windows of the cottage. Her father, a crop of white hair, came to the window and looked out.

Their eyes locked.

Staring at him, she felt like the prophet of doom. It was almost eleven o'clock and she'd come bearing news she knew would keep him awake tonight. What other choice did she have? For once, Kate was glad for the snow. It gave her an excuse to wear a beanie so her father wouldn't see the staples in her head.

He was at the door before she reached it, Jo by his side.

'Hey!' she said. 'I didn't expect to see you. Well, don't just stand there, come in.' Her expression changed from joy to surprise when Hank joined them on the doorstep. 'Well, this is turning into quite a party. What's going on?'

Kate focused on her father. 'Dad, would you mind making Hank a cuppa, or something stronger, while I have a word with Jo in private?'

He did mind and showed it.

He turned and walked away.

Kate felt guilty. She'd dragged him into this and now she was pushing him away. She could tell him it was police business – technically it was – but by morning the press would be all over it and he'd feel cheated.

As Hank followed him into the house, Jo gave her favourite male detective a kiss on the cheek, then grabbed her coat and stepped outside for some privacy. The two women fell into an embrace, the white stuff falling to the ground all around them. Kate held on for a long time. It felt like an age since they had seen each other at breakfast.

'Dare I ask why you're here?' Jo pulled away, her good humour dissolving. 'This isn't you just dropping by to say hello because you can't bear to be without me, is it?'

'No, I have something to tell you and you're not going to like it . . .' Her attention was drawn to the interior of the cottage. Only the living room lights were on. Her father and Hank in there but someone was missing. Two someones. She moved closer, making sure, then turned to look at Jo, a question on her lips. 'Where's James?'

'He just slipped out to walk Nelson. Why?'

'Right . . .' Kate scanned the treeline. No sign of him. 'Which way did he go?'

'That way.' Jo thumbed toward the river.

'How long's he been gone?'

'Kate, stop it. You're scaring me.'

'Sorry . . .' Kate grabbed her hands. 'I didn't mean to frighten you.'

She explained why she'd come and why she couldn't stay. It had nothing to do with the lack of room. She had to get back to the scene of the arson. The house would be under guard all night. Of all the things she might have said, Jo wasn't ready for the reality of what came out of Kate's mouth.

She wept openly, devastated to learn that the home they shared had been deliberately targeted. It had taken them a long time to fully commit. When they did, they'd set out to create their own safe house, a sanctuary where they could chill and enjoy each other's company, away from the stress of their day jobs. In more senses than one, what had happened tonight had torn it down.

'He won't stop until he's caught,' Jo warned.

'Neither will I . . .' Though the fire was too close to home, Kate was philosophical about it. 'Things could've been so much worse. You're safe . . .' James emerged through the trees with Nelson. Kate gave him a massive hug and smiled at Jo. 'See, we're all safe. That's all that matters. The rest is bricks and mortar. It can be repaired. Look, there's a security detail on its way. When they get here, I've got to go.'

James was clueless. 'Will one of you tell me what's going on?'

'You no longer have to pay for the back door,' Jo said. 'We don't have one.'

# 91

Kate moved into an interview room and sat down, waiting for Hope to arrive, in more ways than one. Away from the noise of the interview room, she could think more clearly. Someone had used the room for a break and had left a *Sunday Times* on the table, its headlines guaranteed to sell copies: **HOW I FELL IN LOVE WITH A SERIAL KILLER**.

'Fuck's sake!' Kate said under her breath.

She turned the newspaper over, hiding the article of Elizabeth Kendall's relationship with Ted Bundy. She had no interest in reading about a man who killed thirty women across America.

While the man she was hunting didn't fall into some people's definition of a serial killer, he'd killed three times in separate incidents and had to be stopped. Words associated with motive crowded in on her: jealousy, control, desire, revenge, greed. She didn't think that a psychotic episode had tipped a killer over the edge, bringing the life of a successful businesswoman to a premature end, but it had set off a chain reaction.

Kate's mobile lit up: Stone.

She was glad of the company. 'Hey, David—'

'Where are you?'

'Interview room. Why?'

'Just wondered if you were around.'

'Not for a couple of hours.'

'Whatever it is, good luck.'

'Thanks, I've got a few minutes if you're quick.'

'OK, I've yet to link Max Gilroy as an accomplice but my lot just received an anonymous tip-off that they're following up.'

'Can you be more specific?'

'It seems he had a boyfriend who's devastated by his death.

That might give us leverage to find out who Max had been associating with of late.'

'OK, let me know if it pays off. Anything else?'

'Yeah, a witness rang in who was in Dean Street car park when Walker went over the edge. She claims she saw something, or should I say someone acting suspiciously, who was the size and stamp of the man we're after. We're checking that out too. How's it going your end?'

'Slowly. This one is the mother of all investigations, to be honest. For a while there I had Walker pegged as a suspect. Obviously, I was wrong about that.'

'I've been keeping an eye on stuff. Your man Shepherd seems to fit the bill in terms of wealth and character—'

'Yeah, I thought so too at first, but he's a narcissist whose only mission in life is to make money. That doesn't necessarily make him a killer. There's someone else I'd rather not name until I've checked him out. He claims he met Hannah in Paris in 2004 and kept in touch with her. I'm making discreet enquiries about him.'

'He's a polis?'

'Confidentially, yes.'

'Is that why you're pissed off?'

'No, I just wish I was making more headway. Hank thinks I'm a basket case.'

David laughed. 'You'll get there, Kate. Any one of your theories could be a goer.'

'Or none of them.' There was a knock at the door.

'Hey, our job involves disproving rather than proving guilt.'

'Yeah, I know.' Carmichael popped her head in. Kate held up a finger, asking her to wait a second, then went back to her call. 'David, my witness is here. We'll catch up later.'

Disconnecting, Kate stood up as the door opened a second time, hoping that the woman being shown into the room would reveal exactly who she was up against. While the man she was hunting was at large, Aaron wasn't safe.

Alex Hope was steely-eyed, mid-fifties, silver-grey hair and the body of a woman half her age. Her coat was already off, hung over her left arm. She was casually dressed in jeans and warm, chunky, designer knitwear Kate's salary wouldn't stretch to.

'Why do I feel like I just crawled out from under a stone?' was the first thing Hope said.

Reminding herself to be less transparent, Kate proffered a hand. 'I'm Kate, thanks for coming down. It's good of you.' Rank was unimportant to Kate at the best of times. In the conversation she was about to have, it was redundant. Less formality would build rapport. This witness might have vital information to share. Extending her condolences, Kate invited Hope to sit.

'Good journey?'

'I've had worse.' Hope pulled out a chair and sat down. 'In my experience, trains never run well on a weekend. The heating on this morning's wasn't working.'

'I can offer you a better class of coffee than LNER.'

'It couldn't be worse, but I'm good, thanks.'

Instinctively, Kate warmed to the former military intelligence officer. In terms of experience, they had much in common. When it came to getting the lowdown on the enemy, both were trained in the art of strategy and tactics. Together they would make a formidable team if the DCI played her cards right.

'I hope you gave as good as you got.' Hope was referring to Kate's head wound.

'Yeah, never pick a fight with a BMW 1 Series.'

Hope laughed.

Kate got straight to it, sharing as much information as she could in order to elicit the right responses, making it absolutely clear what she knew and what she was keen to find out. Hope listened intently, without interruption, until Kate had finished speaking. 'So you see my problem. In short, I have a handle on where and when Hannah met her abuser, but little else to go on. I'm hoping you can fill in the gaps.'

# 92

The two women had been talking for around half an hour. Hope said: 'As far as our business arrangement was concerned, Hannah and I conspired together for no other reason than to keep her parents and child safe. Her morale was on the floor but, as time went on, the stronger she became. Kate, if you've formed the impression of a woman worn down by abuse, you're a mile wide of the mark.'

'That's interesting.'

'What is?'

'Another witness told me she was out to humiliate her abuser.'

'Would that witness be a man by any chance?'

'As it happens—'

'Thought so . . .' Hope shook her head. 'Why is it that when a female decides to fight back it's seen as vindictive, a spiteful act motivated by rage, not civic duty? And that the person on the receiving end, usually a bloke, doesn't deserve it? Fuck that. If my perspective counts, Hannah was a woman with a strong moral compass. She was going to stop this man to prevent him from selecting his next victim, do or die.'

Hope looked away.

'Sounds like my kind of woman,' Kate said.

'Yeah, look where it got her.' Hope's eyes flashed with anger and frustration. 'She was fearless, Kate. A force to be reckoned with. She said her intel was good. God knows I tried to wheedle it out of her. It wasn't that she didn't trust me. She'd learned not to trust anyone. She had a strong impulse to take this man down, to treat him as he'd treated her. It wasn't revenge, it was justice. An eye for an eye.'

'She could have got that through us.'

'Exactly what I told her. At home, she took the beatings, made him think she'd learned her lesson. The top and bottom of it was, she was investigating his business dealings. She wasn't interested in him appearing on a domestic assault charge a slick lawyer would plead was provocation, one where he'd walk, ready to beat her or someone else senseless. So yes, her endgame was to destroy him. It was like a drug to her. She had the means and opportunity to do it. She was living on a knife-edge. Ironically, taking the fight to him made her feel alive and less vulnerable. Her words, not mine.'

'Even though he could kill her at any moment's notice?'

'Even then. Tell me you or I would've done things differently? Would we hell. Look, I'm no psychologist, but Hannah thrived on subterfuge, just like us. What she did was high-risk, just like us, but it gave her power she hadn't had for a very long time.'

'What do you know about the bloke she was with?'

'Only that he's set up as a charitable entrepreneur.'

'A front, I assume.'

Hope gave a nod. 'He's well-connected: police, politicians, lawyers were just some of the people he hung around with. He'd once threatened to have Hannah sectioned by psychiatrist friends if she turned against him. He was that confident in his ability to control her. He couldn't.'

'Did she let anything slip in the course of your conversations?'

'Once. She said she couldn't find him linked to any company's board of directors and yet everything else about him seemed legit. He was like a ghost, she said. A very rich ghost. She begged me not to follow her or ask questions she didn't want to answer. She felt terribly guilty for worrying her parents, but she was of the opinion it was better if they stopped searching for her. Full stop.'

'Did she know her mother had passed away?'

'Not as far as I know. I was abroad when it happened. Peter told me when I returned to the UK. Unfortunately, Hannah had moved on by then. My emails bounced back undelivered. I was forced to sit it out and wait for her to contact me. She never did. Her actions may seem unconscionable to you, but they were taken with the best intentions. Peter, Marianne and her boy's safety was paramount. Nothing else mattered. So you see, the fucker you're hunting has taken four lives, not one.'

'I know you didn't mean that literally, but he's actually taken three.'

'What? Who?'

'I can't say. People in his employ,' Kate clarified.

'Jesus! You need to find him.'

'I won't stop until I do.'

'Can I give you a piece of advice?' Hope didn't wait for a reply. 'However many good deeds and donations this phoney philanthropist has doled out, no matter how fireproof he thinks he is, everyone – and I mean everyone – has a weakness. Hannah was his. He may have beaten her, maimed her even, but he adored her. When you catch him, that's what'll wind him up the most.'

'I'll be sure to make use of it.' Discovering the weak points in an adversary was Hope's thing. She'd just given Kate the upper hand and deserved her thanks. Intel like that was gold to an SIO planning interview strategy. 'How we doing for time?'

Hope checked her watch. 'I'm fine for another half hour.'

'Wait here, I have something I want to show you.'

Leaving the room, Kate rushed down the stairs to the exhibits room. When she returned, Hope was nowhere to be seen. Kate was about to panic when she spotted her coat dumped on the floor beside her chair, along with her bag.

The door opened behind her.

'Sorry, I needed the restroom.' Hope sat down, eyeing the package in Kate's hand.

Kate pushed an exhibits envelope across the table. It contained the key that Jo found in the playground at the caravan site.

As Hope studied it, Kate studied her.

Hope looked up, a smile developing. 'I might just be in a position to help you out here. I'll only tell you if you remember to breathe.'

They both laughed.

'Last time Hannah and I met was in Morpeth,' Hope said. 'I was up here on a job. I couldn't put my finger on it, but she wasn't herself. I was worried about her. Despite the promises I made, when she and I split I trailed her to see where she'd go. She only made one detour on the way home. If this . . .' She held up the exhibit. 'Is what I think it is, I know exactly where you'll find what you're looking for.'

# 93

Locksafe Vaults was an independent safe-deposit box facility, hidden away in the market town of Morpeth, close to its seventeenth-century clock tower on Oldgate. The vault provided cutting-edge security for its clientele, 24/7. Conveniently, the place was open on a Sunday afternoon. Kate and Hank had gone there without an appointment and with high hopes, only to have them dashed.

The owner, Craig Davison, was mid-fifties, smartly dressed in a tailored navy suit, white shirt and striped tie. Once Kate explained why she was there, he confirmed that Hannah was indeed a client. He paused before delivering crushing news to the detectives. 'Theoretically, as she's now deceased, I can override the biometric scanner and PIN to get you into the vault. There's no problem with that, but in order to match the key to my own, you'll need her four-digit box number.'

'That's not very helpful,' Hank moaned.

'I'm not being awkward, Sergeant.'

Hank looked at him as if he was. 'Aren't you?'

'No, I'm not. It normally takes a court order to get inside one of these. As you can appreciate, the estate inherits the contents and I'll have questions to answer if anything is missing.'

'We're not after her jewellery.'

Hank was beginning to irritate Kate. As he continued arguing with the proprietor, she turned her back, tuning them out, mentally walking her way through the written list of possessions O'Brien had removed from Hannah's caravan, and the images that went with them.

If only she could hear herself think.

'We're after the man who murdered her,' Hank said.

'I appreciate that,' Davison said. 'I'd ask you to appreciate my situation. Under the sad circumstances the detective chief inspector just outlined, I'm prepared to make allowances, but I'm not a magician.'

'There must be a way round it.'

'There isn't. As I said, I'd like to help you out. My daughter is a police officer. I know only too well how difficult your job is. Mine isn't easy either. I can drill a lock if someone has lost their keys and can prove who they are, but that's not the case here. You can prove ID, and you have a key, but no number. Now do you understand? I'm terribly sorry . . .'

'Not as sorry as we are. We have no clue.'

'Maybe we do,' Kate said.

Hank snapped his head around.

She turned to face Davison. 'Try One. Zero. Four. Five.'

'She's a genius,' Hank told Carmichael as they waited for everyone to arrive for an impromptu briefing. 'Come with me.' He took her by the arm, guiding her into Kate's empty office, drawing her attention to the photocopy of Hannah's note that was posted to the wall, the first words of which were: Friday, 10:45 p.m. 'On day one, Kate queried why Hannah might sit down and pen a letter at that time of night. Now we know she didn't. As inspired guesses go, this is right up there.'

'Brilliant,' Carmichael said. 'So what was in the box?'

Before he could answer, Kate knocked on the window, summoning them.

The incident room was crammed at the best of times. With two teams squashed in, it was standing room only that afternoon. Kate stood out front, facing the room, Stone by her side, Hank and Carmichael directly in front of her. Detectives from the combined Murder Investigation Teams fell silent as she called for order.

'First of all, can I thank those of you who've joined us from a rest day at short notice. I'm sorry to spoil your Sunday roast.

I did it because there has never been a better time to pool resources.'

There were no scowls, no dissenting voices.

Kate had every faith that they were all on board. 'I have no intention of wasting time on trivia, or repeating myself, so pay attention. Three hours ago, acting on information received, Hank and I secured the contents of a safe deposit box that has blown this enquiry wide open. Hannah Swift left us a raft of incriminating evidence against her former abuser, a forty-eight-year-old male.' She uploaded a large image onto the digital murder wall that popped up on the screen behind her. 'This is Dominic Clay, who is now our only suspect.' Using her laptop arrow keys she moved through a slideshow. 'Take a good look. This man is dangerous and will kill again if we don't stop him.' Kate turned to face the detectives. 'The documents we found in the IP's safe deposit box all relate to him. They go back several years and will take time to process.' She held up a hand, stemming a collective moan. 'The good news is the best forensic accountant in the country will be with us later today—'

'Felicity Fairfax?' It was Stone who'd asked the question.

Kate looked at him. 'You know her?'

'We've worked together once or twice.'

'Great, that'll help her settle in. She'll be joined by two senior detectives from the fraud squad and they won't move from my office without someone watching them.' Kate found Carmichael in the crowd. 'Lisa, you will be on their shoulders to ensure that anything found is immediately fed to me and the team.'

'Yes, boss. What about Monaco? Now we have a name—'

'Yes, leave that,' Kate said. 'Harry, reallocate her actions. We may not need to complete that one. There are plenty of images of Clay and Hannah in the dossier. The financial documentation is dynamite. DCI Stone and I are in agreement that it'll sink Clay, stripping him of everything he owns. But it will not convict him of the murders of Hannah, Walker or Gilroy. Put anything that doesn't relate to our main suspect in for referral and get a shift on with forensics. If results are due, chase them up. We need something to link Clay to these deaths.'

Stone was nodding in agreement. There had been a palpable shift of mood since the briefing began. Faces were animated. Notes being taken. Everyone concentrating on what was being said.

'Our priority is to get eyes on Clay,' Kate said. 'I want him found and watched round the clock. He doesn't move without DCI Stone and me knowing about it. For reasons that should be clear to all of you, Hank and I are known to this man. We can take no active part in following him. DCI Stone will run a covert surveillance operation, so get your hands in the air. Unless it's a matter of life and death, we don't touch Clay until the forensics report is in. He's not someone who will roll over. Any questions?'

# 94

Kate left the building in a buoyant mood, without mentioning one vital part of the puzzle that, apart from herself, only two people were aware of: Stone and Hank. One of the last things that Hannah had placed in her safety-deposit box was a receipt for five hundred quid's worth of euros, purchased at an Alnwick bank with cash. No euros were found in her caravan. Neither were they in the box. As of an hour ago, Kate had reason to believe that the money had been sent to Aaron. British Transport Police had been on the blower to Hank, informing him that the boy boarded a train from Settle to St Pancras yesterday where they lost him in the crowd.

Hank had asked them to check Eurostar.

That, in Kate's considered opinion, was a good call.

On Friday, before Aaron took off, French Police had scoped out the family home in Bordeaux, but Kate intended to honour Hannah's plea to find her son. In view of his young age, and a promise Kate had made to herself, she didn't want anyone else to do it. Bright had given her the green light to travel, taking Hank with her.

'So why didn't you tell them where we were going?' he asked.

'Hope said Clay has friends in our organisation. Bright decided we should keep it to ourselves until he's in custody, just in case he got wind of it. Stone will take over while we're gone. I was going to take Jo, but I thought you'd sulk—'

'You bet I would.'

'You're good with kids, not that she isn't, but she has a shedload to do.'

'And I don't?' Hank wasn't buying her excuse. 'What's the real reason?'

'If Clay is one step ahead of us, I'll need your muscle.'

'To carry your bags?' Hank quipped.

'No, you idiot. I'm in no fit state to fight, am I? That's the deal, take it or leave it.'

Hank made a fist, lifting his right arm, showing off his biceps. 'Don't forget to pack me spinach?' he said, making Kate laugh out loud. The adrenaline rush of bringing an offender down was kicking in already.

# 95

Shrouded in mist in the half-light of dawn, Swift's home in Bordeaux was one of the most romantic properties Kate had ever seen. Unused and unloved, the small but perfectly formed, south-facing chateau was magical, complete with a moat and swimming pool. In spite of the silence and stillness of the surrounding vegetation, she imagined laughter, music, people eating oysters on the terrace and drinking champagne. In reality, the area was covered in fallen leaves. Chairs had blown over, shutters were closed, their peeling paint draped with cobwebs.

To the left of where Kate was standing was a stone chapel tower with thick walls and unglazed windows that were, like the door, overgrown with wisteria that would give a spectacular display in a few months' time. As she stood there, wishing she had a key so she could explore the interior, her mood morphed into something darker. It struck her that she was viewing the embodiment of one man's grief for a lost wife. Marianne Briand was much loved. Peter Swift must've been utterly devastated when she died.

Should he choose to care for his grandson, Kate hoped that the chateau would once again mean something to him, kick-starting his life . . . . but first, she had to find Aaron.

As if he'd read her mind, Hank asked how she wanted to handle the search.

She turned to face him. 'I'm not seeking permission, if that's what you mean.'

'The family are a big deal round here, Kate.'

'They're not the only ones,' Kate smiled at him. 'You've been a rock during this investigation, Hank. Stopping me going home on Saturday night probably saved my life, but on this occasion, allow me to break the rules.' She spread her hand. 'We're in the middle of a forest, half a mile from a main road. Who the hell will see us? Besides, if they knew why we were here, I'm sure they'd approve.'

'Do they know?'

'About Hannah's death or Aaron's life?'

'Either, or.'

'Not sure. Peter said he'd take care of it. I'll give him a call later. If he hasn't, or can't bring himself to, we'll do it before we return to the UK. Put your phone on silent, we don't want to spook Aaron if he's here.' Quietly, they picked their way to the front door. It was secure, no sign that it had been opened in a long time, no disturbance of leaves or twigs. Kate whispered. 'You go that way.' She thumbed in the opposite direction. 'I'll go this—'

'No way, I'm not letting you out of my sight.'

She didn't argue.

Knowing what Dominic Clay was capable of, Hank was right to be cautious. They checked the front of the chateau, then walked down the east side in silence, checking the ground-floor shutters to see if any were loose or open. They weren't. Same at the rear. Everything locked and secure.

They turned the corner, heading south toward the front of the house. Hank tapped Kate's arm, pointing toward the pool. The plastic cover was filthy, sunken in the middle where black rotting leaves floated in rainwater. Two parasols lay on the deck, their colours faded, bleached by the sun. One of three steamer chairs had been blown over, but beneath a clump of trees, the pool house door stood ajar.

'Stay here,' Kate said.

'No, I'm coming too—'

'Do as I say. If he's there, I don't want to spook him.'

Kate walked towards the open door, then stopped dead in her tracks, halfway across the lawn. There were signs of recent activity, parallel marks crossing what was once a flower bed d was now a patch of wet mud. In between the two channels was a pair of reverse footprints where someone had walked backwards pulling a heavy weight toward the pool house.

*Oh God.*

The sight brought on a flashback of Hannah's beaten body, causing Kate to stop and catch her breath, Bright's voice calming her with wise words, as it always did in situations like these. He gave her the courage to face her demons when she wanted to look away. He gave her strength when she was too weak to carry on. Turning on her torch, she directed the beam inside the windowless building which, as she got closer, she realised was larger than it had appeared from a distance. As she neared the open door, she noticed a fourth steamer chair had been dragged inside. It lay upturned, on its side . . .

Next to it was a crumpled sleeping bag . . .

Aaron wasn't in it.

## 96

For a long moment, Kate stood at the door, staring at the empty sleep sack. It was cleanly laundered. Everything else in the pool house was covered in cobwebs and a thick layer of dust, including poolside paraphernalia: seat cushions, small tables, deflated airbeds, some chewed at the edges. On a side table were several colourful, dynamically shaped ashtrays that belonged to a different era, one of which lay smashed on the floor.

As she stepped inside, Kate looked down.

Splinters of vintage glass, large and small, were strewn across the hand-cut terracotta tiles. One of them showed fresh damage, presumably where the heavy object had made contact with the floor. There were scuffed footprints in the dust and what looked like a pool of blood.

Someone had been here recently.

Taking a deep breath, Kate moved inside.

Caught in her flashlight was a small area that had been cleared of debris before the glass had fallen or was thrown. A half bottle of water and curled-up crusts of bread were on the floor. Sweeping the torch to the left, Kate noticed a white wire protruded from beneath the upturned chair. Try as she might to suppress her growing fears, all she could think of was that Dominic Clay had beaten her to the boy.

Heart racing, she got down on her knees to examine the wire. It was attached to a mobile phone that lay face down underneath the chair. Photographing it in situ, she put on gloves, recovering the device. Turning it over, she saw that the screen was smashed. Erring on the side of caution, treating the place as if it were a crime scene, she placed the mobile in an evidence bag. As she stood upright, a noise from the rear of the pool house spooked her.

ɔm his position in the garden, Hank saw torchlight sweep ɛft and right in quick succession. He observed Kate back away slowly. When she cried out, he took off, sprinting across the lawn, arms like pistons. He crashed through the door just as she turned to run, almost knocking each other out in the process.

'Aargh!' Cringing, Kate shut her eyes, unable to control her body's reaction to what she'd seen. 'Fuck! Enemies with two legs I can cope with. Those with four freak me out. I just saw three rats the size of French Bulldogs.'

Hank burst out laughing.

What she said next wiped the smile off his face.

'We're too late.'

'What?'

'Take a look.'

As he went inside, Kate almost slid down the outside wall, exhausted.

The investigation meant nothing if she couldn't honour Hannah's last request that she should find and save Aaron from Clay. For the first time in her entire career, Kate knew defeat. She had no idea where to go next. The man was more than a formidable opponent. He was a machine. A winner. He'd worn her down and shown her who was boss. Hannah had fought bravely to protect her son and Kate had failed her.

French voices in the distance.

Kate stood. 'Hank!'

He arrived by her side.

Kate pointed at figures moving towards them through the trees. And suddenly, four gendarmes appeared, weapons drawn.

One of them yelled, '*Aller sur le terrain!*'

'Police Anglaise!' Kate yelled back.

A female gendarme: 'On the ground, now!'

Kate glanced at Hank.

He shook his head.

They were damned if they would.

## 97

Despite his grubby face, the boy who stepped out from the treeline behind the gendarmes was clearly Aaron. His was an angelic face that hadn't yet begun to show the signs of adulthood creeping ever closer. However young he did or didn't look, the sad fact was this kid had been forced to grow up far quicker than most because of the actions of the man Kate assumed was his biological father, though she had no proof of it. Unlike Kate and Hank, the child spoke perfect French. He began to spout forth an explanation to local police that Kate found hard to keep up with.

She caught 'Ma mère . . .' and then the kid got upset.

'Aaron, it's OK. My name is Kate. I've been looking for you.'

The female gendarme who'd spoken English suggested that her crew move away. They fell back like an army detail. She gestured to Hank to follow. It was an order, not a request. There were phone calls to be made, authorities to contact, on both sides of the English Channel. It might take hours to sort out this cross-border shitshow.

When they had gone, Aaron glared at Kate, like he also knew what was coming and didn't want to hear it. She'd have done anything, absolutely anything, not to hurt him. She'd given the death message many times to a parent of murdered children. On the occasions that it was the other way around, there was usually another adult family member prepared to break the news. Not this time. Kate wasn't spared the trauma of telling the boy that his mother was gone. In his heart, he knew it already . . . and yet he still asked.

'She's dead, isn't she?'

'I'm afraid so, yes.'

Aaron looked away, tears rolling silently down his cheeks.

Kate drew him to her. 'I'm so sorry, Aaron.'

She felt like weeping too. After a long while, he pulled away, wiping his tears with the palm of his hand. Kate formed the impression that he'd been expecting this for as long as he was able to remember.

For this child, happily ever after was a myth.

'How did you find me?' he asked.

It wasn't hard, but Kate wanted him to know that he was loved, that he was Hannah's first and last consideration, that in no way had he been abandoned to fend for himself. 'Your mum left me a clue.'

'She told me to wait here for her. I don't mean here exactly.' He pressed his lips together, hanging on but only just, to his emotions. 'I mean inside.'

'You have a key?'

'Yes, it's in my bag, but the chateau is scary at night and there's no electricity. I like it better in the pool house. Last night . . . ' He paused, embarrassed. 'I left my phone in there. Can we go and get it?'

'No need, I have it here.' Now Kate understood the broken glass, the pool of blood. 'You saw the rats, right?'

The wonderful interior of the house was lost on Aaron but not on Kate. It was covered in dust, the furniture hidden beneath large white sheets, but even so it was, without doubt, a magnificent home that contained many original features. Among the objets d'art was a huge photographic print featuring Hannah's parents with their arms wrapped around her. Aaron didn't seem to notice it as he walked by.

He'd obviously seen and got used to it.

In the kitchen, he pulled out a chair, sitting down at one end of a table large enough to seat twelve. There were a couple of sweet wrappers on the tabletop, a crisp packet and an empty Coke can. Replacing them with fresh baguettes, pastries and water, given to her by the gendarmes on the way in, Kate apologised for the lack of choice, promising to feed him properly later.

Aaron looked but didn't touch.

Hank joined them.

'Dig in,' he said. 'You need to eat.'

The lad didn't move or speak.

Kate thought that he was too upset. She gave Hank the nod, hoping that if he got stuck in, the boy would too. Then it dawned on her that Aaron was waiting for her to sit down, a case of public school politeness that was unnecessary but endearing.

She joined him at the table.

After he'd eaten, Kate and Hank spent around an hour talking, answering his questions, making sure that he fully understood what had happened to his mother, without going into detail.

As traumatised as he was, this exceptionally bright lad was able to verbalise his feelings, confirming the detectives' suspicions that Hannah had been supplying him with phone SIMs, deleting texts as soon as they were sent, taking all necessary precautions to conceal his whereabouts, sending him the means to escape. As they suspected, there was an arrangement whereby Hannah would ring once a week and what he should do if she didn't.

Kate stood. 'Aaron, will you stay with Hank a moment, please?'

He seemed overly anxious. 'You're leaving?'

'No, I'm not going anywhere. And when I do, you're coming with me.' She gave a reassuring smile, deciding to level with him, just as his mother had. 'I know you've never met him, but I need to ring your grandfather to let him know you're safe.' His mother's father, she clarified. 'He's desperate for news. Like you, I always keep my promises.'

What he said next surprised her. 'Can I speak to him?'

In that moment, Kate's heart broke a little. 'Of course, if you'd like to.'

'I would. Mum told me a lot about him.'

Kate smiled. 'I noticed his name on the Rowing Club Honours Board at Haltonghyll.'

'He was club captain three years running,' Aaron said proudly. 'No one has ever done that before or since.'

'Is that right?' Kate smiled. 'Sounds like you have a lot to live up to.'

'I hate rowing. I'm in the cricket team though.'

'Give me a minute to explain, then I'll put you on.'

Swift was speechless. He sobbed on the phone, then apologised for doing so. Kate explained where she was, then handed her mobile to Aaron, leaving him to have a private word with the man who'd begged her to support his case for legal guardianship.


Ten minutes later, Aaron joined Kate and Hank outside, returning her mobile. All three sat down on the sunny steps out front. This felt nothing like February. The skies were clear, the temperature set to rise to eighteen degrees, with a slight westerly breeze.

'OK, son?' Hank asked.

'Yes.' Aaron seemed easy in their company. He thanked Kate for letting him speak to his grandfather. She smiled, telling him that Peter was looking forward to meeting him. The lad seemed choked, overwhelmed almost. He pulled his own phone from the pocket of his jeans. 'If this works, I'll show you something.'

Kate watched him open Mail.

He looked up. 'Mum and I used to upload videos sometimes, so we could see what the other was up to, then we'd delete the next day. On Tuesday I found something. I didn't know what it was, so I emailed it to myself before she had the chance to delete it from the cloud.' He tapped on the email. All that was there was an image file with the tiny clapperboard icon in the centre and the identification number: IMG_0545.MOV. 'I was going to talk to her about it on Friday. I think it might be important.'

## 98

'We've got something explosive, David. Go and get him! We needn't wait . . . Yes, positive,' Kate said. 'Do it now. When you have, give me a bell. If it's all the same to you, I'd like Carmichael to make the arrest . . . Clay will be expecting me. Failing that, he'll be expecting someone of higher rank than a DS. Let's not give him what he wants. If we're going to throw the book at him, we need to charge him with everything, including attempted murder of a police officer, in which case I can't take part in the interview.'

'You think Carmichael's ready to lead?'

'Absolutely, she deserves this. Clay won't like being questioned by a female officer. I'll put Hank in there with her and direct operations backstage.' Across the lawn, Kate saw Hank lock the door of the chateau and walk Aaron to the car. 'Look, I've got to go. When I know you have him, and not before, I'll leave Aaron with his grandfather and catch the first flight out of Heathrow. If all goes to plan, we could make Middle Earth by five. That'll give Clay plenty of time to choose a new solicitor.'

Carmichael made the arrest at Clay's home, which meant she could search it or bring in someone to do it for her. She chose the latter. The MIT were now on the clock to gather and organise evidence for her to put to Clay in interview. Actions were being carried out all over the city in a race against time. Kate had also given them a job to do that involved a number plate she wanted ANPR to find as a matter of urgency.

One of Stone's team was interviewing the witness from the Dean Street car park who'd seen a man acting suspiciously before Walker's swan dive off the top and Stone was interviewing Gilroy's boyfriend, Liam Rossiter. He'd known that Max had been up to no good and that he'd recently been well paid for a driving job.

'One night only,' Liam said. 'Max was buzzin' when he came home.'

'Who approached him?' Stone was sure that Clay hadn't.

'Nah, man.' Liam hadn't stopped crying since the MIT picked him up and brought him to the nick for questioning. 'If I tell you, the crazy bastard will kill me too—'

'Not if he's behind bars. C'mon, Liam. You want to catch the man who shot Max, don't you?'

Stone could cope with sob stories. He'd never been much good with sobs. He gave the kid a minute to pull himself together before making the most of his raw emotions. 'Liam, Max didn't deserve to have his life taken away. If you thought anything of him, anything at all, you need to tell me right now. We have someone in custody. If he walks, he'll do a runner and that'll be down to you. It's now or never.'

'All I know is what I saw in the club. There's this guy, Stilts they call him. Shouldn't be hard to find. Tall bloke. Calls himself The Enforcer. Big hat. Cool clothes. Straight out of the nineteen twenties. Thinks he's fucking Al Capone. He scared Max into it.'

'You did the right thing,' Stone said, getting up. 'I'll get someone to take your statement and get you home.'

He couldn't get out of there quick enough to raise the action to find this man.

It was all going on at Middle Earth.

## 99

With Clay in custody, Kate sat down with Hank and Carmichael to discuss strategy. Clay had been arrested for three
murders – Hannah Swift, Max Gilroy and Terence Walker
– and the attempted murder of Kate. She'd been planning to
wait until forensic accountant Felicity Fairfax had completed
her work, but once Aaron had handed over a vital piece of
evidence, she was forced to act.

When they were done, Kate met with Fairfax to get a handle
on the financial matters. With Clay facing murder charges,
that was less of a priority, but Kate was hell-bent on sticking
it to him, dismantling his life for what he'd done to Hannah.
'There's absolutely no rush for this,' she said. 'But it would help
if you could give me a sense of the incrimination evidence
Hannah gave us.'

'Sure,' Fairfax said. 'The dossier she provided is gold dust.
You'd think she worked in the financial sector.'

'Her father did.'

'You can tell. It's organised and chronological. Some years
ago, Clay was into multimillion-pound mortgage fraud, using
false identities, involving hundreds of dodgy IP addresses in
order to hide his digital footprint, leading the authorities to
proxy servers, the profiles of which are in places like Nigeria,
India, Thailand,' Fairfax explained. 'Back in the day, it was a
simple process. Submit offers on properties over the market
value, then default on payment. The cash was then either
smuggled to countries where the banks were less circumspect
or washed clean via other means.'

'I thought financial institutions had got wise to this type of
scam?'

'They did, which caused a dilemma for conmen like Clay,

ing off their money stream, shutting them down.'

'And then he met Hannah.'

'Whose business he decided to exploit,' Fairfax said. 'His plan was ingenious. As you know, Hannah was providing high-end, bespoke sports tours. Her clientele were rich, some of them global celebrities. Clay saw an opportunity to work with her clients in other ways, catering for their sexual desires, sourcing a certain type of man, woman or child. There is evidence of that here. He saw a demand and set himself up as supplier, wherever they happened to be in the world. Recording their vile acts, Clay then issued ultimatums: pay up or he'd out them.'

'And risk exposing himself?'

'He was more subtle than that. He'd start rumours, such as employee exploitation, bullying in the workplace or anything else that made investors nervous. Their company shares would dip. Guess who'd be there to pick them up.'

'At a knockdown price,' Kate said.

'Exactly. Powerful people pay dearly to keep their dirty hands clean. Hannah found one who was and is prepared to speak out. In my experience, others will follow.'

'You can prove that?'

'Hannah did it for me. The fact that he was selling kids for sex is, I suspect, what triggered her quest to bring him down.'

Kate nodded. 'Were you able to follow the money?'

'Kate, I'm not a wizard. Forensic accounting takes time. What I need to follow is the audit trail of his offshore accounts, find out exactly how he moved his money, calculate his worth, what he owns in cash and property. Hannah's given me a start, but I need time to verify her documentation. Everything I've seen so far checks out, but I won't know until I've been through the lot.'

'Crack on – he's facing substantive murder charges and attempted murder. We can add arson with intent to endanger life and criminal damage. That's enough to keep us going. What you're going to do is tap the final nail into his coffin.'

# 100

'The wait is excruciating,' Carmichael said.

Kate smiled at her, then at Hank. 'I remember what it was like, my first big interview.'

'What's the hold-up?'

'Lisa, I know you're dying to get in there, but patience is key.'

'Kate's right,' Hank said. 'We don't make a move until we have to. He won't like being kept waiting, will he? He'll be expecting to walk. Sit back, relax. Let the bastard sweat is my view.'

'When you do go in,' Kate said to Lisa, 'do it with your head chopped off. Make it personal. Think about Hannah's post, the life she built for herself, the sacrifice she made to take him down. We have everything we need to link him to Hannah. Not only did he know her, he lived with her. He flew around the world with her – and we can prove it. By the time Fairfax is finished with her dossier, we'll also know how he moved his money. She reckons we can get him for' – Kate began to count on her fingers – 'fraud worth billions, tax evasion, money laundering, child exploitation and blackmail. There isn't a charge sheet long enough.'

'You're on,' Kate said, half an hour later.

Carmichael gathered a thick file from her desk. 'I'm ready.'

Behind Kate's back, Hank winked at Lisa.

Kate gave her one final piece of advice. 'If Clay takes the interview anywhere that benefits us, by all means go with it, otherwise concentrate on the fact that he murdered Hannah and then gradually introduce the others. If you need to consult with me, take a break. I'll be right next door in the observation room.'

Carmichael smiled at Hank. 'Let's do this.'

...ichael entered the interview room confidently, taking the
...t directly opposite Clay, leaving Hank to face his lawyer,
...ames Holroyd. Giving her name for the tape, she invited
Hank, Clay and Holroyd, to do the same.

The suspect was the epitome of cool.

'Mr Clay, do you understand that you have been arrested for
the murder of Hannah Swift, Max Gilroy and Terence Walker
and for the attempted murder of Kate Daniels?'

'Can I just stop you there, Detective Sergeant? Obviously, I
know of Hannah Swift. We were once in a relationship, but I
haven't seen her for some years, for good reason. The woman
was a bunny-boiler: highly strung, jealous too, unable to stand
the fact that I was more successful than she was. She was also
an unfit mother, which is why arrangements were made to
send our son away to school.'

'Hmm . . .' Carmichael opened the file in front of her. She
flipped a few pages, taking her time before locking eyes with
him. 'Our information is that Hannah made all the arrangements for her son.' Lisa tapped the file. 'At least that's what it
says here.'

'On my instruction. I'm a busy man.'

'Did you ever visit your son at his school, Mr Clay?'

Clay didn't flinch. 'As I said, I'm busy—'

'And a risk-taker too it seems.'

'Excuse me?'

'I'd have thought that a man with your know-how would
think it foolish to hand such an important task to a woman
you described as unstable, quote "an unfit mother" unquote.
Carmichael paused, in no hurry to proceed. 'You don't know
where he is, do you, Mr Clay? Hannah was so terrified of you,
she fled after taking the child out of the school you'd chosen,
boarding him elsewhere to keep him safe.'

'I want to see the SIO. Where is she?'

'None of your business. You can't throw her under a BMW

one minute and expect her to be in good fettle the ⅃.
sides, this is a straight case, one of the easiest murders
ever worked on. It really doesn't require a senior rank.
first victim left us a dossier of incriminating evidence a roo.
would understand. Wouldn't you say so, DS Gormley?'

'Definitely.' Hank never took his eyes off Clay.

'Now,' Carmichael said. 'Where were you on Tuesday the
eighteenth of February between five p.m. and nine p.m.?'

'I was in a restaurant in Durham,' Clay said.

'Ah yes, a table for one. Conveniently, we found the reservation in your house.'

He looked right through her. 'There you go then.'

'Your mobile phone was there but you weren't, were you,
Mr Clay?'

'DS Carmichael,' Holroyd said, 'where's your evidence?'

Carmichael looked at the brief. 'There's an image of that
restaurant on Mr Clay's device . . .' She held up the mobile
in question. 'It's also the only appointment in his calendar.
Excuse me for being cynical, but I find that rather suspicious
for a man of his standing in the community, one who claims
he's too busy to visit his only child.'

'It's a new phone,' Clay said. 'I misplaced my old one.'

'You don't save to the cloud? I hear it's very good.' Carmichael switched her focus to his brief but not before she'd
caught Clay's anxiety over mention of the cloud. He didn't
know what was coming but it was making him sweat. 'Mr Holroyd, we know who had Mr Clay's mobile phone. We found
his associate—'

'What associate?' It was the first time that Clay had reacted.

'All in good time . . .' Carmichael switched focus again. 'Mr
Holroyd, I have to tell you that it's not looking good for your
client. Allow me to demonstrate.'

# 101

Kate and Maxwell had moved to the observation room where they could watch and conduct proceedings if necessary. Neil would act as runner between her and the incident room so she could feed any new evidence to Carmichael in real time.

'I wish I had her instinct and timing,' Maxwell said.

Kate smiled. 'She's a natural.'

They looked on as Carmichael continued. 'For the tape, I'm about to show Mr Clay and his solicitor a video IMG_0545. MOV obtained this morning from a key witness.' Lisa didn't say which witness and neither the suspect nor his legal advisor asked. Tapping a key on her laptop, she uploaded the file onto the smart TV screen behind her, then eyeballed Clay. 'Are you ready?'

He didn't answer, though he'd seen the still image of two headlights frozen on screen.

'Yes, no?' Carmichael glanced at Holroyd.

He had the telltale signs of a worried man.

*And so he should.*

She'd given fair warning of what was to come. From the look of him, he had an inkling that it would sink his client when she ran the video. He stared at her for a long moment. 'Detective Sergeant, I'd like a few minutes with Mr Clay. Now please—'

'Actually, I'd like a word with you outside,' Carmichael said.

Closing her laptop, she scooped it up, then got up and moved toward the door.

Text messages had been pinging into Kate's mobile from detectives on the ground, everyone keen to get in on the act of putting Clay behind bars. Grateful for the adjournme was out of her seat so she could waylay and update Carm and Hank. They arrived in the corridor simultaneously, bu did Holroyd.

Kate hung around, lifting her mobile to her ear as cover.

Ignoring her, Lisa closed the door on Clay and focused on Holroyd. 'Listen, don't be drawn in by the fact that he's a wealthy man. We have so much evidence, by the time we finish with him, he won't have two pennies to rub together. He's not going home anytime soon.'

Holroyd smirked. 'I've been paid upfront.'

'I hope it wasn't a cheque.'

He gave her hard eyes and walked away.

Kate arrived at Carmichael's shoulder. 'What was that about?'

'A bit of one-upmanship.' Lisa grinned.

'You're doing great.'

'I haven't started yet, boss.'

'Yeah, well, Clay will lose his cool when he sees Hannah's video clip.' Kate's mobile rang. She checked the screen, then looked up. 'Go ahead and get yourselves a coffee while you can. I'm going to pop in here and take this call.'

She disappeared into the viewing room.

DC Andy Brown was very excited. 'Guv, the witness from the Dean Street car park has described our man to a T. She only saw him for a second, but said everything was wrong about him. She didn't seem the type to scare easily but said he had evil eyes. Thought you might like to know.'

'Hold on, Carmichael needs to hear this.' Kate looked out into the corridor. Hank and Lisa had already disappeared. She went back inside, shut the door and sat down. 'Sorry, Andy. You were saying?'

'The witness said the guy she saw wore a good coat. Collar turned up. Good shoes. Shiny. Yellow scarf. For all his expensive kit, the guy was wearing a baseball cap with what

.cribed as Arabic writing on it. I've alerted the search
at Clay's house to find it, but I wouldn't hold your
.th.'

Kate's focus was Clay and Holroyd in the interview room.
They had their heads together, whispering conspiratorially.
'Andy, did you say yellow scarf?'

'Affirmative.'

'Jesus! I'm looking at it.'

Carmichael and Hank entered the interview room and sat
down. Lisa checked her watch. 'For the tape, the time is 22.42
on Monday the twenty-fourth of February, 2020. This interview is being resumed at Northern Area Command HQ. I am
DS Carmichael. Also present are . . .'

'DS Gormley.' Hank looked at the solicitor.

The brief followed suit. 'James Holroyd, acting for Mr Dominic Clay.'

Clay didn't speak.

'Not playing? OK . . .' Carmichael did it for him. 'The suspect, Dominic Clay, is also present and has declined to identify
himself.' She was about to run the video clip they had yet to
see. 'Are we all ready to resume?' No one objected. 'Mr Clay,
your ex, Hannah Swift, has supplied us with video evidence
from beyond the grave. I'd like you to watch it now, please.'
She pressed play.

Carmichael paused the video footage. 'That is you and Max
Gilroy, isn't it, Mr Clay? This video is timed and dated: 19.44
on the evening of Hannah Swift's murder, the eighteenth of
February 2020. As you just saw, the video began with the
mirror image of the victim facing the camera. She is standing
inside the caravan in which she was murdered. She then ro-
tates the aspect, capturing you arriving. The owner of the site
had been out for the evening, returning shortly after the video
was taken.' Carmichael pushed a photograph across the table.

'I'm showing exhibits OB1 and OB2, crime scene image show curtains of the same fabric as in the photograph, a. now covered in blood.'

Holroyd swallowed hard.

Clay didn't look down.

# 102

'How long after?' Holroyd asked bluntly.

'Excuse me?' Carmichael knew what he was getting at but wanted him to underline it.

'You said the site owners had been out for the evening and returned shortly after.'

'I did. They were home by nine.'

Client and lawyer had their heads together for a word or two, then moved apart.

'Detective Sergeant, by my calculation, that provides a seventy-six-minute window between Mr Clay arriving and the site owners getting home,' the lawyer said. 'I concur with my client. Anyone could have murdered Hannah Swift during that time.'

'That, if I may say so, is the predictable response of a desperate man.' Carmichael relaxed into her seat, keeping her focus on Clay's brief. 'What do you think the chances are of anyone else wandering in to murder your client's ex-girlfriend, when the man he arrived with drove off in her vehicle and ended up dead in a quarry? There was only one person with enough evidence to finish your client financially. That was Hannah Swift.'

Clay was beginning to unravel.

'Mr Clay, as I alluded to earlier, Hannah Swift supplied us with documents contained in a safe deposit box that will finish you. Who else is out there with that kind of motive? She was terrified of you. She hid her child from you. She's been in hiding for years.'

She switched focus.

'Mr Holroyd, the fact that your client asked a convicted offender to take his mobile to a Durham eatery when he was clearly in Northumberland with Gilroy proves beyond any

doubt that this offence was not carried out in a fit
It was premeditated, planned and executed with no
shown to the victim. It was a prolonged attack in which
was tortured. Stilts – that's the nickname of the offender I ju
referred to – thinks he's a gangster. But when it comes down
to it, he's smart enough to distance himself from murder. He's
already coughed to supplying Mr Clay with a getaway driver.
He chose well. Max was nicknamed after Dutch racing driver
Max Verstappen, the youngest ever to win in Formula 1. Unfortunately, as you know, Max Gilroy is no longer with us.'

Kate watched Clay's response like a hawk, even as the door to
the observation room swung open. Neil Maxwell retook his
seat beside her, passing her a message. Kate continued to listen
in to the interview going on next door . . .

'For the tape, Mr Clay has declined to answer,' Carmichael
said.

'Maybe we'd better watch the video again.' Hank was rubbing it in.

As Carmichael rewound, Kate took the opportunity to read
the note and almost punched the air in triumph. She smiled
at Maxwell then took a photograph of the message which was
handwritten, containing only five words:

We found the cap, guv.

In the interview room, Carmichael pressed play.

Just as the clip came to an end Kate sent Hank the message
Maxwell had given her.

Holroyd almost hit the roof as Hank's mobile began to
vibrate on the table between them. He palmed his brow, embarrassed by such an obvious show of nervousness, avoiding
eye contact with the detectives sitting opposite and his client.
Clay's expression was a toss-up between frustration and sim-
mering hatred.

'Are you going to say anything?' he barked. 'What the hell
am I paying you for?'

feigned sympathy. 'Clay, you did yourself no favours
g rid of Walker. No offence, but Mr Holroyd seems
ble to guide you on this matter. Which is a shame, given
ur penchant for hanging out in the playgrounds of the rich
and famous—'

'Detective Sergeant, is there a point to this tirade?'

A photograph of the cap arrived on Carmichael's phone.

She leaned over and showed it to Hank.

His eyes were back on Clay. 'How was Monaco?'

Clay didn't answer.

'Oh, we know all about you meeting Hannah there. Did you
know that Gilroy was a big fan of F1? Which is why, I suspect,
he bought the cap our colleagues just found in the boot of your
motor. I'm told it's a collector's item, from the first ever Bahrain
Grand Prix.'

Carmichael showed Clay the photograph that had just
pinged into her phone. 'I'm showing the suspect a photograph
of exhibit JM/25. As you can see, it bears the same distinctive
logo our colleagues spotted on the cap of whoever was driving
Gilroy's car up the airport road after Max was shot dead in a
quarry in Northumberland. That was you, Mr Clay.'

'Yes!' Kate said in the observation room. 'She's not asking, she's
telling. He looks chilled enough, but he can't stop the nervous
twitch above his right eye.'

Maxwell agreed, his eyes fixed to the screen.

Carmichael sat forward, elbows on the table. 'I suspect that
when we have that cap analysed it will have Max's DNA and
yours on the inside of it. We have a witness willing to swear on
oath that the cap never leaves his car. As I said at the beginning
of this interview, this one was easy.' She was lying. 'I've hardly
opened my notes.'

'We haven't even started on the attempted murder of our SIO
yet,' Hank said. 'While we're in here with you, our colleagues
are all over the place, evidence gathering. Their attention to

detail is outstanding. They even placed you at the ?. CCTV. I viewed the footage. Fuck me if I didn't walk past you. Give you a thrill, did it? Hope so. It's the la you'll get.'

Carmichael took over. 'Mr Holroyd, your client arrived the hospital within minutes of the ambulance transporting Kate Daniels. She'd been pushed into the road deliberately and was hit by a car. He left two minutes after she discharged herself. And yet he never once approached the reception desk. I'd like to see you talk him out of that one.'

Her eyes shifted to the suspect.

'You're a bit of a voyeur, aren't you, Mr Clay? We also captured you in the crowd outside DCI Daniels' burning home, but we won't bother going there. The footage we have speaks for itself.' She paused. 'You are – I beg your pardon, you were until today a very wealthy man with fast cars, a wonderful home, huge amounts of disposable cash. I suspect your well-heeled friends will run a mile when they find out who you really are. The ones who already know will want to keep you inside for as long as possible. In fact, they're beating a path to our door to give evidence. If you were to leave here now, you couldn't afford the taxi home.'

## 103

From the outset of her investigation, Kate had known she was up against a formidable opponent. There was no doubt about that. No ambiguity in Hannah's note either. Her abuser was the who, though it had taken Kate a while to identify him. She'd known the what, where and the how, but not the why of this triple-hander.

She would never forget Hannah Swift.

Kate stood in the back row during the funeral service. The church was packed to the rafters, Jack and Peggy Shepherd among the mourners. Simon Shepherd was conspicuous by his absence. Café owner Gemma Munro had come to pay her respects, along with villagers who'd clubbed together to pay for a memorial plaque in Hannah's name. It would be hung at St Peter the Fisherman to celebrate her short life.

Along with Alex Hope and Eden from Women's Aid – two women who'd provided crucial evidence to investigators – many of Kate's colleagues were also in attendance, including Stone, whose team had worked tirelessly to bring about a resolution. He was a good bloke. Kate liked him. They nodded to one another as he left with Hank, now the best of friends, on their way to the nearest pub to sink a pint and put the investigation to bed.

Kate sought out Aaron, asking for a moment of his time. They moved away from the crowd for some privacy in the garden of remembrance. It was important to let him know that his mother's last request was to find and protect him and only him. He didn't need to see the note. He didn't ask and Kate didn't offer.

'I have something for you.' She took a small gift box from

her pocket, handing it to him. 'The box is second-hand, old one of mine,' she said. 'But what's inside is yours.' A fla. of recognition as he opened it to reveal the gold locket and the image of his younger self. 'Your mum would want you to have it. The rest of her belongings I'll send on.'

'To my granddad's house, please.'

Kate nodded, so choked by his bravery she couldn't speak.

She'd been tortured by his mother's death, a burden that had lifted slightly by the certainty of knowing that Aaron had someone to love, someone to care for him. Peter had offered him a permanent home and was in the process of securing legal guardianship, though Kate was convinced that the lad's surviving biological parent would make that task as difficult as possible, despite the fact that he was unavailable and, by virtue of his violence, unfit.

The boy had chosen to remain at Haltonghyll to complete his education, though for the first time in his young life, he now had somewhere to go at the end of term. Aaron had told Kate that they planned to return to the chateau in the summer. He was excited to be meeting his French family. Kate walked him back, gave him a big hug and left him with Peter, wishing them well.

Jo was waiting near the gate. Kate suggested a walk to the harbour. They strolled down the hill and sat on a bench facing the sea. 'I never did find anything in Walker's office or his home to link him to Clay.' Kate slipped on her sunglasses. 'Maybe he too had a safe deposit box. Who the hell cares now? He was terrified of Clay.'

'So was I,' Jo said. 'Weren't you?

'Yes, but if you tell a soul, I'll deny it.' Kate looked down, then up. 'Is it wrong that I wanted to beat him senseless? That I wanted him to suffer like Hannah did?'

'No. Yes. No, it's perfectly normal.' Jo linked hands with Kate but couldn't look at her. 'You should be proud that you

pped him of his assets, his memories, his liberty . . . and
u found Aaron. That's everything Hannah asked of you.'

The investigation into Hannah Swift's murder had touched
them both. 'I have a request,' Jo said. 'Come home, take a few
weeks off and put this behind you.'

Kate's phone rang.

The smile slid off Jo's face.

'Don't panic. It's Naylor. Same job. Different force.' Kate
tapped to answer.

'*Le Français est innocent,*' Naylor said.

Kate laughed. 'That is the worst accent I ever heard.'

'Hey, I tried.'

'I know Jean Cassel is clean. Our case has been over for
weeks. What took you so long?'

'My memory is as bad as my French. Sorry, totally forgot
until I read about it in the press. Did you charge Clay with all
three?'

'We did and a whole lot more besides. It was touch and
go for Walker, but we caught a break. Remember that very
expensive silk fibre I told you about, the one forensics didn't
even have on their database?'

'What about it?'

'He was arrested wearing a yellow scarf.'

'Thought you said he was clever.'

'I misjudged him.'

'Doesn't sound like you.'

'Believe me, the only thing he was good at was attacking
those too weak to fight back. Yeah, big mistake . . . yeah, why
not? We'd love that . . .' Kate laughed, turning to face Jo. 'He
wants to take us to dinner at Bouchon.' She was referring to one
of the few French restaurants in the area. 'You OK with that?'

'Oui, madame. So long as we don't talk shop.'

'Jo's in,' Kate said into the phone. 'What time? OK, see you
there.'

Jo held Kate's hand as they walked to the car. They were p~~~ of what they had achieved. Even more so of Hannah. Domi~ Clay was no longer a playboy. He was a remand prisoner who face a judge and jury one day, then rot in a cell wearing a lifer's vest. Hannah had seen to it that he'd never see the light of day. She'd never given up, never given in, never settled for being the victim in all this. Brick by brick she'd built the case against her abuser and, in doing so, she'd left an indelible mark on Kate, Jo and every detective in the MIT.

# Acknowledgements

Many professionals have contributed to this book: Orion's editorial team, sales and marketing, cover designers and a host of others who work hard in the background to make me look like I know what I'm doing. I often don't.

I have fantastic support from my friend and agent Oli Munson at A.M Heath; editor, Francesca Pathak; publicist Alainna Hadjigeorgiou and marketing executive, Lucy Cameron. Not forgetting my copy editor, Anne O'Brien. They all love Kate Daniels as much as I do . . . almost.

Thanks to all who generously recommend my scribbles and shout loudly at every opportunity both in the UK and abroad. It makes an enormous difference. And to readers generally . . . without you, frankly, there would be no point in writing at all.

None of this magic would have happened without the love and support of the best family anyone could wish for: Mo; Paul, Kate, Max and Frances; Chris, Jodie, Daisy and Finn – you are the best part of my life.

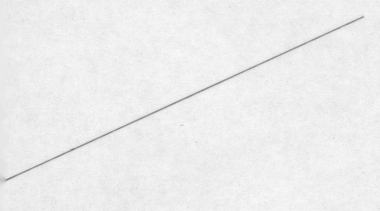

# Credits

Mari Hannah and Orion Fiction would like to thank everyone at Orion who worked on the publication of *Her Last Request* in the UK.

**Editorial**
Francesca Pathak
Lucy Brem

**Copy editor**
Anne O'Brien

**Proofreader**
Kati Nicholl

**Contracts**
Anne Goddard
Humayra Ahmed
Ellie Bowker
Jake Alderson

**Design**
Debbie Holmes
Joanna Ridley
Nick May

**Finance**
Jasdip Nandra
Afeera Ahmed
Elizabeth Beaumont
Sue Baker

**Editorial Management**
Charlie Panayiotou
Jane Hughes
Bartley Shaw

**Audio**
Paul Stark
Amber Bates

**Marketing**
Lynsey Sutherland

**Production**
Ruth Sharvell

**Publicity**
Alainna Hadjigeorgiou

**Sales**
Jen Wilson
Esther Waters
Victoria Laws
Rachael Hum
Ellie Kyrke-Smith
Frances Doyle
Georgina Cutler

# STONE & OLIVER SERIES

### THE LOST

Alex arrives home from holiday to find that her ten-year-old son Daniel has disappeared. It's the first case together for Northumbria CID officers David Stone and Frankie Oliver. But as the investigation unfolds, they realise the family's betrayal goes deeper than anyone suspected. This isn't just a missing persons case. Stone and Oliver are hunting a killer.

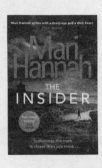

### THE INSIDER

When the body of a young woman is found by a Northumberland railway line, it's a baptism of fire for detective duo DCI David Stone and DS Frankie Oliver. The case is tough by anyone's standards, but Stone is convinced that there's a leak in his team – someone is giving the killer a head start on the investigation. These women are being targeted for a reason. And the next target is close to home...

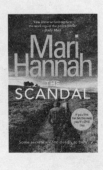

### THE SCANDAL

When *Herald* court reporter, Chris Adams, is found stabbed to death in Newcastle with no eyewitnesses, the MIT are stumped. Adams was working on a scoop that would make his name. But what was the story he was investigating? And who was trying to cover it up? When a link to a missing woman is uncovered, the investigation turns on its head. The exposé has put more than Adams' life in danger. And it's not over yet.

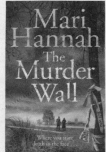
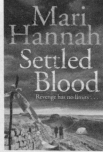
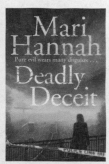

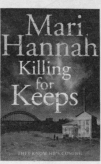
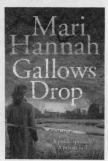

# WITHOUT A
# TRACE

## People don't just disappear …

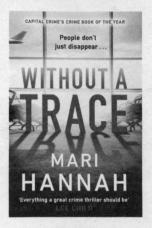

'Involving, sophisticated, intelligent and suspenseful
– everything a great crime thriller should be'
**LEE CHILD**

'A gripping, twisty police procedural – fans of the
Kate Daniels series will love this one'
**SHARI LAPENA**

'Compelling, page-turning suspense. Kate Daniels
is a character to cherish, and Mari is a
writer at the very top of her game'
**STEVE CAVANAGH**